PENGUIN BOOKS

Havana Storm

Clive Cussler is the author or co-author of a great number of international bestsellers, including the famous Dirk Pitt® adventures, such as *Arctic Drift*; the NUMA® Files adventures, most recently *Zero Hour*; the *Oregon* Files, such as *Mirage*; the Isaac Bell Adventures, which began with *The Chase*; and the highly successful most recent series, the Fargo Adventures. He lives in Arizona.

Dirk Cussler, an MBA from Berkeley, worked for many years in the financial arena, and now devotes himself to full-time writing. He is the co-author with Clive Cussler of *Black Wind*, *Treasure of Khan*, *Arctic Drift*, *Crescent Dawn* and *Poseidon's Arrow*.

Find out more about the world of Clive Cussler by visiting www.clivecussler.co.uk.

ALSO BY CLIVE CUSSLER

DIRK PITT® ADVENTURES

Poseidon's Arrow
(with Dirk Cussler)
Crescent Dawn
(with Dirk Cussler)
Arctic Drift (with Dirk Cussler)
Treasure of Khan
(with Dirk Cussler)
Black Wind (with Dirk Cussler)
Trojan Odyssey
Valhalla Rising
Atlantis Found
Flood Tide
Shock Wave
Inca Gold
Sahara
Dragon
Treasure
Cyclops
Deep Six
Pacific Vortex!
Night Probe!
Vixen 03
Raise the Titanic!
Iceberg
The Mediterranean Caper

FARGO ADVENTURES

The Eye of Heaven
(with Russell Blake)
The Mayan Secrets
(with Thomas Perry)
The Tombs (with Thomas Perry)
The Kingdom
(with Grant Blackwood)
Lost Empire
(with Grant Blackwood)
Spartan Gold
(with Grant Blackwood)

ISAAC BELL NOVELS

The Bootlegger (with Justin Scott)
The Striker (with Justin Scott)
The Thief (with Justin Scott)
The Race (with Justin Scott)
The Spy (with Justin Scott)
The Wrecker (with Justin Scott)
The Chase

KURT AUSTIN ADVENTURES

Ghost Ship (with Graham Brown)
Zero Hour (with Graham Brown)
The Storm (with Graham Brown)
Devil's Gate (with Graham Brown)
Medusa (with Paul Kemprecos)
The Navigator
(with Paul Kemprecos)
Polar Shift (with Paul Kemprecos)
Lost City (with Paul Kemprecos)
White Death
(with Paul Kemprecos)
Fire Ice (with Paul Kemprecos)
Blue Gold (with Paul Kemprecos)
Serpent (with Paul Kemprecos)

OREGON FILES ADVENTURES

Mirage (with Jack Du Brul)
The Jungle (with Jack Du Brul)
The Silent Sea (with Jack Du Brul)
Corsair (with Jack Du Brul)
Plague Ship (with Jack Du Brul)
Skeleton Coast (with Jack Du Brul)
Dark Watch (with Jack Du Brul)
Sacred Stone (with Craig Dirgo)
Golden Buddha (with Craig Dirgo)

NONFICTION

Built for Adventure:
The Classic Automobiles of
Clive Cussler and Dirk Pitt
The Sea Hunters
(with Craig Dirgo)
The Sea Hunters II
(with Craig Dirgo)
Clive Cussler and Dirk Pitt
Revealed
(with Craig Dirgo)

Havana Storm

CLIVE CUSSLER
and DIRK CUSSLER

PENGUIN BOOKS

PENGUIN BOOKS

UK | USA | Canada | Ireland | Australia
India | New Zealand | South Africa

Penguin Books is part of the Penguin Random House group of companies
whose addresses can be found at global.penguinrandomhouse.com.

First published in the USA by G. P. Putnam's Sons 2014
First published in Great Britain by Michael Joseph 2014
Published in Penguin Books 2015
003

Set in 12.5/14.75 pt Garamond MT Std
Typeset by Jouve (UK), Milton Keynes
Printed in Great Britain by Clays Ltd, Elcograf S.p.A.

A CIP catalogue record for this book is available from the British Library

ISBN: 978-1-405-93121-2

www.greenpenguin.co.uk

For Thom and Judy Sharp

PROLOGUE
Pursued

Destruction of the U.S.S. Maine

February 15, 1898

Sweat flowed down the exhausted man's face, cascading in heavy drops off his unshaven cheeks. Pulling a pair of thick wooden oars toward his chest, he tilted his head and rubbed a soiled sleeve across his forehead. He ignored the pain in his limbs and resumed a slow but steady stroke.

The exertion alone didn't account for his perspiration, nor did the muggy tropical climate. The sun had barely cleared the horizon, and the still air hanging over Havana Harbor was cool and damp. It was the strain of pursuit that kept his pulse rapid. With vacant eyes, he stared across the water, gesturing with his head to the man behind him in the boat.

It had been nearly two weeks since the Spanish militia first tried to appropriate his discovery, forcing him to flee. Three of his comrades had already died defending the relic. The Spaniards had no qualms about killing and would gladly murder him to get what they wanted. He would have been killed already, except for a chance encounter with a ragtag band of armed Cuban rebels, who provided him safe passage to the outskirts of Havana.

He glanced over his shoulder at a pair of warships moored near the harbor's commercial anchorage.

'*Al estribor,*' he rasped. 'To the right.'

'*Sí,*' replied the squat Cuban seated behind, wielding his own set of oars. He was similarly attired in torn and soiled clothes, his face shaded by a weathered straw hat.

Together, they maneuvered the leaky longboat toward the modern steel warships. The old man scoured the harbor for threats, but he seemed to have finally eluded his pursuers. A safe haven was within his grasp.

They rowed slowly past the smaller warship, which carried a Spanish flag hung from its stern mast, and approached the second vessel. An armored cruiser, it featured twin gun turrets that protruded awkwardly over either side rail. The deck and topsides were painted a straw yellow, offset against a clean white hull. With lanterns still aglow in the dawn's light, the ship sparkled like an amber diamond.

Several sentries patrolled fore and aft, watching over the ship in a high state of readiness. An officer in a dark uniform appeared on a superstructure walkway and eyed the approaching longboat.

He raised a megaphone. 'Halt and state your business.'

'I'm Dr Ellsworth Boyd of Yale University,' the old man said in a shaky voice. 'The American Consulate in Havana has arranged for my refuge aboard your vessel.'

'Stand by, please.'

The officer disappeared into the bridge. A few minutes later, he appeared on deck with several sailors. A rope ladder was lowered over the side and the longboat waved to approach. When the boat scraped against the warship's hull, Boyd stood and threw a line to one of the sailors.

'I have a crate that must accompany me. It is very important.'

Boyd kicked away some palm fronds that concealed a thick wooden crate lodged between the benches. As the sailors lowered additional ropes, Boyd surveyed the surrounding waters. Satisfied as to their safety, Boyd and his assistant secured the ropes to the crate and watched as it was hoisted aboard.

'That will have to remain on deck,' the officer said as a pair of sailors muscled the heavy box to a ventilator and tied it down.

Boyd handed his rowing partner a gold coin, shook hands in farewell, then climbed up the rope ladder. Just north of fifty, Boyd was in strapping condition for his age and acclimatized to the humidity of the tropics from working in the Caribbean each winter season. But he was no longer young, a fact he was loath to accept. He ignored the nagging pains in his joints and the constant fatigue he couldn't seem to shake as he climbed on to the deck.

'I'm Lieutenant Holman,' the officer said. 'We've been expecting you, Dr Boyd. Let me show you to a guest cabin, where you can get cleaned up. Due to security concerns, I'll have to ask that you remain confined to your cabin. I'll be happy to arrange a tour of the ship later, if you like, and we'll see if we can get you on the captain's schedule today.'

Boyd extended a hand. 'Thank you, Lieutenant. I'm grateful for your hospitality.'

Holman shook his hand with a firm grip. 'On behalf of the captain and crew, I welcome you aboard the battle cruiser USS *Maine*.'

A light evening trade wind nudged the *Maine* about her mooring until her blunt bow pointed toward the heart of Havana. The ship's sentries were thankful for the breeze, which alleviated the rank odor of the harbor's polluted waters.

The evening breeze also carried the nighttime melody of Havana's streets – the honky-tonk music from its harbor-front bars, the laughing voices of pedestrians on the nearby Malecón, and the clank of horse and wagons maneuvering through the narrow boulevards. The vibrant sounds were a painful reminder to the *Maine*'s enlisted sailors that they had been denied all shore leave in the three weeks since they had arrived. The ship had been dispatched to protect the American Consulate after a riot by Spanish loyalists, angry at the US support of Cuban rebels battling the oppressive Spanish regime.

Boyd's cabin door shuddered under a loud knock and he opened it to find Lieutenant Holman, dressed in a razor-crisp blue uniform that seemed to defy the humidity.

Holman gave a slight bow. 'The captain welcomes your acceptance to dine with him this evening.'

'Thank you, Lieutenant. Please lead on.'

A warm bath and a long afternoon nap had rejuvenated Boyd. He walked with the confident gait of a man who had beaten the odds. He still wore his field clothes, now freshly laundered, to which he had added a dinner jacket borrowed from Holman. He tugged uncomfortably at the sleeves, several inches too short for his gangly arms.

They made their way to a small officers' mess near the aft deck. In the center of the room, a linen-covered table gleaming with white china and silverware was occupied by the *Maine*'s captain.

Charles Sigsbee was a studious man with a reasoned mind, well respected in the Navy for his leadership qualities. Sporting round spectacles and a bushy mustache, he resembled a bank clerk more than a ship's captain. He rose and greeted Boyd with an impatient gaze as Holman made the introductions.

The three men sat down at the table and a steward appeared, serving a consommé. Boyd ignored a small dog that clung to the captain's side.

Sigsbee turned to Boyd. 'I hope you find your accommodations aboard the *Maine* satisfactory.'

'More than adequate,' Boyd said. 'I am thankful for your courtesy in allowing me aboard on short notice. I can't tell you how beautiful the *Maine* looked when I first sighted her this morning.'

'I'm afraid we're not configured for comfort or guests,' Sigsbee said. 'While our presence in Havana is to effect the transport of Americans at risk, local events seem to have calmed since our arrival. I must say, I was surprised at receiving a communiqué from the Havana Consul asking that you be welcomed aboard for transit back to the United States – with nary an explanation.'

Boyd sighed. 'The local Consul is a family friend from Virginia who was kind enough to intervene. However, it is no exaggeration to say my life was in grave danger.'

'Lieutenant Holman tells me you are an anthropologist from Yale University.'

'Yes, I specialize in the native Caribbean cultures. I just completed a winter field school in Jamaica and made an unplanned detour to Cuba.'

The steward cleared away their empty soup bowls and returned with plates of broiled fish. 'The crate that we brought aboard,' Holman said, 'it was from your excavation?'

Boyd nodded.

'Perhaps,' Sigsbee said, 'you'd care to show us this artifact after dinner and explain its significance.'

Boyd tensed. 'I would rather wait until we get to sea,' he said in a low voice.

'How did you come to arrive in Havana?' Holman asked.

'I left Montego Bay on the steamer *Orion* a fortnight ago, bound for New York. But shortly after we departed, the vessel developed boiler problems. We were forced to limp into Cárdenas, where the passengers were offloaded. We were told we would be delayed at least three weeks while the ship was repaired. I decided to come overland to Havana in the hope of catching a packet boat to Key West. Then the trouble began.'

He took a sip of water, and Sigsbee and Holman waited for him to continue.

'It was the Spaniard, Rodriguez,' Boyd said, his eyes bulging in anger.

'Rodriguez?' Holman said.

'An archeologist from Madrid. He happened to be in Jamaica and visited our camp. Someone must have tipped him off to my discovery, as there he was, traveling aboard the *Orion*, watching my every move. It was no coincidence.' His voice quivered. 'I have no proof, but somehow he must have disabled the vessel.'

The captain frowned. 'So what happened when you landed in Cárdenas?'

'I was traveling with two students and my field assistant, Roy Burns. We purchased a mule and wagon in Cárdenas and loaded the crate and our belongings. We set off for Havana the next day, but while bivouacked that night we were attacked.'

His eyes glazed in a distant stare at the painful memories.

'A group of armed men on horseback assaulted us. They roughed up Burns and me pretty good and took the wagon. Then one of my students went after them with a knife. The fiends ran him through with a machete, then hacked up his classmate. They didn't have a chance.'

'These were Spanish soldiers?' Sigsbee asked.

Boyd shrugged. 'They were armed and wore uniforms, but they seemed to be some sort of insurgent outfit. Their uniforms had no insignia.'

'Probably Weylerites,' Holman said. The extremist faction remained loyal to Spanish Governor General Valeriano Weyler, who had recently departed Cuba after a brutal reign subjugating Cuban rebels.

'Perhaps,' Boyd said. 'They were well equipped but appeared to be irregulars. We found they were camped in a village called Picadura. Burns and I were determined to recover the artifact and followed them to their camp. Burns started a fire to distract them, while I scattered their horses and retook the wagon. Burns caught a bullet in the chest. I had to leave him . . .' His voice trailed off in bitterness.

'I drove the wagon hard through the night, barely escaping their pursuit. At dawn, I hid the wagon in the jungle and foraged for food for me and the mule. I eluded their patrols for three days, traveling only at night on trails I hoped would lead to Havana.'

'Remarkable that you avoided capture,' Sigsbee said.

'Ultimately, I didn't.' Boyd shook his head. 'They found me on the fourth day. The mule gave me away with his braying. It was just a small patrol, four men. They pushed me up against the wagon and had their rifles raised when a volley sounded from the jungle. The Spaniards fell to the ground, cut down to a man. It was a band of Cuban rebels, who happened to be camped nearby and heard the ruckus.'

'They didn't try to take the crate?' Holman asked.

'They were only interested in the dead Spaniards' weapons. They treated me like a *compadre*, seeing, I suppose, that I was an adversary of the Spanish. They stuck with me until the edge of Havana.'

'I'm told the Cuban rebels, while untrained, are tough fighters,' Sigsbee said.

'I can attest to that,' Boyd said. 'After their patrol was killed, the remaining Spanish contingent consolidated forces and came after us with a vengeance. The rebels constantly peppered and harassed them, slowing their advances. When we reached Havana's outskirts, the Cubans dispersed, but one of them contacted the consulate on my behalf. Their best fighter guided me to the waterfront, acquired a longboat, and helped me reach the *Maine*.'

Sigsbee smiled. 'Fortuitous assistance.'

'The Cuban rebels show great hatred to the Spaniards and appreciate the armed assistance our country is giving them. They pleaded for more weapons.'

'Duly noted.'

'Captain,' Boyd said, 'how soon will you be departing Havana?'

'I can't say, but we've been on station for three weeks, and the local unrest appears to have subsided. We have a commitment in New Orleans later this month, which I believe will still be honored. I anticipate orders directing our departure within the next few days.'

Boyd nodded. 'For our well-being, I hope it is soon.'

Holman laughed. 'Dr Boyd, you needn't worry. There's not a safer place in Havana than on the *Maine*.'

After dinner, Boyd smoked a cigar with the officers on the quarterdeck, then returned to his cabin. A nagging uneasiness gnawed at his thoughts. He wouldn't feel safe until the ship left the waters of Havana Harbor far off its stern. Somewhere in his mind, he heard the voices of Roy Burns and his dead students crying a warning from the heavens.

Unable to sleep, he climbed to the main deck, drawing in a deep breath of the damp night air. Somewhere near the bridge, he heard the chimes of a bell signaling the time at half past nine. Across the harbor, revelers were getting a jump on their Mardi Gras celebration. Boyd ignored the sounds and stared over the rail at the calm black waters below.

A small skiff approached the battleship, eliciting a sharp warning from the officer of the deck. The boat's lone occupant, a ragged fisherman, waved a half-empty bottle of rum at the officer and shouted a slurred response before turning the small boat away.

Boyd watched it angle around the *Maine*'s bow, then heard a metallic clink in the water. A small crate or raft was banging against the hull. The wooden object skittered along the ship as if self-propelled. Boyd looked at it, then realized it was being towed by the fishing skiff.

A knot tightened in his stomach. He looked up to the bridge and yelled at the officer on watch. 'Officer of the deck! Officer of the deck!'

A muffled bang seemed to originate beneath the ship, and a small geyser of water sprayed near the bow. Boyd felt two beats of his heart, then there was a titanic explosion.

The Yale professor was flung against a bulkhead as the front half of the ship erupted like an angry volcano. Steel, smoke and flames shot high into the sky, carrying the mangled bodies of dozens of crewmen. Boyd shook off a pain in his shoulder as a rain of debris hammered the deck around him. The ship's forward crow's nest appeared from nowhere and collapsed in a heap along-side him.

Rising to his feet, Boyd instinctively staggered for-ward across the listing deck. His ears rang, drowning out the cries of sailors trapped belowdecks. All that mattered was the relic. Under the red glow of an inferno burning amidships, he staggered toward it. Somehow the crate had escaped damage and was lying secure near the remains of a crumpled ventilator.

A fast-approaching side-wheeler caught his eye. The

steam-powered boat drew alongside the sinking battle-ship, turning briskly and slapping against its hull. Without making a sound, a trio of men in dark clothing leaped aboard.

Boyd thought they were part of a rescue party until one of the *Maine*'s sailors, a machinist who had been standing watch, limped across their path, his singed uniform smoking. One of the borders lunged at the sailor, driving a blunt knife into his side and tossing his crumpled body over the rail.

Boyd was too shocked to react. Then, his mind pro-cessed the meaning. The boarders weren't there to lend aid; they were Rodriguez's men. They had come for the artifact.

The archeologist limped back to the crate and spun to face the attackers. A twisted shovel, flung up from one of the coal bunkers, teetered against a bulkhead. Boyd grabbed it.

The first attacker brandished a bloody knife that glistened under the light of the spreading flames.

Boyd swung the shovel.

The intruder tried to step back, but the water now swirling at his feet slowed his movement. Boyd tagged him across his cheekbone. The attacker grunted and fell to his knees, but his two companions behind didn't falter. They rushed Boyd before he could swing again, knocking the shovel aside. A heavy pistol appeared in the hands of one of the men and he fired point-blank at Boyd.

The bullet struck his left shoulder. The archeologist fell back, and the two men elbowed past him and loosened the ropes that secured the crate.

'No!' Boyd shouted as they began dragging the crate across the sinking deck.

He regained his feet and sloshed after them on weakening legs. The boarders ignored him and hoisted the crate over the side and into the arms of several men in the lighter. One wore a low-brimmed hat to hide his face, but Boyd knew it was Rodriguez.

Woozy from loss of blood, Boyd sagged against the nearest man. The boarder, a short man with cold black eyes, grabbed Boyd's arm. But before he could shove Boyd aside, his face fell blank. A faint shadow crossed his face, and his gaze shot upward.

An instant later, the border disappeared under the towering mass of one of the *Maine*'s twin funnels, which had fractured at its base and collapsed like a hewn redwood. While the attacker was flattened, Boyd was only clipped by the funnel. But his leg got caught under the mass, pinning him to the now awash deck.

He struggled to break free, but the weight was too great. Held underwater, he fought for air, poking his head above the rising water and gasping great breaths as he pulled at his trapped leg.

Beneath him, he felt the ship lurch as the keel sought the harbor floor. As the forward fires licked at the ship's ammunition magazines, sporadic shots zinged around him. Then the bow began a slow descent to the bottom.

Feeling the vessel begin to plunge, Boyd strained for one last breath. His final vision was of the side-wheeler, the stolen crate wedged on its aft deck, steaming rapidly toward the harbor entrance.

Then the *Maine* dragged him down into the blackened depths.

PART I
Mystic Current

The Alta and Diving Bell

I

June 2016

The squat wooden fishing boat had been painted a dandy combination of periwinkle and lemon. When the colors were fresh, they had lent the vessel an air of happy tranquility. But that was almost two decades ago. The weathering of sun and sea had beaten out all semblance of vibrancy, leaving the boat looking pale and anemic against the ominous sea.

The two Jamaican fishermen working the *Javina* gave little thought to her dilapidated exterior. Their only concern was whether the smoky engine would propel them back to their island home before the leaks in the hull overran the bilge pump.

'Quick with the bait while the tuna are still biting.' The elder man stood at the stern while manually deploying a long line over the side. Near his feet, a pair of large silver fish flopped angrily about the deck.

'Not you worry, Uncle Desmond.' The younger man picked up some small chunks of mackerel and slapped them on to a string of rusty hand-forged hooks. 'The sun is low, so the fish still bite on the bank.'

'It ain't the sun that's waiting for the bait.' Desmond

grabbed the remains of the baited line and dropped it over the side, tying off the end to a cleat on the gunwale. He stepped toward the wheelhouse to engage the throttle but stopped and cocked his ear. A deep rumble, like rolling thunder, sounded over the boat's old diesel motor.

'What is it, Uncle?'

Desmond shook his head. He noticed a dark circle of water forming off the port beam.

The *Javina* creaked and groaned from the invisible hand of a submerged shock wave. A frothy ball of white water erupted a short distance away, spraying a dozen feet into the air. It was followed by a bubbling concentric wave that seemed to rise off the surface. The wave expanded, encompassing the fishing boat and lifting it into the sky. Desmond grabbed the wheel for balance.

His nephew staggered to his side, his eyes agape. 'What is it?'

'Something underwater.' Desmond gripped the wheel with white knuckles as the boat heeled far to one side.

The vessel hung on the verge of flipping, then righted itself as the wave subsided. The *Javina* settled back to a calm surface as the wave dissipated in a circular path of boiling froth.

'That was crazy,' his nephew said, scratching his head. 'What's happening way out here?' The small boat was more than twenty miles from Jamaica, the island's coastline not quite visible on the horizon.

Desmond shrugged as he turned the boat away

from the receding eruption's epicenter. He motioned off the bow. 'Those ships ahead. They must be searching for oil.'

A mile from the *Javina*, a large exploration ship tailed a high-riding ocean barge down current. An orange crew boat motored slightly ahead of the ship. All three were headed for the *Javina* – or, more precisely, the point of the underwater explosion.

'Uncle, who says they can come blasting through our waters?'

Desmond smiled. 'They got a boat that big, they can go anywhere they want.'

As the small armada drew closer, the waters around the *Javina* became dotted with white bits of flotsam arising from the deep. They were bits of dead fish and sea creatures, mangled by the explosion.

'The tuna!' the nephew cried. 'They kill our tuna.'

'We find more someplace else.' Desmond eyed the exploration ship bearing down on them. 'I think it best we leave the bank now.'

'Not before I give them a piece of my mind.'

The nephew reached over and spun the wheel hard to port, driving the *Javina* toward the big ship. The orange crew boat noted the course change and sped over, pulling alongside a few minutes later. The two brown-skinned men in the crew boat didn't appear Jamaican, which was confirmed when they spoke in oddly accented English.

'You must leave this area now,' the boat's pilot ordered.

'This is our fishing grounds,' the nephew said. 'Look

around. You kill all our fish. You owe us for the fish we lose.'

The crew boat pilot stared at the Jamaicans with no hint of sympathy. Pulling a transmitter to his lips, he placed a brief call to the ship. Without another word to the fishermen, he gunned the motor and drove the crew boat away.

The massive black hulk of the exploration ship arrived a short time later, towering over the *Javina*. Undaunted, the fishermen yelled their complaints to the crewmen scurrying about the ship's decks.

None paid any attention to the dilapidated boat bobbing beneath them until two men stepped to the rail. Dressed in light khaki fatigues, they studied the *Javina* momentarily, then raised compact assault rifles to their shoulders.

Desmond rammed the throttle ahead and spun the wheel hard over as he heard two quick thumps. His nephew stared frozen as a pair of 40mm grenades, fired from launchers affixed to the assault rifles, slammed on to the open deck and bounced about his feet.

The wheelhouse vaporized into a bright red fireball. Smoke and flames climbed into the warm Caribbean sky as the *Javina* wallowed on her broken keel. The pale blue-and-yellow fishing boat was charred black as she settled quickly by the bow.

For a moment, she seemed to hesitate, and then the old vessel rolled in a faint farewell and disappeared under the waves.

2

Mark Ramsey allowed himself a slight grin. He could hardly contain his sense of euphoria as he sped past the grandstand. The gritty smell of gasoline and burnt rubber tickled his nostrils, while the cheers of a trackside crowd were just audible over the roar of his motorcar. It wasn't just the sensation of racing on an open track that gave him joy. It was his leading position with two laps to go that thrilled the wealthy Canadian industrialist.

Driving a 1928 Bugatti Type 35 Grand Prix racer in a vintage-class oval race, he had been the odds-on favorite. The light and nimble French blue Bugatti, with its iconic horseshoe-shaped radiator, had been one of the most successful racing marques of its day. Ramsey's supercharged straight-eight engine gave him a healthy boost against the competition.

He had quickly separated himself from the field of assorted old cars, save for a dark green Bentley that tailed several lengths behind. The heavy British car, carrying an open four-seat Le Mans body, was no match for the Bugatti through the Old Dominion Speedway's banked turns.

Ramsey knew he was home free. Easing out of the second turn, he floored the accelerator, roaring down the main straightaway and lapping a Stutz Bearcat. A white flag caught his eye, waved by the starter atop a flag stand, signaling the final lap. Ramsey allowed himself a sideways glance at the crowd, not noticing that the pursuing Bentley had crept closer.

Braking and downshifting with the racer's heel-and-toe foot maneuver, he guided the Bugatti in a low arc through the next turn. The heftier Bentley was forced to follow higher, losing precious distance. But coming out of the turn, the Bentley cut a sharp line on to the backstretch and let out a bellow. Equipped with a Rootes supercharger, which protruded from the front crank-case like a silver battering ram, the Bentley howled as its driver mashed the accelerator before upshifting.

Ramsey glanced at a dash-mounted mirror. The more powerful Bentley had closed within two lengths, its imposing blunt radiator filling the image. He held the accelerator down through the backstretch as long as he could, braking late and hard, before throwing the Bugatti into the final turn.

Behind him, the Bentley fell back as its driver braked earlier and entered the turn wide. Its tires squealed as they fought for grip while chasing the Bugatti through the turn. The Bentley's driver was no slouch. He was driving the big demon at its limit.

Ramsey tightened his grip on the wheel and muscled the Bugatti through the curve. His own late braking had sent him on an awkward line through the turn. Trailing his own brakes to hold his turn, he was angered to hear the wail of the 'Blower' Bentley accelerating from behind him.

The Bentley was high on the track, but its driver had aligned its wheels to exit the corner. Ramsey dug hard through the turn, then was flat on the gas the instant he could unwind his steering wheel. The shrieking Bentley had almost closed the gap and was on his rear fender as they hit the homestretch.

It was a classic fight to the finish, pitting light-weight finesse against brute power. The Bugatti's 140-horsepower motor was a hundred fewer than the Bentley, but the British car tipped the scales at a ton heavier.

Both cars surged toward the 100-mile-per-hour mark as they stretched for the finish line. Ramsey saw the flagman wildly waving the checkered flag and he felt his heart pounding. The Bugatti still held the lead, but the Bentley was inching alongside. Racing fender to fender, the two ancient vehicles roared down the track, mechanical dinosaurs from a more elegant age.

The finish line approached and brute power held sway. The Bentley lunged ahead at the last instant, nipping the Bugatti by inches. As the larger car edged by, Ramsey glanced at the Bentley's cockpit. The driver appeared totally relaxed at the moment of victory, his elbow casually cast over the door sill. Breaking protocol, Ramsey charged ahead of the field as the entrants took a cooldown lap before heading to the pits.

Ramsey parked the Bugatti next to his customized luxury bus and oversaw his crew of mechanics as they checked the car and placed it in a covered trailer. He watched curiously as the Bentley pulled to a stop nearby.

There were no trailers or team of mechanics tending to the British car. Just an attractive woman with cinnamon hair waiting for the victor, sitting in a folding chair with a toolbox and a cooler at her feet.

A tall, lean man climbed out of the Bentley and collected a passionate hug from the woman. Pulling off his racing helmet, he ran his fingers through a thick mat of black hair that framed a tan and rugged face. He looked up as Ramsey approached and extended a hand.

'Congratulations on the win,' Ramsey said, muting his disappointment. 'First time anybody's taken me in the Bugatti.'

'This old warhorse found a burst of energy on the last lap.' The driver patted the Bentley's fender. His sea-green eyes nearly matched the color of the car and burned with an intelligence Ramsey had rarely observed. The driver had the look of a man who lived and played hard.

Ramsey smiled, knowing full well it was the driver, not the car, that had beaten him.

'My name's Mark Ramsey.'

'Dirk Pitt,' the driver said. 'This is my wife, Loren.'

Ramsey shook hands with Loren, noting she was even more attractive up close.

'I love your Bugatti,' she said. 'Such a sleek car for its day.'

'Fun to drive, too,' he said. 'That particular car won the Targa Florio in 1928.'

As he spoke, his team of mechanics pushed the French car into the back of a semi-trailer truck. Loren recognized the logo, emblazoned on the side, of a red grizzly bear with a pickax in its teeth.

'Mark Ramsey . . . you're the head of Bruin Mining and Exploration.'

Ramsey looked askance at Loren. 'Not many people know me in the States.'

'I was on a recent delegation that toured your gold mine on the Thompson River in British Columbia. We were impressed by the environmental consciousness that surrounds the entire operation.'

'Mining has had a poor track record, but there's no reason that can't change. Are you a congresswoman?'

'I represent the Seventh District of Colorado.'

'Of course, Representative Loren Smith. I'm afraid I was out of town when the US congressional delegation toured. My misfortune, I should say. What was your interest in the operation, if I may ask?'

'I serve on the House Subcommittee on the Environment, and we are examining new ways of managing our natural resources.'

'Please let me know if there is any way I can be of help. We're always looking at safe ways to mine the earth.'

'That's very good of you.'

Pitt picked up Loren's folding chair and placed it in the rear of the Bentley. 'Mr Ramsey, would you care to join us for dinner?'

'I'm afraid I have to catch a plane to Miami to meet with some clients. Perhaps next time I'm in Washington.' He eyed Pitt with a dare. 'I'd like another go at you and your Bentley.'

Pitt smiled. 'Nobody has to ask me twice to get behind the wheel.'

Pitt climbed in and restarted the Bentley. Loren joined him a moment later.

Ramsey shook his head. 'You don't have a trailer?'

'The Bentley's as good on the street as it is on the track,' Pitt grinned, gunning the car forward. Both occupants waved as Ramsey stared back.

Loren turned to Pitt and smiled. 'I don't think Mr Ramsey was too impressed with your maintenance crew.'

Pitt reached over and squeezed his wife's knee. 'What are you talking about? I've got the sexiest crew chief on the planet.'

He collected his winner's trophy at the gate, then rumbled out of the Manassas, Virginia, track grounds. Passing the nearby Civil War battlefield site, he turned on to Interstate 66 and made a beeline toward Washington, D. C. The Sunday afternoon traffic was light, and Pitt was able to cruise at the speed limit.

'I forgot to tell you,' Loren shouted over the roar of the open car, 'I got a call from Rudi Gunn while you were on the track. He needs to talk to you about a situation he's monitoring in the Caribbean.'

'Can it wait until tomorrow?'

'He called from the office, so I told him we'd stop by on the way home.' Loren smiled at her husband, knowing his disinterest was only a bluff.

'If you say so.'

Reaching the suburb of Rosslyn, Pitt turned on to the George Washington Parkway and followed it south along the Potomac. The white marble edifice of the Lincoln Memorial gleamed in the fading sunlight as he turned into the entrance of a towering green glass building. He drove the Bentley past a guard station and parked in an underground garage near a keyed elevator, which they rode to the tenth floor.

They had entered the headquarters of the National Underwater and Marine Agency, the federal department tasked with stewardship of the seas. As NUMA's Director, Dirk Pitt oversaw a large staff of marine biologists, oceanographers, and geologists who monitored the oceans from a fleet of research ships across the globe. The agency also used ocean buoys, gliding submersibles, and even a small squadron of aircraft, all linked to a sophisticated satellite network, that allowed constant monitoring of weather, sea states, and even oil spills in nearly real-time fashion.

The elevator doors opened on to a high-tech bay that housed the agency's powerful computer center. A quietly humming IBM Blue Gene supercomputer system was concealed behind a high curved wall that faced Loren and Pitt. Extending across the face of the wall was a massive video display, illuminating a dozen or more color graphics and images.

Two men were engaged at a central control table in front of the video wall. The smaller of the two, a wiry man with horn-rimmed glasses, noticed Loren and Pitt enter and bounded over to greet them.

'Glad you could stop by,' Rudi Gunn said with a smile. An ex–Navy commander who had graduated first in his class from the Naval Academy, he served as Pitt's Deputy Director. 'Any luck at the track?'

'I think I would have made the late W. O. Bentley proud today.' Pitt smiled. 'What brings you boys into the office on a Sunday?'

'An environmental concern in the Caribbean. Hiram can tell you more, but there appears to be a pattern of unusual dead zones cropping up south of Cuba.'

The trio stepped over to the control table, where Hiram Yaeger, NUMA's head of computer resources, sat pecking at a keyboard.

'Afternoon, Mr and Mrs Pitt,' he said without looking up. 'Please grab a seat.'

An ardent nonconformist, Yaeger wore his long hair wrapped in a ponytail and dressed like he had just staggered out of a biker bar. 'Sorry to intrude on your weekend, but Rudi and I thought you might want to be aware of something we picked up on satellite imagery.'

He pointed to the top corner of the video wall where

a large satellite image of the Gulf of Mexico and the Caribbean Sea dominated the screen. 'That's a standard photographic view. Now we'll go to a digitally enhanced image.'

A second photo appeared, which overlapped the original with brilliant colors. A bright red band arced across the eastern Gulf Coast shoreline.

'What does the red enhancement indicate?' Loren asked.

'A dead zone, judging by its intensity, off the Mississippi River,' Pitt said.

'That's right,' Gunn said. 'Satellite imagery can detect changes in the light reflection off the ocean's surface, which provides an indication of the water's organic content. The seas off the Mississippi River Delta are a textbook dead zone. Rich nutrients in the river from fertilizers and other chemical runoffs create explosive growths of plankton – algae blooms. This in turn depletes the water's oxygen content, leading to hypoxic conditions that kill all marine life. The area off the Mississippi Delta is a notorious dead zone that's concerned scientists for many years.'

Loren noted the lingering bands of magenta that discolored the coastal waters from Texas to Alabama. 'I had no idea it was so pervasive.'

'The intensity is fairly localized at the delta,' Gunn said, 'but you can see the widespread effects.'

'That's well and good,' Pitt said, 'but we've known about the Mississippi dead zone for years.'

'Sorry, chief,' Yaeger said. 'We're actually focused a little farther south.'

He pointed to a trio of burgundy blotches that dotted the waters northwest of Jamaica. The patches were spread across an irregular line, extending past the Cayman Islands to near the western tip of Cuba.

Yaeger tapped at his keyboard, zooming in on the area. 'What we have is an odd series of dead zones that have cropped up rather suddenly.'

'What does the maroon color signify?' Loren asked. 'And why do the spots get darker as they progress to the northwest?'

'It appears to be another burst of phytoplankton growth,' Gunn said, 'but much higher in intensity than we saw in the Mississippi Delta. They were fast-forming but may be somewhat temporary in nature.' He nodded at Yaeger, who brought up a series of satellite images.

'This is something of a time-lapse view,' he said, 'starting about three months ago.'

The initial photo showed no anomalies. A brightly hued spot appeared in the next image, then two more burgundy patches in the following photos. As each new dead zone appeared, the earlier spots faded slightly.

'There's some sort of sharp impact that is gradually diluted but is soon followed by another outbreak at a different location. As you can see, there seems to be a pattern from southeast to northwest.'

Pitt eyed the multiple dead zones as they progressed.

'What's odd is that they are far from any landmass. They aren't the result of pollution from river runoffs.'

'Precisely,' Gunn said. 'It doesn't make a lot of sense.'

'Could someone be dumping pollutants at sea?' Loren asked.

'It's possible,' Gunn said, 'but why would someone go to all these locations? A criminal polluter would likely just dump in one spot.'

'What got our attention were the related fish kills and the apparent progression of the disturbances toward the Gulf of Mexico. We've found numerous media reports in Jamaica, the Caymans, and even Cuba, reporting large quantities of dead fish and marine mammals washing ashore miles away from the visible zones. We can't say for sure there is a connection, but if so, the impact may be much more acute than appears on the images.'

Loren looked back at the view off Louisiana. 'The Gulf Coast can hardly afford a new environmental catastrophe on the heels of the BP oil spill.'

'That's precisely our concern,' Gunn said. 'If these dead zones begin sprouting in the Gulf of Mexico at the intensity we're witnessing here, the results could be devastating.'

Pitt nodded. 'We need to find out what's creating them. What do our hydrographic buoys have to say?'

Yaeger brought up a new screen, showing a global schematic. Hundreds of tiny flashing lights peppered the map, representing NUMA sea buoys deployed around the world. Linked to satellites, the buoys measured water temperature, salinity, and sea states, with the data constantly downloaded to Yaeger's computer center. He zeroed in on the Caribbean, highlighting a few dozen buoys. None were located near the dead zones.

'I'm afraid we don't have any markers in the wake of the dead zones,' Yaeger said. 'I checked the status of those closest, but they didn't reveal anything unusual.'

'We'll need to get some resources on-site,' Pitt said. 'How about our research vessels?'

'The closest vessel of size would be the *Sargasso Sea*.' Yaeger converted the screen to show the fleet of NUMA-deployed research ships.

'She's in Key West, supporting an Underwater Technology project that Al Giordino is leading,' Gunn said. 'Do you want me to call him and reassign the ship to investigate?'

Yaeger rolled his eyes. 'Al will love that.'

Pitt stared at the map. 'No, that won't be necessary.'

Loren saw the look in her husband's eyes and knew exactly what he was thinking.

'Oh, no,' she grimaced, while shaking her head. 'Not the lure of the deep again.'

Pitt could only gaze at his wife and smile.

The Revolution Day party wound down early. It had been sixty-three years since Fidel Castro and a band of rebels attacked an Army barracks in Santiago, setting off the eventual overthrow of Cuban leader Fulgencio Batista. These days, there seemed little worth celebrating. The economy was still in tatters, food was in short supply, and the technological leaps the rest of the world enjoyed seemed to be passing the country by. On top of that, rumors were rampant, yet again, that *El Comandante* was near his last breath.

Alphonse Ortiz drained the mojito, his sixth of the night, and weaved his way toward the door of the stylishly furnished apartment.

'Leaving so soon?' the party's hostess asked, apprehending him at the door. The wife of the Agriculture Minister, she was a buxom woman buried under a mask of heavy makeup.

'I must be fresh for a speech tomorrow at Martí Airport, recognizing its recent expansion. Is Escobar about?'

'Over peddling influence with the Trade Minister.' She nodded at her husband across the room.

'Please give him my regards. It was a splendid party.'

The woman smiled at the false compliment. 'We're happy you could join us. Good luck with your speech tomorrow.'

Ortiz, a highly regarded Cuban vice president on the powerful Council of State, gave a wobbly bow and escaped out the door. Five hours trapped conversing with half the Cuban cabinet had left him hungering for fresh air. Easing himself down three flights of stairs, he crossed an austere lobby and stepped on to the street. A blast of warm air greeted him, with the sounds of revelers celebrating the national holiday.

Ortiz stepped across the crumbling sidewalk and waved at a parked black sedan. Its headlights popped on and the Chinese-made Geely zipped up to the curb. Ortiz opened the rear door and collapsed into the backseat.

'Take me home, Roberto,' he said to the wrinkled man at the wheel.

'Did you enjoy the party?'

'About as much as I savor a migraine. Stupid fools just want to relive the past. Nobody in our government bothers thinking about tomorrow.'

'I think the president does. He likes your thinking. One day, he puts you in charge.'

It was a possibility, Ortiz knew. There was a short list of possible successors waiting for Raúl Castro to retire in 2018, and he knew his name was on it. That was the only reason he had attended the Revolution Day party and made nice with the other cabinet ministers. When it came to politics, you could never have too many allies.

'One day, I'll be in charge of a rocking chair,' he mused to his driver. He leaned back in his seat and closed his eyes.

Roberto grinned as he pulled into traffic and threaded his way out of downtown Havana. A moment later, a rugged six-ton Kamaz military truck stopped near the front of the apartment building. A soldier in olive drab fatigues emerged from the shadows of an adjacent doorway and climbed into the truck.

He nodded toward the departing black sedan. 'The target is live.'

The driver stepped on the gas, cutting off a motor-cyclist as he veered down the street. A block ahead, the Geely skirted past the Museo Napoleónico before turning on to Avenue La Rampa and driving across the western suburbs. While many high-ranking govern-ment officials lived in luxury city apartments, Ortiz maintained his residence in a modest hilltop home out-side Havana that overlooked the sea.

The traffic and city lights gradually fell away as the Geely motored through an agricultural area of cooperative tobacco and cassava farms. The military truck, having trailed through the city at a discreet dis-tance, closed the gap and rode up tight on the sedan's bumper.

Roberto, who had worked as a chauffeur for sixty of his seventy-five years, didn't flinch. The unlit road was a haven for stray dogs and goats, and he wasn't going to risk a collision on account of an anxious tailgater.

The truck hung tight for a mile until the road curved up a sweeping hillside. With a noisy downshift, the truck drifted into the opposing lane and charged alongside the Geely.

Roberto glanced out his window and noted a star-shaped emblem on the door. A Revolutionary Army vehicle.

The truck surged slightly ahead, then veered sharply into the Geely's lane, smacking into the sedan's front fender.

Had Roberto possessed the reflexes of a younger man, he might have braked hard and quick enough to slip back with minimal damage. But he was a touch too late, allowing the heavy truck to shove the car across the road.

The sedan slammed into a rusty side rail, producing a trail of sparks.

The truck showed no mercy, pinning the Geely against the steel barrier in the hope of propelling it over or through the rail, then down the hillside. But as the vehicles exited the curve, the side rail came to an end, replaced by a series of squat concrete pillars. The sedan slid past the side rail and smashed head-on into the first concrete post.

The car struck with a loud clap that echoed across the landscape. On the opposite hill, a young ranch hand was startled awake by the crash. Sitting upright in an open lean-to he shared with a dozen goats, he peered toward the road beyond. An Army truck was skidding to a halt just past a mangled car. One of the car's headlights still shone, illuminating the truck a few yards ahead. The boy grabbed his sandals to go and help, then stopped and watched.

A man in fatigues emerged from the truck. The soldier glanced around as if ensuring no one was watching, then strode toward the car, a flashlight in one hand and a dark object in the other.

Inside the car, Ortiz groaned from the pain of a separated shoulder and a broken nose, having been flung into the headrest. He gathered his senses as warm blood flowed down his chin. 'Roberto?'

The driver sat motionless, slumped over the wheel. Roberto's neck had snapped, killing him instantly, after he had rocketed into the windshield. The Chinese export car had no air bags.

As reality sank in, Ortiz sat up and saw the Army truck through the shattered windshield. He wiped his bloodied face and watched as the soldier approached, carrying a dark object.

'Help me. I think my arm is broken,' he said as the soldier pried open the passenger door.

The soldier gave him a cold gaze and Ortiz realized he was not there to offer aid. Sitting helpless, he watched as the soldier raised his arm and swung at him with the object. An instant before it crushed his skull, the minister recognized it as an ordinary tyre iron.

4

The diver thrust his legs in a scissors kick, propelling his body swiftly through the clear water. He kept his face down to scan the sandy seafloor that stretched before him like a ragged beige carpet. Detecting a movement on the bottom, he slowed, angling toward the object. It wasn't a fish but something resembling a huge, brightly colored crab.

The creature traveled on long, spider-like appendages that seemed to rotate along its sides. It emitted a faint blue glow from its eyes, which peered coldly ahead. The diver followed the mock crab as it crawled toward a high protrusion of coral. The crab butted against the coral, then backtracked and tried again. Once more the coral stopped its progress.

The diver watched the crab repeat the movement several times before swimming close and swatting its back. Its blue eyes turned black and its legs stopped clawing. The diver grabbed the crab, tucked it under one arm, and kicked to the surface.

He broke the water amid a gentle swell, close to a modern research ship painted bright turquoise. Side-swimming to a hydraulic dive platform off the stern, he deposited the crab and hoisted himself aboard.

Al Giordino was a short man with the burly build of a professional wrestler combined with the toughness of an elder crocodile. His muscular arms and legs fairly burst the seams of his wetsuit as he rose to his feet, spat out his regulator, and yanked off his dive mask. He brushed away a lock of curly brown hair plastered to his forehead and waved to a man on deck to raise the dive platform.

A minute later, the platform creaked to a stop at deck level. Giordino gathered up the crab with an irksome look and stomped on to the deck. He froze at the sight of the crewman who had raised the platform. It was Dirk Pitt.

Giordino grinned at the sight of his boss and old friend. 'Escaped from the tower of power again, I see.'

'Just making sure the NUMA technology budget isn't being spent on cheap rum and dancing girls.'

Giordino shot Pitt a pained look. 'I told you, I've sworn off cheap rum since my last pay raise.'

Pitt smiled as he helped Giordino remove his tank and weight belt. Friends since childhood, the two had worked together for years, forging a bond tighter than brothers. As founding employees of NUMA, their underwater scrapes were legendary within the agency. Giordino now headed up NUMA's Underwater Technology division, spending much of his time field-testing new remote sensing devices and submersible vehicles.

Pitt nodded toward the mechanical crab. 'So who's your arachnoid friend?'

'We call her the Creepy Crawler.' Giordino placed it on a workbench and began stripping off his wetsuit. 'She's designed for extended deepwater survey duty.'

'Power source?' Pitt asked.

'A small fuel cell, which processes hydrogen from seawater. We designed her to crawl across the bottom of the murky depths for upward of six months. We can deploy her from a submersible or even drop her over the side of a ship. With preprogrammed guidance, she will crawl along a directed path until reaching a designated end point. Then she'll float to the surface and emit a satellite signal that tells us where to pick her up.'

'I assume she's recording her travels?'

Giordino patted the mechanical creature. 'This one's loaded with a battery of sensors and a video camera, which is activated at periodic intervals. We have a half dozen more in the lab that can be configured with a variety of sensing devices, depending on the mission.'

'Might come in handy when we get to the Cayman Trench.'

Giordino arched a brow. 'I figured you didn't come down to Key West for lunch and a drink at Sloppy Joe's. Why the Cayman Trench?'

'It's near the heart of a string of dead zones that have cropped up in a line between Jamaica and the western tip of Cuba.' Pitt summarized his meeting with Gunn and Yaeger in Washington.

'Any idea of the source?' Giordino asked.

'None. That's why I want to get on-site and have a look.'

'If it's man-made, we'll find it,' Giordino said. 'When do we leave?'

'Captain says we can shove off in an hour.'

Giordino gave a wistful gaze toward Duval Street and its line of raucous bars, then tucked the Creepy Crawler under his arm.

'If that's the case,' he said with a disheartened tone, 'I'd better find my friend a new brain before she's cast to the depths again.'

He walked across the deck, leaving a trail of wet footprints behind him.

5

The suffocating darkness six hundred feet beneath the surface of the ocean had vanished. Banks of LED lights, encased in titanium housings capable of withstanding the crushing pressure, cast a bright glow on the undulating seafloor's stark landscape. A silver-scaled tarpon swam by and eyed a curious array of scaffolding that towered under the lights before darting into the more familiar blackness.

The structure resembled a lighted Christmas tree that had toppled to one side. Or so thought Warren Fletcher, who peered through a small acrylic window that was as thick as his fist. The veteran commercial diver was perched in a large diving bell that was suspended fifty feet above the seabed by a cable from a support ship.

Working in the alien world at the bottom of the sea fascinated Fletcher. He found an odd tranquility working in the cold dark deep. It kept him active in the grimy, dangerous business of commercial diving years after his original dive partners had retired. For Fletcher, the siren of the deep still summoned.

'You ready for your next dive, Pops?' The helium-rich air circulating through the diving bell gave the voice a high-pitched warble.

Fletcher turned to a walrus-shaped man named Tank who was coiling an umbilical hose across a rack. 'There ain't a day I'm not, Junior.'

Tank grinned. 'Brownie's on his way back, should be up in five.'

As the designated bellman, Tank was responsible for assisting his two divers with their equipment and for manning their life-sustaining umbilicals. The trio would work an eight-hour shift before being hoisted to the surface ship *Alta*. There they were transferred to prison-like living quarters in a steel saturation chamber that maintained the pressure of the seafloor.

Keeping the divers under constant pressure avoided the need for decompression cycles after every dive. Captives of deep pressure, the men were disciples of saturation diving, where their bodies adjusted to an infusion of nitrogen that might last for days or even weeks. At the end of the job, the men would undergo a single extended decompression cycle before seeing the light of day again.

The purpose behind their dives was the age-old quest for oil. Fletcher and his crewmates were several days into a weeklong project to fit a test wellhead and riser on to the seafloor. A drill ship would then hover over the site and bore through the sediment in the hope of striking oil. Fletcher and his cohorts were laying the foundation for the third test well their Norwegian employer had attempted in the last six months.

Under license from the Cuban government, the

exploration company had been given the right to explore a promising tract of territorial waters northeast of Havana. Petroleum experts believed a huge, untapped trove of oil and gas reserves lay off the Cuban coastline, but the Norwegian firm was batting zero. Its first two test wells had come up dry.

'You think the *Alta* will run us into Havana when we pop the chamber?' Tank asked.

Fletcher nodded but was only half listening. His attention focused on a faint light that appeared beyond the wellhead site. He turned and looked down the diving bell's trapdoor, spotting the light of Will Brown working his way up to the chamber. He turned back to the viewport as the other light grew closer, splitting into two beams. As the object approached the base of the wellhead riser, Fletcher could see it was a small white submersible.

The submersible slowly ascended, traveling close enough that Fletcher could see its pilot. The submersible carried a thick plate-shaped disk on its articulated arm like a waiter carrying a tray.

As the vessel rose out of view, Fletcher cocked his head toward the ceiling. 'Shack, who just did a drive-by?'

An unseen voice from the *Alta* replied, 'You got company down there?'

'Just got buzzed by a submersible.'

There was a long pause. 'It's not ours. You sure you ain't seeing things, Pops?'

'Affirmative,' Fletcher said, annoyed.

'We'll keep our eyes open to see if anyone comes 'round to collect her.'

Tank kept reeling in the umbilical as Brown swam closer. The open floor hatch fed through a short tube to a second external hatch, also open. The pressurized interior, fed oxygen and helium from the surface, matched the pressure of the water depth and kept the chamber from flooding.

With his helmet-mounted dive light leading the way, the shadowy figure of Brown approached and popped his head through the interior hatch.

Tank and Fletcher pulled Brown up through the hatch, setting him on the deck with his feet dangling in the water. The diver carefully removed his fins while Tank unhooked his umbilical, which had provided Brown a cocktail mixture of breathing gases and also cycled a stream of hot water through his drysuit.

Removing his faceplate, the diver took a deep breath, then spoke through chattering teeth. 'Cold as penguin crap down there. Either there's a kink in the hot-water line or the boys upstairs turned down the thermostat.'

'Oh, you wanted hot water through there?' Tank pointed at the umbilical. 'I told them you needed some air-conditioning.' He laughed and handed Brown a thermos of hot coffee.

'Very funny.' The diver unclipped a large wrench from his weight belt and handed it to Fletcher. 'I almost

47

have the base flange mounted. You won't have any problem finishing up.'

A loud rumble rattled through the diving bell. A second later, Tank and Fletcher were thrown off their feet as a concussive blast rocked the bell. Tank yelled as Brown's coffee scalded his neck. Fletcher grabbed the umbilical rack and hung on while the diving bell swayed. It felt like a giant hand had grabbed the bell and was shaking it like a snow globe.

'What's going on?' Brown yelled as the other two fell across his prone body.

'Something on the surface,' Fletcher muttered, still gripping the wrench. He felt an upward jerk, then the lights went out and the shaking stopped. His face was near a viewport and he instinctively looked out. For an instant, the wellhead lights were strangely bright, then they blinked out. It took him a second to realize what was wrong. The bell had been jerked toward the wellhead and was falling forward.

'Seal the hatch! Seal the hatch!' he yelled, dropping to his knees.

A small red auxiliary light popped on, providing dim illumination, as an emergency alarm wailed. Brown's legs were still dangling through the exterior hatch.

Fletcher grabbed the diver and pulled him to the side. Tank had regained his senses enough to slam down and tighten the interior hatch. An instant later, the diving bell struck a hard object. A groan of stressed metal beneath their feet reverberated through the interior.

48

The diving bell hesitated, then jerked to one side. Inside, human bodies, heavy dive equipment, and strands of umbilical cords lay crumpled in a heap. An anguished moan was barely audible over the beeping alarm.

'You boys okay?' Fletcher asked, worming his way through a pile of umbilical cord and easing himself to his feet.

'Yeah.' Tank's voice was shaky. The dim light couldn't hide the unadulterated fear in his eyes. He reached up and felt a bloody gash on the top of his ear. 'Brownie, you okay?'

There was no response.

Fletcher groped through the tangle of debris until touching Brown's drysuit. He gripped the material and pulled the diver clear. Brown slumped over, unconscious.

Fletcher pulled down the diver's hoodie and felt for a pulse, feeling a faint flutter. He heard a groan and saw his chest heaving. A golf-ball-sized lump protruded from his forehead, and something about his feet didn't look right.

Pulling away his fins, he could see Brown's left foot dangled at an awkward angle. 'I think he broke his ankle – and got knocked cold in the tumble.'

The two men cleared a space on the sloping deck and stretched Brown out. Tank produced a first-aid kit, and they wrapped his ankle and bandaged his head.

'That's about all we can do until he regains consciousness,' Fletcher said.

Trying to find his bearings, he pressed his nose to the acrylic porthole. The sea was as black as coal, but the interior light cast a faint glow around the bell. They had collided with the riser or its blowout preventer and appeared to be hung up on one of the two structures. A long, slender object wavered in the current, and he shielded his eyes against the porthole to discern what it was.

He tensed in sudden recognition, feeling like a wrecking ball had slammed into his belly. It was a portion of the diving bell's umbilical. Several long coils of it dangled from a riser crossmember. While it was possible the support ship had inadvertently released a length of their drop cable and umbilical, he instinctively knew otherwise. Both lines to the surface had been severed.

Fletcher stepped to a control panel and studied the dials tilted before him. Confirmation came quickly. Electrical power, helium and oxygen gas, communications, and even hot water for the dive suits – all provided from the *Alta* through a jumble of hoses and wires in the umbilical – had ceased. The crew of the diving bell had been abandoned.

Tank started calling the support ship, which could normally hear their every utterance via an open communication system.

'Save your breath,' Fletcher said. 'They've lost the

umbilical.' He pointed out the viewport toward the tangled pile of hose.

Tank stared for a moment as the words penetrated his battered skull. 'Okay,' he muttered. 'Are the scrubbers on? How's our air?'

Fletcher took command, activating an emergency transponder, a top-mounted flashing strobe, and a backup carbon dioxide scrubber, all operated by battery. At a small control panel, he opened the valve on several gas tanks mounted on the bell's exterior and adjusted the breathing mixture. Provided they could keep warm, the bell carried sufficient power and emergency gas for two to three days. Given their proximity to Florida and the Gulf, it was plenty of time for a saturation-equipped rescue ship to reach the site.

'Scrubbers are on. Air mix looks good.' He eyed a mechanical gauge. 'Pressure stable at six hundred and twenty feet.'

During normal operations, the bell's atmospherics were managed by a dive supervision team on the *Alta*. A measured mixture of gases was pumped through the diving bell's umbilical, carefully adjusted as the bell reached operating depth. Helium, rather than nitrogen, was the primary inert gas fed to the divers, as it eliminated the rick of nitrogen narcosis, a dangerously intoxicating effect that can occur deeper than a hundred feet. The bell was fitted with its own external tanks filled with helium, oxygen and nitrogen, for just such an emergency.

Fletcher motioned toward the viewport. 'Since I'm already suited, I'll inspect the exterior.'

'Without any heat, you better make it quick.'

While Fletcher reconfigured his umbilical to operate off the emergency gas supply, Tank slipped into the lockout to open the exterior hatch. The hatch moved only a few inches before striking something metallic. Tank put all his weight against the hatch, but it wouldn't budge. Slipping his hand through the gap, he reached into the water and groped around.

'Best scrap your dive plans, Pops. The bell frame must have bent when we hit bottom and is blocking the hatch. No way we're going to get that open.'

Fletcher had a sinking feeling the dive gods weren't finished invoking payment for some past sin. 'Okay. I'll try raising the ship on the subcom. Why don't you pull out the Mustang suits and see if you can get Brownie into one.'

Tank pulled open a side compartment that contained thick, rubberized survival suits designed for cold-water immersion. He slipped into a cumbersome suit, then tried pulling another on to Brown's inert body. Fletcher activated an emergency radio configured with an external transponder mounted on the exterior of the bell. For the next several minutes, he tried hailing the *Alta*. He got only static.

Without the radiant heating from the surface umbilical, the temperature in the bell quickly cooled. Feeling the chill even in his dry dive suit, Fletcher abandoned the radio to help Tank squeeze Brown into the survival suit. 'They must have their hands full topside,' he said. 'I'll try calling again in a minute.'

'There's no sense in waiting around,' Tank said. 'You saw the slack in the umbilical. The lift line is severed. They're not going to be able to pull us up, but they can certainly acquire us if we make the surface on our own.'

Fletcher considered Tank's words. He was inclined to wait until reestablishing communications with the surface before initiating an emergency ascent, but the silent response from above likely meant a serious situation aboard the *Alta*. Tank was probably right. With Brown injured, there was no point in hanging around the depths.

'All right. Prepare to drop the weights. I'll radio up that we're engaging in an emergency ascent – in case someone can hear us.'

While Fletcher made the call, Tank opened a floor panel. Inside was a pair of T-grips fashioned to a set of external weights clamped beneath the bell. He waited until Fletcher turned from the radio and gave him a nod, then twisted the grips.

There was a slight clink as a pair of lead weights dropped from the bell housing. But only one of the weights fell free to the seafloor. The other remained wedged in place by the bent frame. With a slight shift in balance, the diving bell started a crooked ascent. Fletcher winked at Tank but stiffened when a horrendous screeching echoed through the bell. A rush of turbulence appeared out the side viewport as the bell jolted to a stop.

'We're snagged on the BOP!' Tank shouted.

Both pressed their faces to the port. All they could see was a cascade of bubbles rushing past with the roar of a Boeing 747 at takeoff.

Ascending at an angle, the bell had caught a protruding elbow from the blowout preventer. The steel extension had sliced into the rack holding seven of the diving bell's nine emergency gas tanks. As the bell rose, the blowout preventer severed the tanks' valve connections before jabbing into the base of the rack and snaring the bell in a vise-like grip.

Fletcher jumped to the console and checked the pressure gauges. The normally stoic diver turned gray as he watched eighty per cent of their emergency atmosphere disappear to the surface. Trapped inside the bell ensnared on the bottom, they were now at the complete mercy of a surface rescue.

Tank looked to his partner. 'How bad?'

Fletcher turned slowly but said nothing. The look in his eye told Tank all he needed to know. They had only a few hours to live.

6

Six hundred feet above the diving bell, the Norwegian ship *Alta* was in the throes of death. Thick black smoke covered her forward deck, streaked by sporadic bursts of flame. A large derrick used to feed drill pipe over the side lay collapsed across the deck. Waves came close to washing over the rail as the ship listed deeply at the bow.

Kevin Knight, the *Alta*'s captain, stared out the bridge window at the carnage. Minutes before, he had been monitoring a weather report when a deep rumble sounded in the bowels of the ship. The deck flexed beneath his feet. An instant later, a forward fuel tank erupted in a blistering explosion that engulfed the vessel.

'Sir, the dive shack reports they've lost contact with the bell,' yelled the third officer, whose face trickled blood from a shattered window.

Alarm bells blared, and flashing console lights indicated sections of the ship already flooded. Knight ground his molars as he absorbed the growing damage. There was no avoiding the inevitable.

He turned to the communications operator. 'Issue a Mayday call! Relay that we are sinking and require immediate assistance.'

Knight picked up a transmitter and spoke over the ship's public-address system. 'Fire control teams, report to your stations. All remaining hands prepare to abandon ship.'

'Sir, what about the diving bell?' the third officer said. 'And there are three more men in the saturation chamber.'

'There's an emergency pod built into the saturation chamber. Get the men into it at once.'

'What about the bell?'

Knight shook his head. 'Those boys will have to sit tight for now. There's nothing we can do for them.' He gave the hesitant officer a stern gaze. 'Go get to that chamber. Now!'

The dazed crew and roughnecks made their way aft to a pair of enclosed lifeboats. Several men who were burned or injured had to be lifted into the boats, a task made more difficult by the ship's steep list. Knight raced through the vessel, calling off the firefighters, ordering all men to the boats while ensuring nobody was left behind. At the base of the accommodations block, he found the chief engineer emerging from belowdecks.

Knight yelled over the roar of nearby flames. 'Is everybody out?'

'Yes, I think so.' The engineer was breathing heavily. 'She's flooding fast, sir. We best get off at once.'

Knight shrugged him off. 'Get to the boats and launch them. I'm going to make a final pass forward.'

'Don't risk it, sir,' the engineer yelled. But Knight had already vanished into a swirl of smoke.

The stern was rising precariously as he stepped across the deck. Through the smoke, he caught a brief glimpse of the bow already awash. He ran to the waterline, scanning the deck for any last crewmen. A pair of loud splashes told him the two lifeboats had jettisoned. The realization gave him a sense of relief – and terror.

The acrid smoke burned his eyes and choked his lungs. He called out a last plea to abandon ship. As he turned to move aft, he noticed a boot protruding from behind a deck crane. It was his executive officer, a man named Gordon. His clothes were charred and his hair singed. He peered at Knight through glassy eyes.

The captain tried pulling him up. 'Gordon, we have to get off the ship.'

The exec screamed at his touch. 'My leg!'

Knight saw that one of Gordon's legs was twisted at an obscene angle, a bloodied piece of bone protruding through his trousers near the knee. A knot twisted in the captain's stomach.

A crash disrupted his thoughts as a bundle of drill pipe broke free and tumbled into the water. Tortured groans emanated from belowdecks as the hull strained under the imbalance of the rising stern. The deck shuddered beneath Knight's feet as the ship tried a last-gasp fight to stay afloat.

Slipping an arm around Gordon, Knight tried to

raise the injured man. Gordon let out a raspy grunt before falling limp in Knight's arms. The captain struggled to lift the officer, but his own knees, weakened by an ancient football injury, wouldn't allow it. The two sagged to the deck as a generator broke loose and slid across it, missing the men by inches.

The *Alta* had but seconds left. Knight resigned himself to a mortal ride to the seafloor.

Then a crisp voice cut the air. 'I'd suggest a quick exit before we all get our feet wet.'

Knight snapped his head toward the voice, but a thick cloud of smoke obscured his vision. Then a tall, dark-haired man emerged from the haze, his luminous green eyes surveying the scene.

'Where . . . where did you come from?'

'The R/V *Sargasso Sea*,' Pitt said. 'We received your distress call and came at full speed.'

He looked at Gordon and then at Knight, noticing his shirt's shoulder insignia. 'How bad is your man hurt, Captain?'

'Broken leg.'

A deep rumble shook the ship as its stern tilted higher. Pitt rushed over to the two men, clutching a safety harness attached to a rope. He secured the harness around Knight. 'Can you hang on to him?'

Knight nodded. 'As long as I don't have to walk.'

Pitt hoisted Gordon's limp body and draped it over Knight's shoulder. 'I'm afraid you may have to get a little wet after all.'

He pulled a handheld radio from his belt and called to the *Sargasso Sea*. 'Bring it up gently.'

The deck lurched. 'She's going under!' Knight yelled.

The *Alta*'s captain saw the harness line pull taut as the ship began to slide beneath his feet. He felt a hand shove him as the water rushed up to him. It was Pitt, pushing him toward the rail.

He clung tightly to Gordon as they were pulled underwater. They banged against a ventilator box, and Knight felt the harness jerk as a boil of water rushed around them. The water suddenly calmed as the harness continued to strain against his chest. Then they broke free and were dangling above the waves.

Knight looked up to see a turquoise-colored ship pulling them to safety, the harness line attached to a crane that stretched over the side rail. He tightened his grip on Gordon's body, which felt noticeably heavier. The first officer retched, and his gasps confirmed that he was still breathing.

Knight rotated to see the last of the *Alta*, its bronze propeller cutting the empty sky, just before the ship plunged beneath the surface amid a grumble of twisting metal and escaping air. The ship's twin lifeboats and the floating decompression chamber pod bobbed nearby, safely clear of the sinking ship's suction.

Knight focused his gaze on a ring of bubbling water that marked the ship's demise. A few bits of flotsam drifted to the surface, but there was no sign of the man who had just saved his life.

7

Pitt felt like he was riding the nose of a freight train barreling through a dark tunnel.

After pushing Knight and Gordon clear, he tried to get himself over the rail. But the plunging vessel moved too quickly, and the rush of water threw him against a deck-mounted crane. The acceleration of the sinking ship kept him pinned as the water hurled against him.

He ignored a pain in his ears from the increasing pressure and pulled his way along the crane. A cacophony of muffled metallic sounds vibrated through the water as loose materials smashed into the ship's bulkheads. A severed stanchion came hurtling into the crane, missing Pitt by mere inches.

Reaching the bottom of the crane, he set his feet and launched himself off the corner, stroking furiously toward the unseen side rail. A hard object collided with his leg, then he was free of the maelstrom. The sinking ship rushed past him on its sprint to the bottom, more felt than seen in the dark and murky sea.

The waters around him were a disorienting swirl, but Pitt remained calm. He had been a diver most of his life and had always felt comfortable in the water, as if it were his natural element. Panic never entered his mind. He tracked a string of bubbles rising toward a faint silver glow. Orienting himself, he swam toward the surface but found it receding.

Pitt was being drawn down by the *Alta*'s suction. He swam hard against the invisible force. His head began to throb. He needed air.

His body bumped against something and he instinctively grabbed it. The object was buoyant and, like Pitt, fought the grasp of the ship's suction. As his throat tightened, Pitt knew he must break free and surface quickly.

With his lungs bursting and his vision narrowing, he continued to kick with a fury. He felt no sensation of ascending, but he realized the surrounding air bubbles were not rising past him. He looked up. The luminescent surface was drawing closer, and the water felt warmer. The gleaming surface dangled just beyond reach as every blood vessel in his head throbbed like a jackhammer. Then suddenly he was there.

Bursting through the waves, he gulped in air as his heart slowed its pounding. A small motor buzzed nearby, and in an instant an orange inflatable roared up beside him. The smiling face of Al Giordino leaned over the side.

He laughed as he easily pulled Pitt into the boat. 'That's a new take on riding the range.'

Pitt gave him a confused look, then peered over the side. Bobbing beside them was a bright green portable outhouse from the *Alta* that he had ridden to the surface. Pitt smiled at his dumb luck. 'I think it's what they call ascending the throne,' he said.

The *Sargasso Sea* had already hoisted aboard the *Alta*'s emergency decompression chamber pod and was rounding up the lifeboat survivors when Pitt and Giordino boarded. Captain Knight spotted Pitt and rushed to his side. 'I thought you were gone for good.'

'She tried to take me for a one-way ride, but I managed to hop off. How's your partner?'

'Resting comfortably in sick bay. You saved both our lives.'

'That was quite a fire aboard your ship. Do you know what started it?'

Knight shook his head. The image of the exploding ship would haunt him for the rest of his days. 'Some sort of explosion. It set off the forward fuel bunker. Can't imagine what caused it. Miraculously, everyone seems to have gotten off the ship, even the men in the saturation chamber.' A tortured pain showed in his eyes. 'There are three more men on the bottom. Divers.'

'Were they in the water?'

Knight nodded. 'Working out of the diving bell at depth. The initial explosion severed the lift cable and umbilical. We never had a chance to warn them.'

'We've called the Navy's Undersea Rescue Command,' Giordino said. 'They can have a submersible rescue vehicle on-site in ten hours. We're also searching for any nearby commercial deepwater resources.'

'Assuming no injuries or problems with the bell, the divers should be safe for at least twenty-four hours,' Pitt said. He pointed to a small yellow submarine on the stern deck. 'We best see how they're making out. If nothing else, we can keep them company until the cavalry arrives.'

Pitt turned to Giordino. 'How soon can we deploy the *Starfish*?'

'About ten minutes.'

'Let's make it five.'

8

The two-man submersible dropped below the choppy surface and began its slow descent, driven by the pull of gravity. Pitt barely had time to slip into some dry clothes before Giordino had the *Starfish* prepped for diving. Climbing into the pilot's seat, he rushed through a predive checklist as the submersible was lowered over the side.

'Batteries are at full power, everything appears operational. We are approved for dive,' Pitt said with a wink as seawater washed over the top of the viewport.

Giordino flicked on a bank of external floodlights as they sank past the hundred-foot mark. The descent felt painfully slow. As men who worked in and around the sea, they felt an affinity for the unknown divers lost on the seafloor. Several minutes later, the taupe-colored bottom materialized.

'The current pushed us east during our descent,' Giordino said. 'I suggest a heading of two hundred and seventy-five degrees.'

'On it.' Pitt engaged the *Starfish*'s thrusters.

The submersible skimmed over the bottom, driving against a light current. The seafloor was rocky and undulating but mostly devoid of life.

Pitt noticed the terrain change a short distance ahead. 'Something coming up.'

A parallel band of rippled sediment appeared, stretching across their path like a recessed highway.

'Tread marks,' Pitt said. 'Somebody had some heavy equipment down here.'

Giordino peered into the depths. 'That says we should be close to the wellhead.'

They traveled a short distance before the hulk of the *Alta* appeared in the murk. The bow was crumpled from hitting the seafloor, but the ship was otherwise intact, sitting upright at a slight list. Pitt wasted no time inspecting the ship's damage and circled around its stern. He was immediately met by an underwater junkyard.

Debris from the *Alta* was scattered across a rocky shallow, joined by a conglomeration of pipes, compressors, and cables jarred free at impact. There were large steel gas cylinders, most containing helium or oxygen in support of the *Alta*'s saturation chamber. Dozens of the green, brown and black cylinders lay scattered across the bottom.

As they glided over a buckled tin shed, Giordino called out. 'Strobe light, off to the right.'

Pitt turned the submersible toward the flash. A raised structure, sprouting pipes from its center, partially blocked the light. Pitt navigated around the wellhead riser and blowout preventer to find the diving bell wedged against the structure, jammed at an obtuse angle, with one of its drop weights still in place.

Giordino shook his head. 'They sure got themselves into a nice pickle.'

A small light wavered in one of the bell's viewports. Pitt flashed the submersible's lights as he eased closer, cautious of the wellhead's protruding fittings.

'I think I see two men in there,' Giordino said.

'Let's see if we can raise them on the emergency channel.'

Pitt activated the emergency transponder that operated on the same frequency as the diving bell's. 'Submersible *Starfish* to *Alta* diving bell. Do you read me?'

A high-pitched, garbled voice replied in the affirmative.

'Their helium-speech unscrambler must have been topside,' Giordino said. 'Hope you watched a lot of Disney cartoons growing up.'

The voice of Warren Fletcher blared over the speaker in a Mickey Mouse tenor. Pitt lost much of the verbiage but made out that one man was injured and that the bell had lost most of its emergency gas. He slid the submersible to the side and saw for himself. A half-dozen gas cylinders were piled on the sand below the bell, a large gash evident in the bottles' storage rack.

Pitt eyed the spent tanks. 'They have a serious air problem.'

'Somebody just held up two fingers to the glass,' Giordino said. 'Two hours.'

It was a problem they hadn't expected to confront.

Pitt's objective had been to find the bell and give the men encouragement until a deep-sea rescue team could arrive. But those resources were at best eight hours away. By the time outside help arrived, the men in the bell would be long dead.

'Poor buggers,' Giordino said. 'The Navy's hours away. Those boys will never make it.'

'They can if they swim to the surface.'

Pitt radioed the bell. '*Alta* divers, can you abandon the bell and dive to the surface? We have a deco chamber topside. Repeat, we have a deco chamber topside.'

Fletcher replied in the negative, explaining that the hatch was blocked from the outside.

Pitt and Giordino surveyed the exterior and saw the hatch was blocked shut by the bell's bent base frame, which had also jammed the ballast weight in place.

Pitt studied the heavy-gauge steel. 'No way we can straighten that out. Do you think we can pull them off the riser?'

'It's worth a shot. We can't access the lower frame, where they're pinned. Of course, the bell won't ascend far dragging all that cable.'

'They'll have to break free sooner or later.' Pitt moved the submersible around the diving bell. Approaching from above, he hovered the *Starfish* just above the bell.

Giordino went to work, extending an articulated robotic arm and grasping a secondary lift eye on the bell. 'Got it.'

Proceeding gently, Pitt angled the thrusters down and tried lifting the diving bell. The dive capsule rocked but refused to budge. Pitt tried adjusting the angle of lift, but each time the bell remained fixed to the wellhead riser.

Pitt eased the submersible lower and Giordino released the grip on the lift point.

'That bell probably weighs as much as our submersible,' Giordino said. 'We just don't have enough horsepower to pull it off.'

'She just needs a good tug from above.'

'I agree, but it ain't going to come from us.'

'That's right,' Pitt said. 'It will have to come from the lift cable.'

'You mean raise the cable? There's over six hundred feet of steel cable. It probably weighs ten times as much as the bell. No way we could drag that to the surface.'

'Not drag. Float,' Pitt said with a twinkle in his eye.

Giordino studied his partner. He had seen that look before. It was the never-say-die gaze of a man who had cheated death many times over. It was a look of determination that spouted from his friend like Old Faithful. Pitt didn't know the men in the diving bell, but there was no way he would stand by and let them die.

Giordino rubbed his chin. 'How can we possibly do that?'

'Simple,' Pitt said. 'We just raise the roof.'

9

Feeling as if he had been abandoned to die in a cold steel coffin, Fletcher watched the lights of the NUMA submersible recede across the seafloor.

'They'll be back,' he said, trying to convince himself.

He could do little but focus on his breathing, every inhalation a reminder of their limited air. Like most professional divers, he wasn't prone to claustrophobia, but little by little the diving bell seemed to compress around him.

He gazed at Tank, who had slid to a sitting position beside him and stared at the floor in resignation. To lessen his own anxiety, Fletcher remained standing, his face pressed against the viewport while tracking the submersible. What was it up to? The vessel seemed to be just moving back and forth, stirring up silt. Whatever they were doing, it seemed to have nothing to do with saving him and his partners.

But saving the men's lives was exactly what Pitt was up to.

'Short of a granny knot, that's the best we can do,' Giordino said, sweat dripping off his brow.

He was operating the robotic arm, or manipulator,

which was again clutching a strand of the diving bell's lift cable. Leaving Fletcher and the bell in the shadows, Pitt had traced the length of the cable until finding the frayed end near the sunken *Alta*.

He had Giordino grab the cable end and drag it to the metal shed they had passed in the debris field earlier. The prefabricated welder's shed had stood on the ship's deck but was sheared off when the *Alta* struck bottom. The shed had somehow landed upright. Although heavily dented, it stood fully intact in the soft sand.

With a good deal of finessing, Pitt and Giordino secured the cable around the shed's hinged door, then looped it around the sides and roof several times.

'Won't win us a merit badge for knot tying,' Giordino said, 'but now our kite's got a tail.'

'On to the scientific portion of the experiment,' Pitt said.

Giordino let loose the cable, and Pitt guided the submersible close to the *Alta*. He settled the submersible on the seafloor and watched as Giordino reached with the manipulator and clutched a brown helium tank by its valve.

Giordino gave Pitt a cautionary gaze. 'These babies ain't light.'

'Mere child's play.' Pitt raised the submersible just off the bottom and applied power to the reverse thrusters.

The submersible eased backward. The helium cylinder held firm, then slipped across the sand. Pitt worked the controls until he had dragged the tank alongside the welder's shed, positioning its valve near the open door.

'There's one,' Pitt said.

'Not a popular move with our batteries.' Giordino looked at their gauges. 'We're down to thirty-five per cent remaining power reserves.'

Pitt nodded and maneuvered the submersible toward the next cylinder. They had repeated the process six more times, lining up all seven tanks beside the shed, when Giordino announced they could do no more.

'Power reserves approaching single digits, boss. It's time we think of heading for daylight.'

'Okay, maestro. First open up the tanks, and let's see if this bird will fly.'

Pitt hovered the submersible over the cylinders so Giordino could reach down with his manipulator and open the valves. A cascade of bubbles rushed past the viewport as he opened the first valve. When Giordino had opened the last cylinder, Pitt moved back a few feet and Giordino nudged the tanks forward, allowing the spewing gas to rise into the confines of the welder's shed.

It was a crazy gamble but their only chance of saving the divers. Pitt hoped to raise the cable enough to lift the diving bell off the wellhead structure. To do so, the welding shed would act as a lift bag and pull the cable to the surface.

Pitt maneuvered the submersible until it hovered just above the shed.

'You sure you want to park it here?' Giordino asked.

'We might need to hold it steady, as well as give it a boost. See if you can grab hold of it.'

Giordino reached out the manipulator arm and latched on to a knuckle in the shed's peaked roof. Pitt purged the ballast tanks. A wall of rising bubbles obscured their view and any sensation of movement, so Pitt eyed a depth gauge. The digital readout held steady, then began decreasing a foot at a time.

He grinned. 'We're moving.'

Peering into the distance from the diving bell, Fletcher saw the submersible ascend. For a second, he thought its lights illuminated a small house beneath it. He rubbed his eyes and watched the lights of the submersible disappear, his hopes of escape vanishing with it.

Little did Fletcher know he was attached to the rising structure.

Using the weight of the submersible to balance the roof, Pitt managed to keep the shed level as it filled with gas and attained buoyancy. More importantly, the shed continued to rise while trailing the steel lift cable beneath it. As the structure ascended, the sea pressure would diminish, causing the gas inside the shed to expand. With luck, the expanding gas would provide the needed lift to offset the growing weight of the cable.

'Five hundred feet,' Giordino said. 'We're riding a regular freight elevator.'

'Feels more like a mechanical bull.' Pitt jockeyed the

submersible to one side. He had to constantly work the thrusters to keep the shed's roof level. If the shed tipped, the gas would escape and the whole works would plummet to the seabed.

The odd assemblage continued to rise in a curtain of bubbles. Ascending higher, the expanding helium ultimately displaced all the water in the shed. Its sides began to bulge as the expanding gas sought its escape, streaming out of every crevice, as well as the open door. The shed's ascent accelerated, pushing the submersible with it.

The *Sargasso Sea* had been alerted to stand clear but at the ready. Pacing her stern deck, Kevin Knight stared at the water. A disruption caught his attention and he watched as a circular froth erupted. A few seconds later, the bright yellow NUMA submarine broke the surface, rising completely out of the water. Knight saw that it was sitting on some sort of structure that resembled a tiny house. As it settled slightly and the submersible moved clear, Knight recognized it as the welder's shed from the *Alta*.

At Pitt's direction, the *Sargasso Sea* moved in quickly and snared the looped cable with a crane and hook. The structure was hoisted on to the stern deck as a waiting throng of crewmen secured the cable with clamps and braces. The loose end was unwound from the shed and fed on to a drum winch that had been cleared of its own cable.

As the winch began reeling in the cable, the ship's

lift crane deposited the welder's shed over the side and retrieved the submersible.

Pitt and Giordino had barely climbed out of the hatch when Knight jumped in front of them.

'Are they still alive?'

'For the moment,' Pitt said. 'The bell lost several of its emergency gas cylinders, so they don't have much time to spare.'

The crew waited anxiously as the winch spooled up the cable. No one knew what they would find at the other end. Finally, there was a commotion near the stern rail and Pitt saw the top of the diving bell break the surface.

'Snag it with the lift crane and prepare to transfer it to the decompression chamber,' Pitt said. 'We'll need some welders to cut away the lower frame to access the hatch.'

The bell was hoisted aboard and the crewmen swarmed to work. A technician ran up to Pitt as welders' sparks began spraying across the deck.

'I've spliced the bell's communications cable with our comm system,' the technician said. 'One of the divers inside wants to talk to you. His name is Warren.'

Pitt followed the technician to a console set up near the bell. He picked up a handset as a man inside the bell waved through the viewport.

'Hi, Warren. My name's Pitt. How are you making out in there?'

'A lot better now that I can see some sunshine,'

Fletcher said. 'For a while, I thought we were going to be a permanent part of the wellhead. That was a crazy way to lift us, but I'm sure glad you tried.'

'Apologies for the rough ride. How are your partners?'

'Tank's good, but Brown has a broken leg. He's been in and out of consciousness.'

'We've got a doctor waiting in our decompression chamber, just as soon as we can get you into it.'

'Thanks, Mr Pitt, we appreciate everything. Tell me, though, what happened to the *Alta*?'

'She sank in a sudden explosion. No casualties, thankfully, but nobody seems to know what happened. We'll talk again once we get you transferred to the chamber.'

Fletcher nodded. 'Call me crazy, Mr Pitt, but I saw an unknown submersible shortly before the cable snapped. I think somebody may have deliberately sunk the *Alta*.'

Pitt looked into the diver's hardened eyes and realized it was the least crazy thing he had heard all day.

10

A bright azure sky belied the sorrow that hung over Havana. The source of the melancholy was a funeral procession that crept through the crumbling streets of Cuba's capital, where the calendar seemed fixed at the year 1959. The pockmarked streets, which over the centuries had been trod by Spanish conquistadors, British redcoats, American doughboys, and Russian generals, were lined ten deep by ordinary Cuban citizens. Seemingly every resident of the island had come to bid a final farewell to *El Caballo*.

Fidel Castro Ruz, the fiery father of the Cuban revolution, had finally lost his battle with mortality. It had been nearly sixty years since a young Castro had broken exile and landed on Cuba's southwest tip in a borrowed sailboat with a ragtag army of eighty-one guerrilla fighters. In a coup that was nothing short of miraculous, he'd fueled rural grassroots support and overthrown the Batista government, marching triumphantly into Havana less than three years later.

Castro's love affair with Marxism had failed to transform Cuba into the utopia he had envisioned, however, and his half-century reign, ending in 2008 when he'd passed power to his brother Raúl, had been marked more by political repression and economic suffocation than freedom and prosperity. Yet he remained a revered figure to Cubans, most of whom knew no other leader.

The horse-drawn funeral caisson, escorted by an honor guard in crisp white tunics, inched into the Plaza de la Revolución and eased past a large viewing stand. Cuba's government and military elite took center stage, surrounded by an array of international dignitaries. The best seats were reserved for representatives from Venezuela, China and Nicaragua, along with a handful of Hollywood actors. Raúl Castro stood at attention and saluted his brother as the procession marched past the towering José Martí Memorial.

Raúl and his vice president, a fellow octogenarian who walked with a cane, returned to the Interior Ministry Building for a small reception. The Cuban ruling elite, consisting of the Council of State and the Council of Ministers, along with key members of the National Assembly, the Communist Party and the Revolutionary Armed Forces, assembled in an impromptu line and paid formal respects to President Castro.

A sharp-dressed man with silver hair completed his condolences, then crossed the room, inadvertently brushing into a general engaged with an aide.

'Excuse me, General,' he said, stopping to face the man he bumped.

General Alberto Gutier's hawkish face crinkled as he regarded the man through steady teak eyes. 'Minister Ruiz.'

'It is a sad day for all of Cuba,' Ruiz said. '*El Caballo* was the heart and soul of the revolution.'

Gutier smirked at the mention of Fidel's popular nickname, the Horse. 'One man can start a revolution, but it takes many to sustain it.'

'True, but there can be no advancement of the cause without dynamic leadership.' Ruiz gazed at Raúl's aged vice president, who had been helped to a chair near Castro and was inhaling oxygen from a portable tank.

Turning back to Gutier, he spoke in a low tone. 'It won't be long before a new order will rule Cuba. Vigorous, worldly and progressive.'

'You couldn't mean yourself?'

'Why, what an excellent suggestion,' Ruiz said. 'I'm glad I can count on your support and shall look forward to your continued contributions to the Council during my presidency.'

The two were bitter rivals. Both served in Castro's cabinet, Gutier as Minister of the Interior and Ruiz as Foreign Minister. And both curried the president's favor, knowing the power to rule the country next was within reach. To Gutier's chagrin, Ruiz was widely considered the favorite to replace the ailing vice president and stand ready as Castro's successor.

Gutier gave Ruiz a frigid stare. 'There's a better likelihood that you will be polishing my boots first.'

'Come, now. You really don't expect to ascend the ranks, do you?' He leaned forward and whispered in the general's ear. 'There's a rumor that Minister Ortiz's death was no accident and that the Army was somehow involved. Bad press for you, my dear friend.'

It was Gutier's turn to smile. 'Perhaps it is true,' he whispered back. 'In which case, I hope that you drive carefully.'

The normally glib Ruiz turned his back on the general and meandered toward a group of friendly associates.

Gutier dismissed his aide and looked about the room, trying to hide his contempt. Most of the Cuban leadership consisted of old cronies of *El Caballo* who clung to power with one foot in the grave. Ruiz was right about a new generation waiting in the wings, but what he saw of that crowd repulsed him. They were all like Ruiz, products of a privileged upbringing who spouted revolutionary adages while quietly living like celebrities at the expense of the state.

Not that Gutier didn't enjoy his own trappings of power. He was just used to a more austere lifestyle. With a younger brother, he'd been raised in a Santiago shack by a destitute mother after his father had been killed defending Cuba in the Bay of Pigs invasion. When his widowed mother had married an Army officer, his economic status improved, if not his happiness.

His stepfather was an alcoholic who regularly beat the boys and their mother. Perhaps out of guilt, Gutier's new father introduced his adopted sons to Army life and maneuvered them into officer training school. After years of abuse, the brothers returned the favor when they came of age by strangling the man and tossing his body into the Cauto River. Escaping without suspicion, Gutier and his brother had their first taste of murder with impunity. It wouldn't be their last.

Through cunning and aptitude, the elder Gutier rose quickly through the ranks, establishing a reputation for ruthlessness. He caught the eye of Raúl when the younger Castro commanded the Revolutionary Armed Forces. Promoted to Raúl's staff, he served as an effective, if not always popular, problem solver.

With Raúl's ascension, Gutier was appointed Interior Minister, but only after a more seasoned general suffered a debilitating paralysis after ingesting an unknown toxin.

Gutier bid farewell to a group of assemblymen and departed the reception. Hopping into a Russian-made military truck, he was driven across Havana to a small airfield at Playa Baracoa. He transferred to a helicopter that took him east along the coastline, passing the entrance to Havana Harbor and the heights of Morro Castle. Thirty miles down the coast, the helicopter landed in a field next to a small marina. Gutier was then taken in a launch into the indigo waters of the Straits of Florida.

The launch approached a luxury yacht moored in the bay. An Oceanco-built boat that measured over two hundred feet, its sleek opulence towered over the small launch. Gutier read the vessel's name, *Gold Digger*, in yellow lettering on the stern, as they approached a lowered stepladder. A crew member escorted the general into an air-conditioned salon.

Mark Ramsey was mixing cocktails behind a mahogany bar. 'General, good of you to come. I wasn't sure you would be able to keep our appointment on such a somber day.' He turned off a television monitor that was displaying Fidel Castro's body lying in state.

'My official duties were fulfilled earlier,' Gutier said. 'It may be a somber day for Cuba's history but I think a bright one for its future.'

Ramsey handed him a daiquiri. 'To the prosperity of Cuba.'

'To Cuba.'

Ramsey led him to a dining table scattered with documents, where each took a seat.

'It's been a difficult week,' Ramsey said. 'I lost a drill ship under lease from the Norwegians and you lost a national icon. All this on top of the terrible accident with Minister Ortiz.'

'No man lives forever. Fidel's imprint on Cuba shall remain long-lasting.'

'His absence leaves an inspirational void for your country. Perhaps one that a man like yourself could fulfill.'

Gutier displayed a poker face. 'Man cannot predict his destiny. Tell me about your ship incident and the state of your oil-drilling prospects.'

'The *Alta* was a modern drill ship that specialized in deepwater operations. She was laying the foundation for an exploratory well in quadrant R-29 of our leasehold.' He slid a chart in front of Gutier and pointed to a section northeast of Havana. 'This is one of two areas for which we had acquired oil exploration rights, as signed by Minister Ortiz before his passing. I hope there will be no problem in continuing to honor the agreement.'

'Minister Ortiz represented the Cuban government. The agreement will be honored. Now, what of this sunken ship?'

'An unknown explosion sent her to the bottom in less than ten minutes. The crew got away safely, but three divers were trapped on the seafloor. If not for a passing American research ship, they would have died. As it is, there was no loss of life.'

'That is fortunate. The vessel was insured by the owner?'

'In this instance, the operator was responsible for insuring the ship while it was on the job.' Ramsey's lips tightened at the thought of the deductible that would come out of his pocket.

'When do you plan to return to the site?' Gutier asked.

'Our second leased rig is working on our other site off the western coast. We view that region as lower potential, so we'll transfer operations in a week or two and complete the test well that the *Alta* started.'

Gutier looked Ramsey hard in the eye. 'I would ask that you refrain from any further work in area R-29 for at least three weeks.'

'Any particular reason?'

'It is my desire,' Gutier said gruffly.

Ramsey slid the chart in front of him. 'General, I know it took considerable effort within your government to allow our consortium to come into your territorial waters. I appreciate what you've done for us. But we were given authorization to explore only two small offshore quadrants, neither of which our geophysicists rated highly promising. For us to have success and allow you to develop an export oil market, we need access to additional seafloor.'

'Mr Ramsey, I might remind you that there are other parties seeking the same opportunity.'

'We're talking deepwater operations. It's a different ball game. It'll take you twice as long if you go with the boys from Venezuela or Mexico . . . or the Middle East.'

'But you yourself are a mining engineer.'

'True, my expertise is with mining. In fact, I'm just a limited partner in this joint venture. I'm here only because the venture group's CEO is recovering from a mild heart attack. But I can assure you, our group of Canadian and Norwegian oil exploration experts have extensive experience in the North Sea and Arctic. They'll get the job done. They have deepwater experience you can't find just anywhere.'

'But you have yet to show results.'

'In the oil business, there are no guarantees.'

Gutier gazed at the map. 'Where is it you would like to drill?'

Ramsey pointed to a large area a hundred miles northwest of Havana. 'Given a choice, the North Cuba Basin is at the top of our probability list.'

'I might have some sway to open up a portion for your examination. But I will require something in return.' His dark eyes bore into Ramsey.

'Name it.'

'I understand you recently had some troubles with a mining operation in Indonesia.'

'The trouble was with some Islamic militants. They kidnapped my site mine supervisor and three engineers – in broad daylight off the streets of Jakarta.'

'And they were rescued?'

'All alive and well, thankfully.'

'And their captors?'

'Not so fortunate.' Ramsey offered a wry smile. 'They were killed in a firefight.'

'But not by government forces.'

'No. Why the interest?'

'I have a project that requires some outside military expertise.'

'You have the top forces of the Cuban military at your disposal.'

'True, but this is an external project that requires absolute discretion.'

'Not in the US, is it?'

'No.'

Ramsey nodded.

'I'd like to hire your men,' Gutier said.

'They're not my men. They were hired contractors who specialize in this type of work.'

'Would they work for me?'

'I don't see why not, providing you're not a secret al-Qaeda sympathizer.'

'If it makes you feel better, my mother was a devout Roman Catholic and raised my brother and me as such.'

Ramsey stepped to his desk and returned with a slip of paper containing a name and phone number.

'Maguire?' Gutier read aloud. 'That's it?'

'That's my contact. The phone number – and a Cayman Islands bank account – is all the information I possess.'

'He is a professional?'

'First-rate. I just wouldn't ask him a lot of questions.'

Gutier stood to leave. 'I'm sorry for the loss of your ship. You will have access to the new oil lease site shortly.' He turned and walked out of the salon.

Ramsey didn't move. Staring out the window as Gutier's launch motored away, he couldn't help but wonder if he had just made a deal with the devil.

PART II
Aztlán

The Cenote Codex

II

The rays of the dive light shimmered through the crys-
talline waters, illuminating a coarse limestone wall a
dozen feet away. No detail was too small to see, Summer Pitt thought, amazed at the clarity. Though she
missed the color and warmth of the sea life that made a
usual saltwater dive enticing, she relished the opportunity to dive in perfect visibility. Peering up, she
watched as her air bubbles floated to the surface a hundred feet away.

The daughter of NUMA's Director and an oceanog-
rapher herself, Summer was diving in a cenote near the
coast of Tabasco, a state in eastern Mexico. A natural
sinkhole formed in a limestone deposit, the cenote was
essentially a vertical, water-filled tunnel. Summer had
the sensation of traveling through an elevator shaft as
she descended the fifty-foot-diameter cavern. As the
filtered sunlight waned, she turned her dive light to the
depths below. A few yards away, two other divers were
kicking toward the sandy bottom. She cleared her ears
and pursued the other divers, catching them as they
reached the bottom at a depth of one hundred and
twenty feet.

She swam alongside a dark-haired man whose tall,

lanky body matched her own. He turned and winked, the joy of the cenote dive evident in his bright green eyes. Her twin brother, Dirk, who shared their father's name, always showed an extra jolt of liveliness when exploring the depths.

They finned toward the third diver, a bearded man whose shaggy gray hair swirled around his facemask. Dr Eduardo Madero, an anthropology professor from the University of Veracruz, was carefully examining the bottom. Dirk and Summer had just completed a joint marine project with Madero, assessing an area of coral reefs off Campeche. In appreciation for their help, Madero had invited them to dive in the isolated Tabasco cenote, where he was engaged in his own cultural resource project.

Madero hovered over a large aluminum grid anchored over a portion of the cenote's floor. Small yellow flags with numbered tags sprouted from the sand, marking artifacts discovered during the formal excavation. Most of the targets of Madero's excavation were readily visible.

Easing alongside him, Dirk and Summer aimed their dive lights at the partially excavated section. Summer immediately recoiled. A human skull stared up at her, grinning ghoulishly with brown-stained teeth. A pair of small gold hoops glistened in the sand beside the skull, a pair of hand-fashioned earrings once worn by the smiling owner.

Summer swung her light about, revealing a morbid

assortment of protruding skulls and bones. Madero hadn't exaggerated when he cautioned them before the dive that it was like visiting a graveyard struck by a tornado.

The fact that the cenote had been used for human sacrifices seemed apparent, but Madero had yet to identify its occupants. The location was in a region once inhabited by the Olmecs, and later the Mayans, although Madero could not date any finds to either era. A small ceramic figurine had been dated to 1500 A.D., concurrent with Aztec rule farther north, and close to the time of the Spanish conquest.

Gazing at the exposed skull, Summer envisioned the ceremonial human sacrifice that had taken place centuries before on the cenote's rim. If it was an Aztec ritual, the victim would have been held facing the sky while a high priest plunged a razor-sharp flint knife into the victim's chest and ripped out the still-beating heart. The heart and blood were offerings to the gods, possibly the warrior deity, who ensured the sun's daily travels across the sky.

In some instances, the victim's limbs would be severed and consumed in a ritual meal while the torso was tossed into the cenote. In the case of the Aztecs, human sacrifice occurred daily. The smiling skull looking up at Summer might just be one of hundreds of victims sacrificed from the unknown village that once stood overhead. She shivered at the thought despite the warmth of her wetsuit.

Summer turned and followed Madero as he guided them over several excavation pits, pointing out a basalt grinding bowl, or *molcajete,* that had yet to be cataloged and removed. After several more minutes surveying the grisly bits of human remains, Madero motioned with his thumb toward the surface. Their bottom time had expired.

Only too glad to depart the submerged graveyard, Summer gently swam toward the surface ahead of the two men. As she followed her trail of ascending bubbles, she brushed along the limestone wall. A wayward kick jammed the edge of her fin against a protrusion, nearly pulling it off her foot. To her left, a ledge jutted from the wall and she propped an elbow against it as she readjusted her fin.

She pushed off from the ledge to continue her ascent but felt a smooth shape beneath her arm. She hesitated, examining the narrow ledge, which was crowned with a thick mantle of silt. As she fanned her hand through the water, she brushed away a layer of loose sediment that swirled upward in a brown cloud. As it began to settle, an image emerged through the murk, a painted butterfly.

Madero approached and glanced at the ledge. A glimmer of recognition sparkled in his wide eyes. He gently brushed a gloved hand over the surface, then dug his fingers into the sediment, tracing the object's perimeter. Caught on the ledge during its descent, it had no associated cultural context to warrant a more methodical excavation. He scooped the silt aside, exposing a ceramic container roughly the size of a jewelry box. The lone corner not encrusted with sediment featured a tiny butterfly.

Madero motioned for Summer to take the box and ascend. She gingerly lifted it from its perch like the box was a ticking bomb and then kicked toward the surface.

Their limited time on the bottom didn't require a decompression stop, so she continued finning until her head popped above the calm surface. She floated near a makeshift stairwell as Madero exited the cenote and dropped his dive gear, then returned to take the box from Summer's anxious fingers. Dirk followed her as she climbed up the steps. They quickly stripped off their wetsuits as the steamy heat of the Mexican Gulf Coast enveloped them.

'The water was amazing,' she whispered to Dirk, 'but I could have done without the graveyard tour.'

He shrugged. 'Not the worst place to spend eternity, after losing your heart.'

'What did they do with the hearts?'

'Burned them, I believe. They might have left a few in inventory.' Dirk waved an arm about the surrounding light jungle. Madero had found only scattered remains of a temple structure and an adjacent village near the cenote. Little of it was now recognizable. Only a pair of canvas tents, used by Madero and his associates during their periodic excavations, gave any hint of human occupation.

The archeologist had taken Summer's box to a nearby table. Summer and Dirk approached as he carefully brushed away a layer of concretion with an old toothbrush.

'So what did Summer find?' Dirk asked. 'An old box of cigars?'

'No es una caja de cigarros,' Summer replied with a shake of her head.

Madero smiled. 'Your Spanish is good.' He kept his eyes focused on the box. 'I believe it is in fact something much more remarkable.'

Summer crowded in close to study the artifact. 'What do you think it was used for?'

'I really can't say, but the design certainly appears Aztec. They were wonderful artisans. I've viewed a large number of artifacts but never anything like this.' He set down the toothbrush and tilted the box toward Summer.

'The shape is unique,' he said. 'A perfect square is much more difficult to create out of clay than a round pot. And look at this.'

He pointed to the seam along the edge of the lid, which was sealed with a gray substance.

'Glued shut,' Dirk said.

'Exactly. It looks like dried latex, which is easily extracted from the local rubber trees.' He picked up the box and gently shook it. A light object rattled inside.

'It's remained sealed and watertight despite its

94

immersion,' Madero said. 'The sediments covering the box must have provided a layer of protection.'

'What do you think is inside?' Summer asked.

Madero shook his head. 'There's no telling. Once we get it back to my lab in Veracruz, we can X-ray it, then remove the latex and open it.'

Dirk grinned. 'I still say it's some musty cigars.'

'Perhaps.' Madero set the box down with reverence. 'But I think it could contain something much more significant.'

He picked up the toothbrush and lightly scrubbed the center of the lid, gradually revealing a bright green circular pattern. Inlaid stones of green and blue were impressed into the design. The wing of a bird began to take shape.

'The Aztecs incorporated animals into much of their artwork,' Madero said. 'Eagles and jaguars were popular motifs, representing the warrior classes.'

Summer studied the expanding image. 'It's a bird of some sort, but I don't think it's an eagle. Were other birds used symbolically?'

'Yes, especially exotic tropical birds. Their plumage was highly valued, more so than gold. The emperor and other nobility would commission elaborate headdresses from feathers of a green jungle bird called the quetzal. Then there is Huitzilopochtli. He was the ancestral deity of the Aztecs, perhaps their most important god. He was a patron of war but also of their home of Tenochtitlan. He was the guiding force for the

Mexica in their original migration from Aztlán to Tenochtitlan – what is now Mexico City.'

'And he was associated with a bird?' Summer asked.

'Yes, a blue hummingbird. The image was typically reserved for items of the ruling class.'

Madero blew away the loosened debris and held the box toward Summer. She could now see the stones were pieces of jade and turquoise. They were joined by inlaid bone and pyrite in the shape of a bird in flight. There was no mistaking the animal's stubby wings and long, thin bill.

It was a blue hummingbird.

12

All eyes were focused on the now cleaned ceramic box. Perched on a steel table in a lab adjacent to Dr Madero's college office, its secrets beckoned under a bank of fluorescent lights.

Madero treated the lid's sealed edges with a solvent, then heated the seams with a small hair dryer. The combined effects softened the natural latex and loosened its bond. Madero tested the gooey material with a plastic putty knife.

'It's quite sticky,' he said. 'I think it will open right up.'

Grasping the lid with a gloved hand, he gave it a gentle tug. The lid popped right off.

Standing on either side of Madero, Dirk and Summer leaned close. A small piece of green felt blanketed a square object inside. Madero pulled away the felt, revealing a tablet of coarse pages.

'It looks like a small book,' Summer said.

Madero's eyes were as wide as platters. Using tweezers, he opened the blank top page, revealing a colorful cartoon-like image of several warriors carrying spears and shields.

'Not simply a book.' Madero's voice quivered with excitement. 'A codex.'

Summer was familiar with the Mayan and Aztec codices, pictographic manuscripts that recorded their culture and history, but she had never seen one in person. She was surprised when Madero pulled up the first page and the subsequent ones unfolded in accordion fashion. Each contained a pictorial image with multiple glyphic signs.

'Is it Mayan?' Dirk asked.

'No, classic Nahuatl.'

Summer frowned. 'Nahuatl?'

'The language of the Mexica, or Aztecs. I recognize the glyphs as classic Nahuatl symbols.'

'Can you decipher it?'

Madero unfurled the codex across the table, counting twenty panels. He photographed each panel first and then carefully studied the images. He kept his thoughts to himself as he moved from one panel to the next. The early panels depicted a battle, while later ones showed men carrying a large object. After several minutes, Madero looked up.

'It seems to describe a local conflict. An account of the battle was recorded in stone, which was split in two and carried away for some reason.' He shook his head. 'I must profess to being a little out of my element here. A colleague of mine, Professor Miguel Torres, is an expert in Nahuatl. Let me see if he is available.'

Madero returned a moment later, trailed by two men.

'Dirk, Summer, this is my esteemed associate Dr Miguel

Torres, head of the archeology department. Miguel, my friends from NUMA.'

A bearded man with a smiling cherub face stepped forward and shook hands.

'It is a pleasure to meet you. Congratulations on your amazing discovery.' His eyes darted to the codex. He suppressed his curiosity long enough to introduce the man behind him.

'May I present Juan Díaz of the Cuban Interior Ministry? Juan is here performing research on his own Aztec artifact. Like myself, he is excited to view your discovery.'

Díaz smiled. 'Apparently your find is much more interesting than the small figurine I possess.'

'You found an Aztec artifact in Cuba?' Summer asked.

'It likely found its way there through later trade,' Torres said. 'While Aztec nautical voyages in the Caribbean are a possibility, we have no recorded evidence of any occurrences.'

The professor turned his attention to the codex. 'Eduardo already showed me the ceramic box. A wonderful discovery in itself. But a codex inside as well?'

'Please,' Summer said, 'take a look and tell us what you think.'

The archeologist could barely contain his excitement. He slipped on a pair of cotton gloves and approached the codex.

'The paper is classic *amatl*, constructed from the

inner bark of the fig tree, which was then whitewashed. That is consistent with several known Aztec codices. It is crisp, bright, and in excellent condition. Simply amazing, after being submerged for centuries.'

'Fine craftsmanship from the ancients,' Madero said, 'as we've seen many times before.'

Torres studied the first panel. 'It appears similar to the Borturini Codex at the National Anthropology Museum.' He pointed to several symbols below the image of the warriors. 'That codex dates from the colonial era.'

'Do you mean the arrival of the Spanish?' Summer asked.

'Yes. In 1519, to be precise. That's when Cortés landed near Veracruz.'

Torres initiated a running narrative of each panel. A loose tale quickly emerged from the images.

'The Aztecs are mourning some sort of defeat in the early panels,' Torres said. 'It was associated with a large number of deaths. It is unclear if the opponent was a regional enemy or the Spanish.'

'Or disease?' Madero asked.

'Quite possibly. Smallpox arrived with the Spanish and ultimately killed millions. I think it references a conventional battle, however. In the second panel, we see a group of warriors dressed in feathers and beaked helmets. These were the cuāuhtmeh, or Eagle Warriors, an elite group of skilled veterans.'

Torres pointed to a trail of footprints painted across

several pages that signified travel. 'As a result of the battle, they are taking something of a major journey.'

'Their trip continued on water?' Summer asked, pointing to the next panel, which showed seven canoes at the edge of a body of water.

'Apparently so. The Aztec capital of Tenochtitlan was built on an island in a lake, so we know they used small canoes.'

'These appear significantly larger,' Madero said.

The Cuban Díaz inched forward with interest. 'Numerous warriors are depicted in each boat. It also appears they have loaded provisions aboard. And that may be some sort of sail.' He pointed to what looked like a pole with a loose sheet around it.

'Yes, very curious,' Torres said. 'I'll admit, I've never seen an Aztec depiction of a large vessel like that. We may have to consider the possibility they were navigating in the Bay of Campeche.'

'Or beyond?' Díaz asked.

'That might explain why we found the codex in Tabasco,' Madero said. 'There must have been some connection with their departing or returning point on the coast.'

'There is much we don't know,' Torres said.

They all studied the next panel, which showed the seven canoes heading across the water toward the sun. The following image showed a single canoe returning.

'Now things get interesting,' Torres said. 'The next panel shows an Eagle Warrior, presumably from the surviving canoe, describing his voyage to a stonecutter. Then we see the related images being carved into a large circular stone.'

'It resembles the Sun Stone,' Madero said.

'Where have I heard of that?' Summer asked.

'It was discovered in 1790 during renovations of the Mexico City Cathedral and is now displayed in the National Anthropology Museum. Some twelve feet across, it contains a myriad of Aztec glyphs, many related to known calendar periods.'

'If the scale is accurate,' Torres said, 'this stone would be considerably smaller.'

Dirk looked at the image, still contemplating the canoes from the earlier panels. 'Any idea about the nature of the voyage?'

'The purpose isn't clear, but it appears they were transporting something of great significance. That is implied by the presence of the Eagle Warriors as escorts. Perhaps a special offering to one of the deities.'

'Would that include items of intrinsic value,' Díaz asked, 'such as gold or jewels?'

'The Aztecs valued and traded such objects, and they are reflected in their religious artifacts, so that would be likely.'

The next panel showed the stonecutter with his handiwork, standing in a house, while men wearing steel helmets and breastplates assembled outside.

'And now the Spanish appear,' Madero said.

'Yes, and they want the stone.' Torres pointed to the

next image. 'The stonecutter cuts it in half and tries to hide both pieces. The Spaniards find one piece and then kill the stonecutter.'

The next page showed a stone fragment being loaded on to a ship with a large sail. A monkey was depicted above the bow.

'So the Spanish obtained the stone and loaded it on a galleon,' Summer said. 'It must be now sitting in the basement of a museum in Seville, collecting dust.'

'I'm not aware of any such artifact,' Torres said. 'And the Spaniards got only half the stone. The final panels show more Eagle Warriors transporting the remaining piece and hiding it in a cave beneath a mountain marked with a cow.'

'Any clue where that might be?'

Torres pointed to a page depicting footsteps along a flat-topped pyramid crowned by four large statues.

'That most certainly is the Pyramid of Quetzalcoatl at Tula,' he said, 'which is north of Mexico City. After reaching Tula, the footsteps on the next frame indicate they continued farther. It's difficult to gauge distances, but if the next page represents another day or two's journey, they might have traveled another thirty or forty miles beyond Tula.'

Madero pored over the final image. 'They then buried the stone in a cave, it would seem, near a mountain marked with a cow. That's very curious.'

'That they would try to hide the stone?' Summer asked.

'No, the fact that they drew a cow. Cattle were not native to North America. They were brought over by Columbus.' He stepped to a file cabinet and returned with a folding road map of the Mexican state of Hidalgo. He pinpointed Tula near the map's southeast corner.

'It's probably safe to assume they traveled from the south to reach Tula. The question is, where would they have gone from there?'

He and Torres examined the surrounding place names, searching for a clue.

'Maybe Huapalcalco?' Madero pointed to a town east of Tula. 'An important Toltec city that also represents one of the oldest human occupation sites in Hidalgo.'

'If they were traveling from Tenochtitlan, or the Tabasco coast,' Torres said, 'they wouldn't have needed to pass through Haupalcalco. It's too far east.'

'You're right. Farther north is a better bet.' Madero dragged a finger from Tula, stopping at a town called Zimapán, almost fifty miles north. He stared at the lettering, lost in thought.

'A cow on the mountain,' he said. 'Or is it really a bull? Isn't there an old Spanish mine around there called Lomo del Toro, or Bull's Back?'

Torres's eyes lit up. 'Yes! A very early Spanish silver mine, predecessor to the big El Monte Mine west of Zimapán. I worked on a dig at a village site near there many years ago. The bull's back refers to the rugged top of the mountain. You're right, Eduardo, it fits the description. The cave could be on this very same mountain.'

'Could the stone still be there?' Díaz asked.

The room fell quiet. Madero finally broke the silence. 'It's a remote area. I think the chances are good.'

'There's only one problem,' Torres said. 'The Zimapán Dam, built in the 1990s, flooded the valley floor west of the mountain. If the cave is located on that side, it may be underwater.'

'Underwater, you say?' Madero turned to Dirk and Summer and winked. 'Now, who do we know who could pull off an underwater search of that nature?'

Dirk and Summer looked at each other and grinned.

13

The tranquil expanse of open water appeared much like any other portion of the Caribbean. Only the occasional dead fish slapping against the bow of the *Sargasso Sea* gave hint of anything amiss. The NUMA research ship cut its engines and eased to a drift in the lightly choppy seas.

Two days had passed since they had slipped into Havana Bay under the watchful eye of a Cuban patrol craft and offloaded the *Alta*'s injured crew and oil workers. A Cuban Revolutionary Navy tender had pulled alongside and hoisted a diving bell over to the NUMA ship. The Canadian dive team climbed from the NUMA decompression chamber into the pressurized bell, which was transported back to the Cuban ship, where the men would complete their decompression cycle.

Captain Knight waited for the last of his men to debark, then approached Pitt at the gangway. 'I hate to think of how many men we would have lost if you hadn't responded to our distress call. I can't thank you enough.'

'Lucky thing we were in the neighborhood.' Pitt nodded at the antiquated ambulances beginning to pull away from the dock. 'We would have been happy to drop you in Key West.'

Knight smiled. 'We'll be well treated. We're operating under a contract with the Cuban government, so it's probably better we're here to sort through the repercussions. Hopefully, I'll be able to smooth over the fact that we won't be able to tap that exploratory well for a while.'

'I wish you luck,' Pitt said, shaking hands.

Moving at a measured pace, Knight stepped ashore, then turned and gave the crew of the *Sargasso Sea* a sharp salute.

As the gangway was secured and the mooring lines retrieved, Giordino approached Pitt with a box of Ramón Allones Cuban cigars under one arm.

'How did you score those?' Pitt asked. 'Nobody was allowed off the ship.'

'I made fast friends with the harbor pilot. They cost me two bottles of Maker's Mark.'

'I'd say you got the better end of that deal.'

Giordino grimaced. 'Not if you consider they were my last drops of booze smuggled aboard ship.'

They stood at the rail, watching the historic Malecón slip by, as the *Sargasso Sea* made its way out of the compact harbor. Pitt had set foot in Havana years earlier and was struck by how similar the waterfront appeared, as if the march of time had somehow bypassed the city.

The NUMA ship soon found open water. Shedding its Cuban escort, it beat a quick turn around the island's western tip, backtracking on a southeastern tack toward Jamaica. Reaching one of Yaeger and Gunn's dead zones, the *Sargasso Sea* came to a halt and a flurry of activity began. A team of scientists took water samples, lowering collection devices to varying depths and rushing them to the lab.

In the meantime, Giordino prepped an autonomous underwater vehicle. The torpedo-shaped AUV was packed with sensors and a self-contained sonar system. With a prearranged road map, the device would dive to the bottom and skim along the seafloor in a set grid pattern, mapping the contours.

Pitt watched as Giordino released the AUV from the stern A-frame. 'When will she be back?'

'About four hours. She's on a short leash for the initial run, surveying less than a square mile. No sense in running her crazy until we can determine the source of the dead zone.'

'My very next intent.' Pitt migrated to the bridge, where he had the captain hopscotch the vessel around the area, stopping at half-mile increments for additional water samples. When it was time to retrieve the AUV, Pitt grabbed Giordino and ducked into one of the labs. A dark-eyed woman in a blue lab coat motioned for them to join her in front of a computer monitor.

'Do you have some results for us, Kamala?' Pitt asked.

Kamala Bhatt, the *Sargasso Sea*'s marine biologist, nodded. 'We do indeed.'

She took a seat on a stool. 'As you know, dead zones are common all over the world's oceans. They are typically found near the mouth of rivers carrying polluted runoff. But this site, and the others identified by Hiram Yaeger, are far from land. Our initial testing does show a decrease of oxygen levels, but it is less than we would otherwise expect.'

Pitt shook his head. 'So there is in fact no dead zone here?'

'On the contrary, the toxicity levels are quite high. It just wasn't the animal I expected to find.' She pointed to the computer screen, where a bar graph displayed the composition of one of the water samples. 'The water tests lower for oxygen content than typically found, but there seems to be another factor that is increasing the impact to aquatic life. I had to delve deeper until I found one element out of place. Its concentration is off the charts.'

'What's that?' Giordino asked.

'Mercury. Or methyl mercury, to be precise.'

'Mercury poisoning this far from land?' Pitt asked. 'Are you sure?'

'We've tested all but the last batch of seawater samples, and they all show highly toxic concentrations of methyl mercury. We've found bioaccumulation in the plankton, which then works itself up the food chain. We also sampled a number of dead fish, which seem to be present in large numbers, and confirmed the presence of mercury.'

'Mercury is nothing new,' Pitt said. 'Industrial air pollution has been increasing mercury levels in the oceans for decades. But this is different?'

Bhatt nodded. 'The concentration is exponentially higher. This isn't just some general acid rain but a specific, localized incident. The only comparable toxicity I can find historically is from Minamata, Japan. A factory there dumped twenty-seven tons of methyl mercury into the bay over several decades, resulting in catastrophic damage to nearby residents and local sea life. Nearly two thousand deaths have been attributed to it.'

'But we're fifty miles from land,' Giordino said.

'If I had to guess,' Bhatt said, 'I would say that someone has been dumping industrial wastes out here.'

'If that's the case,' Pitt said, 'the AUV will show it.'

'The concentration was highest in the water sample where the AUV was launched,' Bhatt said.

'She's due up any minute,' Giordino said. 'Hopefully, the litterbugs left a calling card.'

The trio retreated to the stern deck as the AUV surfaced and was hoisted aboard. Giordino downloaded the sonar data on to a portable hard drive and returned to the lab to review the images. He quickly advanced through the AUV's acoustic imagery, which showed hundred-meter swaths of the undulating seafloor. There were rocks, sand, and even occasional dunes, but no drums, crates or other debris. Only an odd series of shadowy lines marred the bottom, concentrated in a slight underwater valley.

'Nothing obvious,' Giordino said, 'though those lines might be worth a closer look. It's difficult to say if they are geological features or man-made.'

'We might be dealing with something that's buried,' Pitt said, 'in which case we've got our work cut out for us.'

'I can reconfigure the AUV to perform a sub-bottom profile. That would give us a limited look beneath the seabed, if the sediment conditions are friendly.'

Pitt stared at the sonar screen, knowing the answer to the mystery was there somewhere. He shook his head slowly. 'No, let's move on. It looks to be a sandy bottom here, which isn't conducive to the sub-bottom profiler. We've got two more dead zones to investigate, and I'll wager the source will be evident at one of those.'

Without debate, Giordino relayed the order to the bridge, knowing from the past that Pitt's intuition was as good as gold.

14

The battered green panel van turned off the dirt road and pulled to a stop on a high bluff. As a cloud of trailing dust settled, Dr Torres climbed out of the driver's seat and spread a topographic map across the hood. Dirk and Summer joined him as he took a black pen and marked an X through a square grid. A half-dozen adjacent grids were already marked.

'That was the last accessible area around the base of Lomo del Toro to survey,' Torres said in a tired voice. 'Aside from the two abandoned mine shafts we crawled through, I'm afraid we've found nothing resembling a cave, or even a potentially buried one.'

'Dr Madero told us it was a long shot,' Summer said.

'True. I wish he was here to see for himself.'

'He was disappointed, but he couldn't get out of a speaking engagement in Mexico City,' Summer said. 'We did promise him we'd give it our best effort.'

Torres nodded. He was certain they were in the right place. He and Madero had spent days studying the codex and comparing it to other Aztec documents, as well as reading contemporary Spanish accounts. Bit by bit, they deciphered additional clues that seemed to confirm the Aztecs had carried the half stone to Zimapán.

One notation indicated they had traveled north, presumably from their capital of Tenochtitlan. Another indicated they stopped at Tula along the way. Tula was an ancient Toltec city near the northern fringe of the Aztec empire, just over twenty miles away. The codex revealed the warriors had traveled two days beyond Tula, traversing a steep ravine, before depositing the half stone in a cave near the base of a cow-shaped mountain. Everything pointed to Lomo del Toro.

But two days of searching the dry, rugged region in Mexico's Central Plateau had led nowhere. After arriving at the mining town of Zimapán, the three drove through the narrow canyon of Barranca de Tolimán, which seemed to align with the Aztec description. At Lomo del Toro mountain, they initiated a search around its perimeter. Much was inaccessible by car, forcing them to hike the rugged terrain. They were now hot, dusty, and tired of dodging rattlesnakes.

They had explored all around the mountain, except for the El Monte Mine facility facing Zimapán, which encompassed the original Spanish digs. With most of its silver and lead deposits having been mined in excavations that stretched back to the sixteenth century, it was now a small operation. Torres conferred with mine officials and a local historian, but no one recalled any stories of an Aztec cave, or even an Aztec presence in the area. Fears that the stone was hidden in an early mine shaft were minimized when they realized the mining operation was high up the mountain.

Torres drank warm water from his canteen and shook his head. 'My friends, perhaps the Aztec cow mountain is located elsewhere.'

Dirk produced a copy of the codex page that illustrated the burial site. He gazed from the mountain image to the imposing heights of Lomo del Toro. 'The ridge highlines look like a match to me.'

Summer gazed at the mountain and agreed. Studying the photocopy, she noticed a faint line beneath the cave. 'What's that?'

Dirk and Torres peered at the line.

'I didn't remember that in the original,' Torres said.

'That's what I thought,' Summer said. 'It became more visible in the photocopy.'

Torres studied the line closely. 'It would appear to be a river or creek.'

Dirk was already eyeing the topographic map. 'The view of the bull is most prominent from either the southwest or the northeast. The northeast area is mostly rolling hills that descend toward Zimapán. To the southwest, where we are now, there's a natural wash running along the mountain's western flank.'

'We've already searched there,' Summer noted.

'But not here.' Dirk's finger followed the wash, tracking beneath a low ridge that jutted from the base of the mountain. A half mile distant, the ridge grew into a high, steep bluff. The wash below disappeared into a large reservoir.

'You think the cave is in this small ridge that stretches off Lomo del Toro?'

'No, I think it's beneath this high bluff.'

'That's underwater,' Summer said.

'It wouldn't have been when the Aztecs were here.' Torres's voice had a new optimism. 'The lake was created by a dam built some twenty-five years ago.'

Dirk dragged his finger to the middle of the reservoir. 'If you were drawing a picture of the cave from this vantage point, the peak of Lomo del Toro would rise above and just beyond the top of the bluff. The codex image would still fit.'

'Yes, yes,' Torres said, his face lighting up. 'Are you up to the task of searching in the water?'

Dirk gave the professor a wink. 'Could an Aztec priest carve a turkey?'

15

They plunged into the reservoir from a shoreline ledge, finding the water cool and the visibility clear. Summer involuntarily shivered in the water that was not as warm as the cenote where they had last dived. She hovered a moment at the ten-foot mark to clear her ears, then swam after her brother, who was already descending rapidly. After Torres had found a path to the water's edge, the siblings had assembled their dive gear in record time, leaving the archeologist to pace the shoreline.

Dirk followed the gradient until it leveled at sixty feet. The lake bed was a bland tableau of rocks and brown mud that resembled a moonscape. Any sign of a riverbed was long since hidden, covered by sediment built up since the dam was constructed. Dirk knew the original watercourse had followed the base of the ridge, and when Summer joined his side, he took off across its steep face.

They could look up the face of the ridge nearly to the surface. They swam in short spurts, methodically surveying the rock wall in the hope of spotting a cave-like opening. Numerous times they were deceived by shadows and narrow fissures that led nowhere. Both were strong swimmers, and with little current in the lake, they quickly advanced several hundred yards along the base of the ridge.

The feature gradually sharpened to a near-vertical rise. Dirk was looking ahead to the next contour when he felt Summer grip his arm. She pointed to the rock incline at his side. A small indentation was visible where his fin had knocked away some silt. He stuck his fingers into the crevice and scooped away a thick handful of mud. The water turned murky, but a minute later it cleared and they could see the indentation was a carved step. Summer ran her hand above the cut and found another hollow. Scooping away the mud inside, she exposed it as another step, carved directly above the first one.

She pointed up the face of the rock and began ascending. Every foot or so, she found another step filled with sediment. About forty feet above her, Summer noticed a dark spot and her heart skipped a beat.

It appeared little different than the rock shadows that had deceived them earlier, but she became more intrigued when a pair of fish emerged from the darkness. Dirk followed Summer as she ascended, following the buried flight of steps. Drawing close to the rock shadow, she saw a thick ledge protruding from the wall above her, obscuring the view farther up.

With a strong kick of her fins, she broached the rim and peered over the top. Just beyond was an oval recess in the rock wall. Neatly concealed by the ledge, and accessible only by the steps when the land was dry, the cave would have been a highly defensible hideaway for its ancient occupants.

Summer waited until her brother joined her on the ledge. She then flicked on a dive light and swam through the slim opening, startling a large bass that darted out of the darkness. Dirk followed her, careful not to scrape the floor with his fins and kick up a cloud of sediment.

The small opening led a short distance before expanding into a house-sized cavern. Removed from the surface light, the interior was black and ominous, save for the thin illumination of their dive lights. The ceiling soared high above them, allowing the divers to float easily while surveying the interior. But there was little to observe. A rock fire pit occupied the center of the cave floor, while an orderly mound of crushed rock was piled against the back wall. There was no sign of the half stone, or any other artifacts.

Dirk swam to a side wall and examined it with his light. Crude scars peppered the surface, indicating the rocks in the pile had been hammered from the wall. He picked up one of the rocks and held it to his dive mask. It was a heavy chunk of granite flecked with silver. Someone had discovered a vein of the ore and made a primitive attempt to mine it. Could it have been the Aztecs?

He pocketed the rock and joined Summer, who was slowly swimming circular laps with her light pointed at the floor. The excitement in her eyes had vanished and she gave her brother a disappointed shake of her head. Dirk pointed toward the entrance and motioned to leave.

Summer followed, keeping her light pointed at the floor. As they crossed the center of the cave, her light caught the fire pit. She had examined it earlier but found only a ring of rocks over a mud floor. Now she noticed there were no charred sticks or signs of charcoal. Nor were the rocks blackened. She hesitated and then noticed the rocks' alignment. They didn't actually form a round pit but were instead positioned in a semicircle.

She reached out and snared Dirk's ankle before he swam out the entrance, then dropped down to the fire pit. He turned his light on her as she glided above the pit and plunged a hand into its center. Summer's fingers drove through several inches of sediment before reaching a hard surface. Sliding her hand against it, she could tell it was flat.

Her pulse quickened as she scooped the mud from the fire pit in thick handfuls. Fine particles rose through the water, deflecting their lights and turning the visibility to soup. Dirk released a shot of air from his buoyancy compensator and descended to the floor, feeling Summer's elbow as she continued to sling mud. He felt her movements stop and they both lay quietly, waiting for the water to clear.

It felt like an eternity to Summer, but it was only a

minute or two before the water began to become clear. She saw Dirk's light appear, then the shape of his wetsuit. Together, they turned their lights toward the fire pit, where Summer's hand still rested. As her fingers came into view, she traced the outline of a large, flat object. Brushing away a thin layer of sand, she pressed her face down to see.

The carved head of a bird gazed back at her, surrounded by an assortment of stylized glyphs like those in the codex. Summer winked at her brother and pointed at the figures.

She had found the Aztec stone.

16

The stone was too unwieldy to carry any distance, so Summer and Dirk left it in place and swam out of the cave. Dirk had carried a small lift bag attached to his buoyancy compensator. He inflated it with his regulator and tied it to a rock near the entrance. The small bag floated to the surface, providing a marker for the cave. Dirk and Summer followed it up, then swam along the ridge wall to where Torres waited impatiently.

The archeologist leaped like a drunken leprechaun when Summer described their find. 'It was carved in a semicircle?'

'Yes,' Summer said, 'exactly as if it had been cut in half. It was full of carved glyphs, just like the ones in the codex.'

'*Fantástico!* Can you remove it from the cave?'

'Yes, but we'll never get it here.' She pointed to a tiny orange speck in the water. Dirk's float bag lay almost a quarter of a mile away.

'We'll have to move the van closer,' Dirk said. He eyeballed the top of the ridge, then borrowed Torres's topographic map. 'If we circle around the back of the ridge, I think we can drive over the top and descend directly above the cave. There's a tapered gully nearby where we could access the lake.'

Summer nodded. 'We could hoist it straight up the face of the bluff. There's a coil of rope in the back of the van we can use.'

Torres laughed. 'We have nothing to lose but my van. Let's give it a try.'

They loaded their gear and drove around the east side of the ridge, following a weather-beaten dirt track that snaked down the hill to the reservoir's dam. Finding a moderate incline to the ridge, Torres turned off the track and drove up the hillside. The ground was hard and compact, providing firm traction for the van's worn tires.

The surface turned to solid rock as Torres reached the top of the ridge. Dirk got out and guided him down the other side and toward the edge, just overlooking the buoy marker. Torres stopped in front of a pile of boulders and stuck his head out the window. 'How's this?'

'Perfect,' Dirk said. 'Just remember to put it in reverse when it's time to leave.'

Torres applied the parking brake and turned off the engine. Summer was already out the door, uncoiling a length of nylon rope. Tying one end around the van's door post, she flung the remaining line over the side, watching as it splashed into the water forty feet below.

'It's a hundred-foot line,' she said. 'Should be just enough to get us there.'

Dirk unloaded their dive equipment and two thin sleeping pads from their camping supplies.

'Can you grab my new camera?' Summer pointed to an underwater Olympus camera within her brother's reach.

Torres helped them haul their gear to the nearby gully, which offered a steep but navigable path to the reservoir. 'Be very careful, my friends,' he shouted as they prepared to enter the water.

'We'll bring it up in one piece,' Dirk replied, knowing Torres's chief concern was the artifact's safety.

He slipped on his mask and stepped into the water, carrying the sleeping pads under one arm. Summer swam past him, retrieving the dangling rope. They met at the lift bag and dove to the cave entrance, another thirty feet down.

At the fire pit, Summer snapped multiple pictures of the stone *in situ*. Setting her camera aside, she helped Dirk muscle the heavy stone on top of one of the sleeping pads. Dirk wrapped the other pad over the exposed side, creating a protective cover, which he secured with Summer's rope. Standing on the cave floor, he pulled the rope to give it a test. With a concerted effort, they slid the bundled stone across the muddy floor.

Nodding at Summer, he dragged the stone out of the cave, while his sister swam above it, guiding it free of any obstacles. Once clear of the entrance, Dirk pushed the stone upright on the ledge, then shot to the surface. They had agreed Summer would stay in the water and monitor the stone's ascent while Dirk and Torres hoisted it to the van.

Dirk hardly had to assist Torres. By the time he had jettisoned his dive gear and hiked to the van, Torres was pulling like a madman. Adrenaline was clearly pumping through the archeologist's veins. But his aged muscles began to fade as the stone broke the lake's surface and Dirk pitched in for the remaining distance. Summer exited the water and joined the out-of-breath men as they removed the rope and pads.

The white half disk glistened under the afternoon sun. Torres dropped to his knees and grazed his fingertips across the surface. The glyphs were crisply cut, though along the edges they had worn thin.

Summer could see the glyphs were carved in bands that would have encircled the entire stone before it was cut in two. 'Can you read what it says?'

'Portions,' Torres said with a nod. 'This section relays an important journey across the water. Though we are missing half the stone, I suspect we'll be able to piece together much of its intent.' He smiled. 'Between this stone and the codex, you've given a pair of old archeologists quite a few years of steady work.'

'Just promise us,' Dirk said, 'you won't keep it all stored away in a dusty archive.'

'Heavens, no. This will easily be the centerpiece at the university's museum. Which reminds me, were there any other artifacts?'

'No, I checked when I photographed the stone,'

Summer said. 'Oh, no!' she burst out suddenly. 'My camera! I left it in the cave.'

'I'll get it,' Dirk said. 'I need to retrieve my float marker anyway. Maybe you can scavenge something to eat from the cooler while I'm gone.'

'No,' Torres said, 'we shall have a celebratory dinner in Zimapán, and the tequila shall be on me.'

Dirk grinned. 'A better offer I haven't had in a month of Sundays.'

He hiked to the water's edge, donned his tank and mask, and swam to the float. He took a quick glance up and noticed an odd swirl of dust rising atop the ridge. Thinking nothing of it, he emptied his buoyancy compensator and sank beneath the surface.

17

The white Jeep Cherokee came barreling up the ridge like a speeding cheetah, its tires chewing up the incline with ease. Reaching the summit, it made a hasty bee-line for the university van. The Jeep's driver didn't bother picking an easy descent but drove straight down the ridge and slid to a stop in front of the van. A patch of loose gravel skittered over the edge of the rock face into the water below.

Summer casually kicked the sleeping pad over the stone and stepped in front of it as three men hopped from the Jeep. Each wore a baseball cap, sunglasses, and a black scarf wrapped around his face. Two held automatic handguns, which they leveled at Summer and Torres.

'What is this?' Torres snapped. 'We have no drugs or money.' Though they were far south of the major drug cartel homeland states, Torres knew the violent organizations had a long reach.

'Shut up, old man, and stand aside,' one of the gun-men said. He waved his pistol at Summer. 'You, too.'

Torres and Summer backed away as the other gun-man stepped forward and threw back the cover from the stone.

'Is this it?' he asked.

The unarmed man stepped closer with a measured ease that was in marked contrast to the two men holding weapons. Clearly older than the others, he was the obvious group leader.

He studied the Aztec stone with a patient gaze. Satisfied, he nodded at his accomplices, then pointed to the back of the Jeep. The nearest gunman, who wore a red shirt, opened the deck lid and then joined the other man. They holstered their weapons and hoisted the stone off the ground.

'No!' Torres shouted. 'That's an important historical artifact.'

He stepped forward and shoved the nearest man, who lost his grip on the stone and fell backward. The other gunman let go as the stone thumped to the ground. In an instant, his pistol was back in his hand. Without hesitation, he raised and fired three shots into Torres's chest.

Summer screamed as the archeologist staggered back. His eyelids fluttered and then he fell to the ground. Everyone else froze as the sound of the gunshots echoed off the surrounding hills.

'*Imbécil!*' the trio's leader cried. He grabbed the gun and pointed at the stone. '*Rápidamente.*'

The two gunmen ferried the stone to the back of the Jeep as their boss kept a watchful eye on Summer. She knelt beside Torres but quickly realized he was dead.

'You killed him for a carved stone!' she cried, rising to her feet.

The two gunmen returned and spoke with their leader in low voices. One produced a knife and cut a short length from the rope. He then reached over and grabbed one of Summer's wrists.

She swung her opposite elbow and slammed it into the man's jaw. As he tumbled back, she took a step to run but froze as a gunshot rang out.

It was the group's leader, firing a shot into the side of the van inches from Summer. He eased the gun sideways, taking aim at her. 'The next one won't miss.'

Logic, and the thought of her brother in the water below, overcame her anger. She remained still as the woozy gunman rose and bound her wrists behind her. After a quiet conversation with the leader, the gunman in the red shirt approached Summer. 'Where is the other man who was with you?'

Summer stared straight ahead and said nothing. The leader strode to the edge of the bluff and stared into the water. Dirk's float bag bobbed directly below. The water was clear enough that he could just make out the ledge fronted the cave. He gazed back to the mass of small boulders in front of the Jeep. They were in perfect alignment.

He pointed at Summer and motioned toward the Jeep. Red Shirt grabbed her arm and pushed her into the backseat, then helped the other two drag Torres's body and roll it off the bluff. Summer grimaced as the body hit the water below with a sickening splash. The man with the knife then went to work on the van, slashing each of its tires.

Satisfied with their handiwork, the three men returned to the Jeep. Red Shirt climbed in the back and held a pistol on Summer, while the other two sat in the front. The leader took the wheel, but instead of backing up, he let the Jeep roll forward against one of the blockading boulders. He put the Jeep in low gear and eased the accelerator, shoving the boulder forward. Smaller rocks in front of it began sliding over the bluff, raining down into the water below. The boulder soon gave way, tumbling into the lake.

The Jeep backed up and took aim at an adjacent wall of rocks stacked high near the edge. The driver nudged at the pile, backing up hurriedly when one slammed on to the hood. Another push broke loose a lower supporting rock and the entire pile cascaded over the side, taking with it a thick chunk of the cliff. The Jeep nearly joined the avalanche, but the driver shifted into reverse and gunned the engine just in time. He turned and headed up the ridge as several tons of rock and debris slid down into the reservoir.

Summer sat stoically, anger showing only in the creases of her eyelids. As the lake vanished in a swirl of dust behind them, she could only pray silently for her brother's safety.

18

It was a small clay bowl that saved Dirk's life.

He had left the float bag in place while he swam into the cave to retrieve Summer's underwater camera. He found it next to the fire pit. As he reached to grab it, his hand dipped into the silt and brushed something smooth and round. Finding a grip, he pulled free a small pottery bowl with the faint image of a snake carved on the bottom.

Slipping the bowl into a pocket on his BC, he probed for more artifacts. He felt nothing but ooze. As a grinding rumble sounded overhead, he glanced toward the cave entrance in time to see its blue glow turn dark. Seconds later, he was enveloped in a cloud of murky water.

Dirk swam blindly to the entrance, feeling his way along the cave floor until colliding with a large rock that blocked his way. As the sediment began to settle, he saw a gap of light to one side. He moved to the opening as a second rumble sounded above him. He considered darting out but hesitated when he heard a large splash. Shining his light through the opening, he saw a cascade of rocks tumble on to the ledge before a new cloud of sediment snuffed out his view.

Dirk could feel the vibration through the rocks as they piled up. It was several seconds before the slide subsided. The rocks from the ridge had knocked loose a large subsurface outcropping, which dumped even more tons of debris on to the ledge. Buried under the avalanche, the cave's tiny entrance was completely sealed.

Dirk backed away from the entrance and examined his air pressure gauge. The needle hovered just above the red low-air warning marker. He had five, maybe ten minutes of air left.

Trapped in an underwater cave with little air, it would have been a perfect time to panic. But Dirk suppressed any such fears and took a calm breath of air, assessing the situation.

His initial urge was to attack the rock pile and try to dig free. Perhaps Summer was already preparing to dig on the other side. But logic told him he would never make it. The thundering avalanche had dropped so much rock, he would exhaust his air supply long before tunneling out.

If that was his only option, so be it. Then he looked up. The cave ceiling rose in twin fissures that angled up nearly twenty feet. He decided to take a quick look.

Gripping his flashlight, he kicked upward, following the first fissure until it converged in a narrow, jagged point. He backtracked and swam up the second fissure, finding a similar cathedral peak. The walls and fissure appeared to be solid rock. He turned and descended, almost missing it. But out of the corner of his eye, he caught a tiny speck of light.

Swimming closer, he found its source, a small pinhole in the rock wall leading to the lake. He pulled out a Randall dive knife strapped to his thigh and poked the tip into the hole. The light expanded as a small chunk of rock flaked away. Dirk began jamming the knife into the hole, gradually increasing its diameter to the size of a softball.

It was a way out, he knew, but he faced the same dilemma. Could he excavate a large enough hole before his air ran out? He had already used three minutes' worth. With limited time, the knife alone wouldn't do the job. He'd need more leverage.

He swam down to the cave floor, approached the ore pile, and searched for a stone he could use as a hammer. He spotted one with a blunt side and plucked it from the pile. Beneath it was a green rock with a near-perfect wedge shape. Intrigued by the shape, he picked it up, then realized that it wasn't a rock. It was too heavy for its size and had a perfectly round hole in its underside.

Dirk held it close to his mask and recognized it as an oxidized copper ax head used to chip ore from the cave walls. The Aztec had been skilled stone carvers, he recalled, crafting statues and temples from the local basalt. Neighboring Mixtec craftsmen in Oaxaca, advanced in the skill of metallurgy, would have traded copper-based tools with the Aztecs. Though the wood handle had disintegrated, the copper head of the ancient ax was still solid.

He quickly swam back to the fissure and put both objects to work. Placing the business end of the ax head next to the opening, he struck the blunt side with the round stone. Muffled by the water, the impact registered as a loud click. Dirk struck it again and a chunk of rock broke away from the opening. The ancient Mixtec metallurgists had mixed tin with the copper when they forged the ax, producing a hard bronze-like metal that was surprisingly effective at cutting stone.

Feeling resistance from the air drawn through his regulator, he began pounding madly at the copper chisel. He didn't have to check his pressure gauge to know he was drawing on his final air reserves. Striking hard caused the rock wall to stubbornly break away in fist-sized pieces. Pulling the loose rock away revealed a hole that was a foot in diameter.

Dirk took a breath and nothing came through the regulator. His tank was completely dry.

Without hesitating, he pounded the chisel as hard as he could. More fragments fell away, but the opening was still too small. His lungs tightened as a pounding in his head mimicked his banging on the rock. Through the vibrating ax head, he could feel a slight give in the rock wall. But the small, ancient ax felt like a ball-peen hammer tapping against the Hoover Dam.

He dismissed the fear of drowning, slipped off his BC, and removed the steel air tank. Grasping it by the neck, he smashed the bottom against the rock. The wall vibrated but nothing more. He smashed it again. And again. The tank collided with a clatter as Dirk released what little air he had left in his lungs. With a desperate plunge, he tried once more, summoning every ounce of strength.

This time, a small crack appeared – then suddenly a three-foot chunk of wall fell away.

Almost too shocked to react, Dirk let go of the tank and kicked through the hole. The surface was only ten feet away. He stroked upward and broke into the blinding sunlight with a rush, gasping and sucking at the fresh air. He floated in the water for nearly a minute before the oxygen was replenished in his blood and his breathing eased. Trying to relax, he stared at an empty sky, ignoring something in the water that brushed at his side. When his breathing slowed, he turned to see what was nudging him.

It was the body of Dr Torres.

19

Dirk reacted quickly, swimming to a small rock outcropping and towing Torres's body behind him. Once on land, he noted the three bullet wounds in the professor's chest.

Dirk looked up toward the van and shouted Summer's name. There was no reply. Then he saw a small cloud of dust wafting over the ridge. He ditched his mask and fins, fumbled through Torres's pockets for the keys, and sprinted up the hill. He saw the frayed rope tied to the vehicle and knew someone had come for the stone. Glancing with fear at the water below, he saw no sign of Summer's body. She must have been abducted.

Disregarding its four flat tires, Dirk started the van, turned it around, and mashed on the gas. The van lurched ahead, its flattened tires thumping against the wheel wells. Despite the uneven traction, Dirk coaxed the vehicle to the top of the ridgeline. Far below, he spotted a white Jeep driving north on the old dirt road.

He fought the urge to turn down the ridge and follow the Jeep. It would be impossible to catch it in the van's disabled state. He'd already lost one of its shredded tires. Assuming the van reached the road, the many patches of soft sand would surely snare it for good.

From his review of the topo map, Dirk knew the road wound around several hills along the base of Lomo del Torro before curving west and leading across the Zimapán Dam. The dam spanned a narrow gorge at the ridge's far end. If he could coax the van along the top of the ridgeline, he would cut off a mile or two and possibly catch the Jeep before it crossed the dam.

He punched the accelerator and rumbled across the ridge's rounded peak. One by one, the remaining tires shredded off. The steel wheels let out a grinding wail, and every bump and dip rattled through the chassis. Dirk felt like he was riding a jackhammer. In the side mirrors, he could see a trail of sparks erupt whenever the wheels scraped over solid rock.

The ridgeline gradually narrowed, forcing Dirk on to a side ledge that held level for a short distance. The ledge narrowed, then vanished altogether in a jumble of small boulders. Dirk swerved up the slope but struck a patch of soft sand. Feeling the rear wheels start to bog down, he had no choice but to turn downhill to maintain momentum. Narrowly missing one boulder, he slid into a tight ravine. The van heeled to its side, nearly toppling over before an opposing rut rocked it back upright. The van thumped over some smaller rocks, then again found even ground.

Dirk feathered the throttle as the ridge began to

taper. Ahead and below him, he could discern the narrow Zimapán Dam. He drove hard down the increasingly steep slope, then slammed on the brakes and spun the wheel. The bent and pitted wheels skidded, digging ruts through the hard-packed surface before the van rocked to a halt. Dirk climbed out and peeked past the hood.

Just three feet in front of the van, the ridgeline dropped away in a sheer cliff. A hundred feet below was the dam's western approach. An aged asphalt road ran across the top of the concrete structure, curving up another ridge on the opposite side. It was easy to see why the dam had been built here. The steep, narrow gorge was easily obstructed.

The thought was of little consequence as his eyes followed the road to the east. The white Jeep was just seconds away.

20

Summer sat still in the backseat, but behind her back her hands worked furiously. The rope around her wrists was still damp from immersion in the lake. The moisture lubricated her wrists while making the rope more tensile. With every bounce of the Jeep, she flexed and pulled, stretching the binding a millimeter at a time.

Already growing tired of guarding her, Summer's backseat captor reached over and locked her door and then holstered his gun. Nevertheless, he stared at her with suspicion, or perhaps it was attraction. She countered with a verbal bombardment of questions. From the obvious – 'Where are you taking me?' – to the frivolous – 'Where did you buy that scarf?' – she harangued the guard. Each query was met with stony silence. The chattering worked as he ultimately turned his head away from her and stared out the window.

Summer eased back the commentary. No point pushing her luck. The gunmen hadn't hesitated to kill Torres and easily could do the same to her. She was encouraged that the three thieves still kept their faces masked despite the heat. If she could stay calm until they reached a town, maybe she could leap from the car and find refuge. But first she'd have to work free of the rope binding.

Her wishes came true sooner than she hoped. The road gradually improved until the Jeep's tires met pavement. They'd arrived at the dam, where the road narrowed as it wound across the top of the structure. The driver sped up, then suddenly cursed and stood on the brakes.

As the Jeep shuddered across the pavement, all four occupants shot forward. The hard braking worked in Summer's favor. Her left hand slipped loose, and as she fell back into her seat, she quickly worked the rope off both wrists. She hadn't seen the reason for the sudden stop. As she peered out the side window, she gaped in horror.

The green university van had shot off the side of the cliff directly overhead and was descending toward them like a Tomahawk missile. The van arced past the Jeep, striking the edge of the road ten feet ahead, where it smashed nose-first before tumbling hard on to its roof. The compressed vehicle slid another dozen feet before coming to a rest – blocking the roadway – amid a pool of leaking engine fluids.

The Jeep was still skidding when Summer unlocked her door and flung herself out. She hit the pavement running and sprinted to the van, shouting her brother's name. As she approached the flattened vehicle, her stomach clenched in a knot. Nobody inside could have survived the impact.

She approached the inverted driver's-side window and crouched to peer inside. There was no one to be seen. The knot in her stomach instantly released.

She had no time to react as she felt the van move. The Jeep had pulled up and the driver was attempting to nudge the wreck aside. Summer stood as the van slid a few inches past her only to find her backseat companion approaching with his gun drawn.

She meekly raised her hands while scanning for signs of Dirk. The sun was in her eyes, but the cliff looked too steep for someone to descend. Seeing no movement on the road they had taken, she glanced in the opposite direction.

They were positioned atop the dam, the reservoir's blue waters lapping at its concrete face twenty feet below her. Oddly, the terrain on the other side of the high, narrow dam appeared completely dry. There was no powerhouse or any sign of water releases into the steep, tight gorge called El Infiernillo Cañones.

Summer looked back at the guard. With an angered expression, he motioned for her to return to the Jeep. She nodded and took a half step forward when an impulse for survival kicked in. It may not have been her best chance at escape, and perhaps it was no chance at all, but she went for it all the same. With a quick side-step, she lunged to the guardrail and leaped. The guard reacted instantly. Reluctant to fire his weapon after his earlier tongue-lashing, he grabbed at her with his free hand, just snaring the cuff of her pants. Caught off balance, he was pulled to the rail. He refused to let go of her but couldn't halt her momentum with his faint grip. As his legs clipped the rail, he plunged over the side.

They tumbled and hit the water together with a loud splash. Summer tried to swim deep, kicking away from the guard. But he maintained his grip on her leg while using his other hand to swing the butt of his pistol at her. She felt like she was in an underwater wrestling match. Figuring that she was the better swimmer, she stroked deeper while kicking to break free of his grasp.

Her hand slapped against the dam and she felt the concrete surface skim across her fingers. The movement was faster than she expected. They were being pulled by a strong underwater current. As the water rapidly darkened, she realized they were being drawn down toward the base of the dam.

A new worry filled her senses. What was causing the undertow? There was no powerhouse or external water flow out the back side of the dam. In the absence of a spillway, there should have been nothing dangerous about diving down the dam's interior face.

The fear of drowning overtook her fear of the guard. She relaxed in his grip and then aligned with his efforts to kick to the surface. But the water turned darker, and an increasing pressure in her ears told her they were being drawn deeper into the lake.

Through the murky water, Summer detected a circular opening, about fifteen feet in diameter, that was sucking them toward it. She realized it was a spillway, cut through the base of the dam. The Zimapán Dam had in fact been built to generate hydroelectric power, only its generating station was located at the end of a tunnel some thirteen miles downstream.

The spillway inlet had a grate to keep out large debris, but years of neglect had left it mangled. Nearly half of the grate had been battered inward, allowing an unfettered flow of water.

Summer and the guard saw what was coming and fought to swim clear. But the suction grew stronger, pulling them faster to the opening. Abandoning her instincts, Summer did the unthinkable. She swam toward the inlet.

The guard glanced at her in disbelief, panic filling his eyes as he fought the relentless pull. Too late, he realized Summer had made the smart move. Swimming hard with the flow, she angled across the current just enough to reach the intact section of grating. She snared a metal crossmember and yanked her body toward it.

She slammed against the grate, nearly knocking the last breath from her lungs. The water pressure pinned her alongside some logs, a tire, and other debris. She turned her head as the guard came hurtling past. His scarf and sunglasses had long since been ripped away, and Summer saw the stark terror in his eyes as he failed to break free of the suction. In an instant he was gone, sucked down the black hole where the swirling waters drowned his final screams.

At least someone will be able to recover my body, Summer thought as a yearning for air overpowered her senses.

Clinging to the grate in final desperation, she wondered what was happening atop the dam and if her brother was still alive.

21

Dirk was very much alive, despite a pounding heart and aching lungs. More by luck than ballistic trajectory, he had launched the van off the bluff and on to the path of the fleeing Jeep, aided by a rock on the accelerator and a rope holding the steering wheel. He didn't wait for the dust to settle before sprinting downhill in pursuit.

He had to backtrack a hundred yards to find a path to the road below. The gradient would have been precarious for someone in hiking boots but was borderline suicidal for someone at a full run wearing water shoes. Several times Dirk lost his footing, tumbling and sliding down the loose terrain. Only his wetsuit protected him from serious injury.

During his descent, he could not see the dam and could only hope the Jeep would still be there. Not that he had a plan of any sort. Weaponless against armed men, he had little hope of stopping them. But he had to find out if Summer was with the men – and still alive.

As he neared the bottom of the cliff, he caught sight of the dam and nearly froze. Summer was standing near the crumpled van. Suddenly she leaped into the lake with a gunman in tow. Distracted by the sight, Dirk lost his footing and fell hard down the hillside.

The tumble cost him valuable seconds. By the time he regained his footing, the Jeep had squeezed past the overturned van. The driver stopped and peered into the water. He stared a moment, then shook his head. Seconds later, the tires spun and the Jeep shot across the dam, its rear end weighed down by the stolen artifact.

Finally reaching the road, Dirk raced to the dam. Blocked by the battered van, the Jeep's driver never noticed him in his mirror as he drove up the hill. At the smashed vehicle, Dirk peered into the water. Calm and flat, it gave no indication of the human turmoil below.

He raced to the van and pried open a rear door. The interior was a jumbled mess, but he found Summer's dive tank, BC and mask. He slipped on the equipment and popped open the tank's K valve. Something nagged at him and he retrieved the rope. One end was still secured to the doorframe, so he tied the loose end to a D ring on his BC. Hopping over the rail, he plunged into the cool lake.

He flicked on a small light attached to the BC and followed a trail of sediment particles rushing into the depths. Soon he felt the pull of the current. He kicked hard, accelerating with it while searching for Summer.

Still pinned to the grate, she had managed to pull herself to its upper edge. She had been underwater for more than a minute and was approaching a state of hypoxia.

Had there been a ladder or anything else to grip, she

might have pulled herself clear of the suction, but all she found was the smooth face of the dam. A flood of desperate, confusing thoughts surged through her mind, pleading for her to try to escape. Perhaps there was hope at the other end of the spillway? She began prying her fingers off the grate when something caught her eye.

A faint light came from above. The light quickly grew brighter until it was joined by a figure flying toward her. Hope and agony struck simultaneously as she recognized Dirk rushing past her and through the open grate. Oddly, his eyes seemed to smile as he vanished into the black hole.

An instant later, she saw the light wavering in the spillway. Through its flashes, she detected a taut rope leading from her brother up to the surface. He reappeared a moment later, hoisting himself hand over hand until reaching the top of the spillway opening. Summer was a few feet to his left, frozen to the grate, her face turning blue.

Bracing his feet against the concrete surface, he pushed off with all his might, springing toward his sister. He released one hand from the rope and reached for her torso. Feeling his touch, she grabbed his hand, then wrapped her arms around his waist.

She yanked the regulator out of his mouth and jammed it into her own, sucking deep breaths. Dirk inflated his BC, pulled them a few feet up the rope, and waited for Summer to pass back the regulator. They shared the tank's air as Dirk muscled them up the face of the dam. The spillway's suction gradually waned until they could kick to the surface.

'That was a nasty surprise down there,' Dirk said after they broke into the sunshine.

'You're telling me. I was about two seconds away from finding out what's at the other end of the spillway.'

'Likely the spinning turbines of a hydroelectric plant.'

Summer shuddered at the fate of the gunman who had been sucked through the tunnel. 'I think I've had my fill of this reservoir.'

She swam to the side of the dam, grabbed the rope, and hoisted herself up. Dirk followed suit, gladly ditching the tank and BC when he reached the van.

Summer gazed at the empty road that curved up the hill. 'They shot and killed Dr Torres, then stole the stone.'

'Any idea who they were?'

She shook her head. 'There were three of them. One went in the water with me and was sucked through the spillway. They all made an effort to conceal their identities.'

'Professional artifact thieves who weren't afraid to kill.'

Summer kicked at a small stone. 'Dr Torres was killed before he even had a chance to decipher the stone. Now it's gone. I guess we'll never know what it says.'

'Madero can still figure it out.'

'Not without the stone.'

'We still have something almost as good.' Dirk rummaged through the interior of the mangled van. A moment later, he crawled out clutching something.

Summer glanced at it and her face turned red. 'No, you didn't!'

Dirk could offer only a crooked grin as he held up the smashed housing of Summer's new underwater camera.

22

The house phone rang and rang, and rang some more. St Julien Perlmutter didn't believe in answering machines, voicemail, or even cell phones. To his way of thinking, they were all intrusive annoyances. He particularly had no use for such devices on the rare occasion he left his Georgetown house, which usually meant he was eating at one of the capital's finer dining establishments or engaging in archival research at a national library.

Fortunately for the caller, Perlmutter was at home, searching for an ancient tome on one of his many bookshelves. A behemoth of a man, he was perhaps the foremost maritime historian on the planet. His breadth of knowledge on ships and shipwrecks was legendary, while archivists drooled for the day Perlmutter would expire and his collection of letters, charts, journals and logbooks might be subject to acquisition.

Dropping into a stout leather chair beside a rolltop desk, he reached for the phone on the tenth ring. Like most objects in his house, the handset was a marine relic, having once graced the bridge of the luxury liner *United States*.

'Perlmutter,' he answered in a gruff voice.

'St Julien, it's Summer. I hope I didn't catch you in the middle of a meal.'

'Heavens, no.' His voice instantly warmed. 'I was just searching for a firsthand account of Christopher Columbus's fourth voyage to the New World.'

'A serendipitous era,' she said.

'The Age of Discovery always was. I had the pleasure of dining with your father recently. He said you and Dirk were working in Mexico.'

'Yes, we're still here. And we could use your help. We're trying to track down a Spanish ship that would have sailed from Veracruz in the early days of the conquest.'

'What was her name?'

'I'm afraid we don't know. The only clue to her identity is a drawing from an Aztec codex, a copy of which I just emailed you.'

While Summer relayed the discovery of the codex and their travails with the Aztec stone, Perlmutter turned on his desktop computer and pulled up the image.

'Rather slim pickings,' he said. He studied the cartoonish image of a sailing ship with a monkey floating above its bow. 'Do your Aztec experts have an interpretation?'

'Nothing definitive. The monkey may relate to the cargo, its route, or possibly a moniker for the ship's name. We hope it's the latter.'

'It's possible, although during that time the Spanish were more apt to name their ships after religious icons.

Fortunately, the records of the early Spanish voyages are fairly stout.'

'It's the stone we're after, so if you have any thoughts on where it may have ended up, we'd certainly be interested. It obviously has some deep significance to someone.'

'Regrettably, many among us will go to unsavory lengths in pursuit of a simple dollar. I'm sorry about your friend. I do hope you and Dirk will be careful.'

'We will.'

'As for the stone, I've been through all the major Spanish maritime museums and don't recall any mention of such an artifact. I suppose it could have ended up in a private collection. I'll make some enquiries.'

'Thanks, Julien. We'll be sure to bring you back a bottle of your favorite tequila. Porfidio, if I remember.'

'Summer, you are an angel. Just don't let your renegade father near the stuff or it will be a dry bottle before I get within sight of it.'

Perlmutter hung up the phone and stared at the image of the galleon on his computer. As he stroked his thick gray beard, his mind was miles away. Four thousand miles, to be exact.

'There's only one place to start, my fine furry friend,' he said aloud to the image of the monkey. 'Seville.'

23

Pitt gazed out the *Sargasso Sea*'s bridge window as a large container ship passed to the north. Another twenty miles beyond it lay the green coastline of southern Cuba. He wondered if the toxic effect of the mercury was already encroaching on its shores.

The NUMA research ship was approaching the third dead zone identified by Yaeger. Pitt was bristling at their failure to identify a source. The second site, a hundred miles northeast of the Cayman Islands, had yielded no answers. This current area, like the last, showed extreme concentrations of methyl mercury, though at slightly decreased levels. Because the mercury was more dispersed, it had taken the scientists two days to narrow the peak toxicity to a four-square-mile area.

The muted sounds of efficiency on the bridge were broken by the deep voice of Al Giordino grumbling through an overhead speaker. 'Stern deck. AUV is aboard. I repeat, AUV is aboard. Please proceed to the next grid area.'

Pitt beat the captain to the transmitter. 'Bridge acknowledged. I'll meet you in the theater in five minutes for today's matinee.'

'You bring the popcorn, I'll bring the Milk Duds. Stern deck out.'

By the time Pitt made his way to the wet lab on the main deck, Giordino was scrolling through the AUV's sonar images on a large-panel display. Pitt noticed the seafloor was much more dramatic than the earlier sites, with rocky outcroppings and undulating hills and valleys.

He took a seat next to Giordino. 'Your AUV got a workout on this run.'

'That's what she's made for.' Giordino pointed to an insert on the screen that portrayed the overall search grid and their relative location. 'If the drift estimates are correct, there's a high probability the source of the mercury release is within the quadrant just surveyed.'

'Let's hope there's a visible indicator this time,' Pitt said.

They reviewed nearly an hour of sonar images. While the seafloor did flatten, no man-made objects were apparent. Finally, Pitt noticed a shadow on the seabed and had Giordino halt the scrolling.

'Zoom in on that streak,' he said. 'It looks like a linear path across the bottom.'

Giordino nodded and enlarged the image. 'There's an even pair of lines. They look too precise to be geography.'

'Let's see where it goes,' Pitt said.

Giordino resumed scanning. The faint lines appeared in greater concentration in a section of the grid that dipped into a large depression. Pitt was tracking the change in depth when Giordino froze the image.

'Well, lookie here,' he said. 'Somebody lost a boat.'

A dark, slender object rose from the bottom, casting a short shadow. Familiar linear tracks edged nearby.

'It looks long and lean,' Pitt said. 'Perhaps a sailing boat that's partially buried.'

'The AUV was running at a low frequency to scan a wider path, so the definition is on the weak side. That blur of a boat looks to be about thirty feet long.'

'Doubtful it's our mercury source but maybe worth a look.'

Giordino resumed scrolling until the AUV's records came to an end. Pitt noted the vehicle's last recorded depth before it returned to the surface.

'I'm afraid that's all she wrote,' Giordino said. 'Some shadowy lines and a small boat.'

Pitt poked a finger at the now blank screen. 'The AUV's depth recorder indicated something of a depression in the middle of that grid. It may be nothing, but if that area is the source of the mercury contamination, it might be worth examining from a broader spectrum. Can a mosaic image of the entire survey grid be assembled? Or at least major blocks of it?'

'Piece of cake. All it will take is a little seat time at the keyboard.'

'Fine, but you better pass it off to someone else. You've got a more immediate job.'

'What's that?'

'Firing up the ship's submersible,' Pitt said. 'I want to see for myself what's happening down there.'

24

My friends, I am glad to see that you are well."

Dr Madero's relief at seeing Dirk and Summer barely registered in his voice. His face formed a gaunt mask of shock and angst as he ushered them into the lab beside his university office.

'We feel terrible about Dr Torres,' Summer said. 'If I hadn't found the codex . . .'

'No, no, it is a remarkable find. Besides, I can say with certainty that Miguel died doing what he loved best.' His voice turned nearly to a whisper. 'I'm only sorry that the police have been unable to apprehend the killers.'

'They fished one of them out of the river below the hydroelectric plant,' Dirk said. 'Unfortunately, he was so pulverized, there wasn't much left to identify. Do you have any idea who would have killed Dr Torres for the stone?'

Madero shook his head and grimaced. 'It could be forces from anywhere, maybe even outside the country. We've had lots of problems around Tula with the black market trade of Toltec relics. The thieves probably don't even know what they have.'

'I got the distinct impression,' Summer said, 'they knew exactly what they were after.'

'I will remain hopeful that the stone will be recovered,' Madero said in a weak voice, 'and Miguel's death avenged.'

'At least we have the photographs, even if my camera will never work again.' She shot her brother a cross gaze.

'I thought it was a disposable,' Dirk said.

'Yes, it is something.' Madero retrieved a folder with Summer's photographs of the stone. He displayed one that had been enlarged to show details of the glyph.

'Can you tell us what the stone represents?' Summer asked.

'Much along the lines of the codex.' Enthusiasm returned to his voice. 'As you can see from the alignment of the glyphs, the stone was cut or broken in half, your piece representing the left-hand segment. The angular designs along the perimeter represent the sun, which symbolizes life and the present era in Aztec lore. The design is very similar to the Aztec calendar stone, except that the interior glyphs are carved in a top-to-bottom narrative rather than concentric circles.'

'Do the glyphs match those on the calendar stone?' Dirk asked.

'More similar to the Stone of Tizoc. It was a sacrificial altar stone, elaborately carved, but also of a commemorative nature. Yours appears to be carved from the same material, a volcanic rock called andesite. While the altar stone is full of proper names, titles and places, your stone represents more of a narrative tale.'

Summer looked at Madero with anticipation. 'And what exactly is the tale?'

'Regrettably, we only have half, but we can make some speculations.' Madero took a deep breath and pointed to the top of the stone, where several rows of glyphs filled the surface within the sun border.

'Here we see skeletal glyphs, which indicate death and sorrow. Like the codex, it is not clear if this is the result of some regional battle or the arrival of the Spaniards. Then we find an image of Huitzilopochtli, the ancestral deity and war god. He appears to be directing an important procession of some sort, the meaning of which is evidently on the other half. And both the Eagle and Jaguar Warriors again signify an importance to the traveling group.'

Madero rubbed his eyes, then turned back to the image. 'Next we find some glyphs indicating water and fishing, which are interspersed with our familiar tracks, indicating travels. The interval spacing suggests to me a voyage, as the codex indicated, that possibly lasted over a week. Then things get interesting.'

At the bottom of the glyphs was a rounded blank space along the stone's broken edge. Madero pointed out a jagged line running beneath it and two irregular circles inside.

'This is some sort of map. It is my belief they carved an image of their destination. From the portion we can see, it was some sort of bay that contained a number of islands. Unfortunately, we would need the other half of the stone to complete the picture.'

'Could that simply be a rendition of Tenochtitlan?' Dirk asked.

'From what we know, the shape of Lake Texcoco doesn't seem to match. I had the same thought, particularly when I saw this.'

He pointed to the image of a bird's head and neck that ran off the broken edge.

'A flamingo?' Summer asked.

'Or maybe a crane,' Madero said, 'signifying Aztlán.'

'Professor Torres told us about Aztlán,' Dirk said. 'It was the Aztecs' ancestral homeland, described as an island within a lagoon.'

'Aztlán, the "place of the cranes," believed to be somewhere north of the Aztec empire, from where the Mexica originally emigrated.' Madero stared at the stone. 'I may be falsely extrapolating, but along with the reference to Huitzilopochtli, the message seems clear. A group of important Aztecs made a pilgrimage to Aztlán. The codex would seem to confirm the trip was made across water and that the voyage was successful.'

'Why the pilgrimage?' Summer asked. 'And what were they transporting?'

Madero shrugged. 'With only half the stone, we'll be left with an eternal mystery.'

'It may not be for long,' Dirk said.

'What are you saying?'

'We have a lead on the other half of the stone.'

Madero turned pale and Summer laughed.

'It's still a long shot,' she said. 'I consulted a family friend in Washington, St Julien Perlmutter, who's an expert marine historian. He has an associate at the General Archives of the Indies in Seville, who produced a registry of ships that sailed to the New World in the early sixteenth century. One of the ships was named the *Bad Bear*.'

'I don't understand,' Madero said.

'I didn't either, at first,' she said. 'I sent Perlmutter a copy of the codex page that showed the galleon with the glyph of the monkey. He went through the ship rolls, searching for some connection to a monkey or other primate, but came up empty. Fortunately, Perlmutter's a stubborn man and he kept looking for an angle. He found it when he researched the word for monkey in Nahuatl.'

'*Ozomahtli,*' Madero said.

'Exactly. He found what he thinks could be a link to a vessel called the *Oso Malo*, or *Bad Bear*.'

Madero smiled. 'They do sound similar. It wouldn't be a stretch to think the Aztecs misinterpreted the Spanish sailors' name of their ship. That may be an inspired correlation by your historian.'

'He's been known to work miracles for the right motivation.'

'But identifying the ship won't produce the stone,' Madero said.

'It might in this case,' Summer said, 'as the fate of the *Oso Malo* is rather compelling. She made only one voyage to Veracruz, in 1525. On her return trip to Cádiz, she sailed into a hurricane and had to make for Jamaica. She nearly made it, before foundering on the north shore.'

'Was the wreck salvaged?'

'We don't know yet,' Dirk said, 'but we intend to find out. Summer and I are flying to Jamaica tonight. We're scheduled to return to work aboard a NUMA research ship in three days but will use the intervening time to locate and explore the wreck site.'

'We hope any historic salvors would have been interested only in precious metals or jewels and would have tossed aside a broken old stone.' Summer pointed to the photo. 'At least we know what we're looking for.'

Madero looked at the twins and shook his head. 'The link to the ship is tenuous at best. I think you are chasing a fantasy. Please, let it rest. Once the first stone is recovered, the academic community will learn of its existence and we shall receive all kinds of leads to the second fragment. It is no doubt in a museum somewhere.'

'Perhaps,' Summer said, 'but there is no harm in looking. Besides, I'm not going to Jamaica just so my brother can lie on the beach and drink rum for three days.'

'Spoilsport,' Dirk muttered.

'You two be careful,' Madero said quietly.

'We will, Eduardo.' Summer shook his hand. 'We'll let you know exactly what we find.'

Madero stood motionless as they departed the lab, then turned stiffly toward his office. Out of its shadows, Juan Díaz emerged, holding a gun. A younger man behind him crossed the lab and locked the door to the hallway.

'A very enlightening conversation,' Díaz said. 'I'm so glad we happened to be here. Your friends are quite helpful. Perhaps they will be as helpful in locating the second stone as they were in discovering the first.'

Madero stood quietly, fury seething in his eyes. Only moments before Dirk and Summer arrived, Díaz had appeared in his office with the gun to demand the codex. The realization that the Cuban had murdered Torres struck him with a bolt of anger. 'The link to the shipwreck in Jamaica is pure speculation,' Madero said. 'You'd be wasting your time going there.'

'I admire your attempt at dissuasion, but we both know it's an entirely reasonable hypothesis.'

He stepped close to Madero and eyed him. 'You neglected to tell your friends the true value behind the stone. Why is that? Are you going to plunder your friends' riches?'

Madero clenched his teeth. 'I was just trying to protect them from harm.' He looked at Díaz, a rugged-framed man whose black eyes gyrated like a hungry hawk's. 'How do you know what the stone says?'

Díaz smiled. 'I happened to make my own find,

which brought me to Dr Torres. A stroke of good fortune, really, that you happened to share your discovery of the codex. Now, where exactly is that fine document?' The Cuban raised his pistol at Madero.

Madero cautiously slipped a hand into his pocket and produced a key ring, then unlocked a steel cabinet. The Aztec codex, tucked in its felt lining, lay inside a small plastic bin. Díaz gave a slight nod to his companion, then snatched the container.

His attention focused on the codex, Madero didn't detect the other man lift a stone Olmec statue off the lab bench. With a wide swing, the man brought the statue down across the back of Madero's head. Madero melted to the ground.

Díaz stepped over the prone body and turned to his partner. 'Wipe your prints off that statue. If we are lucky, the police will think his American friends killed him and stole the codex.'

With a look of smug satisfaction, he tucked the container under his arm and strolled out of the building.

25

The moss-colored water washed over the *Starfish*, snuffing out the bright Caribbean sunshine. Pitt monitored the ballast tank from the pilot's seat, while alongside him, Giordino checked the power and life support systems.

'Estimated bottom depth is twelve hundred feet,' Pitt said.

Giordino yawned. 'Nearly enough time to slip in a nap before we get there.'

The deepwater submersible descended by gravity alone, making for a lethargic ride to the seafloor. The descent seemed even slower for Giordino, who was deprived of a nap as Pitt needled him about his latest girlfriend, a well-known Washington attorney.

'At least I'm not married to a politician,' Giordino countered.

Pitt halted their descent as the sea bottom came into view. Giordino let out a low whistle. 'Looks like somebody was building a freeway down here.'

They had dropped on to one of the shadowy linear images they'd seen on the sonar. In person, the lines were much more defined and clearly not a natural geographic feature. They could only be mechanically made tracks.

Pitt guided the submersible to a wide set of parallel marks and hovered over them. 'Someone's been down here with some heavy equipment, all right.'

'The indentations are over ten feet across,' Giordino said. 'I don't know of many vehicles large enough to make that kind of a track.'

Pitt shook his head. 'It's not from an oil or gas well operation. Somebody was conducting a large-scale mining operation.'

'You think someone was down here scooping up manganese nodules?'

'A good bet. Probably high in gold content.'

Pitt thrust the submersible across the scarred seabed, where two different track marks crisscrossed a wide area. 'Do those second tracks look familiar?'

'Now that you mention it, they look an awful lot like the tracks around the *Alta*'s diving bell.'

'My thoughts exactly.'

As Pitt circled away from the tracks, he noticed the water depth decrease slightly. The depression they'd seen in the sonar image was evident out the viewport in the form of a bowl-shaped indention that dropped sharply at its center. The tracks were most prevalent around this center point.

'Do you think they blasted here?' Giordino asked.

'Kind of looks that way.'

'Whoa, ease off the gas a second. The water temperature just spiked about fifty degrees.'

Pitt eased off the thrusters, nudging the submersible toward the center of the depression.

'Temperature's still rising,' Giordino said. 'Up to one hundred and forty degrees, one-fifty, one-sixty . . . now dropping.' He tracked it for another minute. 'It peaked at about one hundred and sixty-five degrees.'

'It's a thermal vent,' Pitt said, 'right in the heart of their mining grid.'

'Makes sense. Deepwater vents are known for their rich surrounding minerals.'

'I bet this one comes with a high dose of mercury.'

'That must be the source,' Giordino said. 'Odd that we've never run across high levels of mercury in other hydrothermal vents we've examined.'

'Might have something to do with the explosives. There could be a pent-up base of mercury beneath the vents that's dispersed by a blast.'

'Makes sense. If it's a natural deposit that was disturbed, that would explain why we didn't find any overt evidence at the other two sites.'

'If we look closer,' Pitt said, 'I bet we'll find the same telltale tracks and man-made depressions.'

'Now we know what to look for, let's get back to the ship. I'd like another look at the last two sites' sonar records.'

'Sure,' Pitt said, 'but first one quick detour.'

Circling the depression, he scanned the depths before goosing the submersible toward a slender brown object jutting from the sand. Hovering above it, they could see it was neither a ship nor a sailboat. It was a large log.

'So much for my sunken boat,' Giordino said. 'It's just a big log that rolled off a cargo ship.'

'Not so fast,' Pitt said. He circled to the other side, where they could see it was actually a dugout canoe.

'Will you look at the size of that?' Giordino said as he reached up and activated an external video camera. 'It must be over thirty feet long.'

'That's a major league dugout canoe,' Pitt said. 'It must have been used for inter-island travel.'

The canoe was half buried and facing away from the depression, but its interior was free of sand and debris. Pitt eased the *Starfish* along its length, allowing the video camera to capture a thorough record of the vessel.

'I count ten benches,' Giordino said, 'wide enough to seat two oarsmen each, with plenty of cargo room to spare.'

'Probably used by the local Taíno Indians for trading goods.' Pitt pointed to the hull. 'Looks like they knew how to modify a canoe for the open seas.'

Carved planks had been pegged to the topsides of the canoe, creating a freeboard that extended an additional ten inches. Both stem and stern featured raised angular end pieces that had been attached to the base log.

'I don't know what they were carrying,' Giordino said, 'but it's a cinch it wasn't mercury.'

Pitt nodded. As he swung around the end of the canoe, the submersible's thrusters blew away a patch of loose sand, exposing a small rectangular stone.

Giordino caught sight of the object. 'Something on the bottom there.'

'I see it. Why don't you try to bring it home?'

Giordino was already activating the controls of the manipulator, extending its silver claw as Pitt brought the *Starfish* over the object. He easily grasped the stone and pulled it from the sand. As he held it to the viewport, he and Pitt could see it was a carving of a native warrior. The image had squat legs, a large nose, and wore a breechcloth.

Pitt glanced at the carving before purging the ballast tanks to surface. 'Possibly of ancient vintage,' he said.

'He kind of reminds me of our high school wrestling coach, Herbert Mudd,' Giordino said.

Pitt grinned. 'I'll wager young Herbert there would have an interesting story to tell, if he could talk.'

The carved warrior remained clutched in the manipulator's claw, peering into the cockpit as the submersible rose to the surface. Although Herbert would leave the talking to others, the little stone statue would ultimately have a lot to declare.

26

The pinging melody from a sidewalk steel drum band greeted Dirk and Summer as they exited Montego Bay's Donald Sangster International Airport. Summer listened a moment, then dropped a five-dollar bill into the band's Rastafarian-knit collection hat, eliciting a nod from the trio. She hustled to catch up to Dirk, who was shrugging off an aggressive taxi driver before making his way to the rental car kiosk.

'Space B-9,' he said to Summer, dangling a set of car keys.

Stepping toward their assigned parking spot, they found a Volkswagen Beetle convertible. 'A Beetle?' Dirk asked with a pained expression.

'Best the office could reserve on short notice.' Summer grabbed the keys away from her brother. 'I think they're cute.'

'Cute and functional don't always go hand in hand.' He stuffed their suitcases into the small trunk. It was too minuscule to hold their dive gear, so Dirk wedged their equipment bags into the backseat floor.

He shook his head. 'We've still got to pick up our magnetometer and some dive tanks.'

'We can just stack things up,' Summer said, lowering the top.

She slid behind the wheel on the car's right side and passed her brother a road map. 'I'll drive and you can navigate our way to the dive shop.'

As Dirk climbed in the passenger seat, he grunted something about needing rum. Summer drove the car around to the air cargo office, where they picked up a small crate. She then headed south toward Montego Bay. Summer melted into the late-afternoon traffic. Steering down the road's left lane, a vestige from Jamaica's British colonial past, she drove with a focused vigilance.

They motored another five minutes before Summer pulled off the road, her knuckles white. In that short span, they'd been nearly sideswiped by a moving van and rear-ended by a bread truck. 'They drive like crazy here!' she blurted.

'Too many potholes,' Dirk said, 'or maybe just too much pot.' He hopped out and stepped to the driver's door. 'I'll take it from here, if you like.'

'Gladly,' Summer said, sliding to the passenger seat.

Dirk took off, a grin forming as he joined the aggressive drivers. Where Summer felt intimidated, Dirk felt a challenge, one he fulfilled at home by racing a 1980s-era Porsche in local sports car club events.

They found the dive shop near one of the luxury hotels on Doctor's Beach and rented four air tanks, which they piled on top of their other gear in the VW's backseat. Reversing course, they passed by the airport, leaving the outskirts of Montego Bay behind them as they followed a narrow coastal road along the north shore.

They passed a conglomeration of resorts and scenic plantation houses, a reminder of Jamaica's slave-produced sugar industry that prospered in the eighteenth century. The traffic and development withered as the road skirted the jungle-kissed waters of the blue Caribbean.

Summer checked the road map. 'White Bay should be coming up.'

The road wound through a dense patch of jungle before opening above a shallow cove ringed with white sand. Dirk turned on to a narrow dirt road, escaping a tailgating taxi that had been pestering him since they left the dive shop.

The dirt road curved past a lane of ramshackle houses to a band of beachfront cottages that lined the cove. Mostly foreign-owned vacation retreats, the cottages appeared sparsely occupied.

'The rental agent said the third house on the left.' Summer pointed to one of the bungalows. 'The yellow one there, I think, with the white trim.'

Dirk nodded and pulled into the bungalow's open carport. A gentle surf rocked the beach just a few dozen yards in front of them. 'Accommodations right off the wreck site,' he said, gazing at the waterfront. 'Can't get more convenient than that.'

'The keys are supposed to be under the mat and the house already stocked with groceries, so we can stay put and work until the *Sargasso Sea* makes port.'

'And a workboat?'

'A Boston Whaler with extra fuel tanks is supposed to be waiting at a pier around the cove.'

They unloaded their belongings into the modest two-bedroom bungalow, opening all the doors and windows to catch the afternoon breeze. After hauling the dive tanks down to the beach, they walked to the nearby pier.

They found the workboat tied to the pier, appearing as though it had been sitting there for years. Its fiber-glass finish was dulled by the sun and its brightwork was consumed by rust. 'Looks like it was built during the Civil War,' Dirk said.

'Same goes for the dock.'

They stepped single file on to the rickety pier, which was little more than a handful of narrow planks atop some rock pilings. Dirk placed their dive tanks in the boat and pulled the starter on the outboard motor. The engine fired on the second pull. 'Not the *Queen Elizabeth*, but it'll do.'

'The cove is smaller than I expected,' Summer said as they walked back to the cottage under a setting sun. 'It looks less than a mile across.'

'With luck, we ought to get it surveyed in a day.' Dirk stopped and stared into the waves. Like his father, he was drawn by an almost primeval need to explore the sea. The remains of the *Oso Malo* were calling just off shore.

They rose at dawn and shoved off from the dock under a cool breeze. Dirk opened the crate they had picked up from the airport and unpacked a towed magnetometer unit. Once they were under way, a fish-shaped sensor was towed behind the boat. The cable was attached to a small processing station with an audio monitor, which would signal the presence of ferrous metal objects with a high-pitched buzz.

Using a handheld GPS unit to mark their path, Dirk drove the boat in narrow survey lanes across the cove while Summer monitored the magnetometer, adjusting the length of the towed cable to keep the sensor from grounding on the bottom. On their third lane, the monitor shrieked – it was a large target. Dirk cut the motor and Summer jumped over the side with mask and fins for a quick investigation. She surfaced a minute later and climbed into the boat with a frown.

'Somebody lost a nice anchor, but it's much too new to be from a Spanish galleon.'

'We can fish it out later.' Dirk restarted the motor.

They surveyed until midday, stopping only for a quick lunch at the cottage. Returning to the dock, Summer motioned offshore. 'Looks like we have some competition.'

A faded green skiff with a lone man aboard was bobbing off the cove. Clad only in a pair of cutoffs, the man waved at Summer, then slipped on a mask and jumped over the side, clutching a speargun. A minute later, his head popped above the surface for a quick breath of air, then he disappeared again.

Dirk sailed the Boston Whaler to their last position in the middle of the cove and motioned to Summer. She lowered the magnetometer and they resumed surveying as a bank of low clouds rolled in, offering respite from the hot sun. The magnetometer buzzed with small targets here and there but found nothing of consequence. After two more hours, they drew near the other boat. The Jamaican diver pulled himself on to his boat with a long string of silver fish tied to his waist and guzzled a drink of water from a plastic jug. He smiled broadly at the Boston Whaler. 'What you looking for, mon?'

Dirk slowed, forcing Summer to reel in the magnetometer.

'A Spanish shipwreck,' he said. 'Supposedly sank in this cove in 1525.'

The man nodded. 'Samuel show you.'

Without another word, the Jamaican pulled up his anchor and started the motor on his skiff. He chugged offshore, veering slightly east before cutting the motor and tossing out his anchor. Dirk pulled up alongside and followed suit.

'It here,' Samuel said. 'Forty feet water.'

'Kind of you to show us,' Dirk said before introducing themselves. 'This cove apparently has good fishing all the way around,' he added, eyeing Samuel's speargun and catch.

Samuel smiled. 'All Jamaica good fishing.'

The water was still shallow enough to make out the bottom, and Dirk could see the rising green shape of a coral reef a few yards to the side. The winds began kicking up as a squall crept in from the northwest, turning the surface gray.

Samuel stood in his boat and motioned to Summer. 'Pretty lady come with me. I show you wreck.'

'Please do,' she said. She pulled on her mask and fins and slipped into the water first.

Samuel jumped in and dove straight to the bottom. Summer caught up and followed him as he swam a short distance, then pointed to the seafloor. At first, all she saw was a crusty bottom. A subtle mound then took shape, which stretched into the nearby coral mass. Summer fanned away the soft sand, exposing a pair of smooth, rounded rocks. With a tinge of excitement, she recognized them as river rock, often used for ballast in early sailing ships. The large mound in front of her was ballast from a ship that had sunk a long time ago.

Her ears began to pound, telling her it was time to surface. She glanced at Samuel, who was calmly digging in the sand, then kicked to the surface. It was a few short strokes to the Boston Whaler, and she grabbed its anchor line as the boat jostled in the growing seas.

'Any luck?' Dirk asked, poking his head over the side.

'It's a wreck, all right. Plenty big and all covered up. He put us right on top of its ballast mound.'

'Sounds just what we're looking for.'

Samuel surfaced a second later. 'Is this the wreck you want?'

'I think so. What do you know about it?'

Samuel shook his head. 'Not much. It's called the Green Stone Wreck. People say green stones in its cargo washed up on the beach for many years a long time ago. That is all I know.'

He tossed Dirk a small stone he had dug from the bottom. It was smooth and dark green and had a radiant luster. Dirk looked at it for a moment before sticking it in his pocket and helping Summer aboard. Samuel climbed on to his boat just as the first sprinkles from the squall began to pepper them.

'Thanks, Samuel. This looks like the wreck we're searching for. We'll find out tomorrow when the weather clears and we can take a better look.'

Samuel flashed a toothy smile. 'I bring tanks tomorrow. We work together. You pay me one hundred dollars.'

Dirk nodded. 'You have a deal. But only if you throw in one of your snappers for dinner.'

Samuel picked out the largest fish from his stock and tossed it on to the deck of the Whaler.

'See you in the morning.' He winked at Summer and motored off through the rainstorm.

Dirk turned toward shore and sped to the dock, bouncing hard over the rising swells. The rains struck heavily, dousing the siblings.

'The wreck site looks pretty old,' Summer shouted. 'You think Samuel gave us the *Oso Malo*?'

'I know he did.' Dirk fished the green stone from his pocket and tossed it to his sister.

'That's green obsidian,' he said. 'It was probably mined in Mexico. Dr Madero showed me an Aztec spearhead made from the stuff. He said it was a highly valued commodity to the Aztecs. Seems likely the Spaniards would have exported some of the stuff during their early days of conquest.'

Summer examined the stone and nodded. 'If it had any value, they probably would have loaded it aboard a galleon.'

They tied up the boat and walked back to their cottage, wearing confident grins despite the pelting deluge.

27

'I think Samuel likes you,' Dirk teased as they walked toward the pier the next morning.

'Well, he's a good swimmer,' Summer said. 'And he does have nice teeth.'

'Nice teeth? That's what you look for in a man?'

'Some things are non-negotiable. Bad teeth is one of them.'

'Haven't you heard of corrective dentistry?'

'I suppose you're right. Bad teeth are probably easier to fix than a bad personality.'

They hopped in the boat and motored into the cove. The rainstorm had long since passed, leaving a nearly flat sea. True to his word, Samuel was waiting at the wreck site with a small stock of air tanks. Dirk pulled alongside and tied up to his boat as Summer gazed over the side. She could see clear to the bottom, easily spotting Samuel's anchor wedged in the sand.

'Good morning,' the Jamaican said. 'You enjoy the fish?'

'Yes, though my brother overcooked it. I see you brought plenty of air.'

'You ready to dive?'

'Yes, we are,' she answered. 'I'm happy to see you've brought us better weather.'

'My pleasure.' Samuel grinned. 'So, what you look for? Gold or silver?'

'Sorry to disappoint you but there's no treasure, at least as far as we know. We're looking for a carved round stone.'

Samuel's broad mouth turned down. 'Okeydokey. I help you find that, too.'

They dove to the bottom, where Dirk and Summer surveyed the ballast mound. Using a reeled tape measure, they computed its width and length to the point where it was swallowed by a large coral outcropping. Dirk motioned toward the surface.

'I wasn't counting on a hungry swath of coral,' he said after climbing into the boat.

Summer floated in the water alongside Samuel. 'According to St Julien's data, the *Oso Malo* was seventy feet long. We've got at least half that length clear of the coral.'

'I guess thirty-five feet is better than nothing.' Dirk yanked the starter pulley to a gas-powered water pump that he'd rented the day before after canvasing a half-dozen dive shops in Montego Bay. He threw an intake hose into the sea and passed a second nozzle and hose over to Summer. 'You ready to dig?'

'Give me a second to hit the bottom.' She inserted her regulator and submerged. Dirk gave her time to position herself at one end of the ballast mound, then turned on the valve that cycled seawater through the pump.

A blast of water sprayed out the nozzle in Summer's hand, which she used to jet away the loose sand covering the ballast mound. Samuel watched as she began clearing a foot-wide path along the top of it, revealing a pile of smooth river rock.

Blasting away the overburden was slow and physically taxing, so the three took turns manning the waterjet, working in thirty-minute shifts.

Summer documented the excavation with a new underwater camera that Dirk had bought her and recorded notes in a journal. It took the better part of the morning to reach the coral abutment, where they exposed a portion of the ship's timbers.

After lunch, they scoured a second trench a few feet to the side. Dirk had nearly completed a third trench on the opposite side when the jet stopped spraying. He surfaced to find the pump motor silent.

'Did you shut it off?' he asked Summer, who sat next to Samuel by the pump.

'No, it ran out of gas.' She sloshed a near-empty fuel can. 'We've barely enough left to get back to shore.'

Dirk pulled himself aboard, stripped off his dive gear, and allowed himself a moment's rest. 'I think that pretty much ends it anyway. I had nearly finished the third test trench. With the three, the odds were good we would have exposed the stone if it was there. I'm afraid that if it's still on the wreck, it's embedded some-where in the coral.'

Summer frowned. 'If it's in the coral, we'll never find it.'

'You still have many interesting artifacts,' Samuel said. He pointed to a towel spread on the boat's floor-boards. It was covered with objects exposed by the test trenches, mostly pieces of broken porcelain and cor-roded nails and fittings. Several chunks of green obsidian also glistened in the sun.

'At least nothing suggests the wreck is anything other than the *Oso Malo*,' Summer said. 'This should make for a nice exhibit at the National Museum of His-torical Archaeology in Port Royal.'

'We find stone tomorrow,' Samuel said.

'No, Dirk's right.' Summer shook her head. 'The stone should have been visible on top of the ballast mound. It's just not there – or lost to the coral. I'm afraid we must leave Jamaica tomorrow anyway.'

Dirk fished out his wallet from a dive bag and gave Samuel two hundred dollars, thanking him for his help.

'You two crazy,' he said with a smile. 'If you must leave, then Samuel buy you drink first.'

'At the moment, I'd like nothing better,' Dirk said.

They pulled up anchors on their respective boats and motored to the stone pier. Under Samuel's direc-tion, they piled into the Volkswagen and headed toward Montego Bay. They had driven but a short distance when he had them pull up to a small building. A faded sign on the roof proclaimed it the *Green Stone Bar & Museum*.

'Green Stone,' Summer said. 'That's what you called the wreck.'

'Yes. Maybe they have your stone. I know they have cold beer,' Samuel said with a grin. 'I live in the next village over.'

The bar was empty, save for a black dachshund sleeping in the corner. To Dirk's and Summer's surprise, the interior was filled with nautical artifacts. Rusting anchors, cannonballs and porcelain dishes adorned the walls, while a dusty fishing net covered the ceiling. A high wooden shelf sagged under dozens of pieces of green obsidian identical to those they had found on the wreck site.

'These artifacts must be from the *Oso Malo*,' Dirk said, examining a pewter plate stamped with a three-towered castle beneath a crown – a Castilian mark.

The sound of clinking bottles emanated from a back room, and an old man emerged with a case of beer. His hair and beard were dusted white, but he moved spryly in a loud aloha shirt.

'Afraid I didn't hear you come in,' he said. 'What can I get you kids to drink?'

'Two Red Stripes, and a daiquiri for the lady,' Samuel said, smiling at Summer.

'Works for me,' she said.

They moved to the bar as the man mixed Summer's

drink and passed chilled bottles of Red Stripe beer to Dirk and Samuel. They smiled when the old man opened a third beer for himself.

Taking a sip of the Jamaican brew, Dirk motioned toward a barnacle-encrusted sword mounted over the bar. 'We were on the wreck of the *Oso Malo* today, but it looks like you beat us to it.'

The bartender's eyes lit up. 'I haven't heard her called by that name in years. She was always known locally as the Green Stone wreck, or the Emerald Wreck, although, of course, there were no emeralds on her.'

'What do you know of the green stones she was carrying?' Summer asked.

'Simply green obsidian. It's a pretty rock, but there's nothing inherently valuable about it. Of course, the sixteenth-century Spaniards may have felt differently. It was apparently prized in Mexico, so they loaded up a ship with the stuff. Unfortunately for us,' he said with a twinkle in his eye, 'they sent the gold and silver in another direction.'

'We understand,' Dirk said, 'the ship was sailing from Veracruz to Cádiz when it ran afoul of a hurricane.'

'That's right. She blew aground just off White Bay. Despite being so close to shore, most of the crew drowned. Only four men made it ashore alive, later finding refuge at a Spanish settlement called Melilla.'

'Did the Spaniards salvage the wreck?' Dirk asked.

'Not as far as anyone knows. It took three years before the survivors even made it back to Spain. By then, the ship was all but forgotten, since she wasn't carrying gold or silver. She lay there undisturbed for almost four hundred years until discovered by an American archeologist around the turn of the century.'

'An American?' Summer asked.

'Ellsworth Boyd was his name. He had excavated a number of early Taíno Indian sites on the island. He was conducting an excavation in the area when the locals told him about the stones fishermen pulled up in their nets. He came to the bay and hired Jamaican free divers to pull up what they could.' He waved a hand toward the rock-laden shelves. 'Lots of green obsidian.'

'Do you know what became of the other artifacts they recovered?'

'You're looking at most of them. Boyd shipped a few items to the Yale Peabody Museum in New Haven but the bulk remained here. This stuff would have probably gone, too, but Boyd died shortly after the excavation. Some of his associates, my great-uncle included, decided to establish a museum here in his honor. It became a bit neglected over the years, but after inheriting owner-ship, I've done what I can to keep it going.'

Dirk revealed their interest in the ship. 'Do you have any recollection of a large semicircular stone with Meso-American inscriptions that may have come off the wreck?'

The bartender gazed at the ceiling. 'No, I can't say that rings a bell. But you might want to take a gander at Boyd's journal of the excavation.'

Summer's eyes widened. 'He left a record of his work on the *Oso Malo*?'

The bartender nodded. 'Yes, it's quite detailed.'

He stepped into the back room and emerged a minute later with a thin leather-bound book caked with dust. 'Been sitting on the shelf awhile,' he said, 'but you're welcome to borrow it.'

Summer cracked the cover and read aloud the handwritten title page: '"A record of the excavation of a Spanish shipwreck in White's Bay, Jamaica, November 1897–January 1898, by Dr Ellsworth Boyd."'

She flipped through the pages, finding detailed entries and elegant hand-drawn images from each day of the excavation.

She gasped. 'This is fabulous. If he found the stone, he surely would have recorded it in this journal.'

Samuel leaned over Summer's shoulder to view the journal. 'This your lucky day.'

Dirk drained his beer and slapped the empty bottle on the bar. 'Let's order some dinner and see what the good doctor has to tell us.'

'I'm afraid we don't serve food here,' the bartender said, 'but there's a good seafood joint down the road called Mabel's. Their grilled snapper is a winner. You can take the journal with you.'

'Thank you,' Summer said. 'That's very kind of you, Mr . . . uh . . .'

'My name's Clive, but most people call me Pops,' he

said with a wink. 'Keep the book for as long as you like. I ain't going anywhere.'

Samuel paid for the drinks, and the trio stepped outside into the fading glow of the late-afternoon sun.

'Join us for dinner, Samuel?' Dirk asked.

'No, must get home before the wife gets angry.' He shook Dirk's hand, then gave Summer a hug. 'Good-bye, my friends. I hope you find what you are searching for.'

'Need a lift?' Summer asked as he started to stride away.

'No thanks. I walk from here. Good-bye.'

Dirk and Summer waved as they climbed into their car.

'To Mabel's?' Dirk asked.

Summer nodded, clutching Boyd's journal tightly in her hands. 'Let's hope the grilled snapper there is served on a stone platter.'

28

Slightly larger than a walk-in closet, Mabel's Café was an open-air diner shaded by a high thatched roof. An early dinner crowd of locals had already infiltrated the place, forcing Dirk and Summer to scramble to find an empty table facing the ocean. A brassy waitress with braided hair brought them a couple of Red Stripes and they both ordered the house snapper. While they waited, Summer opened the journal and began devouring its contents.

'Boyd writes that he was searching for the remains of an early Spanish settlement on the Martha Brae River when he was told of the Green Stone Wreck. With the help of some local fishermen, he located the site. He says a large portion of the hull was visible from the surface, which he attributes to the force of a hurricane that struck the island a few months earlier and uncovered the wreck.'

'He's probably right,' Dirk said. 'Little of the wreck would have survived in these warm waters if exposed to the elements for four hundred years.'

'Boyd didn't have the resources to hire hard-hat divers, so he relied on local free divers to excavate the site. Working through the winter, they retrieved and cataloged over a thousand artifacts.'

Summer turned the page to find a drawing of the wreck as Boyd found it. The entire keel and crossmember supports were visible, as were several sections of the hull.

Dirk eyed rows of ballast rock and noted a small coral outcropping near the stern. 'Looks nothing like that today. At that point, the coral was just encroaching the site.'

'A lot can change in a hundred years,' Summer said.

The waitress arrived with their plates of grilled snapper, accompanied by a side of boiled okra and *festival*, a cylindrical blob of fried dough. Summer dug in with a fork in one hand while continuing to scan the journal.

The succeeding pages described the daily results of the excavation, with occasional drawings of the more interesting artifacts. Aside from the ship's heavy iron fittings, including anchors, chains, and a pair of small cannon, the bulk of the raised artifacts were chunks or carved pieces of the Mexican green obsidian.

Near the end of the journal, Summer turned the page and nearly choked on a mouthful of okra. In the center of the page was a rough rendering of a large carved stone in the shape of a semicircle.

'He found it!' she gasped.

Dirk gazed at the drawing and smiled.

'Looks like a perfect match to the stone you found at Zimapán. Unfortunately, he didn't make a very detailed drawing.'

Summer nodded. Aside from the partial image of a

bird, Boyd had depicted no detail from the stone. She flipped ahead to the last page but found no additional illustrations.

'No luck,' she said. 'He must have known it was Meso-American. I wonder why he didn't devote more attention to it.'

'What does the narrative say?'

Summer recited the remaining text.

'On January 26th, Martin, our lead diver, uncovered a large inscribed stone that was originally thought to be ballast. With considerable effort, the stone was raised off the bottom and towed to shallow water, where it was brought ashore. The stone appears to be one half of a larger round artifact that was deliberately split in two. Subsequent surveys of the wreck site by the divers failed to locate the other half.'

'I share in his frustration,' Dirk said with a shake of his head.

Summer continued reading.

'The stone is Mexica, as Roy Burns has identified its carvings as Nahuatl glyphs. Its shape and design appear similar to the Calendar Stone, although at a fraction of its size. Its meaning is as yet unknown, although Roy is successfully translating sections at this time.'

'Tell us something we don't know,' Dirk said.

Summer skimmed the remaining pages. 'The next

few days were spent winding down the excavation and cataloging artifacts,' she said. "But there's a bit more on the stone. On January twenty-ninth, he writes:

> *'Roy has spent the last days studying the Mexica stone and making detailed drawings. His interpretation is necessarily incomplete, but he believes the stone is a map to an island depository associated with the deity Huitzilopochtli. He is quite excited about it, and has taken to calling it Boyd's Emperor Stone. Quite ridiculous, I'm afraid.*

'Those are his words,' Summer said. 'No indication of what's on it, or even a rendering of the map.'

'Burns is right,' Dirk said. 'There's obviously significance to this island depository. Too bad he didn't give us his piece of the map.'

'This is interesting.' Summer turned to the last page. 'The final entry is dated February 1st:

> *'We received an unwelcome visitor to the camp today in the form of Julio Rodriguez, who apparently has been in Jamaica on a dig near Kingston. He immediately enquired about the Mexica stone. He must have a spy in our local work crew. Fortunately, the stone has already been crated and was out of view on a wagon. Roy and I told him nothing, which stoked his ire and he departed in a tiff. Once again, he is seeking glory on the backs of other men's toils. Thankfully, we are departing Port Antonio tomorrow, and will be able to decipher the stone's full meaning back in New Haven.'*

Summer closed the journal. 'That's the last entry.'

'So our hunch stands. The second stone is most likely collecting dust in a back room of the Yale Peabody Museum.'

Summer scrunched her nose. 'I don't know. Boyd seems to recognize its importance. One of them must have published a paper on it.'

'I suppose,' Dirk said, 'but it could be as forgotten as the stone.'

'We can email St Julien and the museum tonight,' she said, 'and do more digging when we get aboard the *Sargasso Sea* tomorrow. Assuming Dad doesn't have a mountain of work waiting for us.'

Finishing their meal, they paid the bill and hopped into the VW for the short ride back to the cottage. Turning on to the coastal highway, they were approached by a battered pickup that rode up on their bumper. Dirk accelerated, but the truck hung on his tail.

Summer glanced in the mirror at the truck's rusty grill bouncing dangerously close behind. 'This guy makes a New York cabbie look polite.'

Dirk nodded and pressed deeper on the gas. The winding road broke into a straight stretch that was free of oncoming traffic. Dirk edged the Beetle to the shoulder and slowed to let the truck pass. But the driver kept on Dirk's bumper.

'The guy can't take a hint,' Dirk muttered, forgoing the courtesy and speeding up.

'Maybe he's taking the highway advice to heart,'

Summer said, pointing at a weathered road sign that proclaimed *Undertakers Love Overtakers*.

The road wound down a small hill and over a bridge that spanned a marshy creek. As they reached the bridge, the truck finally made its move and pulled alongside the Beetle.

Dirk glanced at a tough-looking Jamaican in the passenger seat who flashed an unfriendly grin. Then the man leaned out the truck's window, pointed a pistol at Dirk, and pulled the trigger.

29

The shot whistled by as Dirk instantly stood on the brakes. The truck swerved hard over, smacking into the Volkswagen and driving it toward the meager bridge railing. The Beetle's left fender tore through the guardrail, shattering its wooden supports like they were toothpicks.

Dirk downshifted, fighting to keep the wheel straight. Summer let out a yelp as they veered off the shoulder, the left tires half hanging over the edge. The popping of the gunman's pistol sounded over the fray. The Beetle's windshield shattered as Dirk and Summer ducked low in their seats.

Amid a screech of grinding metal, the VW fell back before the heavier truck could knock it into the creek. Dirk snapped the wheel right, barely escaping a plunge off the road. Finding no oncoming traffic, he swerved into the far lane and stomped on the accelerator.

The Beetle's turbocharged four-cylinder engine howled as the small car shot past the slowing pickup. The truck's driver reacted quickly, gunning his own engine. A well-tuned 5.7-liter Mopar Hemi under the hood belied the truck's shabby appearance and gave it more than enough juice to give chase.

'How did they track us here?' Summer yelled, gripping the dashboard as Dirk pushed the Beetle hard through a tight curve.

'I don't know, but they're serious about finding the other half of the stone.'

The VW hit a large dip in the road and bounded into the air. The rear bumper scraped the pavement on their return to earth, sending a trail of sparks flying. Summer turned and watched the pickup wallow through the same dip, its driver nearly losing control.

The Beetle was faster through the corners, but the truck easily gained ground on the straight stretches. Charging down a straight section, the truck approached and smacked the rear end of the Volkswagen. The Beetle skittered, but Dirk maintained control and gained separation on the next bend.

'Do you know where this road goes?' Summer shouted.

'I know it runs along the north coast to at least Port Antonio, but that's a ways off. If we come to a sizable town first, we can try and lose them or find the police.'

Summer noticed a road sign indicating that the town of Ocho Rios was eighteen kilometers ahead. 'Maybe we can find police there.'

The VW approached some slower traffic, which Dirk hopscotched between oncoming vehicles. The truck followed suit but lost ground in the process. Dirk was forced to slow as they entered the town of St Ann's Bay, the site of the island's first Spanish capital. A handful of ornate Georgian buildings peppered the town center, giving Dirk and Summer promise of finding police assistance. Their hope was short-lived as the sound of gunfire again erupted behind them.

'Get down!' Dirk said, glancing into the rearview mirror.

The pickup had somehow bypassed a row of cars and was right behind them. The passenger was now leaning out the side window, firing. Whether by faulty aim or the mistaken belief that late-model Beetles were still rear-engined, the shooter fired three rounds harmlessly into the trunk.

Dirk stomped on the gas and blasted through a stop sign, barely avoiding a fruit truck. 'Apparently our friends don't hold the local constables in high regard.'

'We'll have to try for Ocho Rios,' Summer said. 'I think that's a port of call for cruise ships, so there will definitely be a police presence.'

Dirk maneuvered past a stopped bus and sped out of the town, leaving the truck wedged behind. The coastal road cleared of traffic, and Dirk nudged the Volkswagen north of ninety miles per hour. In another ten minutes, they'd reach the larger city.

'Try calling the Ocho Rios police,' Dirk said. 'Find out where they are and tell them we're coming.'

'Nine-one-one?' Summer asked.

'I think it's the inverse here, one-one-nine.'

Summer started to dial when Dirk stood on the brakes, causing the phone to fly out of her hands.

Rounding a bend, he had spotted a tour bus stopped on the road ahead. Oncoming traffic had also stopped, allowing a throng of tourists returning from the beach to clog the road while boarding the bus. Additional buses up the road were exiting a side parking lot.

'This isn't good,' Dirk said, seeing there would be no quick resolution to the bottleneck. He quickly scanned the road for a possible exit or point of concealment.

They had only one choice. Just shy of the bus, a small dirt road angled into the jungle. If Dirk could get the VW up the road before the pickup turned the corner, their pursuers might think they'd gotten ahead of the stopped traffic.

Dirk let off the brakes and accelerated toward the parked bus.

Summer threw her hands on the dash to brace for an impact. 'What are you doing?'

She fell silent as he stomped on the brakes and yanked the car in a blunt right turn. Screams erupted from the frightened tourists boarding the bus, but their cries were muted by the Beetle's screeching tires as it slid in an arc, then shot up the dirt road. Dirk held his breath as the car bounded up and into the jungle. He glanced to his right and down the highway to see if they had been detected.

The nose of the pickup appeared just around the corner, pursuing at high speed. A second later, the Volkswagen was lost under cover of the thick brush. The car bucked and shimmied over the rut-filled road, which looked like it hadn't been used in the last decade.

'Do you think they saw us?' she asked.

'I don't know, but I sure hope not. We're certainly not going to outrun them on this road.'

A hundred yards behind, the pickup's driver had missed seeing the Volkswagen turn. But he didn't miss the fresh skid marks that led to the side road nor the light cloud of dust floating above it. With a shark-like grin, he wheeled on to the side road and barreled up its washboard surface.

Ahead, the road climbed through thick foliage that clawed at the VW's blue paint. Summer saw a vine-covered sign with an arrow pointing to *Dunn's River Lookout*. As they turned through a tight switch-back, she peered behind them and caught a faint glimmer of steel through the bushes. 'Bad news. They're still on our tail.'

Dirk nodded, battling the Beetle to keep it from getting high-centered. He had no idea where the road would lead, but he knew their time on it would be short.

'Worst case, we stop and take to the jungle,' he said. 'Head downhill to the road. If we get split up, let's meet at the Green Stone Bar.'

Summer tried to smile. 'First drink's on you.'

Dirk coaxed the Beetle up a short hill, then stopped. The road ended in a clearing just wide enough for a car to turn around. Tall trees encircled the clearing except to their left, where a shallow river rushed by. They were effectively boxed in as the pickup truck roared up the hill behind them.

Dirk looked at his sister.

'It would seem,' he said with a grimace, 'that we've reached the end of the line.'

30

Summer gazed at the loose sandals they both wore, dreading a sprint through the jungle. Hearing the roar of the approaching pickup, she reached for the door handle. 'We better get going.'

Instead, Dirk put the car in gear and drove forward. 'Wait,' he said, looping the car around the dead end. He angled toward the wide, shallow river and stopped at its gravel bank.

'What are you doing?' Summer asked.

'That's Dunn's River.'

The rusty sign down the road had registered in Dirk's mind. He knew that one of the major tourist attractions in Jamaica was *Dunn's River Falls*, a terraced waterfall that visitors enjoyed climbing by linking arms in large groups. It explained the bevy of buses below.

'Let's get across the river,' he said. 'We can hike down the other side and hop on a tour bus at the bottom.'

Too late, an engine roared and the pickup came flying over the crest. The truck was traveling much too fast – on a collision course with the Volkswagen. Dirk punched the accelerator, driving off the bank and into the river.

The truck just slipped by the VW as the driver mashed on the brakes and slid to a stop in front of a mature mango tree.

Inside the Beetle, Dirk kept the accelerator down and continued across the river. The bed was relatively flat and shallow, and the car easily bounded toward the opposite side.

'Don't these things float?' Summer asked.

'You're thinking of the original Beetle,' Dirk said. 'I don't know about the new models. Nor do I want to find out.'

They had slogged about thirty feet across the river when they heard a splash behind them. To Summer's dismay, she saw the pickup truck follow them into the river. Another pop sounded behind them, and Dirk heard a whistling an instant before the dashboard disintegrated in front of him.

'We're not going to beat them across,' Summer said, her voice tightening.

Dirk came to the same conclusion. He hadn't counted on the pickup following them. With its lower clearance, the VW would bog down or stall sooner than the truck. Glancing in the mirror, he yelled at Summer to hang on, then turned downriver.

They had entered the river above the head of the falls and it was only a short distance to the first rocky terrace – about a three-foot drop to a small pool. With the Beetle's drive wheels still finding traction, he centered the car with the falls and drove off the edge.

The front wheels struck an inclined rock that pitched the car's nose up and the car landed in the pond nearly upright. The impact sent a wave splashing over the falls beyond.

Though the water nearly covered the wheels, the Volkswagen kept running, and Dirk steered it forward. He and Summer looked back to see the pickup truck hesitate at the top of the falls, then follow them.

'They're crazy,' Summer shouted over the water's roar.

Dirk shook his head. 'Guess we need to be crazier.'

He coaxed the VW across the pond to the next falls. Unlike the first, it was a continuous descent of nearly seventy feet that angled down a series of terraced ledges. Dirk checked to ensure his sister was safely buckled in, then aligned the Beetle and drove over the edge.

The initial plunge was the sharpest, a ten-foot drop on to a narrow terrace. The VW landed nose-first, crunching the front end, but bounced up and forward. The air bags deployed with a puff of white smoke as the car skipped over the next ledge.

The Beetle bounded like a hopping frog down a long series of inclines and ledges. A group of tourists watched in shock as it tumbled past them. It caromed from one boulder to another, its tires bursting and suspension imploding, yet it remained upright. Momentum carried the VW down a long, slick rock, where it slid thirty feet through a rush of water.

Dirk and Summer's wild ride ended at a final set of

steeply terraced falls. The battered Beetle descended the incline amid a screech of metal. Striking the bottom terrace, it did a slow forward flip, splashing wheels-up into a large pool. The inverted car floated peacefully for a moment – and then sank from view.

A nearby Jamaican tour guide abandoned his clients and waded toward the steam and bubbles that marked the VW's resting place. He froze as something under the water grazed his shin. Then the tall, lithe figure of Summer emerged, clutching a red journal. A second later, Dirk popped to the surface a few yards away and swam to his sister.

The Jamaican gasped. 'You both alive? It's a miracle.'

'The miracle is called an air bag,' Dirk said. 'You okay, sis?'

Summer gave him a weak smile. 'I've got a wrenched shoulder and a sore knee, but everything else seems to be working.'

'Look out!' One of the tourists pointed toward the top of the falls.

Dirk and Summer saw the pickup tipping over the ledge. The driver had pursued the Volkswagen to the precipice of the second falls, then stopped to watch the Beetle's descent. But a boulder underneath had given way, leaving the truck teetering on three wheels. The driver tried backing up but more rocks broke loose. The truck hung in midair for a moment, then plunged over the falls.

With its heavier front end, the truck hit the first

terrace nose-first and flipped over. Crashing down the next incline, the truck then somersaulted all the way down the falls. Wheels and bumpers went flying in all directions. The passenger was tossed out the window midway, his body colliding with a limestone boulder that snapped his spine.

The driver rode the pickup all the way to the bottom as it struck the pool with a colossal splash. The cab was completely pulverized. As the truck settled into the water, Dirk knew the driver was dead.

'Might be a good time to get out of here,' he said, grabbing Summer's arm and pulling her to the river-bank. They staggered past a group of stunned tourists, who stared at the truck's sunken remains as if waiting for its dead occupant to emerge.

Climbing down the remaining falls, Dirk and Summer found a Montego Bay resort hotel bus idling in the parking lot and casually boarded it. They hunkered down in the back row, trying to avoid the gaze of the tourists following them, who chatted excitedly about the vehicles they saw plunge down the falls.

When the bus got under way, Summer noticed her brother's wide grin. 'What's so amusing? We almost got killed back there.'

'I was just thinking about the look that will be on that guy's face.'

'What guy?'

'The guy at the car rental counter when we tell him where to collect the Volkswagen.'

31

The bungalow was dark as the intruder crept on to the porch at two in the morning. He stopped and listened for sounds from within. All was silent, aside from the lapping of the nearby surf. He gently placed his palm on the knob and twisted. It turned freely. He eased the door open an inch and peered inside.

The room was almost pitch-black. An open rear window allowed in just a hint of ambient light, revealing that both back bedroom doors were closed. It was better than he had hoped.

The intruder slipped into the house and closed the door behind him. He took a tentative step forward – and a bright floor lamp snapped on. Wheeling around, he squinted toward it. Through the spots dancing in front of his retinas, he saw Dirk sitting in a chair facing him, holding a speargun in his lap. A row of empty beer bottles on an adjacent coffee table testified to the patience of his ambush.

'It's quite a nice weapon,' Dirk stated. He pointed the loaded speargun at the man. 'A KOAH. They cost about six hundred dollars in the States. Not the tool I would expect a simple fisherman from Trelawny Parish to carry, let alone leave behind in his boat.'

'They pay me well, Mr Dirk.' Samuel's bright teeth gritted in anguish.

'How about you drop your gun,' Dirk said. It was a command, not a request.

Samuel nodded, pulling a Smith & Wesson revolver from his waistband and setting it on the floor.

'I like you and your sister,' the Jamaican said, rising slowly. 'I not come to hurt you.'

'But you would for a price.'

'No.' Samuel shook his head.

'I don't think your friends had the same conviction. Are they both dead?'

Samuel gave a solemn nod.

Dirk swung the speargun toward the coffee table. Partially hidden by the beer bottles lay the red journal of Ellsworth Boyd. Dirk placed the tip of the speargun on the book and nudged it toward Samuel. 'Here's what you're after. Go ahead and take it.'

Samuel hesitated.

Dirk glared at him. 'If you had asked a few more questions while we were drinking at the Green Stone Bar, you could have saved us both a lot of trouble.' The fatigue of the day's events, along with the beer, showed in his bloodshot eyes.

Samuel extended an unsteady hand toward the journal.

As his fingers grazed the cover, Dirk slapped down the speargun's tip. 'One thing I need to know first. Who's paying you?'

'A man in Mo Bay I work for sometimes.'

'What's his name?'

Samuel shook his head. 'He's my cousin. Just middle-man, not important to you.'

'Then who's paying him?'

Samuel shrugged. 'The top boss man? He's from Cuba. And he likes antiquities and shipwreck artifacts, like you. That's all I know.'

'A Cuban, you say?'

'Yes. He flew here in Army plane, not stay long.'

Dirk nodded and released the journal.

Samuel gently picked it up and tucked it under his arm. 'I got to know,' he said. 'Where's the stone that everybody wants?'

'Most likely in an American museum. Where your Cuban friend won't be able to touch it.'

Samuel shrugged. 'I hope you find it first, not him. My cousin says he's crazy.'

The Jamaican backtracked to the door and turned the handle. 'Good-bye,' he said, his eyes staring down in shame.

'Good-bye, Samuel.' Dirk clicked on the speargun's safety and set it down.

Samuel closed the door behind him.

A minute later, Summer emerged from her bedroom wearing an oversized Scripps Institute of Oceanography T-shirt. She covered a yawn. 'I thought I heard voices.'

'I just gave Samuel the journal.'

'You what?'

'It's what Díaz was after. Now he doesn't need to kill us in our sleep.'

'Juan Díaz, the Cuban we met in Mexico?'

'One and the same. He hired Samuel to monitor us and paid for the thugs in the pickup. No doubt he's behind the theft of the stone at Zimapán.'

'Díaz . . .' A look of bitter disappointment crossed her face. 'He was the leader of the thieves who took the stone? How could I have been so blind?'

'We met him only briefly. You told me they all wore disguises and that the top guy hardly spoke.'

'Still, I should have recognized him.' She sat on the couch in shock. 'He's responsible for the death of Dr Torres. But why would a Cuban archeologist kill over an Aztec artifact?'

'He may not even be an archeologist. It could be he's operating an artifact smuggling operation. There's big money in black market antiquities. Both sections of the stone together could be worth a lot of money to a collector . . . Or it could be something else.'

'What's that?'

Dirk stared at the speargun with a faraway gaze. 'Perhaps, just perhaps, Díaz knows exactly what the Aztecs were carrying when they sailed to Aztlán.'

PART III
Cuba Libre

Underwater Mining Operation

32

Dirk and Summer had barely stepped aboard the *Sargasso Sea* when the engines rumbled to life and the research vessel sailed out of Montego Bay's sparkling waters.

'No R and R for the crew in sunny Jamaica?' Summer asked her father after greeting him with a warm hug.

Pitt shook his head. 'We're headed for the north side of Cuba and I want to get there as soon as possible.'

'He's a regular Captain Bligh,' Giordino said.

Pitt shifted his eyes toward Giordino. 'There might be certain crew members who can't be trusted on a rum-producing island like Jamaica.'

Giordino shook his head. 'Ye of little faith.'

'We got your email describing the dead zones,' Dirk said. 'Have you learned anything more?'

Pitt led them to the wardroom, where poster-sized photos were taped to a corner bulkhead. 'These are seafloor images of the three dead zones we surveyed. Photomosaics, actually, stitched from individual images recorded by the AUV. As you can see, there is a symmetrical depression at the center of each zone. We didn't identify the source of the toxicity until Al and I took the *Starfish* down for a closer look at one of them and found a hydrothermal vent at its center.'

'The thermal vents we've explored in the Pacific are rich in minerals and highly acidic,' Dirk added, 'but not broadly toxic.'

'These are. They are in relatively shallow water for a thermal vent, less than a thousand feet, which may contribute to the problem. We're finding methyl mercury plumes over ten miles long.'

'Mercury?' Summer asked.

Pitt nodded. 'Surprising, but it shouldn't be. The largest source of mercury in the environment comes from the volcanic eruptions. Two hundred and fifty million years ago, give or take a few weeks, the seas were completely poisoned by mercury from volcanic activity, to the extent that virtually all marine life was killed off. Hydrothermal vents, we know, are nothing more than a vestige of underwater volcanic activity. For whatever reason, the mounts and ridges in this part of the ocean are rife with mercury.'

'Now that you mention it,' Dirk said, 'I recall reading about an underwater volcano off the southern tip of Japan that's spewing a high concentration of the stuff.'

'Same principle in effect here,' Pitt said.

Summer pointed at one of the photos. 'It's odd that there's a similar depression around each of the thermal vents.'

'That's no coincidence,' Pitt said. 'We're quite sure the craters were formed by man-made explosions.'

'Why would someone blow up a thermal vent?' she asked.

'Someone,' Giordino said, 'was ploughing up the bottom in the name of sub-sea mining.'

'Of course.' Summer nodded. 'Hydrothermal vents are often surrounded by rich sulfide ore deposits.'

'Looks like somebody tried panning for gold in a serious way,' said Dirk.

'That's our guess,' Pitt said. 'They blasted open the vent, then sent down mining equipment to vacuum it all up.'

'Walking away with the gold,' Summer said, 'and leaving an environmental mess in their wake.'

'So who's responsible?' Dirk asked.

'We don't yet know,' Pitt said, shaking his head. 'Hiram ran a check on all known sub-sea mining ventures, and associated ocean lease agreements, and found nobody operating in this area. Legally, at least.'

'Could it be the Cubans?' Summer asked.

'Possibly,' Pitt said, 'but we don't think they possess the technology. They'd have to contract for the equipment and that would find its way into the public record. But we do have one clue.'

'What's that?' Summer asked.

'These tracks.' Pitt pointed to a mass of parallel lines that crisscrossed the depression. 'Al and I saw similar tracks near the wellhead where the *Alta* sank.'

'And those tracks looked fresh,' Giordino said.

'Was it the company that's drilling for oil?' Dirk asked.

'I contacted the captain of the drill ship and he said

they had no equipment that could have created those tracks.'

'So you think whoever blew these three vents is working on the other side of Cuba?' Summer asked.

'It's the best we have to go on,' Pitt said, 'so we're heading back to the Florida Straits. About twenty miles off Havana.'

'That's a precarious spot for a toxic mercury problem,' Dirk said, 'right at the head of the Gulf Stream.'

'That's what has us worried. A major mercury plume there might carry up Florida's east coast, and beyond.'

A crewman entered the wardroom and approached Summer. 'Miss Pitt, your teleconference is ready. There's a Mr Perlmutter waiting on-screen.'

Summer smiled at her brother as she jumped from her chair. 'Maybe he found the stone,' she said, before following the crewman to a nearby video conference room.

'The stone?' Giordino asked. 'What were you two up to in Jamaica?'

Dirk described their encounter-laden quest for the two Aztec stones since deciphering the codex, eliciting a grave look of concern from Pitt.

'There must be something valuable waiting for the person who puts the two pieces together,' Giordino said. He rubbed his chin a moment. 'You said Aztec stone? You should meet our friend Herbert.'

Giordino stepped to a corner table, where the statue they plucked off the bottom was serving time as a paperweight for some sonar records. He grabbed the statue along with a handful of photos.

'Say hello to Herbert.' He set the statue on the table in front of Dirk. 'We found him in a large canoe near one of the vents. Our shipboard archeologist thinks it could be Aztec.'

Dirk studied the figurine with a hint of recognition. The warrior's strong profile and costume had a distinct familiarity.

'Dr Madero showed us a similar statue in his university's museum. It looks a lot like one of the Aztec deities.' He looked at Giordino with curiosity. 'You said you found this on a canoe?'

Giordino nodded and slid over the photos. 'Images we took from the *Starfish*, at a depth of twelve hundred feet.'

'The stone depicts the voyage of several large boats on a pilgrimage to the Aztec's homeland,' Dirk said. 'Dr Madero told us that while the Mayans were known to trade at sea, there's no record of the Aztecs traveling offshore.'

'Then either the canoe is Mayan or somebody needs to change the history books.'

'Did you find any other artifacts with the canoe?' Dirk asked.

'No,' Pitt said. 'But those mining vehicle tracks ran right up to it, so someone else may have picked it over.'

Summer returned to the room, showing a defeated look on her face.

'No luck with the stone?' Dirk said.

'None of it good. It's not at Yale, or anywhere else in the US, as far as St Julien can determine. It seems that Ellsworth Boyd, the archeologist who found half the stone, never made it back home. Shortly after departing Jamaica, he was killed in Cuba. Believe it or not, he died in the explosion that sank the USS *Maine*.'

'What was he doing aboard the *Maine*?' Giordino asked.

Summer shook her head. 'Nobody knows. St Julien's going to do some more digging. He seems to think there's a chance the stone was with him aboard the *Maine*.'

The group fell silent as they contemplated the sunken warship that instigated the Spanish–American War.

Dirk finally looked at his father with a devilish smile. 'You said we're heading to a spot about twenty miles off Havana?'

'That's correct.'

'That should put us right in the ballpark.'

'The ballpark for what?'

'If my history serves,' Dirk said, 'the place where the *Maine* now lies at rest.'

33

When the armored cruiser *Maine* blew up unexpectedly in February 1898, killing two hundred and sixty-one sailors, there was an immediate siren call for war. Though the cause of the spark that triggered her powder magazines to detonate still remains a mystery, contemporary fingers all pointed at Spain. Jingoistic fever, fanned by a strong dose of yellow journalism, quickly incited a declaration of war.

The resulting Spanish–American War was itself a short-lived affair. Within months, the American Navy had crushed the Spanish fleet in battles at Santiago and Manila Bay. In July, Teddy Roosevelt's Rough Riders won the day at San Juan Hill, and by August a peace agreement had been brokered between the antagonists.

After the war's end, the genesis for the conflict was oddly forgotten. The mangled remains of the *Maine* sat mired in the silt of Havana Harbor for more than a decade, her rusting main mast standing forlornly above the waves. Commemorative interest, and a desire to clear a harbor obstruction, finally prompted Congress to approve funds to raise the vessel.

In an engineering feat that many predicted would

fail, the Army Corps of Engineers constructed a coffer-dam around the wreck and pumped away the water. The mud-covered ship that emerged was a devastated mass of twisted metal. The engineers cut away the damage and sealed the breach. In March of 1912, the ship was refloated and towed offshore, where she was sunk with her colors flying.

Sitting on the bridge of the *Sargasso Sea*, Pitt studied the hundred-year-old coordinates of the wreck site, marked on a digital map of the Cuban coastline.

'They sank her about four miles from shore. That may have been considered the high seas in 1912, but today the territorial limit is twelve miles. We dally around the site and we're liable to become permanent guests of the Cuban Revolutionary Armed Forces.'

Giordino exhaled a cloud of blue smoke from a lit cigar. 'I wonder if they allow smoking in their prisons.'

Summer stood near the helm with her brother, staring at a calm expanse of blue water. 'We could survey the wreck remotely,' she said.

Giordino nodded. 'Shouldn't hurt anyone's feelings if we sent an AUV to find the wreck and take a few passes. Depending on how the ship struck the bottom, we might get some good looks at her.'

'Okay,' Pitt said. 'But we've got bigger fish to fry at the moment. I'll give you twelve hours, then we're off to the *Alta*'s wreck site. And just don't let the Cubans end up with my AUV.'

Dirk paused. 'What about your Creepy Crawler, Al?

216

If we get a fix on the wreck with the AUV, couldn't we send in one of your crawlers to investigate?'

'With a transponder in the water, we can operate it in real time from the ship. It would be a good test of its abilities.' Giordino sat upright, setting aside his cigar. 'I might even be able to rig a deployment device so the AUV could drop it over the site and save time.'

Pitt knew an American-flagged ship lingering near Cuban waters, especially near Havana, was liable to attract unwanted attention. As soon as Giordino had his AUV launched an hour later, he repositioned the *Sargasso Sea* several miles outside Cuba's territorial limit.

Under Giordino's programming, the yellow AUV sped to the *Maine*'s last-known coordinates and dove to the bottom, initiating a survey grid with its sensors on alert for a large magnetic object.

After six hours, the AUV completed its survey and made a beeline for the NUMA research ship. The vehicle was hoisted aboard and its data pack removed. With the Pitt family crowded around him, Giordino reviewed the results. A square diagram filled with vertical lines appeared on the monitor, sprinkled with amoeba-shaped bubbles.

'We've got a handful of small magnetic anomalies. And a large one in lane 14.' Giordino pointed to a large red splotch.

'Let's take a look at the sonar images,' Pitt said.

Giordino brought up the sonar record and scrolled rapidly until a data table in the corner indicated lane 14.

'The magnetic target was near the top of the lane,' he said, slowing the video to its recorded speed.

A gold-tinted rendition of the seafloor appeared. The sonar system created shadowy images of rocks, mounds and other features that rose from the seabed. The record scrolled a short distance when a dark trapezoidal shape appeared on one side of the screen. Giordino froze the image. 'There she is.'

Summer and Dirk leaned in for a closer look. There was no mistaking the elegant tapered stern of the ancient warship. The opposite end was oddly blunt where the Army Corps had cut and inserted a flat bulkhead to refloat the ship. The *Maine* appeared to be sitting upright on her keel with just a negligible list.

The sight sent a chill up Summer's spine. 'She looks intact and quite accessible. Al, do you think you can get a Creepy Crawler on her?'

'Problem solved,' Giordino grinned. 'While the AUV was running its grid, I had the machine shop fabricate a harness with a timed release. The AUV can carry the crawler to the site and circle a few minutes until the timer activates. The crawler will deploy a transponder when she bails out, which will allow us to walk all over the *Maine*. If your stone was left on the ship, we just might find it.'

'How do you know,' Pitt asked, 'that it wasn't blown to bits in the explosion or ended up in the harbor?'

'The fact is, we don't know if it was destroyed in the explosion,' Summer said. 'As for it ending up in the harbor, Perlmutter told us the refloating of the *Maine* was very well documented. They even dredged all around the wreck site. There was no indication of its recovery.'

'So what makes you think it's still on the ship?' Giordino asked.

'Two items give cause for hope. First, the recovery team was focused on refloating the ship. The *Maine*'s powder magazines were located forward, so the bow section suffered the worst damage. The engineers spent the bulk of their effort there, cutting away the damage and installing a bulkhead. The work crews in the stern just cleared away mud in the search for human remains. I'd like to think they would have left in place a heavy old stone.'

'Assuming,' Pitt said, 'it was carried on the stern of the ship.'

'Our second point of hope there is the archeologist, Ellsworth Boyd,' Summer said. 'Though he died in the blast, his body was recovered intact, indicating he wasn't near the epicenter. As a guest, he would have had a stateroom in the stern. If he wasn't near the worst of the explosion, there's hope that the stone wasn't either.'

'I think I like my odds in Las Vegas better,' Pitt said, shaking his head. 'All right, you might as well get to it.'

Giordino chuckled. 'Don't worry, boss. I have a good feeling that Herbert won't let us down.'

34

Giordino's release system worked as advertised. Two hours later, they were watching in fascination as the Creepy Crawler scurried up a rise of sand and clawed its way on to the deck of the *Maine*. The crawler's video camera showed a bare metal hulk, covered in only a light blanket of marine growth.

Giordino guided the crawler across the steel deck footings, now minus the inlaid teak that originally graced the ship. He battled with the crawler's low level of lighting and an annoying time delay between his movements on a joystick and the device's reaction, but he soon had it scurrying about the wreck.

The *Maine*'s remains were a ghostly tomb of corroding steel, the decks starkly empty. The robot crept into the stern superstructure, which had housed the officers' and captain's quarters. Where paneling and carpet once covered the interior, now there were only gray steel bulkheads. Most of the hatch doors had been wedged open, allowing free view of the empty cabins that had been home to sailors now long dead.

Giordino maneuvered the crawler down a companionway to the berth deck and into an empty wardroom.

There was little to see other than some small cut-glass lighting fixtures that still clung to their ceiling mounts. Finding nothing that resembled a large stone, Giordino guided the crawler back to the main deck and exited the aft structure. He had bypassed the engine room and some coal bunkers, which everyone agreed were unlikely storage places for the stone.

'I think we've seen all there is to see.' He stretched the tired fingers that were operating the joystick.

'Nothing remotely resembling the stone,' Dirk said. 'It probably didn't survive the explosion.'

Summer nodded. 'I guess we'll never know the full Aztec tale.' She turned to Giordino. 'Thanks for the effort, Al. If nothing else, you've captured some amazing footage of the old battlewagon.'

'All in a day's work,' he said, sharing in their disappointment.

'How are you going to get your crawler back?' Dirk asked.

'I'll send it walking toward Key West. If we're still in the neighborhood in a few days, we can pick it up on the fly.'

As he spoke, the crawler caught a leg on a twisted ventilator that was pressed against the aft superstructure. Giordino had to reverse course in order to free the device.

'Hold up.' This came from Pitt, who had been standing silently behind the others, watching the video.

'Go back to where you got hung up.'

Giordino reversed the crawler a few steps. 'Something catch your eye?'

'There, against the bulkhead. Can you zoom in with the camera?'

Giordino nodded and tapped a keystroke. The video display enlarged, revealing a metallic object wedged between the bulkhead and the damaged ventilator.

'It's a gun,' Giordino said.

He finessed the camera controls to focus on the weapon. Pitt stepped to the monitor for a closer look. It was an open-frame revolver, showing only slight corrosion on the barrel and grip though missing its original wooden stock.

'It looks like a Lefaucheux,' Pitt said, 'a French cartridge revolver that was a common sidearm with the Union cavalry during the Civil War.'

'It looks to be wedged pretty tight under that mangled ventilator,' Giordino said. 'It must have gone unseen when they cleaned up the ship for refloating.' He brought the crawler a step closer, magnifying the image even more.

'What is an old French revolver doing on the *Maine*?' Summer asked.

Nobody had an answer until Giordino refocused the image. In fuzzy letters, a faint engraving could be seen on the barrel.

'"F. de Orbea Hermanos, Eibar 1890,"' Pitt read. 'That would be the manufacturer.'

He turned to Summer with an arched brow. 'You were close. The correct question would be, what is an old Spanish revolver doing aboard the *Maine*?'

35

'Have you found your way to the bottom of the pile yet?'

St Julien Perlmutter looked up from his table in the central research room of the National Archives to see the smiling face of the facility's chief military records archivist.

'Very nearly, Martha, very nearly. I apologize for the heavy workout. The files on the *Maine* are more extensive than I anticipated.'

'Lord knows, I can use the exercise.' Martha rested a hand on one of her ample hips. 'Let me know if there's anything else I can pull for you.'

'Martha, my dear, you are pure ambrosia,' Perlmutter said with a smile.

It was his third day in the research room, poring through century-old documents. Although already familiar with the *Maine*'s sinking, he was fascinated at reading the official inquiry into the disaster and its supporting documentation, including vivid accounts by survivors and reports of the ship's damage from Navy hard-hat divers. Possible causes for the explosion, ranging from a smoldering coal bunker to a bursting boiler, were all dismissed by the inquiry board in favor of a suspected external mine.

At first, Perlmutter found no mention of the archeologist Ellsworth Boyd, so he jumped ahead to records of the salvage and refloating of the warship in 1912. Detailed engineering reports, rich with black-and-white photographs, documented the construction of the cofferdam around the wreck, the removal of human remains, and the refloating of the ship and her second sinking.

Throughout the reports, Perlmutter found no mention of Boyd's artifact.

He perused a remaining file of naval communiqués related to responses in Havana immediately after the explosion. He was nearing the end of the folder when he found a letter from the chief forensics officer at Brooklyn Naval Hospital addressed to General Fitzhugh Lee, the Consul General of Cuba. The narrative was brief:

March 18, 1898

Dear General Lee,

 Enclosed under seal is a copy of Dr Ellsworth Boyd's recent autopsy report, as requested.

     Yours obediently,
     Dr Ralph Bennett
     US Naval Hospital, Brooklyn

Perlmutter studied the letter, wondering why an autopsy would have been performed on Boyd. His research instincts told him there was more to the story. Closing the file, he called to Martha.

'All finished?' she asked.

'I'm done with these materials but I'm afraid the quest continues. Can you see what Uncle Sam is holding in the way of some nineteenth-century diplomatic correspondence?'

'Certainly. What did you have in mind?'

'The file of one General Fitzhugh Lee, while engaged as Consul General to Cuba, in the year 1898.'

'Let me check. Those might be at the Library of Congress.'

The archivist returned a few minutes later, beaming. 'You're in luck, Julien. We have a file for him in the archives bearing the dates 1896 to 1898. I put a rush order to have it pulled, but it will still take an hour or two.'

'Martha, you are a peach. Two hours would allow an enjoyable lunch at the Old Ebbitt Grill. Can you join me?'

'Only if we make it an hour,' she replied with a blush. 'I *am* on the federal payroll, you know.'

'The most civil of servants,' Perlmutter said, standing and bowing. 'After you, my dear.'

When they returned an hour and a half later, the files were waiting in the archivist's bin. Refreshed from a lunch of oyster stew and crab cakes, Perlmutter dove into the records.

The correspondence from Fitzhugh Lee, a Civil War

veteran and nephew of Robert E. Lee, was voluminous. The papers covered his 1896 appointment to the post in Havana by President Grover Cleveland until his evacuation from Cuba in April 1898 at the onset of the war with Spain.

Perlmutter skimmed through a hoard of letters describing growing tensions with the Spanish ruling force and growing resistance from the ragtag Cuban rebels.

Working through a flurry of communiqués surrounding the *Maine*'s destruction, he was surprised to find a copy of Boyd's autopsy. The one-page document, a simple narrative of the examination, revealed a startling discovery. Boyd had not died from the *Maine*'s explosion. Instead, his death was attributed to a gunshot wound to the chest, in conjunction with evidence of partial drowning.

Perlmutter sniffed for more clues and found them an hour later in the form of a letter from the *Maine*'s captain, Charles Sigsbee, to Lee. The handwritten letter said, in part:

> *I am in receipt of the report on Dr Boyd. It would seem to confirm Lieutenant Holman's report of a skirmish on the quarterdeck immediately after the explosion. Holman believes there was a brief fray over Boyd's crate. He didn't realize that Boyd was mortally wounded but had assumed he was abandoning ship to board the steamer. I have no way of confirming your suspicions about those responsible, but perhaps*

that can be ascertained with the apprehension of the steamer.
This might also affirm the supposition that the Maine *was*
destroyed on account of Dr Boyd's relic. It seems a sad vanity
that war will accrue on account of the treasure from a long-
deceased empire. C. D. Sigsbee.

'Treasure?' Perlmutter muttered to himself. 'It's always treasure.'

He waded through Lee's remaining papers, discovering another clue: a War Department communiqué to Lee dated a week after the *Maine*'s sinking. Lee was informed that the USS *Indiana* had engaged the steamer *San Antonio* in the Old Bahamas Channel off Cuba's northeast coast.

The *Indiana*'s captain reported with regret that the vessel was sunk in deep water during an attempted apprehension. While the contraband was lost, a survivor, Dr Julio Rodriguez, disclosed his assessment of the suspected repository site before he succumbed from wounds received during the engagement. The location was marked classified and sent to the War Department for strategic evaluation.

Perlmutter put down the letter, aghast at the implications. He now had more questions than answers. But he knew the Pitts' pursuit of the Aztec stone carried considerable significance.

He perused the remaining documents in the file, nearly overlooking a one-page letter on White House stationery dated 1908. It was clearly misfiled, he thought, recognizing the sweeping signature of the President at the bottom. But perusing the shortly worded Executive Order, he felt a tightening in his throat.

An hour later, he bundled the Lee papers and carried them to the return counter, where Martha was finishing with another customer.

'I am most grateful for your assistance, Martha,' he said. 'That should conclude my studies for today.'

'Find anything astounding that will bring you back tomorrow?'

'Indeed.' Perlmutter's eyes were aglow. 'A whole new cause for the Spanish–American War.'

36

'It might be meaningless, but I thought it was worth passing along.'

Rudi Gunn's blue eyes glistened on the ship's video conference monitor as he waited for a reply a thousand miles away.

'Any input is helpful,' Pitt said, 'when you're chasing gremlins.'

'When you told me about the depressions at the heart of the toxic zones,' Gunn said, 'I had Dr McCammon in the geology department scan the region for seismic events. Within the past six weeks, there has been an event near each of the three sites, measuring 4.0 on the moment magnitude scale, or just under 3.0 on the Richter scale.'

'That sounds significant,' Giordino said, pacing in front of the screen.

'Not necessarily. There are about a thousand seismic events a day around the world, but in this instance there appears to be a correlation.'

'I assume the seismic readings could be registering an underwater explosion,' Pitt said.

'Absolutely. About six hundred to eight hundred pounds of TNT could produce an equivalent reading.

Dr McCammon showed me similar readings from known land-based mining operations.'

'That's another shred of evidence that someone is blasting open the thermal vents,' Pitt said.

'There are a limited number of underwater mining systems in operation,' Gunn said, 'but we haven't tracked one to the Caribbean yet. Most seem to be deployed in Indonesia.'

'Given the environmental damage they're causing,' Pitt said, 'it's little wonder they are flying under the radar.'

'One more thing,' Gunn said. 'You mentioned you were headed back to the site of the sunken drill ship?'

'That's right. Al and I noticed some bottom tracks that matched with marks we found around the vents.'

'We checked that area for seismic events and found there was a small rattle in the region just four days ago,' Gunn said. 'Your hunch may be a good one.'

'We're nearly there, so we'll know soon enough. Thanks, Rudi.'

Gunn nodded and his image vanished from the monitor. Pitt turned to Giordino seated next to him. 'Is the *Starfish* prepped for business? I'd like to start with another look at those tracks we saw near the *Alta*.'

'Standing by and ready to go.'

Twilight had settled over the ocean when the *Sargasso Sea* arrived at the spot of the *Alta* disaster. The surface waters were surprisingly crowded. Less than a half mile away, the lights of another vessel could be seen, standing on station. A second vessel appeared to be just east of it.

Pitt turned to the research ship's captain. 'Do we have identification of the vessels?'

The captain peered into a large radarscope, which typically provided a neighboring vessel's name with its location and heading via a satellite tracking system called AIS. He looked up at Pitt and shook his head. 'No identification is registering. They must have their AIS systems turned off.'

Pitt nodded. 'Try them on the radio and advise them we will be deploying a submersible in the area of the wreck.'

The captain hailed the nearby ships but received only radio silence. 'Do you want to wait and deploy in the morning?'

'No, we'll go as soon as you are on station. After all, it's always dark on the bottom.'

Thirty minutes later, Pitt headed to the stern deck cradle of the *Starfish* but was stopped along the way.

'Mr Pitt?'

Pitt turned to find Kamala Bhatt stepping out of a side lab carrying a binder. 'We just pulled a water sample when the ship stopped. I ran a quick test to check for methyl mercury.'

'What did you find?'

Pitt didn't have to ask, he could see the answer in her eyes.

'The numbers are off the charts.'

37

Clad in a blue jumpsuit, Pitt crawled through the hatch of the deepwater submersible. Squirming into the pilot's seat, he was surprised to find his daughter at the copilot's station. 'You nudge Al out of riding shotgun?' he asked.

'Why should he have all the fun?' she replied. 'Of course, it will cost me a box of cigars when we make port. On top of that, I had to tell Dirk that you weren't deploying for another hour to get him out of the way.'

'What kind of a daughter do I have?'

She smiled. 'One who likes to get wet.'

They completed a predive checklist, then radioed the bridge that they were ready to deploy. Giordino activated a crane that lowered the *Starfish* into the water. With lights ablaze, the submersible sank slowly beneath the surface.

Pitt eyed his daughter as she reviewed the readouts on the console and radioed the ship that they were proceeding to descend.

'I don't think we've taken a ride together,' he said, 'since I taught you how to double-clutch my '33 Packard.'

'Thank goodness submersibles don't come with

clutches.' She shook her head at the memory. 'My left leg was sore for a week.'

When the bottom came into view, Pitt adjusted the ballast and engaged the thrusters.

'Is the wreck south of us?' she asked.

'Unless it crawled away. Maybe we can spot it on the sonar. Al said he configured a new system on the *Starfish*.'

Summer reached to an overhead panel and triggered a handful of switches, beating her father to the punch. 'It's a forward-looking, multibeam system with a range of three hundred meters,' she said. 'Dirk and I tested it in the Mediterranean last month and it worked quite well.'

A small monitor began showing a multicolored image of the seabed in front of them. Summer adjusted the sonar's frequency to increase the range.

Pitt shook his head. 'I knew I've been spending too much time in Washington.'

He adjusted the thrusters and sent the submersible skimming over the seafloor. As they traveled south, a dark smudge appeared at the edge of the monitor. A minute later, the *Alta* rose up before them. Her bow was crushed from colliding with the seafloor while her topsides were charred from fire.

'Al and I saw the tracks off her opposite side,' Pitt said as he guided the submersible down the length of the wreck.

'She sank due to the fire?' Summer asked.

'An explosion in the forward fuel bunker sent her

to the bottom. There's a mystery as to what, or who, set it off.'

He slowed the *Starfish* as they approached a hole in the lower hull a few feet back from the bow.

'Pretty sizable blast,' Summer said. 'Internal or external?'

'Interesting question. I'm sure the insurer will be asking the same.'

He maneuvered the submersible around the bow and across an undulating stretch of sand. The *Starfish*'s lights soon illuminated the set of tracks Pitt had seen on the earlier dive.

'Do they look like the same tracks you saw by the thermal vents?' Summer asked.

'They do. Let's see where they lead.'

Pitt accelerated forward, gliding over the tracks while startling an occasional deepwater fish.

Summer watched the sonar monitor. 'Multiple targets directly ahead.'

'I see them,' Pitt said. He wasn't looking at the sonar but at a sprinkling of lights that pierced the darkness ahead.

The seafloor gradually descended and Pitt could see that the lights were centered at the base of a bowl-shaped crater. Two large vehicles came into view, both brightly illuminated. Each was creeping across the seabed, emitting large clouds of silt out their back ends. They were deep-sea mining vehicles, operated from the surface via thick, black power cables.

'Those things are massive,' Summer said, 'as large as a Greyhound bus.'

'At least we caught them in the act,' Pitt said. 'Now we can find out who's causing all the damage.'

Pitt turned off the lights of the *Starfish* and moved closer to the vehicles, the nearest of which was called a bulk cutter. It looked like an overgrown tractor with a giant roller for its snout.

The roller was a rotating cutting drum affixed with tungsten carbide teeth that could chew apart rocks and hardened sediment. The tracked vehicle would ingest the rubble and expel it out of a large tube at the back. The second vehicle, similar in size but minus the roller drum, was a collecting machine. It would follow the bulk cutter and suck up the slurry, pumping it to the surface through a thick Kevlar hose.

Pitt closed with the bulk cutter, admiring its robot efficiency as it churned across the seabed an inch at a time. Summer captured the image of the slate-colored vehicle with the onboard video camera, knowing that few manufacturers could build such a specialized machine.

Pitt was edging alongside for a better view when a bang erupted from the rear of the submersible. The *Starfish* drifted laterally, knocking against the side of the cutter. Pitt reversed the submersible's thrusters, resulting in a second clang from behind.

Summer turned to peer out a small rear viewport. 'It's an ROV. It rammed us.'

'It just took out our main thruster.' Pitt toggled a pair of side thrusters to maneuver out of the way.

The submersible started to turn when another bang rang out and the *Starfish* was again shoved toward the bulk cutter.

'It's intentionally pushing us toward the bulk cutter,' Summer gasped.

Pitt felt the effects through the steering yoke. The ROV had smashed into and disabled one of the remaining side thrusters. Before the ROV could strike again, Pitt pivoted the *Starfish*, spinning away from the bulk cutter. The ROV's bright lights shone through the submersible's canopy. Pitt could see it was a large, deep-water ROV, box-shaped and better than twice the size of the NUMA submersible. The vehicle came charging at them again.

Striking the *Starfish*'s bow off center, it again drove the weakened submersible sideways, shoving it against the bulk cutter just behind the cutter drum.

Pitt reached between their seats and pulled a grip toggle that released an emergency ballast weight. The submersible ascended at once, then came to a crashing halt.

Near the top of the bulk cutter, a large manipulator had been extended. As the *Starfish* collided into it, the robotic arm moved down and pinned the submersible against its side.

Pitt kicked the remaining side thruster and applied full reverse power. The *Starfish* just slipped from under the manipulator when the ROV came up from the side and smashed into their top. Their instrument lights flickered as the submersible keeled over.

At the same instant, the manipulator dropped down and slid through the base frame of the *Starfish*. Its claw grabbed on to a section of tubing and closed shut.

Pitt frantically worked the thruster controls, but they proved useless. The bulk cutter had a solid grip on them and there was nothing they could do about it.

'It's going to ram the glass!' Summer shouted.

The ROV had repositioned itself directly in front of the *Starfish* and was rushing toward the acrylic viewport. At the last second, the ROV ascended, striking the top of the submersible and sliding along its roofline. The ROV then backed away, sporting a scruff of yellow paint and some dangling wires.

Pitt looked at the wires. 'It's our emergency transponder. So we can't communicate with the surface.'

'Are they going to leave us here to die?' Summer whispered.

'Only they know the answer to that,' Pitt said, staring out the viewport.

Like an all-seeing apparition, the ROV floated before them, its lights glaring into the submersible in a blinding taunt of death.

38

'We've lost contact with the *Starfish*.'

'Be right there,' Giordino said.

Hanging up a wardroom telephone, he called over to Dirk, who was examining the results of additional water samples while the submersible was on its dive. The two raced to a tiny control shack on the stern deck.

A communications technician greeted them with a sober nod. 'Both data and communications quit about five minutes ago. I've tried multiple frequencies and links but am getting no response.'

'Any indication of trouble beforehand?' Giordino asked.

'Negative. The last operating specs were fine. Summer radioed a few minutes earlier that they had located the *Alta* and were following some underwater tracks leading southeast.'

'Give me a mark on their last telemetry.' Giordino moved to a monitor that displayed a chart of the area. The technician tapped into a keyboard, pulling up the submersible's last-recorded coordinates, which appeared on the chart as a red triangle.

'That's about a thousand meters south of us.' Giordino motioned out a side window toward the lights of the ship in the distance. 'In the same direction as our friends over there.'

'I'll call them from the bridge and find out what they're doing and whether they have any resources in the water,' Dirk said, rushing out the door.

'Have the captain reposition us over the *Starfish*'s last coordinates,' Giordino said. 'I'll have an ROV ready to deploy in five minutes.'

It took ten minutes for the ship to be repositioned. Dirk hailed the nearby vessel but received only a brief rebuff. Without identifying itself, the ship replied that it was engaged in seabed testing, had not seen the *Starfish*, and ordered the NUMA ship to stay a half mile clear.

The *Sargasso Sea*'s captain promptly ignored the request, rushing his ship within a quarter mile of its position in hopes of locating the submersible.

Giordino lowered his ROV over the side, spooling out its lift cable as fast as the drive winch would allow. Dirk sat in the control shack, watching its video feed. Halfway down, the ROV's camera briefly picked up some faint lights in the distance, then lost them.

At six hundred feet, Dirk activated a joystick and navigated the ROV in a small circle as the seafloor came into view.

Giordino stepped into the control shack a minute later. 'See anything?'

'Caught a flash of lights during the descent at about two hundred feet. Looked too dispersed to be the *Starfish*.'

'That ship is up to no good. Take a look at those bottom tracks.'

The ROV hovered over a slew of tread marks that crisscrossed the bottom. Dirk guided the ROV toward the heaviest concentration.

'Something off to the right,' Giordino said.

Dirk pivoted the ROV, its camera picking up a distant flicker of lights. 'Let's go have a look.'

While Giordino remotely played out additional cable, Dirk powered toward the lights. It didn't take long to see they didn't come from the *Starfish*.

The lights twinkled from the massive collecting machine that was designed to vacuum up crushed rock. The big vehicle sat idle, its bulk cutter partner nowhere in sight. Standing watch nearby was the large, square ROV, hovering a few meters off the bottom.

As the NUMA probe drew near, the collecting machine rose off the bottom amid a cloud of silt. A thick pair of cables began hoisting the machine on a slow journey to the surface. Dirk tracked its motions for a short distance, then broke away as the other ROV came to investigate.

The two ROVs eyed each other warily for a minute. The larger vehicle then turned and chased after the ascending machine to the surface.

'Seabed testing, my foot,' Giordino said. 'They're absconding with most of the seafloor.'

'Dad and Summer surely must have snuck up on their operation.'

'Seems a little unusual that they suddenly packed up and headed for the surface. All we can do now is keep searching.'

They piloted the ROV across the bottom for another two hours, repositioning the *Sargasso Sea* several times to expand the search area. They found no trace of the missing submersible.

Giordino frowned. 'I can't believe we haven't heard a peep from their emergency transponder.'

'Is it external?' Dirk asked.

'Mounted on the sub's roof.'

Dirk turned to the communications technician. 'Have you been recording the ROV's video feed?'

'Yes, as per standard procedure.'

'Replay the footage where we stared down the other ROV.'

The technician rewound the feed.

'Freeze it there,' Dirk said. He and Giordino crouched close to the monitor.

'There,' Dirk said, 'at the bottom of the ROV. There's a couple of dangling wires that look out of place, and a small piece of plastic wedged just below.'

Giordino tensed. 'That looks like part of the transponder's housing. And there's yellow scuffing on the ROV's frame.'

A shadow of anger descended over Giordino's normally jovial face. He stood and stepped toward the door. 'Let's get that ROV back on deck *now*! I think it's time we pay our neighbors a visit.'

39

The churning cutter head, the internal pumps and conveyors, and the creeping steel tracks all came to a stop.
The big mining vehicle spat out a final mouthful of
gnarled rocks and fell silent.

Peering out the *Starfish*'s viewport, Summer felt
more unnerved than ever. After a minute, she turned
to her father. 'Do you think they'll just hold us here
until we run out of air?'

Pitt shook his head as he focused on shutting down
all nonessential systems. 'It won't happen. The *Sargasso
Sea* will find us first. Dirk and Al will have an ROV
down here before you know it.'

'That monster ROV may try to disable it, too.'

'We'll just have to hope they see us first.'

The chance never occurred. At the same moment
Giordino's ROV hit the water, the bulk cutter
was yanked off the seabed, with the *Starfish* clutched
to its side. Twin cables spooled around a massive
drum winch on the surface ship pulled the vehicle up,
giving Pitt and Summer the sensation of riding an
elevator.

Halfway to the surface, they noticed the lights of the
NUMA ROV traveling in the opposite direction. Pitt

grabbed a flashlight and clicked an SOS out the view-port, but the ROV quickly vanished from sight.

A short time later, the bulk cutter broke the surface alongside the mining support ship. The large vessel had disengaged its dynamic positioning system after both mining vehicles had left the bottom and drifted over a mile from the *Sargasso Sea*. The ship turned its starboard side away from view of the NUMA ship.

A massive A-frame, mounted amidships, hoisted the bulk cutter clear of the water. On the opposite side of the deck, a matching A-frame awaited the retrieval of the collecting machine.

Pitt and Summer peered out of the submersible through the glare of dozens of work lights strung above the ship's deck. Their arrival was met by curious stares from a handful of crewmen in hard hats who guided the bulk cutter across the deck and into a semi-enclosed hangar. A contingent of soldiers in green fatigues quickly surrounded the submersible, armed with AK-47s.

'Not the welcoming committee I was hoping to see,' Pitt said.

'Cuban Army soldiers?' Summer asked.

'I believe so,' he said, noting a white star over a red diamond insignia on one of the uniforms.

A soldier shone a flashlight into their faces, motioning them to exit the submersible. Pitt followed Summer to the hatch, stopping at a tool locker and slipping a small folding knife into his pocket before climbing out.

They were greeted silently by the soldiers.

Pitt countered by exploding in mock anger. 'What have you done!' he yelled. Stepping to the rear of the sub, he pointed to the mangled thrusters. 'Look at the damage. I want my ship notified at once.'

The soldiers' hesitation ended when a dog-faced officer appeared on the scene with an authoritative air. 'Take them below and secure them!' he barked. Turning to one of the ship's crew, he added, 'Get that submersible concealed.'

With their assault rifles drawn, four of the soldiers prodded Pitt and Summer away from the *Starfish*. As they passed the bulk cutter, Pitt saw a small red logo painted on the side: a grizzly bear carrying an ax in its teeth.

They were escorted down a companionway into an open work bay that housed the now recovered ROV. A technician procured a pair of cable ties, which the guards used to secure the captives' wrists behind their backs. Pitt and Summer were shoved to the floor with their backs against a bulkhead.

The Army officer, a man named Calzado, appeared a short time later in the company of one of the ship's officers. The two argued loudly while gesturing toward the captives. Then both left the bay.

'What was that all about?' Pitt whispered. Though he understood the Spanish spoken, he had been blocked from view of the quarreling parties by one of the guards.

'I don't think the ship's captain is too happy that we were brought aboard. I caught something about breaching security on the project. I think they're going to move us.'

Summer's words proved prophetic. A half hour later, the pair were marched back up to the main deck. An aged tugboat was tied alongside the mining ship, astern of a wooden barge stacked high with ore from the seabed. Pitt and his daughter were led aboard the tug and into a cramped cabin, where a guard kept watch with the door open.

'Did you see the *Sargasso Sea* when we boarded?' Summer asked.

'No. We must be turned away from her. I'm sure they'll be looking for us by now.'

'But they won't know where to track us,' she replied in a down voice.

They heard the tug's motor rumble to life. A few minutes later, the stubby boat got under way, shoving the barge ahead of it through the rocky seas. Into the night they sailed, leaving the NUMA ship, and freedom, in their wake.

40

The large workboat cut its engines and slowed to a drift under a cloudy night sky. A few faint lights tickled the horizon far to the south, but the ocean around them was empty. The boat's skipper checked the radar system to ensure there were no unseen vessels about. Satisfied they were alone, he picked up a handheld radio.

'Bridge. We're at the drop zone. You're clear to deploy.'

Standing on the open stern deck, James Maguire replied instantly. 'Roger. Proceeding to deploy.'

The mercenary turned to a tall, muscular man smoking a cigarette at the side rail. 'Okay, Gomez. We're clear to drop.'

The two stepped to a large covered object strapped to the deck. They released the ties and pulled back a tarp to reveal a dilapidated coastal fishing boat powered by a small, rusty outboard motor. Or at least that's how it looked.

The boat was actually constructed with a Kevlar composite that made it virtually indestructible. The exterior had been molded and painted to resemble bleached wood suffering from rot.

'Are we fully gassed up?' Maguire asked.

Gomez checked a pair of concealed fuel tanks near the

bow and nodded. The tanks fed two 150-horsepower horizontal motors concealed beneath the bench seats that powered twin jet impellers mounted on the hull.

Maguire opened a set of false floorboards and performed a quick inventory check with a flashlight. One compartment contained a mini arsenal of pistols, assault rifles and an RPG launcher, plus ammunition. Another contained an assortment of dive gear. Maguire loaded a third compartment with a heavy plastic bin he brought from his cabin.

Sealing up the floorboards, he called to Gomez. 'Let's get her wet.'

Gomez stepped to a small crane and hoisted the boat by its lift straps over the side and into the water.

Maguire eyed its name, *Surprise,* lightly painted in yellow on the stern, before climbing aboard. He released the lift straps and handed them to Gomez, who stowed them aboard the ship, then joined Maguire in the boat.

Maguire started up the inboard motors and radioed the workboat's bridge. '*Surprise* is away. We'll see you in forty-eight hours.'

'Roger that,' the skipper replied. 'We'll be waiting right here, catching some rays.'

Maguire laid on the throttle and the faux fishing boat shot away into the night. The mercenary aimed the bow toward the distant lights of Grand Cayman Island, bounding over the choppy black sea on a mission of death.

41

The *Sargasso Sea*'s Zodiac approached at a whisper, only the slap of the waves against its hull signaling its presence. Giordino was thankful for finding an electric motor aboard the research vessel, one used by the ship's scientists when examining ecologically sensitive areas. He was less enamored with the fact that he was piloting a bright orange inflatable across a moonlit sea. The ship's maintenance crew had hurriedly slapped a coat of black paint on the inflatable in the name of stealth, but much of it had fallen victim to the salt spray.

Giordino guided the Zodiac toward the mining ship, which was now holding position a mile east of the *Sargasso Sea*. The vessel was illuminated from stem to stern with bright floodlights that revealed an impressive, modern-built ship with multiple hydraulic A-frames, pumps and conveyors designed for sub-sea mining. Beyond the mining ship, Giordino saw the lights of a second vessel receding to the south.

He approached the ship from the stern to avoid observant eyes on the bridge while searching for a means to gain access. His luck held when he spotted a ladder that had been lowered off the starboard flank.

As the Zodiac drew closer, he read the ship's name on the transom, *Sea Raker*.

Dirk sat on the bow, dressed in black and holding a coil of rope. Figuring their chance of detection was less with a quick strike, Giordino held the throttle down and gunned for the ladder. The inflatable bounced against the side of the ship. Dirk leaped to the ladder, tied off the inflatable, and scrambled up the steps. Clearing the ship's rail, he ducked behind a crane and waited for Giordino.

Giordino tumbled to Dirk's side a minute later. 'How we looking?'

'Not good. We just missed a pair of guards on patrol that are headed up the port rail. They were uniformed and carrying assault rifles.'

'Assault rifles on a mining ship. Lovely,' Giordino said, angered at the notion they had arrived unarmed.

'We better keep a low profile. It looks like there are a few scattered work details still about as well.'

'That may not be a bad thing, if we can mix with the locals.'

Dirk spied an enclosed operator's cab affixed to the crane they were hiding behind. 'I think I see something.'

He crept to the cab door, climbed inside, and found a work coat draped over the operator's seat and a hard hat hanging from a hook. He grabbed both and returned to Giordino.

'Too short for me,' he said, holding up the jacket. 'You're elected to join the ship's crew.'

Giordino squeezed his torso into the coat and pulled the hat low. 'This should pass muster. Let's go see what we can find.'

He stepped on to the deck and moved along the starboard rail as if he'd worked aboard the ship for years. Dirk followed a few paces behind, holding to the shadows. They passed beneath a massive conveyor apparatus used to offload ore, then approached the bulk cutter machine's hangar.

Several crewmen were milling about, some wearing full protective suits and breathing devices. Giordino stood at the fringe until a lone crewman carrying a clipboard stepped in his direction. Giordino waved him over as if to point out a problem with some equipment. When he drew near, Giordino put his hand on the man's shoulder. 'Where's the man and woman from the submersible?' he asked.

The crewman gaped at Giordino a moment, then jabbered a litany of his own questions. Dirk materialized behind him and grabbed his arms, allowing Giordino an unfettered punch to the man's chin. The man instantly fell limp.

'That wasn't very sporting,' Giordino whispered, rubbing his knuckles.

'The consequence of a wrong answer.' Dirk dragged the crewman behind a large drum winch and stripped him of his jumpsuit and clipboard. He rejoined Giordino, moving forward along the deck. They stopped and ducked into the side of the hangar when they noticed a pair of armed guards approaching from the other direction.

Dirk and Giordino approached the bulk cutter and pretended to inspect its steel treads. The guards paid little attention as they strolled past. Once they were out of sight, Giordino started to exit the bay, but Dirk grabbed his arm.

'Al, over here.'

Dirk pulled him aside as a grease-stained mechanic walked by. He waited a moment, then steered Giordino to the other end of the bulk cutter. At the back of the hangar was a large oblong object covered in canvas tarps. Dirk pulled back a corner and saw a familiar yellow shape underneath. 'It's the *Starfish*,' he said. 'They brought it aboard.'

Pitt and Summer weren't trapped at the bottom of the sea. In all likelihood, they were alive and well somewhere aboard the ship.

'Why would they bring them aboard and hide the fact?' he asked.

'Who knows? Maybe they're mining here without authorization.'

They exited the hangar and peered toward the forward section of the ship.

'They probably have them locked in a cabin,' Giordino said. 'Let's see if we can find them.'

They made their way to the six-storey accommodations block near the bow. Entering an open side door, they searched the first two floors, finding a galley, a wardroom and several storage lockers. At that late hour of the night, there were only a few sleepy crew members about, waiting for their shifts to end. On the third level, they stumbled into a lounge fronting the crew's cabins. Three off-duty soldiers sat playing cards. Giordino eyed the adjacent corridors to the cabins. Finding them empty, he smiled at the soldiers and led Dirk to the companionway.

One of the cardplayers gave a cold stare to the two strangers in ill-fitting jumpsuits, but his partners kept their focus on the card game at hand.

'Lucky for us,' Giordino said as they broached the fourth level, 'it doesn't appear as if the ship's crew mingles with the Army boys.'

'Not so lucky, we're running out of accommodation quarters.'

They found the fourth floor identical to the third, minus the cardplayers. There was no sign of visitors under guard.

As they ascended toward the fifth level, an alarm sounded. After thirty seconds, the siren ceased and a stern voice barked through the public-address system in rapid-fire Spanish.

'I think somebody woke up and wants his threads back,' Giordino said.

'Don't tell me that jackhammer right of yours has lost some steam.'

He shrugged. 'We all have our off days. Let's take a quick look at the fifth floor, then hit the road.'

They scrambled up the stairwell to the next level, which was split between officers' cabins on one side and senior crew members' on the other. A few groggy-eyed ship's personnel were staggering from their cabins. No guards were visible, so they turned back toward the stairwell. A soldier came bursting on to the floor. He took one look at Dirk and Giordino and shouted, '*Alto, alto!*'

Giordino recognized him as the cardplayer from the third level. He also saw that he was unarmed. Stepping up to the man, Giordino grabbed him by the collar and threw him across the room. The soldier nearly came out of his shoes before slamming into a side wall and slumping to the floor.

'Let's go,' Giordino grunted, turning around and ducking down the companionway. Dirk followed on his heels.

The stairs were empty, and they raced to the bottom and darted out the door. Giordino exited first and ran straight into an armed soldier heading the other way. The two men bounced off each other, stumbling to the ground.

Though the soldier took the harder fall, he reacted quicker. Bounding to his feet, he thrust his assault rifle into Giordino's chest and shouted, 'Don't move.'

Giordino could only scowl as he eased his hands up in surrender.

42

Dirk stepped from the stairwell at the moment the two other men collided. He leaped back into its cover as the soldier stood up, not having noticed Giordino had a partner. Pounding footfalls and a murmur of voices overhead told him reinforcements were coming down the stairs. With little time to lose, he took a deep breath and waited for Giordino to set him up.

Raising his palms, Giordino feigned innocence and chatted nonstop to divert the soldier's attention. 'What are you doing?' he cried. 'I need to check the main hydraulics. Put your gun down. I'm no intruder.'

He faked an injured leg from the collision and hobbled to the side rail, leaning on it for support. The soldier pivoted to track his movements, repeatedly calling for him to halt. He relaxed slightly when Giordino finally stopped and again raised his arms up high.

It had taken Giordino just a few seconds to get the soldier turned around so his back was to the stairwell. Dirk reacted instantly, leaping from the stairs and charging toward the soldier like an angry bull. Dirk made no attempt to wrest the gun away; he simply lowered his shoulder and barreled into the man.

The soldier caught his approach from out of the

corner of his eye and twisted with the gun just before Dirk smashed into him.

The soldier went tumbling toward Giordino, who in turn tagged him with a hard punch to the gut.

The soldier squeezed the trigger on his AK-47 before he fell, spraying a half-dozen shots harmlessly into the deck plate.

The combined blows had knocked the wind out of him and he fell to the deck atop his rifle, gasping for air while clutching his stomach.

'Appreciate that,' Giordino said to Dirk. 'Now, let's get out of here.'

They sprinted down the starboard deck, but the gunfire had awakened the ship. Armed soldiers and crewmen came flooding out of the accommodations block.

Dirk and Giordino had run only a short distance when shots began flying past them. Ducking for cover, they slipped back into the hangar that housed the bulk cutter.

The hangar was now empty, save for a lone electronics technician on a raised platform checking a control panel. Giordino surveyed the platform, then motioned toward the stern.

'Make for the boat,' he said to Dirk. 'I'll slow them down.'

'You'll never make it.'

'Look for me over the side.'

Dirk knew there was no point in arguing, so he bolted across the hangar and slipped out to the stern.

Giordino approached the steps to the control platform. Alerted by the gunshots, the technician turned
with a petrified look as Giordino stormed up the steps.
'You can't come up here,' he yelled.

Giordino saw the man was terrified. Waving his
thumb over his shoulder, he said, 'Get lost!'

The technician nodded. Nervously slipping past
Giordino, he fled down the stairs and out of the hangar.

Giordino turned to the control panel, which served
as a testing station for the bulk cutter. Green lights
showed there was a live power connection to the
vehicle. He tweaked an assortment of dials and knobs
until he found a pair of dual controls that made the
machine stir beneath him. He jammed the levers forward and the bulk cutter began creeping forward on its
heavy tracks.

Giordino adjusted the controls, slowing the cutter's
left track and pivoting the machine until it faced the
ship's bow. Satisfied with its angle, he found and activated the vehicle's cutter drum.

A pair of armed soldiers peeked around the side of
the hangar as the cutter drum ground into the side
wall. The wall burst off its mounts and collapsed on the
men as the cutter bulled forward. One man rolled clear
and grabbed the arm of his companion, but the compressed wall had pinned him to the deck. The man let
out a warbled cry as the cutter drum drove forward,
grinding him, the wall, and the deck surface into a
bloodstained mixture.

The cutter ground forward across the starboard deck, blocking the soldiers who rushed from amidships. Giordino descended the platform and ran aft. He could see the stern rail ahead when suddenly two soldiers appeared in front of him. They knelt and opened fire with their assault rifles.

Giordino didn't wait for them to take aim. Without missing a beat, he stepped to the side rail, grabbed it, and vaulted over the side.

A spray of bullets peppered the rail a second later as Giordino plunged safely into the sea. He dug hard into the water, swimming deep and away from the ship. He traveled twenty yards before surfacing for air, and to take a quick look.

Dirk's voice filled his ears. 'Grab the line and hang on!'

A large dark object speckled with orange whisked by Giordino's head. He felt a rope sliding by his body and he clamped on to it with both hands.

He was immediately ripped forward, dragged across the surface as a spray of water pounded his face. His arms felt like they were being ripped from their sockets, but he hung on for nearly a minute. Whenever his head broke the surface, he heard the intermittent crack of distant gunfire. He was choking on water and out of breath when the rope in his hands finally fell slack.

He trod water a moment while catching his breath. The inflatable nudged up beside him and Dirk leaned over and offered a hand. Sporadic gunfire still sounded but in diminishing intensity.

Giordino lunged aboard and spat out a mouthful of saltwater. 'Thanks for the keelhauling,' he sputtered.

'Sorry. I figured it was the fastest way out of Dodge. They nicked our inflatable pretty good, but we're well out of view now.'

Giordino saw two of the Zodiac's five airtight compartments were sagging. 'They're certainly gun happy.'

'Guess they weren't too crazy about your shipboard mining demonstration.'

Giordino looked back toward the *Sea Raker*, several hundred yards distant. Somebody had pulled the power on the bulk cutter, but only after it had chewed up thirty feet of deck. He could just make out contingents of armed men swarming around the ship like a hive of bees.

Dirk hit the throttle and turned for home.

As they bounded over a rising sea, Giordino grimaced at the chaotic scene behind them. Their foray had been a complete failure. Somewhere aboard the mining ship, Pitt and Summer were being held captive, and now they would be hell to rescue.

43

A half-moon was still kindling the night sky when the tugboat carrying Pitt and Summer throttled down its engine. Pitt nudged his daughter awake as the boat scraped against a dock and its motor shut down.

She yawned. 'How long was I out?'

'An hour or so.'

'Great. So we must be in Key West by now.'

The guard at the door had stood, stone-faced, the entire journey. Little changed in his demeanor as he held the captives in the cabin another full hour. Finally, another soldier arrived, and together they marched Pitt and Summer off the tug and on to a long dock.

Summer scanned the area. 'Funny, this doesn't look like Florida.'

They had landed along a rugged stretch of verdant coast. Scattered lights were visible on the hills beyond, but the immediate landscape seemed isolated. A pair of illuminated buildings faced the extended dock, set in the base of a protected rocky cove.

The dock itself was massive, extending nearly four hundred feet. Pitt noticed the steel platform was painted a teal gray, which would make it hard to see from overhead. The tugboat was tied up just behind the large oceangoing barge it had pushed to shore. The barge held a mountain of ore, the now dried slurry that the *Sea Raker* had mined from the ocean floor.

As Pitt and Summer were marched along the dock, a contingent of workers approached from shore. Most wore military fatigues, like the soldiers on the *Sea Raker*. A few were attired in hazmat suits with breathing devices. These men began maneuvering into place a large conveyor system that would offload the barge's cargo.

At the end of the dock, Pitt paused to eye several high mounds of ore already onshore, presumably awaiting shipment to a smelter. The barrel of an assault rifle nudged him in the back as a reminder that he wasn't there to sightsee.

They were led past a helicopter pad and a two-storey dormitory building to the doorway of a small, low-roofed structure. Inside, it was configured as a contemporary executive office space, complete with plush carpeting and paneled walls.

Summer's eyes perked up at the sight of some Meso-American artifacts displayed in a glass case. She could give them only a cursory glance before they were shoved into a small office containing an empty desk and two stuffed chairs. The door was left open and an armed guard took his position at the threshold.

'At least we get a modicum of comfort before they pass out the blindfolds,' Pitt said. He sank sideways into one of the chairs, his wrists still bound behind him.

'That's not funny.' Summer took the other seat and leaned toward her father. In a low voice she asked, 'Why do you think they brought us here?'

'Guess they didn't want us in the midst of their mining operation. Maybe they just want us out of the way until they're finished working around the *Alta* site.'

'But the *Sargasso Sea* isn't going to stand by and do nothing.'

'They might not have a choice if the Cuban Navy shows up.'

'That's not going to go over well with Al.'

'There's not much he can do about it. If the military is running the show here, we'll probably have to wait for some sort of political resolution.' He leaned back in the chair. 'We might just have to sit tight and relax until they can barter us back.'

Summer shook her head. 'They're not going to be able to conceal the damage from the mercury releases.'

'That's true. There's something else bothering me. Did you see the shore workers dressed in hazmat suits and breathing devices?'

'They must know about the mercury in the sediments.'

'Maybe, but there was something else. Their suits had clipped to them small monitoring devices – like the pocket dosimeters used by sailors on nuclear submarines.'

Summer thought for a minute, then shook her head. 'No, you may be right. I remember examining the geological makeup of a thermal vent in the East Pacific Rise. There were concentrations of uranium and some rare earth elements in the surrounding basalt.' She looked at her father. 'Could it be they're mining uranium from the thermal vents?'

Pitt nodded. 'It would explain the high degree of security. And maybe why the *Alta* was sunk.'

'You think the Cubans created that hole we saw in the side of her hull?'

'One of the men on the diving bell said he saw an unknown submersible just before the drill ship sank.'

'But why would the Cubans be interested in mining uranium? They don't have the technology to create a weapon.'

'I don't know,' Pitt said.

They both fell quiet, overcome with a feeling they had stumbled on to something much more sinister than they knew.

44

Giordino shook his head in frustration. 'Are we anchored to the seafloor?'

Although the lights of the *Sargasso Sea* glistened a short distance away, it seemed they could not draw close to the NUMA ship. The inflatable's tiny motor was overwhelmed, first by its deflated sections, then by a breeze that had stiffened since their departure. Their voyage to the *Sea Raker* had taken less than fifteen minutes, but they were approaching an hour on the return.

'She's at full throttle.' Dirk squeezed the motor's handgrip tight for good measure. 'The headwind isn't helping.'

On the bridge of the *Sargasso Sea*, Captain Malcomb Smith scanned the waters between the two ships with a pair of binoculars. 'There, I see them!' he said to the helmsman on graveyard shift.

'Are Summer and Mr Pitt with them?'

'It's too dark to tell. I'm going down to meet them at the boom crane to find out.'

The captain made his way to the port side rail, where two crewmen were waiting with a crane to retrieve the inflatable. Smith caught a glimpse of the boat as it cut around the stern and turned up the ship's flank. It hung tight against the hull, hiding within the ship's shadow as it approached the crane.

Smith stepped to the side rail and leaned over, anxious to see if Pitt and Summer were aboard. Instead, he saw a boat full of black-clad commandos, followed a short distance behind by a second boat. The first inflatable raced to a stop as a pair of grappling hooks attached to rope ladders flew over the ship's rail. Two commandos sprang up the ladders and vaulted the rail.

The NUMA captain reacted with a shout, shoving the nearest intruder over the rail and back into the boat below. The second commando, the team's leader, didn't wait for a repeat performance. He leveled a pistol at Smith and pulled the trigger.

A hundred yards away, Dirk and Giordino heard the popping of gunfire. Although they hadn't seen the commandos race by, they could guess what was happening.

A few yards from the ship, Dirk swung the inflatable wide around its bow. Under the glow of the ship's lights, he could see the two assault boats tied amidships with a lone sentry guarding them.

Giordino pointed at the guard, and Dirk nodded. Turning away from the ship, he steered the inflatable in a wide loop until they could see the back of the sentry and then he turned the boat home. With their electric motor, they could approach with stealth.

The sentry was focused on the ship above when Dirk's inflatable came out of nowhere and rammed him broadside. Giordino leaped off the bow and was on the man before he knew what had happened. Lifting the guard off his feet, Giordino slammed him down. His head smacked the housing of the outboard, knocking him out cold. Giordino wasted no time, tearing the rifle from the guard's hands and scaling the side of the ship.

By the time Dirk maneuvered his inflatable alongside the hull and climbed over the side rail, Giordino was out of sight. Moving forward, he recoiled as he tripped over the bloodied body of a crewman, lying facedown.

The ship was oddly quiet, the main deck deserted. Where were the other commandos – and Giordino?

Figuring Giordino would head for the bridge, he followed suit, heading down the deck until he found the port stairwell – and stepped right into the barrel of a waiting pistol.

Too late, he saw the companionway was cramped with bodies. Captain Smith sat on the steps with a dazed seaman, nursing a bloodied shoulder and leg. Giordino, sporting a nasty gash on his head, stood with a pair of scientists under guard by two commandos.

Then came Calzado, the commando leader, who held his pistol at Dirk's cheekbone. 'Good of you to join us. I missed making your acquaintance aboard the *Sea Raker.*'

Dirk had no reply as another commando thundered down the steps, stopping at Calzado's side.

'The bridge is secure, sir,' he reported. 'We have complete control of the ship.'

45

Dirk and Giordino hoisted Smith to his feet and half carried, half dragged the wounded captain out of the stairwell. A trail of blood followed across the deck as Calzado marched them at gunpoint to the stern. They found the remaining scientists and crew being herded, under armed guard, into two of the ship's labs. Calzado motioned for them to join the group being squeezed into the nearer wet lab. Inside, Dirk found the ship's doctor and brought him to the captain.

'What are our casualties?' Smith asked in a weak voice as the doctor examined the shoulder wound. The captain looked like he would pass out at any moment.

The ship's first officer, a gangly man named Barnes, responded first. He wore only his skivvies, having been rousted from his bunk at gunpoint. 'Assistant Engineer Dyer was killed on deck, sir. We have at least four other serious injuries but none life-threatening.'

'Did the bridge get off an emergency call or beacon?'

Barnes shook his head. 'No, sir. They stormed the bridge before anyone knew what was happening. The helmsman reported they were unable to issue any kind of emergency signal. The boarders are still holding Ross on the bridge.'

Captain Smith turned to Giordino. 'Did you see any signs of Summer or Pitt?'

'We found the *Starfish* on board their ship, next to their seabed mining equipment. They must still be aboard.' He refused to consider a less positive outcome.

The captain wheezed. 'Who in blazes are they?'

'The ship is named *Sea Raker*,' Giordino said. 'It's staffed like a destroyer, not a mining ship. Armed soldiers all over the place. They look to me like Cuban regulars.'

Confirmation came a moment later when the door to the lab burst open. Calzado stepped across the threshold and regarded the cramped bay with a surly glare.

'The *Sargasso Sea* has been seized for violating the territorial sovereignty of Cuba,' he said in clipped English. 'You are now prisoners of the state.'

'We haven't entered Cuban waters,' Barnes said.

Calzado looked at the first officer and gave a cold smile. 'It is my duty to warn you that any attempt at escape or interference with the operation of the ship will be met with severe consequences. You will stay here and remain quiet.'

He turned on his heels and marched out. A pair of commandos slammed the door closed and locked it.

'That's a load of bunk,' Barnes said. 'We are positioned over five miles from Cuba's territorial limit.'

The ship's engines rumbled, and they could feel the vessel get under way.

'If we're not in Cuban waters now,' Dirk said, 'we will be shortly.'

Smith closed his eyes as if asleep, but he spoke in a firm voice. 'Let's not tempt fate. Headquarters can still track us and will be alerted when we don't report in. There will be help headed our way in no time. I want everyone to stay put and do as the man says.'

For Giordino, the words fell on deaf ears. He was already pacing the lab like a caged tiger, calculating a way to pounce on his captors.

46

Pitt and Summer were detained in the office for half a day, until they heard several men enter the office complex. The newcomers convened in an adjacent executive office. With its thin walls and both doors left open, the two captives could hear every word.

'All right, Molina, what is the great emergency that required my presence today?'

Juan Díaz put his feet on a large mahogany desk and looked down his nose at the mining operations manager seated across from him. Despite his own time in the Revolutionary Army, Díaz had an open disdain for the military.

'*Comandante*, you always stated that the mining operation is to be conducted with absolute secrecy,' Lieutenant Silvio Molina said. Though Díaz no longer held military rank, the militia on-site addressed him in deference to his powerful family connections.

'Yes, of course,' Díaz said. 'You and your men were handpicked to oversee the operation on account of your loyalty to the general.'

'During our excavations last night, we had an intrusion at the Domingo 1 site.'

Díaz glanced at an oversized map of the Florida

Straits pinned to one wall. An irregular circle, drawn in green and denoted Domingo 1, was marked northeast of Havana. 'Go on.'

'An American marine research ship named the *Sargasso Sea* arrived at dusk and moored near the wellhead site –'

'The *Sargasso Sea*?' Díaz said. 'Wasn't that the vessel that was nosing around after the drill ship was sunk?'

'Yes, it is a vessel of the National Underwater and Marine Agency. They were the ones that picked up the survivors of the *Alta*.'

'What are they doing back at the site?'

'I don't know.' Molina shrugged. 'Perhaps they are performing an inspection for the Norwegian owners of the ship. Or perhaps they are CIA.'

'The destruction of the drill ship was made to look like an accident,' Díaz said. 'Those were your orders.'

'And it was so accomplished. But I warned you it could attract unwanted attention.'

'We're on a schedule, and we needed more time to complete the excavation. If the late Minister Ortiz hadn't given them that sector, of all places, to drill in, we would never have had a problem. We had no choice but to remove them from the site.' Díaz scowled. 'I see that the barge is offloading a new shipment. What are our latest stockpile figures?'

'Including the current barge load, we estimate a total of two hundred and eighty tons in readied stockpile. The customer supply ship is arriving in the morning to collect the first half order of two hundred and fifty tons.'

Díaz stood and approached the wall map. In addition to the green circle, there were two red circles twenty and thirty miles farther north into the Florida Straits. He motioned toward them. 'The thermal vents at Domingo 2 and Domingo 3 are each ten times the size of Domingo 1. They will easily provide the balance of our delivery, if our yield percentages are accurate.'

'Domingo 1 has proven better than anticipated,' Molina said. 'We've seen uranium oxide content in excess of fifty per cent, which far exceeds the highest known yields from any terra firma mines, even those in Athabasca, Canada.'

'The very reason we pursued the high-cost operations of undersea mining. When will the *Sea Raker* be finished at the current field?'

Molina looked at the floor. 'That's uncertain. They had completed eighty-five per cent of the field operations but are standing by at the moment while repairing damage to the ship.'

'What damage?' Díaz asked.

'It was the American research vessel. While we were conducting excavation operations, they sent down a submersible that approached our bulk cutter machine. We were able to remotely acquire the submersible and bring it aboard the ship.'

'You what!' Díaz said, flying out of his chair.

'It was recording our operation. Calzado, on the *Sea*

Raker, reported that his men concealed the submersible on the ship and sent its two pilots ashore this morning with the barge. A short time later, two men from the NUMA ship boarded the *Sea Raker,* apparently in search of their comrades. They were discovered but escaped. And they caused some damage with the bulk cutter before they got away.'

Díaz's face had turned red. 'So this NUMA ship is aware of our operation and knows we captured their submersible?'

'Calzado reports that he and an armed party have taken control of the American ship. He doesn't believe they had a chance to issue a call for help.'

Díaz stared at him. 'You did all this without my authorization?'

'It was an urgent military operation and the hour was late. I did wake the general and obtained his approval.'

Díaz glared at the lieutenant. 'You don't think the Americans will miss their research ship?'

'The vessel has been relocated closer to shore. If they raise trouble, we can accuse them of spying in our waters.'

'This has endangered the entire operation just as we are in the final stretch.' He stared at Molina with cold determination. 'We must accelerate the excavations at Domingo 2 and 3 at once. I will see if our customer will make early acceptance of the second delivery.'

'The *Sea Raker* can proceed to the next two fields and set the explosives while the bulk cutter is repaired.'

'When can they resume mining?'

'Within twenty-four hours, if not sooner.'

'Do it,' Díaz said. 'Do it now! We may not have even that long before the American ship becomes a major liability. I'm returning to Havana to meet with the general. Have the *Sea Raker* moved to the Domingo 2 site at once.'

As he rose to leave, Molina stopped him. 'What about the submersible pilots we captured?'

'Are they still on the barge?'

'They're right next door.'

Díaz took his seat with an exasperated sigh. 'All right, let me see them.'

47

Pitt and Summer had heard every word. They were shocked at the news that the *Sargasso Sea* had been captured. Pitt was less surprised about the intrusion and damage aboard the *Sea Raker*, obviously Al and Dirk's handiwork.

The stakes were suddenly much higher. Absconding with a nosy submersible was one thing, but boarding and commandeering a NUMA ship was something else. The secrecy and paranoia meant the mining project was a high-stakes operation – with even greater environmental consequences at risk from the two untapped thermal vents.

'If those other two vents are ten times larger than the one at the *Alta* site,' Summer said, 'what happens when they blast those open? Rudi said they already had a report of elevated mercury levels near Andros Island in the Bahamas.'

'Multiply the existing contamination by twenty and you've got a full-blown environmental catastrophe,' Pitt said. 'As Rudi pointed out, there's an exponential risk to marine life due to migrating species passing through the mercury plumes.'

'During the BP oil disaster, the great fear was that the spill would reach the Florida Straits and carry up the East Coast,' Summer said. 'The danger here is much worse. If the toxins are released in the middle of the Florida Straits, the methyl mercury could spread through the food chain and contaminate fish stocks from Texas to New England.'

Two armed soldiers roused them from their chairs and escorted them to the room next door.

'These are the two people who were spying on our mining operation,' Molina said as they were brought into the office.

Díaz nearly fell out of his chair at the sight of Summer. She was equally shocked to find her captor was Juan Díaz, but she found her words first.

'*Professor* Díaz,' she said with a sarcastic emphasis on the title. 'I didn't know your anthropology skills included murder and kidnapping.'

'There is much about me you don't know, Summer Pitt,' he said.

She started to respond, then looked past Díaz. Resting on a sturdy table in the corner of the office was the Aztec stone she had discovered at Zimapán. The horror of the events that followed came flooding back. 'You murdered Dr Torres in cold blood.'

Díaz responded with a cold smile.

'You know this woman?' Molina asked.

'Yes. We have a shared passion for Aztec history.' He

walked over to the stone and grazed his fingertips across its surface. 'A pity the other half didn't remain aboard the wreckage of the *Oso Malo* in Jamaica.'

'Yes,' Summer said, regaining her composure. 'Ironic, actually. The other half ended up in Havana, destroyed on the *Maine*. It was under your nose all along.'

'Yes, I, too, discovered that Dr Boyd was aboard the *Maine* with the other half of the stone when the ship blew up. Still, you have been very helpful in providing data on where the treasure may still lie.'

'What treasure?'

Díaz stared at her. 'You mean, you don't know the stone's significance?'

He let out a bellowing laugh as he stepped to a bookcase filled with small stone carvings and artifacts. He picked up a figurine and set it on the desk in front of Summer. 'Only a fool would risk his life for the sake of science.'

It was a figurine of a dog made of solid gold. The design had an ancient look, which Summer suspected was Aztec. 'Where did you steal this? The Veracruz University Museum of Anthropology?'

'It was discovered at the bottom of the sea during one of our mineral surveys.'

'On a long canoe,' Pitt said, 'about thirty miles northwest of Montego Bay.' He had kept silent as the others talked, trying to edge closer to the wall map. A jab from a guard's rifle kept him from discerning its markings.

Díaz bristled at the comment. He picked up the

figurine and returned it to the shelf. Then he stepped over to Summer. Reaching down, he grabbed a fistful of long red hair and yanked her head forward. 'Tell me – now! – why are you here?'

Pitt lunged across the room, his hands still pinioned behind his back, and plowed his shoulder into Díaz.

Díaz sprawled back across his desk as the two guards jumped on Pitt and held him back. Molina unholstered a Makarov pistol and leveled it at Pitt.

Díaz staggered to his feet and glared at Pitt, then regarded Summer. 'A family resemblance, it seems. Your daughter?' he asked Pitt.

Pitt said nothing, appraising him with contempt.

'Perhaps she can entertain my men during your stay.' Díaz turned to the soldiers. 'Get him out of my sight – now!'

The soldiers dragged Pitt out of the office, leaving Summer alone with Díaz and Molina. Díaz opened a desk drawer and pulled out a knife with a carved obsidian blade. He showed it to Summer, then pressed its blade lightly against her cheek. 'Now, where were we?'

Summer gritted her teeth. 'We are tracking the outbreak of mercury pollutants.'

Díaz nodded and pulled away the knife, leaving a thin trace of blood.

'Your mining operation has released toxic plumes that are destroying large swaths of marine life,' she said. 'The plumes are visible by satellite. We tracked the latest one here and came to investigate. The mercury is creating a huge environmental risk.'

Díaz nodded. He was aware of the methyl mercury toxins being released from his underwater blasting but was indifferent to its consequences. 'Perhaps the mercury is problematic, but it will dissipate over time.'

'Irreparable harm has already been done to marine life. And your mining here, in the Florida Straits, could have serious effects throughout the entire Gulf of Mexico and the Atlantic Coast.'

'Harmful to the US, in other words? That is no concern of mine.' Díaz laughed. 'I'm afraid you are too late for that.'

He stepped to the Aztec stone and admired it a moment before tapping it with the obsidian knife. 'Yes, too late for that. But maybe . . .' He tapped the stone once more. 'Maybe you will be here with me when I recover the second stone and complete the message of the Aztecs.'

48

The pilot killed the smoky outboard motor, allowing the skiff to drift with the current. A man on the bow tossed a purse seine net over the side, allowing the movement of the boat to spread its floats. Taking a seat on the forward bench, he made a show of regulating the net's lines. Hesitating a moment, he waved a hand across his nose while gazing at the catch in the bottom. 'Man, these fish have gone bad.'

Seated by the outboard motor, James Maguire laughed. 'Hopefully, they'll deter anyone from searching the boat.'

In ragged T-shirts and dirty baseball caps, the pair looked like local Cayman Island fishermen. They certainly didn't resemble hired mercenaries. Maguire was in fact a former Marine Corps sniper and CIA field operative. Marty Gomez was an ex–Navy SEAL. Only a keen observer would notice the paltry catch they had hauled in over the past six hours, due in part to Maguire intentionally slicing a hole in the center of the net.

While Gomez made a show of yanking on a snagged net, Maguire slouched in the stern and raised a compact pair of binoculars to his eyes. He focused on a small white yacht moored to a buoy a hundred yards away. There was nothing remarkable about the boat, except for a crisp Cuban flag that flapped above its flybridge.

Maguire shifted his gaze to two Revolutionary Armed Forces patrol boats just beyond, which circled the yacht in a slow, continuous loop.

'We're losing daylight,' Gomez said. 'Are you going in?'

They had spent the better part of the day inching close to the yacht. A few hours earlier, one of the guard boats had whisked by for a look but took no interest in the derelict craft.

Maguire looked from one patrol boat to the other, then lowered his binoculars. 'Those boys look half asleep. My grandma could probably pull off the job in a pink rowboat. Anchor us down and I'll be on my way.'

Gomez lowered an anchor beneath the net lines and tied it off.

Reaching beneath the pile of rotting fish, Maguire retrieved a plastic box containing a small dive computer. Activating a digital compass, he took a sighting of the yacht and programmed a path to its estimated position, then strapped the mechanism to his arm.

'Ready to roll.' He removed his hat and sandals. 'Give me some cover.'

'Roger.' Gomez stood with an armful of netting, blocking Maguire from view of the patrol boats. 'I'll keep the lights on.'

Maguire took a last look at the yacht and slipped

over the transom. He swam beneath the boat, its underside not looking anything like its shabby topside appearance. He pulled himself past twin impellers and a set of extending hydrofoils, which had propelled the *Surprise* at over forty knots during its offshore voyage from the workboat the night before.

The boat's slick hull now resembled a rack from a sporting goods store. Maguire grabbed a tank and buoyancy compensator that hung from a hook and popped the regulator into his mouth. A mask and fins came next, then a weight belt. Once outfitted, he swam over to two other concealed items. The first was a hardened plastic box affixed to the hull with a large suction device. He twisted a grip handle, pulled it clear of the boat, and attached it to his BC. Then he grabbed a small diver propulsion unit dangling from a rope. Taking a bearing from his dive computer, he held the water scooter in front of him and powered it on.

He whisked through the water, angling the scooter until he was thirty feet deep and beyond clear view of the surface. The visibility was good, allowing him to see well ahead as schools of fish darted out of his path. Tracking his progress on the computer, he hesitated at reaching his designated end point. The seafloor was empty, so he continued another fifty feet before spotting his target, a large concrete mooring block. His line was true, he had just underestimated the distance.

Powering off the scooter, he set it on the mooring block and ascended a chain that ran to a metal float overhead. Looking up, he could see the outline of the yacht floating above him. He checked its orientation, then moved amidships just aside of the keel line and brushed some marine growth from a small area on the hull. He secured the suction device, along with the plastic box containing five pounds of high explosives and an electric detonator.

He unwound a thin spool of wire attached to the detonator and stretched the wire down to the mooring float. With some plastic ties, he secured it to the float chain and carefully ascended. Just beneath the surface, he affixed a small receiver to the base of the float and extended a flat wire antenna out of the water, plastering it to the side of the float with a wad of putty. With a reassuring tug on the wire, he swam back down the chain and retrieved his underwater scooter.

Ten minutes later, he was alongside Gomez, guiding his skiff down the coast under a setting sun, just another tired Cayman fisherman bringing home his meager catch.

49

A thousand thoughts raced through Pitt's mind, but foremost was concern for his daughter's safety. Pitt's children had been raised by their now deceased mother, so he had missed their childhood upbringing. When Dirk and Summer entered his life as young adults, he had instantly bonded with them. Working together at NUMA had instilled a trusting relationship, allowing their shared love of the sea to draw them even closer. Although Pitt knew his daughter was a tough and savvy young woman, her safety still tugged at his heart.

He focused on the more immediate problem. He had been thrown into an empty storage closet near Díaz's office, secured with a thick door and a sliding-bolt lock. Save for an overhead light fixture attached to the plaster ceiling, the tiny room was bare.

His wrists were still bound behind his back with the cable tie. But that was no barrier, as the Cubans had never searched him. Stretching out on the floor, he lay on his side and twisted his arms until he worked a hand into his front pocket. The penknife from the *Starfish* was buried deep, but he grasped it and pulled it out. Working by touch behind his back, he opened the blade and sawed through the tie.

Once free, he rose to his feet and massaged his wrists while studying the closet door. Again his luck held. Though it was locked on the outside, the door opened inward, held in place by three tubular hinges. Pitt again went to work with the penknife, prying two pins from their hinges while loosening the third. Then it became a waiting game.

Pitt could still hear voices in the office and he sat and waited for silence. Once he heard the slide of the bolt latch, he jumped back from the door, pocketing the loose pins and hiding his wrists behind his back. A guard stuck his head in and tossed a bottle of water and an empty bucket toward Pitt, then departed.

When an hour of silence had passed, Pitt pried the last pin from its hinge. Working the knife blade into the doorframe, he wedged open the back side and peered through the crack. He could see no one. Grasping the door, he yanked it into the closet and pulled the bolt free of its latch. He slid the bolt over and replaced the door on its hinges, securing it with one of the pins. Finally, he stepped out of the closet and locked the door behind him.

But the office complex wasn't empty. He heard two men conversing down the corridor, so he headed the other direction, toward the entrance. He checked the office where he and Summer had first been held, but the room was empty. Summer, he suspected, was no longer in the building.

The voices grew louder, so Pitt ducked into Díaz's open office and closed the door behind him. He stepped to the wall map showing the Florida Straits. The chart had three circles marked in red and green. The smallest he recognized as the location where the *Alta* had sunk. With a sense of dread, he saw that the two red circles were farther offshore, near the center of the strait. They could only be the next thermal vents targeted for destruction and they were in the worst possible location.

At the center of the Florida Straits, the Florida Current was in high gear, generating a northeast flow in excess of three knots. Pitt knew counterclockwise gyres spun off the current, cycling water to the eastern Florida shoreline. He followed the path of the Florida Current as it curled up the coast to join the Gulf Stream. Miami Beach appeared on the map barely a hundred miles away. The miners couldn't have picked a worse location if they'd intentionally tried to commit environmental sabotage.

With a sinking feeling, Pitt envisioned the invisible tide of death. If the thermal vents were blown and the mercury release was of the expected magnitude, the devastation would be wholesale. Contaminated waters, dead marine life, and extinguished fish stocks could plague the entire East Coast. It would make the BP oil spill look like a minor nuisance.

He briefly perused the desk, spotting a calendar with several handwritten notations. An entry marked the imminent arrival of a vessel named *Algonquin*. Below the ship's name was the notation '250 tons at 45% yield.'

Pitt rifled through the desk drawers, finding only routine paperwork and a crude obsidian knife. He palmed the knife when he heard voices outside the door.

The voices receded, and he stepped to the shelf of artifacts. The collection of clay pots, stone carvings and gold jewelry was stacked high. A mahogany paddle sat on the top shelf, a reproduction, Pitt presumed, of one used with the Aztec canoe. At the far end of the shelf, he noticed a framed drawing of a page from a Meso-American codex.

Picking it up, Pitt saw that it showed a man in a green feather headdress lying facedown. In the background, two men wearing eagle-beaked head coverings were loading a chest into a small canoe. Pitt gazed at the drawing for a long while, then considered the half stone next to it.

'Well, I'll be . . .' he muttered, patting the stone in understanding. 'No wonder the big fuss.'

He put the stone out of his mind, focusing on locating Summer and figuring a way to halt the blasting of the thermal vents. But first he had to find his way out of the building. As far as he could tell, there was only one entrance. It was sure to be guarded.

Pitt opened the door to Díaz's office and listened. The corridor was silent, the back-office occupants having apparently left the building.

Testing the waters, he stepped into the hall and made his way toward the foyer. He froze after seeing an armed guard standing by the front receptionist desk, looking out the window. There was too much distance to approach undetected, so Pitt backtracked down the hall – with an idea.

He returned to Díaz's office and studied the phone. It was an older executive model with push buttons for multiple lines. Pitt lifted the receiver and began pushing the buttons until a ringing erupted from the front reception. He set the receiver on the desk, moved to the shelf, and removed the mahogany paddle.

Pitt stepped into the hall and crept toward the foyer. The phone continued ringing at the reception desk as the guard paced its perimeter with a look of annoyance. After five minutes, the irritation became too great and he picked up the receiver. *'Hola? Hola?'*

When there was no response, he slammed down the receiver. Detecting a movement behind him, he spun around to find Pitt in a home run swing with the paddle. It struck him on the side of the head, knocking him on to the receptionist desk. He sprang forward in a daze, only to collect another blow to the opposite side of his skull that laid him out.

Pitt grabbed the limp body and dragged it to the locked closet. Pulling him inside, he removed the man's camouflage jacket and pants and slipped them on over his own clothes. He locked the man in the closet and made his way to the front of the building, grabbing the soldier's AK-47 for good measure.

He peered outside, finding the immediate area quiet. Treading cautiously out of the building, Pitt moved in a frantic hunt to find his daughter.

50

Admiral Raphael Semmes awoke with a start. His ears prickled at a distant sound and he let out a low growl.

The twenty-pound tabby cat rose from his floor pillow, stretched his legs, and hopped on to a king-sized bed. Approaching his sleeping master, he brushed his whiskers against the man's cheeks and began meowing.

St Julien Perlmutter roused from a dream and pushed the cat from his face. 'What is it, Admiral?'

The cat responded with a loud meow, then hopped off the bed and waited near the doorway. Perlmutter took notice and dragged himself out of bed. His cat wasn't prone to feeble neediness. Indeed, he had proven himself something of a fine house guard. Once, he had alerted Perlmutter to a forgotten strudel burning in the oven. Another time, he garnered his owner's attention when some neighborhood kids tried to take his vintage Rolls-Royce for a joyride.

Pulling on a robe and slippers, Perlmutter walked to the door, then hesitated when he heard a sound downstairs. From a display shelf above his dresser, he pulled down a large marlinespike. Nearly the size of a truncheon, the polished metal pin had been used by seamen during the age of sail to splice heavy ropes. With his de facto weapon, Perlmutter stepped down the stairs as quietly as his large frame could muster.

At the base of the stairs, he saw the glow of a penlight coming from his study. He stepped to the doorway and was reaching for the light switch when Admiral Semmes meowed loudly. The penlight's beam swung to the doorway, shining in Perlmutter's eyes.

He shielded his eyes from the light. 'What's going on here?' the marine historian boomed.

He heard a scurrying of papers, so he reached once more for the light switch.

Before he could flick the switch, a heavy book was flung at him and struck the side of his face.

Perlmutter shook off the blow and charged into the dark room, shouting, 'Heathen!'

The penlight blinked off, but Perlmutter stepped toward its source and swung the marlinespike in front of him in a wide arc. He cut only air, then was struck hard by a body blow to the side.

He reacted with a swipe of his free hand, clasping the jacket of the black-clad robber. Perlmutter yanked and the man flew into him. He was barely half Perlmutter's size and squirmed like a snake.

Perlmutter brought the marlinespike around and jabbed the blunt end into the man's ribs, causing a sharp cry. He tried to put his weight to use by grasping the man in a bear hug, but the intruder slipped free and retaliated with a kick to Perlmutter's knee.

Perlmutter buckled and staggered back, stepping on the tail of his cat. Admiral Semmes shrieked and clawed the floor as Perlmutter tried to dance clear. His feet became entangled and he tripped to one side. His head caught a corner of his desk and he crashed to the floor as the intruder bolted out the front door.

The next thing Perlmutter felt was Admiral Semmes's tongue lapping his face. He slowly sat up and rubbed the bump on his head. After a few minutes, the throbbing pain eased enough for him to stand. He flicked on the lights to inventory the room.

A front window had been jimmied open, providing the burglar entry. Yet little in the study had been disturbed. Valuable antiques and ship artifacts were left untouched, as was his collection of rare books. Everything was in its place, except for the leather-bound copy of *Moby-Dick* that had been hurled at him.

He checked his desk drawers, but they had not been touched. As he examined the desktop, he realized there was something missing – his file on Ellsworth Boyd and the sinking of the *Maine*.

He sat down and was about to call the police when Admiral Semmes jumped in his lap.

'Well, Admiral, it would seem the Pitts have stirred up a bit of trouble with the *Maine* and the Aztec artifact. It's a good thing I had already digested the complete file.'

The cat poked his head at Perlmutter's hand and he obliged by stroking the cat's back.

'I will say our tag team wrestling left a bit to be desired. But your early-warning system was superb. It's extra milk for you in the morning, my good friend.'

Admiral Semmes looked at him and purred.

51

Pitt spied a flurry of activity around the dockside facility. The ore barge had been emptied of its original cargo and was now being loaded with small wooden crates and large bins filled with heavy canvas sacks.

He stopped in the shadows and watched a team of men in a guarded storage pen load the sacks, which resembled dry concrete mix. Red signs marked *Explosivos* hung nearby. The sacks likely contained ANFO, or ammonium nitrate/fuel oil, a common industrial bulk explosive, while the small crates contained TNT. The explosives would soon be on their way to the *Sea Raker* for blasting open the thermal vents.

Pitt made his way past the pen to the two-storey building. He saw that the lower level was used for operations support. An equipment locker and a machine shop faced the water on the near side. At the far end was an open garage with a utility truck parked out front. The upper level looked to be barracks for the soldiers – a likely holding place for Summer.

He spotted a side stairway, crept to its base, and started climbing.

When he was halfway up, the door to the second level burst open and a soldier rushed out with a toolbox. There was little Pitt could do, so he simply lowered his head and picked up his pace. The soldier stormed past him without a glance.

At the top landing, Pitt took a deep breath and stepped inside. A dim corridor stretched before him, with multiple rooms on either side. All the doors were open except for one at the far end. Opposite the room, two soldiers leaned against the wall, smoking cigarettes.

Pitt walked toward them, trying to appear casual as he tightened his grip on the assault rifle slung over his shoulder.

Noting his approach, one of the soldiers spoke rapidly to his companion, then darted out an opposite exit, fearful he was about to be caught goldbricking. The other soldier extinguished his cigarette and stood at attention.

Pitt approached quickly, asking from a distance, *'Cigarillo?'*

The soldier reached into his pocket before realizing something was amiss. The approaching man was taller than any soldier he knew, his uniform was several sizes too short, and his craggy face was too mature for his rank.

Rather than extending a hand for the cigarette, the stranger jammed his rifle into the soldier's chest. Before he had a chance to react, Pitt commanded him, 'Drop your weapon.'

The guard nodded and let his rifle slip to the floor.

Pitt nudged him toward the door and told him to open it. The door was unlocked. The guard twisted the knob and flung it open. Summer was seated on a bunk inside, visibly working to free her bound wrists. She froze, then did a double take as Pitt entered with the guard ahead of him.

She gave him a tired smile. 'You join the Revolutionary Armed Forces?'

'The Boy Scouts wouldn't have me.'

Keeping his gun leveled on the guard, Pitt handed Summer his penknife. 'You okay?' He noted the light cut on her cheek.

She nodded. 'Received some idle threats from our host but was otherwise stuck here counting flies all day.'

'I think you'll need his cap and jacket.' Pitt motioned toward the guard.

Summer appropriated his attire. 'What do we do with him?'

'Tie him up. You can use those bedsheets, but start with this.' Pitt handed her the shoulder strap off his rifle.

She wrapped the man's wrists together behind his back, then stripped the sheets off the bed. She secured one around his elbows, then shoved him on the bed and tied his ankles together with the other. She finished the job by gagging him with a pillowcase.

'You did that very well,' Pitt said.

'I've had a bit of experience on the other end lately.'

297

Summer slipped on the guard's jacket and hat. Before they exited the room, Pitt retrieved the man's weapon from the floor and handed it to his daughter.

'I've never fired one of these.'

'You won't need to. Just act like you know how.'

They exited the building by the rear stairwell and ducked behind a dumpster to reconnoiter the dock.

'How do we get out of here?' she asked.

'The tug.'

Summer looked at her father and shook her head. 'Why don't we just sneak down the coast and find another boat? They'll be all over us here.'

'Because of the thermal vents. They're loading explosives aboard the barge right now in preparation for blowing the next two vents. We can't let that happen.'

Summer had heard that firm tone in her father's voice before. She knew there would be no changing his mind. And, rationally, he was right. If the Cubans blew up the thermal vents, it would cause an environmental catastrophe of untold proportions. They had to be stopped and there was no time to spare.

She just wished the job could fall to someone else. 'What did you have in mind?' she asked.

'Try to ignite the explosives on the dock – or on the barge. If we're lucky, maybe we can sink the barge with it. During the confusion, we'll slip out on the tug.'

'And if we're not lucky, we'll be blown sky-high?'

Pitt smiled and shook his head. 'The explosive

they're loading, ANFO, has a low volatility. Getting it to blow requires a secondary detonation. The best we can hope to do is ignite it and hope it burns like crazy.'

'"Crazy" is the operational word, all right.' She noticed her father's calm demeanor and her fears fell away. 'Okay, what can I do?'

Pitt rapped his knuckles against the trash bin. 'I need you to do a little dumpster diving while I round up some transportation. We could use an empty bottle or two, and perhaps a small open container. I'll be right back.'

Before she could answer, he rushed back to the barracks building and stepped to the front side. A short distance away, the storage garage was still open and the gas-powered utility cart parked in front. Pitt lingered near the side of the building as a truck loaded with explosives rumbled past on its way to the barge. Once it passed, he crept toward the open garage. Voices sounded from inside, where a pair of mechanics were overhauling a truck engine.

Pitt ignored the men and approached the cart. Releasing its emergency brake, he pushed it past the open garage door. The cart rolled easily, and the mechanics didn't notice the sound of crunching gravel under its tires. Pitt pushed it past the building and up to the dumpster.

Summer's head popped up from inside, a look of relief on her face when she saw that it was her father.

'Any luck?' he asked.

Summer nodded. 'Three empty rum bottles, a coffee can, and a pair of rats that nearly gave me cardiac arrest.' She passed the containers to Pitt, then leaped out of the dumpster like an Olympic high jumper.

Pitt held up the empty rum bottles. 'They didn't even leave us a last shot.'

'I'd trade a case of rum for a hot shower.' Summer wiped her hands on the borrowed fatigues.

Pitt had Summer stand watch while he went to work. He opened the utility truck's hood and located a rubber fuel line. Pulling it from the carburetor, he let the gas drain into the coffee can, then transferred it into the rum bottles, filling each half full. He reinstalled the fuel line, then sliced several lengths of cloth from his camouflage jacket. He stuffed these into the bottle tops, completing a trio of Molotov cocktails.

'Truck coming,' Summer whispered.

They ducked behind the cart as an empty truck rumbled to the pen for another load of explosives. Once it had passed, Pitt stood and placed the bottles in the back of the cart.

'The dock's clear,' he said. 'Let's get down there before the truck comes back.'

'How are we going to light the bottles?'

'Get behind the wheel and hit the starter for a second when I tell you.'

As Summer slid into the driver's seat, Pitt gathered some dry leaves and sticks and placed them in the coffee can. A thin layer of gasoline sloshed at the bottom, ensuring fuel for the fire. Pitt picked up the can and carried it to the cart's engine. He pulled a spark plug wire, dangled the end inside the coffee can, and motioned for Summer to turn the key.

A blue spark spat from the cable end and ignited the fuel in the bottom of the can. Pitt jammed the wire back on to the plug and jumped into the passenger seat with his canned campfire. Summer restarted the cart and drove down a short hill to the dock.

The barge was still tied up, with the tug astern. Summer drove on to the dock, thankful there were no soldiers nearby. Several men were working around a crane that was loading the barge with crated explosives. Others were positioned aboard the barge, securing the crates.

'See if you can get us past the crane without stopping.' Pitt hid the coffee can and bottles at his feet.

Keeping her head down, Summer maneuvered the cart past the stacked crates and around the crane. The soldiers were too busy loading the barge to pay any attention, save for the crane operator, who looked askance at Pitt's ill-fitting uniform. When Summer had made it past two stacked crates of explosives, Pitt told her to pull over.

Partially concealed by the crates, he grabbed a bottle and lit the rag with his coffee can fire. Stepping to the edge of the dock, he hurled it toward the center of the barge.

The bottle shattered against the top of an open bin, sending a shower of flame over the top sack of ANFO.

Pitt had barely hopped into the cart when he heard someone yell, 'Hey!' Just in front of them, two armed soldiers appeared.

'Go,' Pitt whispered.

Summer floored the accelerator, aiming the utility truck at the two men. The first jumped clear but the second hesitated. Summer clipped him in the thigh, sending him reeling to the side.

Pitt turned to see the first soldier regain his balance and raise his rifle. Quickly lighting the next rum bottle, he flung it to the ground in front of him. The glass exploded in a small fireball that engulfed the soldier's legs. A short burst of gunfire riddled the back of the cart before the soldier dropped to the ground and rolled to douse the flames.

'Where did they come from?' Pitt asked.

'I think they were loafing on the other side of the crate. Tug's just ahead.'

Pitt lit the final Molotov cocktail and flung it at the last stack of crates on the dock, engulfing it in flames.

Summer skidded to a stop in front of the tugboat and they both hopped out of the cart.

'Release the stern line,' Pitt said, 'then go to the wheelhouse and see if you can start her.'

'What if someone's aboard?'

'They probably won't be armed.' He patted the AK-47 under his arm.

Pitt ran to free the bow and spring mooring lines, then jumped on to the tug's narrow deck. He raced to the bow, where several towlines from the barge were wrapped around a trio of bollards. The lines had been drawn tight and Pitt worked feverishly to release them.

Ahead of him on the barge, he heard the cries of men trying to douse the flames, while others ran to quell the dock fire. It would be short order before the two injured soldiers would alert the others of their presence. He was relieved to hear the tug's diesel engine churn to life behind him.

Freeing the last of the barge lines, he scrambled across the squat deck and dashed to the wheelhouse, clutching the AK-47. Bursting through an open side door, he stopped in his tracks.

The wheelhouse was cramped and dim, but he could clearly see Molina standing with an arm locked around Summer's neck and a pistol held to her temple.

'Put down your weapon,' Molina said. 'It is not time to leave just yet.'

Behind him, he heard the sound of additional men charging from the dock and boarding the tug. Pitt could only look at his daughter in anguish as he slowly dropped his weapon to the deck.

52

'Rudi, you're here early.'

Vice President James Sandecker burst into the foyer of his office in the Eisenhower Executive Office Building like a rabid hyena. A fitness fanatic, he was dressed in a black jogging suit and followed by two out-of-breath Secret Service agents in similar attire.

'I wanted to catch you first thing.' Rudi Gunn was seated waiting on a sofa. 'How was your morning run?'

The worst-kept secret in Washington was that the Vice President took a three-mile run around the Mall at five-thirty every morning, much to the chagrin of his security detail.

'A D. C. cab nearly T-boned one of my boys here, but otherwise it's a glorious morning to be pounding the pavement.'

Sandecker opened the door to his office and waved Gunn in as the two agents waited outside for plainclothes replacements. The Vice President took his place behind a massive desk built from the timbers of a Confederate blockade runner. A retired admiral, Sandecker had been the founding head of NUMA, and Gunn had been one of the first he had hired. He still considered NUMA his baby, and kept close relations with Gunn and Pitt. 'What brings you here so early?'

'It's the *Sargasso Sea*. She was operating in the Florida Straits, about thirty miles northeast of Havana. Voice and data links have now been nonresponsive for more than twenty-four hours.'

'Any distress calls or emergency beacons?'

'No, sir.'

'She's captained by Malcomb Smith, isn't she?'

'That's correct.'

'He's a good man.'

'Pitt and Giordino are also aboard.'

Sandecker pulled out a thick cigar, his lone vice, and lit it up. 'What were they doing off Cuba? You weren't helping the CIA, were you?'

'No, nothing like that. They were tracking a series of toxic mercury plumes that have cropped up in the Caribbean.' Gunn explained the sites they'd surveyed off the southern coast of Cuba. 'Pitt believes the mercury plumes are the result of an underwater mining operation targeting hydrothermal vents. We've traced seismic events to each of the areas consistent with the signature of land mining explosions.'

'Underwater blasting?'

'That's what we think. Pitt was tracking some activity at a site in the Florida Straits when we lost contact.'

'Who's responsible for the mining?' Sandecker asked.

'We don't know yet, but we suspect Cuban involvement.'

'Have you searched for the ship?'

Gunn nodded and pulled a photo from an attaché case. 'Satellite imagery from six hours ago indicates she's still afloat.'

Sandecker looked at the dark image, which revealed two light smudges near its center. 'Can't tell much at night,' he remarked.

Gunn pulled out a color infrared image, which showed two oval bands of red in a sea of blue. 'We're confident that is the *Sargasso Sea*, alongside a ship we believe is called the *Sea Raker*. We backtracked through satellite images from the previous week, which confirmed the *Sargasso Sea*'s movements.'

'So who owns this *Sea Raker*?'

'A Canadian company called Bruin Mining and Exploration,' Gunn said. 'The ship is operating under lease to a Panamanian-registered entity with no real history. A rep from Bruin said he thought the ship was involved in a mining project off the west coast of Nicaragua but couldn't confirm where the ship was currently located.'

'Has anybody tried contacting this *Sea Raker*?'

Gunn nodded. 'Yes. The Coast Guard cutter *Knight Island* out of Key West was dispatched to the area. They radioed the *Sea Raker* but received no response.'

'So you think this *Sea Raker* may have boarded the *Sargasso Sea*?'

'That's my guess.'

'Why didn't the Coast Guard sail up alongside and see for themselves?'

'At last check, both vessels are sitting five miles inside Cuba's territorial waters. The *Knight Island* pushed the envelope and crossed the line to within sight of both vessels but then was challenged by a Cuban Navy corvette.'

Sandecker blew a ring of smoke toward the ceiling. 'So we need to put the hammer down on the Cuban government.'

'It's a presumed act of piracy.'

'If you assume the *Sea Raker* is in fact controlled by the Cubans. And if you assume that Pitt wasn't dallying in their territorial waters to begin with.' They both knew Pitt's tendency to bend the rules if a situation called for it.

'The tracking data suggests they were operating outside the territorial limit when contact was lost. At this point, it doesn't matter. We need to go get them.'

Sandecker rolled the cigar between his fingers, then placed it in an ashtray. He looked at Gunn with troubled eyes. 'I'm sorry, Rudi, but there's nothing we can do.'

Gunn recoiled from his chair. He knew Sandecker regarded Pitt like a son. 'What do you mean, there's nothing we can do?'

Sandecker shook his head. 'There are other events in play that involve the President. At the moment, we can't afford to stir the pot with the Cubans. That means no Navy, no Coast Guard, and no State Department. And no cowboy rescue attempts from NUMA. Check with me in another forty-eight hours and I'll see what I can do.'

'They might not have forty-eight hours.'

'My hands are tied.' Sandecker rose from his desk. 'If you'll excuse me, I need to shower and dress for a cabinet meeting in forty minutes.'

Gunn could only nod. He shuffled from the office with an angry despair. By the time he exited on to the street, his despair had turned to resolve. He dialed a number and waited until a gruff voice answered.

'Jack, this is Rudi. How soon can you meet me in Miami?'

53

The warmth of the morning sun only added to Maguire's fatigue. The mercenary pulled his hat down low over his eyes and let his mind wander. After an all-night reconnaissance of the white yacht, he and Gomez were bleary-eyed. They'd earn their paychecks shortly, he thought, envisioning the celebratory plate of crawfish étouffée he would enjoy upon returning to his home in Baton Rouge.

'I have a small boat heading toward the target.'

Maguire cocked open a tired eye. Gomez was hunkered down below the gunwale at the other end of the skiff, looking through a pair of binoculars.

'How many aboard?' Maguire asked.

'Three, plus the pilot. One looks like our man.'

Maguire looked toward the shoreline. The skiff was positioned two hundred yards offshore of the white yacht as they engaged in more pretend fishing. The former sniper wielded his own binoculars and zeroed in on an aqua speedboat racing from shore. One of the yacht's security patrol boats peeled off on an intercept course. But rather than challenge the speedboat, it looped alongside and escorted it to the yacht.

'Better start the video,' Maguire said. 'Let's see if we can get a positive ID.'

While Gomez swapped his binoculars for a video camera, Maguire pulled out a waterproof satchel and retrieved some photos. They all showed the same person: a short, fit, older man with gray hair, glasses, and a thin mustache. Most were distant shots, none particularly clear, but it was all they had been provided with. Maguire passed the best one to Gomez. 'What do you think?'

Gomez had already studied the photos. He took a glance, then checked the video camera's zoomed-in display screen. 'The guy in the gray suit looks like our boy.' He took a second look at the photo. 'You know, there's something familiar about him.'

Maguire nodded as he took another look at the speedboat – and the man in gray. The hair, the glasses, even the clothes seemed to match the photo. Alone, that wouldn't be enough for his usual precise manner of doing business. But his employer had told him to expect the target to visit the yacht in the morning and there he was. He reached into his satchel and powered on a small transmitter.

The speedboat slowed and pulled astern of the yacht. Gray Suit's two companions climbed up a stepladder first and helped the older man aboard. From their cropped hair, hefty builds and ill-fitting suits, Maguire could tell they were a security detail. They escorted the older man into the main salon, then returned to the speedboat. With the patrol boat at its side, the speedboat raced back toward shore.

'Strange that his security detail left him aboard alone,' Gomez said.

'He's probably got a girlfriend on the way, or maybe one already waiting for him in the master cabin.'

'If so, she must be invisible. I haven't seen any sign of life aboard in the last twenty-four hours.' He looked at his partner. 'Video's still running.'

Maguire nodded, then pressed a red button on the transmitter as casually as flipping a light switch.

It sent a radio signal to the antenna Maguire had wrapped around the mooring buoy the day before. The transmission triggered a battery-induced charge to the detonator caps in the plastic case suctioned to the yacht's hull. Their detonation in turn ignited the five pounds of plastic high explosives.

A low bellow echoed across the surface as the yacht rose out of the water in a fountain of smoke, flame and debris. By the time particles of the yacht began raining in a wide, circular swath, Gomez had the skiff's outboard motor started. Any remnants of the yacht that didn't disintegrate in the blast quickly vanished under the waves.

As Gomez motored the skiff away, Maguire observed the scene with a morbid satisfaction. No man could have survived the blast, he thought. Then there came another rumble, this one from his stomach. All he could think about was crawfish étouffée.

54

General Alberto Gutier's large corner office in the Interior Ministry Building was a model of vanity. The large-windowed suite, commanding a prime view of Havana's Plaza de la Revolución, was plastered with photos of himself. Some showed Gutier as a handsome young officer commanding troops in Angola. Others showed him speaking with one – or both – of the Castro brothers. A few even showed Gutier with his own brother. But most were solo portraits of the man, gazing into the camera with mercurial poses of self-importance.

A look of aggravation registered on the flesh-and-blood face of Gutier as his younger brother strolled into the office. Juan Díaz, who had been given his late stepfather's surname while a boy, helped himself to a seat in front of Gutier's massive executive desk.

'You leave the country for a week, and when you return, there is nothing but chaos,' Gutier said. 'You know I can't afford any exposure with the mining operation – especially now. What is going on up there?'

'An American research ship, the *Sargasso Sea*, came snooping around the Domingo 1 site as we were concluding extractions.'

'Isn't that the same vessel that happened by when you sank the drill ship?'

'The *Alta*. Yes, that was happenstance. But there was no happenstance in their return to the site. If they are to be believed, they were tracking plumes of mercury that are being released in the sea when the thermal vents are blown.'

'I told you that was a mistake to sink the drill ship.' Gutier scowled.

'If we didn't clear the site, we couldn't complete our excavation. And if we didn't complete the excavation, we would fall short of our promised delivery.'

'You are naïve,' Gutier said. 'This vessel is CIA, and they've discovered our deal with the North Koreans.'

'I don't think so. I've confirmed that the mercury releases are occurring. Quite a large disturbance has been created from the Domingo 1 site.'

'Will that be of harm to Cuba?'

'No, the currents will carry it northeast.'

'That is good but no proof of the Americans' intentions.'

'The vessel's history tracks to strictly oceanographic projects,' Díaz said. 'And we found no weapons or covert equipment aboard the ship. As you know, one of its submersibles was caught examining our excavation. Two men from the American ship then snuck aboard the *Sea Raker* and caused some damage. Commander Calzado felt it imperative to launch a counterassault, which you authorized. This was successful and the research ship has been relocated to our territorial waters.'

'There was no choice,' Gutier said, 'but now we are playing with fire.'

'I feel the same, but it has already been done. There has been no outcry from the Americans yet, so we still have time to bury things.'

Gutier relaxed slightly. 'This still has the potential to blow the lid on our entire project.'

'I've performed some calculations,' Díaz said. 'We now have sufficient quantity to exceed by twenty tons our first delivery, which, incidentally, is scheduled for pickup tomorrow. I've taken the liberty of accelerating our final shipment to three weeks from today. Our customer has arranged for shipping accordingly.'

'That's two months earlier than we agreed.'

'Yes, but the ore at Domingo 1 has proved a much higher grade than the previous sites. The customer will accept a reduced quantity on the second shipment if the ore contains a uranium oxide content exceeding thirty per cent. We're seeing amounts surpassing fifty per cent, and I expect Domingo 2 and 3 to show similar yields. I've sent explosives to the sites in order to open the vents as soon as possible. If we blow the vents and begin extraction immediately, we can meet the shipment schedule. We just need to keep the Americans at bay until then.'

'You are asking a lot, but I suppose we have little choice,' Gutier said. 'What about the mercury poisoning? I believe Domingo 2 and 3 are much larger thermal vents.'

'Yes, it could create an environmental disaster for the Americans.' Díaz stared up at a portrait of his brother, wearing his finest dress uniform while astride a black stallion.

'Alberto, it was I who discovered the uranium deposits during our oil surveys with the Mexicans. I was merely investigating the possibility of mining gold or silver from the vents. The existence of uranium – and in such high content – was a complete surprise. Yet it was you who saw the potential to use it to strengthen Cuba in the world. Our own leaders are not even aware of what you have accomplished.'

'Which makes it all the more damaging if things are revealed too soon.'

'You knew the risks when you engaged the North Koreans. Trading a thousand tons of high-grade uranium ore for a pair of tactical nuclear missiles was a bold gesture – and it remains such.'

'Bold but risky,' Gutier said. 'I regret to say it was not even my idea. The Koreans wish to enlarge their nuclear arsenal and are short of the raw materials to do it. The issue just happened to surface while we were discussing a small-arms trade. Still, it is a brilliant proposal.'

'A nuclear-armed Cuba will no longer be a pushover for the Americans,' Díaz said.

'We will take a rightful seat among the world's powers.' Gutier clenched his fist, recalling their father's death at the Bay of Pigs invasion. 'Unfortunately, the deal can still unravel quickly.'

'Not with half the order going out tomorrow. But what of your own status? I thought you were anticipating some movement soon.'

Gutier checked his phone. 'I am waiting for news at any moment.'

'The people look up to power,' Díaz said. 'Bringing these weapons to Cuba will make you the country's most powerful man. You will have achieved something that even Fidel could not.'

The words played on Gutier's ego and his anger softened. 'I am still concerned about this American ship and the possible repercussions.'

'We can say they were defecting.' Díaz smiled. 'Convert the ship to our own use and quietly send the crew to a political prison.'

Gutier stared out the window, searching for a better idea. His phone beeped and he found an anonymous email with a video file attached. He played the twenty-second clip and a wide smile crossed his face.

'This changes matters.' He held up his phone and replayed the video.

Díaz watched as a man boarded a yacht, which moments later blew up in a massive fireball. A shocked look crossed Díaz's face. 'That man on the boat – he looks a lot like Raúl.'

'It is Raúl. He was in the Cayman Islands for a meeting of the Community of Latin American and

Caribbean States. I had privileged information that he would be staying aboard a yacht owned by the Cayman's deputy governor.' Gutier beamed. 'It would seem there was an unfortunate accident.'

Díaz shook his head in disbelief. 'My brother, *that* is a risky operation.'

'It was handled by outside elements. Professionals who have no interest in talking even if they thought they were killing somebody else.' Gutier gave a wry smile. 'My only regret is that Foreign Minister Ruiz was not aboard. He was scheduled to have joined Raúl but canceled at the last moment.'

'An audacious action nevertheless. On the heels of Fidel's passing, it will be a great shock to our country. Perhaps it is best that Ruiz was not there as suspicions might have been directed at you. On the other hand, you are still left in a precarious situation. The foreign minister is a lock to succeed Raúl, once our feeble vice president succumbs. You will not be able to maintain your position of power when that happens.'

Gutier showed no concern. 'Perhaps you have provided the means to prevent that from happening.'

'What are you saying?'

'The Americans. They played right into our hands. Ruiz has made no secret of his desire to make peace with the United States and expand trade and tourism. His affection for America has always been his vulnerability. We'll exploit it by implicating this NUMA ship in the death of Raúl.'

Díaz's face lit up. 'Of course. The public will go berserk if they think the Americans killed Raúl. We can make it look like a planned coup, an attempt to install the foreign minister as head of the government.'

'Just the whiff of a connection would be enough for the Council of State to turn their back on Ruiz,' Gutier said. 'If not, I may be able to call on enough comrades in the military to back me in a temporary takeover while the charges are investigated.'

'The only thing better would be if you could claim credit for capturing the assassin,' Díaz said, his eyes dancing with inspiration. 'Forget the research ship, we can go one better. I'll give you the American in charge, a man named Pitt, who was aboard the submersible. We can pin the assassination on him.'

Gutier considered the prospect. 'Yes,' he said, 'we can certainly manufacture evidence to link him to the explosion. We'll have a public trial, which would boost anti-American sentiment . . . and assure in the process that Ruiz is disgraced.'

'And it will allow us to proceed with our deal with the North Koreans. But what should we do about the NUMA ship?'

'I have heard of no private enquiries from the American government,' Gutier said.

'Nor has there been any public reaction.'

'Then sink the ship with all hands,' Gutier said. 'It would be better not to have a chorus of denials. We can say it was lost in an accident. Or if the Americans resist, we'll claim it was a CIA ship in our waters supporting Raúl's assassination and the attempted coup. In the meantime, take a military helicopter to the facility to retrieve the prisoner and I'll arrange for it to appear as if he was apprehended in the Cayman Islands.'

As Díaz nodded, there came a knock at the door. A portly secretary entered the office with a troubled look on her face. 'I'm sorry to interrupt, sir, but there's been a news report from the Cayman Islands. It seems a boat the president was visiting caught fire and was damaged. There's speculation that the president may have been injured.'

Gutier nodded at his brother and rose to his feet. 'This is terrible news,' he said, escorting the secretary from the office. 'We must find out the truth of the matter at once.'

55

The Russian-built Mil Mi-8 helicopter flew in fast over the hills, slowing as it came to the clandestine mining facility. The pilot approached the concrete landing pad and set the chopper down on its center. He let the engines idle as Díaz unstrapped himself and hopped out of an open side door.

Molina waited to greet his boss, an armed guard at his side. Díaz turned to peruse the dock as he stepped off the helipad. The barge and tug were gone, replaced by a Liberian-flagged bulk carrier named *Algonquin*. The shore crew was busy working the dock conveyor, loading uranium ore into the ship's holds.

'I'm happy to see that the *Algonquin* has arrived on time,' Díaz said. 'The barge is safely away?'

Molina nodded. 'The fires were extinguished without incident. She has already met up with the *Sea Raker*. They should begin laying explosives at the Domingo 2 site within a few hours.'

'Good. Where are the Americans?'

'Follow me.' Molina led the way to the open garage on the lower level of the barracks. Pitt and Summer sat on a bench in an empty corner, with two armed guards positioned a few feet in front of them.

Díaz approached with a twisted sense of amusement. 'I understand you enjoyed some extracurricular activities while I was gone. Your attempt to damage the barge and dock was futile, I am happy to report. Our excavation will continue unabated.'

'Blowing up those thermal vents will poison the seas for a thousand miles,' Pitt said. 'Cuban waters and beaches won't be immune.'

'You are wrong, Mr Pitt. The Florida Current will carry it all to American shores. It will be your country's problem, not mine.'

Pitt gave him a steely gaze. 'It will be your problem when the world discovers you caused it intentionally as part of your uranium mining operation.'

Díaz chuckled. 'That's not about to happen, my friend. Now, on your feet.'

The guards jabbed their assault rifles at Pitt. He rose, and Summer followed suit.

Díaz looked at her and shook his head. 'I'm afraid you won't be going with him this time.' He turned to the guards. 'You will be escorting him to Havana. The helicopter is waiting.'

Summer looked him in the eye. 'Why are you taking him to Havana?'

'Oh, didn't you know?' Díaz gave a reptilian grin. 'President Castro is dead and your father has been implicated in his assassination. He will be going to Havana to stand trial.'

'That's absurd!'

'Not at all. Numerous witnesses will place him at the scene.'

Díaz nodded at the guards, who pushed Pitt forward.

Summer stepped in front of the guards and embraced her father.

He gave her a reassuring look as he whispered in her ear to keep calm. But his insides were churning. He had no regard for his own plight, but the last thing he wanted was to leave his daughter behind with Díaz. The guards gave him no choice and he was forced toward the helipad.

Prodded into the helicopter, he was buckled into a bench seat beside the open cargo door. The guards took seats opposite him. One leaned forward and gave the pilot a thumbs-up sign. The rotor spooled up, and a few seconds later the transport helicopter rose into the sky. Pitt looked down in helplessness as he watched Summer being escorted into the office building with Díaz and Molina. Then the mining facility slipped away beneath him, replaced by an empty expanse of blue ocean.

The Cubans reconvened in Díaz's office, where he took a moment to admire the Aztec stone. 'I received an interesting report from a contact in the United States,' he said to Summer. 'Your friend, Perlmutter, is quite a fruitful historian.'

She glared at Díaz. 'Did you hurt him?' she asked with fire on her tongue.

'He is perfectly fine, although short of a few documents. Documents that indicated the other half of the stone was not destroyed on the *Maine* after all.'

'So the treasure is still in play?' Molina asked.

'Very much so.'

Summer held her temper. Her father had started to describe a link he had discovered in the office between the stone and a lost treasure. But the guards had forced him to sit silently.

'So where is the other stone?' Molina asked.

'If Perlmutter's data is correct,' Díaz said, 'the stone was stolen from the *Maine* during her sinking. It was presumably placed aboard a steam packet named *San Antonio* that immediately left Havana. The American Navy apprehended her off the East Coast, but the vessel sank before they could recover the stone.'

Díaz smiled. 'According to the naval records, the *San Antonio* lies in fifty fathoms, some fourteen miles due east of Punta Maisí.'

'You can locate the wreck with the oil survey ship *Kelowna*,' Molina said. 'She's still under charter for another month.'

'Actually, I'm sending you to go find the wreck, Silvio, just as soon as the *Algonquin* leaves the dock.' He glared at Summer. 'I will personally oversee the remaining excavations to ensure there are no more interruptions.'

'I will notify the crew of the *Kelowna* at once.'

Díaz passed a paper to Molina. 'Here are the *San*

Antonio's presumed coordinates. Take the *Kelowna* and initiate survey operations until you locate the wreck. I'll join you as soon as I am able.'

'If we find it first, we shall do nothing until your arrival.' Molina nodded toward Summer. 'What about the girl?'

Díaz looked her up and down and smiled. 'The girl shall be coming with me.'

56

The Army helicopter flew low over the water, hugging the northern coastline of Cuba a hundred yards offshore. Its thumping rotor caught the attention of those below, eliciting friendly waves from solitary fishermen in small boats and young children playing in the surf.

Pitt stared out the open cargo door, computing his odds of escape. The helicopter had a three-man flight crew, plus the two guards. He had little chance of overpowering all five. The open door gave a potential opportunity, though a plunge to his death wasn't what he had in mind. He studied the helicopter more closely.

The aged Mi-8 was a classic military transport helicopter, capable of ferrying twenty-four soldiers in its long cabin. Pitt observed that this particular craft had been modified for search-and-rescue operations. A rescue basket, along with stacks of life preservers, was stowed in the aft fuselage, while a spooled-cable winch was mounted above the open cargo door. Pitt casually glanced at the Spanish-labeled controls on the winch, identifying a lever that raised and lowered the lifting hook.

Pitt found the rest of the interior of classic military

design: bare-bones, with exposed bulkheads. An ex–Air Force pilot with a keen mechanical aptitude, Pitt tracked a myriad of cables and hydraulic lines that crisscrossed the interior. When his foot knocked against a small fire extinguisher beneath his seat, a crude plan came together. Foolhardy though it might be, it was better than facing a firing squad in Havana.

It would all come down to timing – and the men across from him. The guards were professional soldiers, but they had been on duty most of the previous day and night. One was already dozing, while the other regarded Pitt through tired eyes.

Pitt gave the soldier his best disinterested look and closed his eyes. Placing his hands in his lap, he pretended to sleep. He held the pose for several minutes before risking a peek. The second soldier was still awake but had shifted his body to gaze out the forward cockpit window.

With tiny, incremental movements, Pitt unclasped his seat belt, covering the act with one hand. He shifted in his seat, dropping the other hand beneath his knee until it grazed the fire extinguisher. The guard looked his way for a moment and Pitt froze. But then he resumed staring at the rushing water below.

Pitt slowly tightened his fingers around the fire extinguisher, took a deep breath, and sprang from his seat. He swung the steel canister in a wide arc. But rather than attacking the guards, he smashed the base of the extinguisher into a side bulkhead. It wasn't just a random strike. He had targeted a pair of stainless steel lines that crimped under the heavy blow.

'Hey!' The open-eyed guard looked at Pitt like he was deranged. He reached for the rifle on his lap, but Pitt was quicker. He flipped the extinguisher around, yanked its safety pin, and squeezed the handle, shooting a stream of monoammonium phosphate into the faces of both guards. As the first guard blindly raised his gun, Pitt hurled the extinguisher at him for good measure.

'*Adiós,*' he said as he smacked the rescue hoist lever down. Pitt grasped a small ball hook that unraveled from the cable winch, took a quick step, and dove out the open cargo door.

It took a few moments for the guard to wipe his eyes clear and train his rifle on the prisoner. By then, Pitt was gone.

'Land the helicopter at once!' he shouted to the pilots.

The pilot ignored him as a ribbon of red lights flashed across the cockpit controls and the helicopter began bucking in the air.

'She's not getting any fuel,' the copilot said. 'Both engines.'

The pilot checked the gauges. 'But the external tanks are full.' He switched the fuel supply from one external tank to the other, but it made no difference. The helicopter's twin motors continued to sputter.

Pitt had chosen his target well, crimping the twin

steel lines near the engine cowling labeled *Combustible de aviación*. Unfortunately for the pilot, they fed the motors fuel from both external tanks. Pitt had correctly guessed the internal tank had been emptied on the flight in, though its reserve contained enough to keep the motors running for a few minutes. With only seconds to react, the pilot couldn't see past the fact that he knew the external tanks were still full.

The chopper's motors coughed and sputtered, then died in quick tandem. Only the sound of the cockpit alarms and the dying whine of the rotors now cut the air.

The pilot pushed the nose forward and tried to coax out a glide, but the heavy armored craft would have none of it. The big chopper swooped a short distance, then dropped like a sack of concrete.

It struck the water nose-first, the cockpit instantly crumpling, while the main rotor sheared off and tumbled across the surf. The open fuselage bobbed for a second, then plunged under the waves, carrying all of its occupants to the depths below.

57

Jumping from the cargo door, Pitt nearly lost his grip on the rescue line. The ball hook dug into the back of his hands, painfully preventing him from sliding off. With his arms outstretched over his head, he dangled just beneath the skids as the helicopter began to convulse.

The winch gradually fed out more cable, but he cursed its slowness. He had hoped to drop quickly to a jumping point, but he was still too high. He had no choice but to wait for the line to descend – as the helicopter above him engaged in a slow dance of death. Fortunately, the guards were too preoccupied to throw the winch lever and halt his descent.

The line jerked sharply as the helicopter stuttered and slowed. It was all Pitt could do to keep a grip on the steel hook and cable as he swung wildly beneath the chopper. Though he and the helicopter had both lost altitude, he was still dangerously high.

He glanced up, seeing the helicopter's main rotor slow as the motors sputtered – and then quit altogether. When the pilot dipped the nose into a shallow dive, the rescue line fell slack. Pitt dropped almost twenty feet before the line snapped taut, nearly ripping his arms from their sockets.

He was dragged forward and down as the helicopter briefly accelerated under the force of its dive before losing all momentum. The motion caused Pitt to swing ahead of the chopper. Fearful of being crushed under it, he let go of the line and tucked into a ball.

Though now only thirty feet above the water, he was still propelled forward at a high speed. He smacked the ocean hard, tumbling underwater before fighting his way to the surface.

Pitt gasped. The impact knocked the wind from him. He tried to stretch and swim, but a pain shooting from his shoulder kept him from extending his left arm over his head. He kicked and clawed with his good right arm to keep afloat.

He looked in time to see the helicopter cartwheeling past just a few yards in front of him. He ignored the hissing from the helicopter as its remains sank. Instead, he set his sights on an empty sand beach in the distance. Easing into a sidestroke, he swam several yards before seizing up in pain.

He paddled slowly, feeling a crosscurrent carrying him toward a wave-battered stretch of shoreline. With a determined breath, Pitt turned toward the sand beach and began kicking and stroking against the current. The pain surged through him, but he forged on until a ripple of white foam beckoned at the surf line. His feet touched bottom, and he staggered toward a thick stand of foliage up the beach. A warm trickle flowed down his neck and left shoulder and he realized the cable hook had gouged him when he jumped.

Pitt staggered exhausted to the bushes. Approaching a tall banyan tree, the exertion, pain and loss of blood finally reached their zenith. He fell to his knees and collapsed in a heap on the soft sand.

58

'Captain to the bridge, please. Captain to the bridge.'

Bill Stenseth retrieved the handheld radio that blared with the call and held it to his lips. 'Aye, on my way.'

The veteran sea captain abandoned his morning inspection of the engine room and climbed to the *Caroline*'s bridge. As one of the newest research ships in the NUMA fleet, the *Caroline* was built with a central moon pool and a massive A-frame on its stern for deploying a myriad of underwater vehicles. Like all NUMA ships, the vessel's hull was painted turquoise.

A young officer in a starched white uniform approached Stenseth the instant he stepped on to the bridge. 'Sorry to bother you, Captain, but we received an odd message over the radio.'

'What is it, Roberts?'

'An incoming aircraft has requested we pick up three divers in the water off our port bow.'

Stenseth glanced out the bridge window. The *Caroline* was sitting at anchor in a gentle swell less than a quarter mile from a small Bimini island called South Cat Cay.

'There's nobody in the water that we've been able to see,' Roberts said.

'Who made the call?'

'We don't know. They wouldn't identify themselves.'

A seaman on the far side of the bridge pointed toward the bow. 'Incoming helicopter, sir.'

Stenseth stepped on to the bridge wing and watched as a white helicopter approached at low altitude. It was a commercial Bell 407 civil utility helicopter, commonly used by law enforcement and for offshore transport.

The chopper circled the *Caroline* once and hovered off its port bow, dropping almost to wave height. A side door slid open and three men in dive gear leaped out, splashing into the water below. A large orange container was tossed out after them. The helicopter rose from the surface, waggled its main rotor, and took off in the direction it had come.

Stenseth watched the men surface near the ship. 'Get a Zodiac in the water – now!'

Before the *Caroline*'s crew could deploy the inflatable boat, the divers swam to the ship's stern with their container in tow. A dive platform was lowered and the men climbed aboard with their equipment.

Stenseth waited at the rail as the platform was raised to deck height. The shortest of the three divers stepped forward and extended his hand to the captain as he pulled off his dive mask. 'Hi, Bill. Good to see you.'

Stenseth looked agape as he recognized the man normally seen wearing horn-rimmed glasses. 'Rudi, is that you?'

Gunn smiled and motioned to the other divers. 'My

apologies for the surprise visit. I think you know Jack Dahlgren and Pierce Russell.'

'Yes,' Stenseth nodded at the men. 'But why the air drop? We could have picked you up onshore.'

'Time is of the essence. Plus, when you are defying the Vice President of the United States, you want as few people to know as possible.'

'Know what?' Stenseth asked.

'It's the *Sargasso Sea*. We have reason to believe she's been hijacked near Havana. For reasons that are beyond my pay grade, Vice President Sandecker has refused to issue help – and in fact ordered us not to intervene.' Gunn shook his head. 'But I can't do it. The crew may be in danger, so we've got to find out what's going on.'

'Aren't Pitt and Giordino aboard?'

'Yes, which makes things more unnerving. The ship went silent a couple of days ago. They were investigating an undersea mercury plume and may have stumbled on its source.'

'The Cubans?'

'We don't know.'

'So that explains the anonymous commercial helicopter ride.'

'The pilot thinks we're here on a secret mission to track dolphins. He wasn't too happy about making a round trip from Miami and dropping us in the sea, but he was well paid for his services.'

'You're really sticking your neck out, Rudi, but I'll be

glad to help,' Stenseth said. 'Pitt has saved my bacon on more than one occasion.'

'I knew I could rely on you.'

'What can we do to help?'

Gunn pointed across the ship's open deck. A sleek underwater vehicle with a fiberglass hull was parked on a wooden cradle.

'I need you to tell me two things,' Gunn said. 'First, that the *Bullet* over there is fully operational. Second, that you can get the *Caroline* under way within the hour.'

It was Stenseth's turn to smile. 'The *Bullet* just needs a full tank of gas and she's ready to run. As for the *Caroline*, if we're not headed to Cuba at flank speed in twenty minutes, you can have my job.'

'Thanks, Bill. Every second may count.'

'We're on it.' Stenseth took a step toward the bridge, then hesitated. 'By the way, what's in the orange box?'

Gunn's eyebrows arched as he replied to the captain with a straight face.

'Insurance.'

59

Summer sat on the dock in the morning sun for over an hour, an armed guard close by. Her thoughts centered on her father and what had become of him.

As sweat trickled down her brow, a blue dot appeared on the horizon, growing ever larger. It eventually morphed into a sleek crew boat, which raced to the dock under the power of twin turbocharged diesels. Summer was escorted into its air-conditioned passenger cabin, where she watched as several small crates of high explosives were loaded on to the stern deck.

Díaz and Molina appeared on the dock a short time later. They shook hands, then Díaz hopped aboard and the boat roared away from the dock. Summer suppressed a chill as he entered the cabin and took a seat next to her.

'A slight deviation in plans,' he said. 'We will be making a short stop at your old vessel, the *Sargasso Sea*.'

'I may return to the ship?'

Díaz laughed. 'No, my dear. I don't believe you will want to. You shall be joining me instead on the *Sea Raker*.'

'You don't know the damage you'll create by destroying those thermal vents.'

'You don't know the money and power I'll forgo if I don't.' He smiled. 'Of course, it may turn out to be a pittance compared with what our Aztec stones are concealing.'

'What makes you so sure?'

'It's the reason I went to Mexico. Our survey ship discovered the canoe near Jamaica, on which the gold figurine was found. We now know from your codex that the canoe was one of many that sailed from the Aztec empire. Dr Torres was kind enough to confirm the figurine was of a known Aztec design. There must have been much more on the other canoes.'

'A single gold figurine seems like a leap of faith to me,' Summer said.

'It was the only artifact remaining with the canoe. I believe the canoe sank slowly, allowing the crew to escape to the other canoes with most of their cargo.'

'Perhaps. But you now have the location of the other stone. Why don't you stop this insane blasting of the thermal vents and go recover the treasure?'

'And let you and your father go?'

Summer looked into the dark, sadistic eyes of Díaz and found anything but sympathy.

'No, I think not,' Díaz said, answering his own question. He rose to his feet. 'You see, my brother and I have a larger destiny to fulfill.'

He strode off to the bridge as the *Sargasso Sea* appeared before them, leaving Summer to wonder about the identity of Díaz's brother.

The twin commando inflatables were still tied alongside the NUMA ship as the crew boat pulled next to a drop-down accommodation ladder. The crates of explosives were transferred aboard first and then Díaz climbed to the *Sargasso Sea*'s main deck. The commando leader Calzado met him at the rail.

'Any problem with the ship?' Díaz asked.

'No, sir. The prisoners are secure and the ship is quiet. We've been awaiting further orders.'

'Molina tells me that no communications were made by the vessel during the assault.'

'We caught the bridge crew unaware, so we believe that is true. A US Coast Guard vessel pestered us on the radio for some time when we relocated the ship, but they were turned away when we alerted a Cuban Navy patrol craft in the area.'

'Very well.'

'Sir, we just received a call from shore ops. They received a report that a helicopter departing the facility earlier this morning went down near Puerto Escondido while en route to Havana.'

'Any survivors?'

'Unknown. Army forces and a dive rescue team have been called to the site. Updates will be provided as they learn more.'

Díaz's face tightened. Could Pitt have had a hand in the crash? But all was not lost. If Pitt was dead, perhaps he could substitute Pitt's daughter as a suspect in Raúl's death.

He turned and pointed to the explosives stacked on the deck. 'The general has ordered the destruction of the ship. Where is the American crew?'

'They are being held in two locked laboratories near the stern.'

'Keep them there. Your orders are to scuttle the ship with all hands after nightfall. There are to be no survivors. Do you understand?'

The commando nodded. 'It will be done. No survivors.'

60

The crew imprisoned in the *Sargasso Sea*'s wet lab recoiled when the lone door was flung open. One of the ship's helmsmen, a diminutive man named Ross, was shoved through the door, clutching a large cardboard box. A pair of armed commandos followed him in and scanned the room from behind the muzzles of their assault rifles. They nudged Ross forward to distribute the box's contents.

'Ross, is that you?' Captain Smith asked from the back of the bay. He was seated in a desk chair with his feet propped on a stool and his chest wrapped in gauze. While he was still weak, his eyes were bright and alert.

Ross made his way to the captain, passing out bottles of water. He moved gingerly, sporting a black eye and a bruised cheek.

'Sir, the ship's been relocated nine miles off the coast. A crew boat came alongside a short time ago. My Spanish is a little spotty, but I think one of the commandos on the bridge said they brought some explosives aboard and they intend to sink the ship tonight with us on it.'

Smith's ashen face seemed to pale further, then a swell of anger turned his cheeks red. 'Keep that to yourself, Ross.'

'Yes, sir.'

'What do you know of the crew being held in the other lab?' Giordino asked.

'They seem to be holding up fine except for Tyler, who's lost a lot of blood. They let me drop a box of provisions there before I came here.'

'Is that what's in the box?' Smith asked.

'Yes, a bit of a mad mix of food stores. They gave me ten seconds in the galley, so I grabbed whatever was within reach.'

'You!' One of the guards motioned to Ross. 'Hurry up. And no talking.'

'Distribute that to the rest of the crew,' Smith said.

Ross nodded, passing out apples and water as he made his way up front. The guards escorted him out of the lab and locked the door behind them.

The captain motioned to Dirk and Giordino. 'We're in a tight fix,' he said in a low voice. 'Any ideas?'

'It's a sure bet we're supposed to ride the ship to the bottom,' Dirk said. 'Unfortunately, there's not a lot of options.'

'There's no way out of here on our own accord.' Giordino waved his arm around the lab. Immediately after being locked up, he'd examined every square inch for an escape route. But in the absence of a blowtorch, there was none. The lab was essentially a big steel box with a single entry point. 'Our only chance will be to jump the guards next time they open the door.'

Dirk nodded. 'It's all we can do.'

Smith shook his head. 'There are always at least two armed men at the door. You'll both get killed.'

As he spoke, the captain squirmed in his seat, causing his legs to slip off the stool and crash to the floor. The pain wrenched through his shoulder and he cursed.

Standing closest to him, Dirk helped readjust his seat. As Dirk bent down, he noticed that a lower shelf on the lab bench held a large bottle of iodine and several other reagents used by the lab's scientists. As he examined the bottles, an idea formed.

'Captain, about Al's suggestion . . .' He rose to his feet, clasping a few of the bottles. 'What if I can improve our odds a bit?'

61

Pitt came to amid a clamor of voices. He rubbed his eyes, shaking off a grogginess that made him forget where he was. He rolled on to his elbows, and the sharp pain in his left shoulder instantly restored his memory of the helicopter crash. He peered through a low hedge of bushes to locate the source of the shouting.

It came from some divers on a military dive boat working a short distance offshore. A small inflatable cruised the shoreline, presumably looking for survivors. He was stunned at their sudden arrival, then glanced at his Doxa wristwatch and realized he had been out for nearly two hours. He touched his hand to the gash on his neck and shoulder, feeling a mass of dried blood. No wonder he'd passed out.

From the commotion on the dive boat, it seemed the rescue team had located the remains of the helicopter. Pitt watched as five body bags were passed over the boat's rail to a team of divers in the water. It wouldn't be long before someone would realize there had been a sixth person of interest aboard the chopper.

Pitt took stock of the terrain. He had staggered into a small grove of bay cedar shrubs growing beneath a banyan tree. It was the only significant cover for thirty yards around. The open beach stretched for a half mile to his left, while a boulder-strewn bluff blocked passage to his right. Behind him was an open, rocky incline that rose toward the inland jungle a short distance away.

Pitt was considering a path up the hill when he heard the sound of brakes squealing just above. He spied the top of a canvas-covered military truck pull to a stop near the jungle fringe. There was a road atop the hill. But for now it was out of reach as a squad of Revolutionary Armed Forces soldiers dispersed from the truck and began combing down the slope toward the beach.

Pitt moved to the corner of the thicket and crawled under a large bay cedar as a pair of soldiers trod by. They didn't linger but instead proceeded through the thicket and on to the beach. But something caught the attention of one of the soldiers. He stopped and looked down, examining the sand at his feet.

It was Pitt's footprints. They led one way from the surf, up the beach and into the thicket. Pitt watched as the soldier slowly traced the prints back to the banyan tree. The ground was firm around the base of the tree, the prints less distinct. The soldier pivoted around as he searched the area. There was no way Pitt could avoid detection, so he took to the offensive. Waiting until the soldier turned away, he sprang from the bush.

It took Pitt two steps to reach him undetected. He swung his fist, delivering a blow that struck just above the soldier's belt, forcing him to stagger. The soldier spun around to bear his assault rifle, but Pitt was ready. He grabbed the barrel and jammed it to the soldier's chest, then delivered a blow to his face with his free hand.

The soldier dropped to his knees, letting go of the rifle. Pitt snatched the weapon and turned it on the soldier, who he now saw was a boy barely seventeen – likely an unwilling conscript, certainly not on the order of Díaz's highly trained men. The hapless soldier gazed at Pitt with a look of fear.

'Get!' Pitt ordered in a low voice.

The soldier scrambled to his feet and staggered toward the beach. Pitt took off in the other direction, up the hill as fast as his rubbery legs would carry him. He didn't look back when he heard the young soldier shouting to his comrades but ducked when a burst of gunfire shattered some rocks at his side.

Armed with the soldier's AK-47, Pitt sprayed the beach with a short salvo, then continued up the hill. His return fire bought him a few more seconds, just enough time to approach the top of the incline before the shooting from below resumed, this time from multiple sources. He gambled that the other soldiers were equally young and inexperienced marksmen and he continued racing to the top. A ribbon of lead chased him the last few steps, but he was able to dive over the ledge and out of sight.

He rolled into a shallow gully that abutted a narrow paved road. The empty military truck sat a short distance ahead. Thoughts of commandeering the truck vanished when he saw two soldiers setting up a checkpoint behind it. They dropped their barricade posts and peered over the side ledge to see what the shooting was about.

Pitt rose and sprinted across the road. He nearly made it unseen, but one of the soldiers caught his movement and yelled. Pitt countered by firing a short burst in their direction, then raked the truck's engine compartment while continuing across the road. The rifle's half-loaded clip ran dry, and Pitt ditched the weapon as he ducked into the jungle scrub.

He had no time to hesitate. Soldiers from the beach began pouring on to the road behind him. The barricade guards pointed to where he had gone and the soldiers converged on his last position.

Pitt sprinted a dozen yards into the foliage, then turned sharply to the right and ran parallel to the road. He stopped for a second and picked up a rock, which he hurled in the opposite direction. The noise of it striking a tree elicited a crack of gunfire and a pursuit, he hoped, in the wrong direction.

After some hundred yards, he angled to his right until brief glimpses of the road appeared. He approached the fringe and took a peek back down the road.

An old sedan coming from the opposite direction had been stopped at the barricade. Nearer to Pitt, a pair of soldiers were walking along the road, peering into the jungle every few yards. He saw some movement behind him and knew there was no time to rest.

Ducking back into the jungle's protective cover, he

continued running parallel to the road. A minute later, he tripped and fell, his weakened legs failing to clear a dead branch. As he pulled himself to his feet, he heard the car coming down the road.

Thinking fast, he grabbed the branch and dragged it toward the road. He found that he was at the tail end of a curve that obscured both the barricade and the approaching car. He quickly dragged the branch into the middle of the road, then dove into some bushes on the far side as the car rounded the corner and slammed on its brakes.

Pitt recognized the vehicle as a 1957 Plymouth Fury, one of thousands of aged American cars that ordinary Cubans continued to drive as a result of the decades-long trade embargo. Though its body was bruised and its hubcaps mismatched, the chrome bumpers still sparkled and its white paint shone from years of polishing that had buffed it nearly down to the primer.

The two-door hardtop was driven by an older man and woman. They climbed out and dragged the branch off the road. As the couple returned to the car, Pitt emerged from the bushes and held his empty hands out in front of him. He found himself looking into the faces of a gracefully aged Cuban couple who were both smartly dressed.

'Hola!' The man took a step back.

'Hello,' Pitt said with a smile. 'I am desperate for a ride. Sorry to trouble you.'

The woman studied Pitt, noting the wound on his shoulder, the bloodied clothes, and the haggard yet pleasing face. 'Are you hurt?'

Before he could answer, she rushed to his side and led him to the car. She turned to her husband. 'Salvador, hurry, help this man into the back of the car. We have to get him home.'

Just as they pulled away, Pitt saw two soldiers pop out of the jungle, where he had stood seconds before, and stare at the old car rumbling down the road.

62

The Plymouth turned off the pockmarked paved road and on to an equally rutted dirt lane. Pitt's shoulder ached with every pothole, the car's tired suspension relaying each bump in full. Something beneath him in the backseat scratched at his side with every jostle.

After a rough patch of gravel, the car finally stopped and the motor shut off.

The woman, though tiny, possessed a domineering presence. Her full cheeks and wide eyes suggested the beauty of her youth.

'We are here, *señor.*' She turned to her husband. 'Salvador, take this man inside and get him cleaned up. He shall join us for dinner. I just hope he didn't mangle the chickens.'

After helping Pitt out of the car, she reached into the backseat and pulled out a dead pair of whole chickens whose claws had been the source of Pitt's discomfort. Perusing them with satisfaction, she marched into a small house perched along the sloped drive.

Pitt looked at the man and grinned. 'You married a powerful woman.'

'Maria? She is as strong as an ox in all ways. Once

she makes up her mind, there is no changing it. I learned long ago to avoid the sharp tip of her horns.'

Pitt laughed. 'Sounds like sage advice.'

'My name is Salvador Fariñas.' He extended his hand.

'Dirk Pitt.'

'Come this way, Mr Pitt, and we'll get you cleaned up as Maria asks.'

Fariñas led Pitt to the pitched-roof house, which had a tired and faded façade. Its position on a steep bluff offered a commanding view of the ocean. Pitt saw the paved road a half mile below and the shoreline of a small bay some distance beyond.

Inside the house, Pitt was surprised to find a stylish interior. Dark Saltillo tile covered the floor, supporting a mix of modern furniture. A huge picture window facing the ocean illuminated the stark white walls, which were curiously bare. A single brightly colored painting occupied an empty wall next to a fireplace. Pitt admired the depiction of a fisherman displaying his catch, painted in the style of Gauguin. 'That is quite good.'

'Maria painted it. She was a famous artist in Havana many years ago. Regrettably, that is the only work of hers we now possess.'

'She has a gift.'

Fariñas guided Pitt to a cramped bathroom shower and left him with soap and towels. It took nearly twenty minutes to scrub away the dried blood and the pain of his injuries. Borrowing some bandages and a fresh shirt from Fariñas, he looked and felt like a new man when he stepped into the main living quarters.

Maria had plucked and cleaned the chickens and was busy cooking. Fariñas offered Pitt a glass of *aguardiente*, a harsh, locally fermented rum, which he downed with gratitude.

'To your kindness to strangers,' Pitt said when his host filled their glasses again.

'You are most welcome.'

'Salvador, may I ask if you have a telephone?'

Fariñas shook his head. 'We are fortunate to have reliable plumbing and electricity, but the phone lines haven't reached us. And Maria refuses to purchase a cell phone.'

'It's urgent I make an international call.'

'I can take you to Santa Cruz del Norte after supper. You should be able to make a call from there.'

Maria stepped from the kitchen with her paella-like dish, *arroz con pollo*.

'Please, sit down. And, Salvador, please open a bottle of Soroa for our guest.' She turned to Pitt. 'It's a local white wine I think you will enjoy.'

They sat and ate. Having not eaten a full meal in two days, Pitt devoured three platefuls of the chicken and rice. 'You are as excellent a chef as you are a painter, Maria.'

'That is kind of you to say. You know, Mr Pitt, there are rumors that President Castro has been murdered.'

'Yes, I have also heard that.'

'A guard at the roadblock said an American has been implicated and had escaped custody in the area.'

Pitt looked her in the eye. 'I would be that American. And I assure you I had nothing to do with Castro's death. But I may know who did.'

Maria looked at him with a hint of disappointment.

Her husband guffawed. 'You needn't worry, Mr Pitt, about Maria turning you over to the Army. Many years ago, she served three years in custody for a painting that was deemed disrespectful to the state.'

'It is true.' Maria's eyes filled with fire. 'An imbecile Army colonel running the Ministry of Culture took offense to a painting I did of a gun emplacement filled with flowers. They destroyed my studio and confiscated all of my work, locked it away in the ministry building.' She pointed to the lone canvas. 'That is the only painting I kept hidden from them.'

'Why don't you paint again?' Pitt asked.

An inward look crossed Maria's face. 'When they stole my work, they stole a part of me, a part of who I am. I set down my brush that day and vowed never to paint again as long as the state suppressed my work.'

She looked at Pitt with envy. 'Cuba has lived for too long fighting a blanket of oppression against its own spirit. Perhaps change is finally in the air. I pray the change will be only for the good.'

'When power is up for grabs,' Pitt said, 'the first casualty is often liberty.'

'There are always dark forces at play, it seems. Tell me, Mr Pitt, what are you doing in Cuba?'

Pitt described his search for the mercury poisoning and his capture by the *Sea Raker*. He relayed the urgency of halting the destruction of the thermal vents. His anguish showed when he mentioned his daughter was still being held captive.

'We will help you return to your ship,' Maria said. 'Salvador, help me wash the dishes and then we will take Mr Pitt to Santa Cruz.'

Pitt helped clear the plates, then ambled to the picture window, where a seaman's telescope was trained on the waterfront. The sun was low as he gazed out the window and noticed a large luxury yacht moored offshore. Taking a closer look through the telescope, he spotted an odd banner flying over the bridge. Focusing the lens, he was startled to see the flag featured a red bear clutching an ax in its teeth.

'Are you ready to leave?' Fariñas approached with the car keys.

'A slight change of plans.' Pitt pointed out the window. 'Can you get me to that yacht moored in the bay?'

Fariñas gazed at the vessel and nodded. 'I have a cousin with a boat who can run you over. You sure they'll let you aboard?'

Pitt smiled. 'I'll bet a Bentley that they will.'

63

Precisely thirty miles due south of Key West, two boats approached each other for a late-afternoon rendezvous. Both were nondescript cabin cruisers, the likes of which flooded the Florida coastlines every summer weekend. But rather than being sailed by half-drunk doctors sporting sunburns, both were crewed by professional security men carrying concealed weapons. Three miles distant, a pair of Apache attack helicopters kept a discreet eye on the proceedings.

The boats approached each other cautiously like a pair of wary boxers facing off in the ring for the first time. A light breeze ruffled small flags above each pilothouse, one Cuban and the other American.

As crewmen swapped lines and tied the boats side by side, Vice President James Sandecker emerged from the cabin of the American boat and stepped to the side rail. He extended a hand to a gray-haired man on the other boat.

'Good afternoon, Mr President,' Sandecker said.

Raúl Castro shook Sandecker's hand with a firm grip. 'It is an honor, Mr Vice President.'

'Please, call me James. May I come aboard?'

'Of course.' Castro maintained his grip on Sandecker's hand as the Vice President hopped boats. The Cuban president regarded Sandecker up close, noting he was shorter than he appeared on television. But there was something of a revolutionary fire in the man's blue eyes that he instantly admired.

'Call me Raúl,' he said. 'Come, let us sit on the stern deck and talk.'

Sandecker waved off his Secret Service detail, and Castro did the same to his men. The two leaders stepped to the stern and sat beneath a shade canopy.

'Bring us some rum brandies,' Castro called to an aide before addressing Sandecker.

'James, I thank you for agreeing to see me. I never expected that the government of the United States would warn me of a threat on my life. On account of you, I am alive today. I would like to thank you, and your President, for saving me from death.'

'The President was disturbed when our intelligence people pieced together the details of the assassination attempt, particularly since it occurred out of your country. The President and I are pleased you are safe and well.' Sandecker cleared his throat. 'The President feels this would be a good opportunity to advance our relationship from the shadows of the Cold War.'

Castro nodded, staring out with a distant gaze. 'This, too, has been heavy on my heart since my brother died. At one time, my country needed Fidel as much as he needed the people. But that day is long past. For all of the good that Fidel accomplished, he didn't allow Cuba to grow. It is past time for our people to prosper.'

He looked Sandecker in the eye. 'James, as you know, I have announced I will not seek reelection in 2018. I intend to appoint Foreign Minister Ruiz to succeed me. He is a strong proponent of introducing market economics and improving relations with your country.'

He took a deep breath. 'In my remaining days in office, I have decided to pave the way for his initiatives.'

'We have a two-and-a-half-century history of free market democracy. We can help lead you down the right path.'

A burden seemed to lift from the shoulders of the old Marxist. 'It is not an easy thing to abandon the road of the past, but at the same time, it can be liberating.'

An aide arrived with the rum brandies, and the two drank a toast to their improved relations.

'Raúl, I have a question,' Sandecker said. 'Unofficial reports are circulating widely that you were killed in the Cayman Islands. Why have you not gone public and dispelled those rumors?'

Castro's eyes clouded with anger. 'We still don't know who hired the mercenaries to conduct the attack. If those responsible believe I am dead, they will soon act in a way that identifies their guilt.'

'A sound tactic,' Sandecker said, 'but I think I can point you in the right direction.' He reached into his shirt pocket and handed Castro a folded sheet of paper. 'We were curious as well and performed a trace on the funds paid to the mercenaries. Tracking the payment backward from the drop account, we found it had been flushed through no less than three Cayman Islands accounts, each at a different bank. The trail then led through a Venezuelan bank, and finally to a national account in Havana. That's as far as we could get. You'll note the account is a registered repository of the Interior Ministry.'

Castro studied the paper wide-eyed. 'Gutier! Of course. He has a history of extremism, and his ambition is legendary. If I were out of the picture, he could rely on the support of the Army to strong-arm his way to the presidency. It's no secret he covets my job. I guess he couldn't wait . . . or stand to see Ruiz take my place.'

'I'm sorry,' Sandecker said. 'Treachery from within is hard to face.'

'No, I thank you for revealing this rabid dog. I've always had my reservations about the man, but he is a capable leader who has served the state well for many years.'

'Does his role in the military create any complications?'

'Absolutely not. My Minister of the Revolutionary Armed Forces has stood with me for forty years.' He softened his tone. 'I'm sorry, James, but the loss of loyalty is difficult to bear.'

'I understand. It is your matter to resolve.'

'The positive is that it has created a building block to our friendship.' Castro finished his drink.

'Agreed,' Sandecker said. 'Still, there are two issues on our side of the fence that may prove a hindrance in moving ahead.'

'What would that be?'

'The first comes from Asia. We've received a troubling communiqué from our friends in the South Korean National Intelligence Service. They got wind of a rumored deal between Pyongyang and your country. A source alleges that Cuba is providing North Korea a large quantity of high-grade uranium oxide for use in their enrichment facilities. In exchange, North Korea is offering you a small number of tactical nuclear weapons.'

'What?' Castro popped out of his chair. 'That is preposterous. Your intelligence is completely mistaken.'

'You have had some small-arms trades with North Korea in the past.'

'True, but they were minute quantities. We have very little business with North Korea. I assure you, James, I have no knowledge of such an agreement. We have no uranium mining on our island to begin with. And we certainly have no need, or desire, for nuclear weapons.'

'I am happy to hear that. Intelligence errors do happen, and anything out of North Korea tends to be unreliable.'

Castro nodded. 'That must be the case. It is a mad proposition, but fear not. Now, you indicated there was another matter that concerned you?'

'Yes, a secondary issue of great concern to me personally. It's our NUMA research vessel *Sargasso Sea*. You are holding it captive in Cuban waters.'

A blank look fell over Castro's face. 'What do you mean?'

Sandecker explained the sudden loss of communications and the satellite photos showing it afloat in Cuban territorial waters.

Castro shook his head. 'I'm sorry, James, I know nothing of this. Are you sure the vessel hasn't just experienced equipment problems?'

'The satellite photos show no evidence of fire or damage. And the ship has multiple means of communication. We sent a Coast Guard vessel to investigate, but they were driven away by a Cuban Navy vessel. We believe the *Sargasso Sea* has been apprehended by hostile forces.'

'It is possible a regional naval unit is responsible, but this incident has not been reported in Havana.'

'There are fifty people aboard, some of them close friends. I'd take it as a personal favor if you could let me know what's going on.'

'Of course. I understand your concern. I promise to look into the matter immediately upon my return to the capital.'

A short distance off the stern, a large fish jumped out of the water, catching both men's attention.

'Do you like to sport fish, James?' Castro asked.

'It's been a few years since I battled the big ones,' Sandecker said.

'You and I, we must go fishing on our next visit. The blue marlin in the Florida Straits is the best in the world.'

'Reason enough to meet again soon,' Sandecker said, standing and shaking hands. 'I can think of nothing I'd like better.'

64

Riding in the passenger seat this time, Pitt joined the elderly couple for the drive down the hill in the Plymouth. He wore a borrowed straw hat and sunglasses as a minor attempt at cover. There were no roadblocks along the way, though they spotted a speeding military truck as they crossed the paved road.

Fariñas drove through a neighborhood of run-down block houses before stopping at a pink one near the water. An ebullient man with large ears emerged and Fariñas introduced him as his cousin.

'My boat is this way,' the man said. 'Come, I can run you over right now.'

Pitt shook Fariñas's hand and gave Maria a hug. 'I won't forget your kindness.'

'Keep up the good fight, Mr Pitt,' she said. 'And good luck to you and your daughter.'

The cousin led him to a small fishing boat beached on the sand. They dragged it into the water and climbed aboard. A rickety outboard was started and a few minutes later they pulled alongside the stern of Mark Ramsey's yacht, *Gold Digger*. A muscle-laden crewman appeared and motioned for them to move away.

'Is Mark aboard?' Pitt shouted.

'Who wants to know?'

'A Bentley driver by the name of Pitt.'

The crewman gave Pitt an annoyed look, then spoke into a handheld radio. His features softened when the radio squawked a minute later and he waved the boat alongside. Pitt thanked Fariñas's cousin and hopped aboard.

'Mr Ramsey will be pleased to see you in the salon.' The crewman guided Pitt across the open stern deck and through a pair of French doors.

Dressed in a sport shirt and slacks, Ramsey sat at a table, poring through a stack of seismic surveys. He stood up and greeted Pitt with a warm smile. 'You're a long way from the track, Mr Pitt. How on earth did you find me here?'

'Your red grizzly bear logo. I remembered it from your car hauler in Washington. I've also seen it on another vessel in the area, a mining ship called the *Sea Raker*.'

'Yes, that's our flagship deep-sea mining vessel. But you must be mistaken. The *Sea Raker* is operating under charter in the Pacific off Nicaragua.'

He showed Pitt to a chair, noticing his disheveled appearance and the bandage on his neck. 'What exactly are you doing here?'

'In a word, mercury. I was tracking the dispersal of toxic mercury plumes that have occurred in the Caribbean. They are being created by the destruction of undersea hydrothermal vents. Your ship, the *Sea Raker*, is responsible for the damage.'

Ramsey shook his head. 'No, the *Sea Raker* is in the Pacific.'

'I was aboard her two days ago not thirty miles from here. We were investigating the seafloor in a submersible and were abducted by one of the ship's mining machines. We were brought aboard the *Sea Raker* a short time before being taken to shore. I managed to escape, but my daughter is still being held prisoner.'

'Why would the *Sea Raker* abduct you?'

'Because they are blowing up thermal vents in order to mine deposits of uranium buried within them.'

Ramsey looked at Pitt like he'd just stepped off a flying saucer. 'Uranium? You're mad. The ship was chartered to mine gold off Nicaragua.'

Pitt shook his head. 'Perhaps they started with gold, but they've graduated to uranium in the Caribbean. They have a stockpile down the coast that was being loaded aboard an outbound freighter just today.'

'That can't be. I know uranium deposits coexist with other minerals, but I've never heard of it being commercially mined undersea. Why would they be doing so?'

'You'd have to talk to a Cuban named Juan Díaz.'

'Díaz? He took possession of the ship on behalf of a Panamanian venture. You know him?'

'He seems to be running the show. And he's the one holding my daughter.'

Ramsey could see from the intense look in Pitt's eyes that he was telling the truth. 'I'm so sorry,' he said in a shaken voice.

'That's not the worst of it. High-grade uranium ore apparently exists in the deep core of the thermal vents in this region. Somewhere within the layers of sediment is a concentration of mercury, probably laid down during the Triassic Period. Díaz and his Cuban Army pals have blasted open several vents in the Caribbean – and one nearby – that have released large plumes of mercury,' said Pitt. 'As we speak, they are preparing to blast a pair of very large thermal vents in the middle of the Florida Straits. If they succeed, the mercury plumes will likely expand to the Gulf Stream. It will be the environmental disaster of the century.'

Ramsey sank into his chair with the look of a shattered soul. 'I've built my career on prudent mining, using the least invasive environmental techniques possible. I would never have provided my equipment and expertise had I known that's what they were up to.'

He shook his head slowly. 'I should have known something wasn't right. They were extremely secretive about their mining plans, which isn't unusual when gold is at stake. But everything was handled as a military operation. They insisted on crewing my ship with their own men. I never imagined they could create such harm in the few months that they've leased the *Sea Raker*.'

'There's also a high likelihood they were responsible for sinking the drill ship *Alta*.'

Ramsey stared at the plush carpet, overwhelmed by what he'd been told. 'You say they are about to blast more vents? What can we do to stop them?'

'Two things,' Pitt said. 'Get this yacht to the *Sea Raker* as fast as you can and find a way to sneak me aboard. In the meantime, please show me to a radio. I'd like to call my ship.'

65

The Domingo 2 hydrothermal vent emerged like a shattered kaleidoscope amid a barren desert. At a depth of twelve hundred feet, the surrounding seabed was a cold, muddy plain devoid of life and color.

The *Sea Raker*'s auxiliary cutter had excavated a linear trench near the vent's core as a place to deposit the bulk explosives. At the trench's epicenter, a narrow, deeper cut had been made for inserting the high explosives.

A suspended platform, filled with the crated bags of ANFO explosives, was lowered nearby. The bulk cutter, using its heavy manipulator arm, clasped one of the crates and transported it to the trench. In a few hours, more than five thousand pounds of explosives had been laid in the heart of the thermal vent.

On the surface, Díaz's crew boat approached the marionette-like operation performed by the *Sea Raker*. Summer noted the bright deck lights were reflecting off the water as dusk settled over a calm sea. The barge, still laden with explosives for the second thermal vent, was tied alongside the mining ship's port flank. As they approached the barge, they saw the auxiliary cutter machine, finished with its seafloor ditch digging, being hoisted back aboard.

The crew boat tied up aft of the barge, and Díaz climbed a lowered ladder. Summer remained seated in the passenger bay as two soldiers boarded the boat. One took up position in the pilothouse while the other grabbed her elbow and escorted her aboard the *Sea Raker*.

A mining engineer greeted Díaz, then led them to a large prefabricated building on the center deck. Summer felt like she had entered a smaller version of NASA's fabled Houston Control Center. Multiple rows of manned computer stations filled the room, all facing a giant video screen. Each workstation controlled an element of the sub-sea mining operation, with the collector, cutter machines and ROVs operated by toggled panels and joysticks. Video feeds from each underwater device fed into the multiscreen video board.

Summer observed the live underwater footage from two ROVs, while the two raised cutter machines showed deck shots from their multiple cameras.

Díaz took a seat in a leather armchair in front of the video screen while Summer was escorted to a nearby bench.

The mining engineer stood in front and spoke to Díaz. 'We have completed trenching and placement of the base explosives. We are well positioned at the vent, so the deployment went quicker than expected. As you probably saw, both the bulk cutter and the auxiliary cutter have been returned to the ship.'

Díaz pointed to the screen. 'But the high explosives have not yet been set?'

One of the cameras on the bulk cutter showed several crewmen coiling a long, tube-shaped charge about the deck.

'The bulk cutter still needs to place the TNT sleeve and detonator into the base of the thermal fissure. Then we'll be able to fire. We should be ready to lower the charge and the cutter in about ten minutes.'

'Very well. I'll watch the operations from here.'

The engineer nodded as a nearby phone rang. He answered and passed the receiver to Díaz. 'The captain has a question for you from the bridge.'

As Díaz took the call, the engineer stepped to one of the work consoles and conversed with its operator.

Summer was alert to it all. Since entering the control center, she had seen that the operators were too engaged in their duties to pay her any attention. With Díaz and the engineer temporarily occupied, she looked about for her guard. He was leaning against the wall at the side of the room, watching the underwater video feeds.

Summer quietly got up, stepped to a door on the opposite side, and slipped out, only to come face-to-face with another guard, his hand on the bolt of his rifle. He backed her into the control room, shoving her with his gun muzzle digging into her stomach.

Díaz witnessed the act and marched over with a shake of his head.

'A valiant, if fruitless, effort,' he said.

'Why don't you just let me go? I can't halt your under-sea destruction now.'

'You don't care for our hospitality? Then have it your way. You can indeed depart the *Sea Raker*.' He sneered. 'Only it won't be aboard my crew boat.'

66

Pounding the seas at almost thirty knots, Ramsey's *Gold Digger* located the *Sea Raker* on its radar in less than two hours. Pitt spent the intervening time trying to hail the *Sargasso Sea* but was met with only silence. Even a last-minute call to Rudi Gunn at NUMA headquarters went unanswered.

The last vestiges of daylight streaked the western horizon as the *Sea Raker* loomed ahead. Ramsey radioed the mining vessel, then turned to Pitt.

'They were quite surprised and very unhappy to hear from me. They tried to beg off a visit since they are conducting operations. They didn't explain what they are doing here.' He rubbed his chin. 'I said, being just as surprised finding them in the Caribbean, that it was just a brief social call and I certainly wasn't here for an inspection, so they agreed. They'll be rather shocked if you're part of the boarding party.'

'Too many people might recognize me coming in the front door,' Pitt said, peering at the mining ship and adjacent barge. 'I'll have to try the back door. Can you position yourself off *Sea Raker*'s port bow and shield your launch from the ship when you deploy it?'

'Not a problem.' Ramsey relayed the request to the yacht's captain, then gave Pitt a handheld marine radio. 'You're on your own, I'm afraid. We'll loiter about the area a few miles away until we hear from you.'

'Thanks, Mark.' Pitt shook the Canadian's hand.

'Watch yourself. And good luck.'

The *Gold Digger* turned away from the *Sea Raker* as its launch was lowered off the stern. Ramsey and his hefty bodyguard sat on the forward bench as the pilot engaged the outboard and sped toward the mining ship.

On the *Sea Raker*'s opposite deck, Díaz and his crew were engaged in their own launching exercise, deploying the bulk cutter. Dangling at its side like an ornament on a Christmas tree was the *Starfish*, suspended by the cutter's manipulator. Both machines were quickly swallowed by the sea as the ship's drum winch released a steady stream of support cable. Díaz watched them submerge into the black water, then stepped to the opposite side of the ship to greet Ramsey.

The *Gold Digger*'s launch sailed along the ship's port rail to its lowered ladder. Ramsey and his bodyguard leaped on to the ladder and up the steps to the *Sea Raker*'s deck. Díaz was there waiting with several armed soldiers standing loosely behind him.

'Mr Ramsey, a pleasant surprise.' Díaz's tone was anything but pleasant.

'Hello, Juan. I was on my way to New Orleans when my captain spotted you.'

'I'm glad you can visit. Come, let's have a drink.'

Díaz led him forward to the ship's wardroom, where an attendant fixed them drinks.

'What are you doing in Cuba?' Ramsey said. 'You're supposed to be working off Nicaragua.'

'The site proved to be a disappointment. We decided to redeploy here for some test excavations that looked promising from an earlier seismic survey.'

'Do you have authorization to dig here?' Ramsey asked.

'The approvals have been made through the necessary channels.'

'I admire your efficiency. How is the ship working out?'

'She's been outstanding. We had a learning curve on managing the excavation equipment, but now we are operating at high efficiency.'

'Yes, that's why I would have preferred you use my crew.'

Díaz ignored the comment. 'I'm sorry you didn't come at a more opportune moment. We are just deploying one of the cutters for a test run.'

'Could I see your seismic survey data? I've been studying a lot of undersea terrain in this region lately. Perhaps I could be of help.'

'I'm afraid the data isn't aboard ship.'

Ramsey saw through the lie. 'Have you completed an environmental impact assessment for this area?'

'Our scientists have determined there is no impact.'

'Even with blasting?'

'Blasting?' Díaz replied with a wary look. 'We are not conducting any blasting.'

'Our charter specifies full environmental impact assessments and minimally invasive operations in the course of any mining activity. I've built a lifetime's reputation on safe and friendly mining techniques. I must insist that the contract stipulations be followed.'

'Of course. I'll have the reports sent to you next week.'

Díaz drained his drink and rose to his feet. 'It was nice of you to stop by, Mr Ramsey. I hope you have a pleasant journey to New Orleans.'

Ramsey slowly finished his drink. With a sick feeling, he realized that everything Pitt had told him about Díaz was true. He had signed away his ship to mercenaries under the protection of the Cuban government – and they were about to unleash a vast environmental disaster. The situation left him with little recourse.

'It is later than I thought,' Ramsey said. 'Thank you for the drink, Juan. I best get going.'

They exited the wardroom and returned to the deck. Walking past the bulk cutter hangar, Ramsey noticed a crewman in a hazmat suit sweeping up some seafloor residue. It made him think of Pitt and he glanced over the rail at the barge tied alongside.

Bidding Díaz good-bye, he climbed down to his waiting launch and cast off toward his yacht. As the illuminated outline of the *Sea Raker* receded behind him, Ramsey kicked at a loose tarp on the floorboard and muttered to the breeze, 'Good luck, Dirk Pitt. You're going to need it.'

67

Crouched behind a pallet of explosives on the barge, Pitt watched Ramsey's launch sail away as his mind returned to his daughter. The discovery that Díaz was aboard the *Sea Raker* changed everything. It gave him hope that Summer might be aboard, but it also changed his strategy. He'd planned to sneak aboard and somehow disable the mining equipment. But if Summer was aboard, he would have to find her first.

With Ramsey's help, he'd made it this far. Covered by a tarp, he'd hidden on the floor of the launch as Ramsey visited the *Sea Raker*. While the Canadian met with Díaz, the launch's pilot idled the boat off the mining ship's side and let it drift astern. When a few nosy ship hands at the rail grew bored and wandered off, the pilot eased alongside the barge and signaled Pitt. With a quick leap, he boarded unseen.

He crossed the barge, moving quickly from crate to crate. A heavy white powder littered the deck, which he knew was the ANFO from some spilled bags. The barge was only half full of crated explosives, indicating a large portion had already been deployed on one of the thermal vents. The delivery means was in service a few yards ahead of the barge: a steel-grated platform suspended by a thick drop cable. Pitt watched as several crewmen loaded a long, coiled tube on to the platform and lowered it over the side.

He made his way to the rear of the barge and climbed aboard the *Sea Raker* when he spotted no one about. The ship was otherwise alive with activity. He could only assume the crew was preparing to blow the thermal vent. An uneasy feeling began to creep over him. He might be too late to prevent it.

He shook his doubts aside, knowing his top priority was to find Summer.

He crept forward, holding to the shadows, but progressed only a short distance when a work crew came up behind him, lugging a replacement cutter head for the auxiliary mining machine. One man tripped under the burden, twisting his ankle and dropping his end of the weight. A supervisor, straining under the load on the opposite side, noticed Pitt standing nearby.

'You, over there. Come give us a hand.'

Pitt was trapped. If he assisted the men, the bright deck lights would reveal he wasn't part of the crew. If he ignored the supervisor, he would create an undue suspicion.

Spotting a door to a nearby prefabricated structure, he took a chance. Shrugging at the supervisor, he motioned toward the door, stepped over and turned the handle. His luck held and the door opened. He ducked inside as the supervisor shouted a curse in his direction.

Pitt had expected to walk into an equipment locker but found himself at the back of the mining control room. Multiple video images illuminated the big screen while chatter from computer station operators rattled off the steel walls. Pitt eased into a dark corner when he saw Díaz directing the operation from his armchair down front.

Several ROVs flitted about the sea bottom, displaying the massive cache of ANFO explosives piled into the slit trench. One ROV turned upward, its camera capturing the arrival of the bulk cutter as it dropped to the seabed and vanished in a cloud of sediment.

The current blew the water clear as the ROV moved in for a closer view. When it turned to capture the side of the cutter, Pitt nearly choked. Clasped by the cutter's manipulator and held to its side like a bread basket was the NUMA submersible *Starfish*.

Yet it wasn't the appearance of the *Starfish* that startled Pitt. What took his breath away was the sight of his daughter, sitting alone and helpless in the pilot's seat of the stricken submersible.

68

Ninety minutes.

That was the remaining life of the *Starfish*'s battery reserves. Once the power failed and the carbon dioxide scrubbers ceased, Summer would die a slow death from asphyxiation. Unless hypothermia from the cold struck first.

When Díaz and his men forced her into the submersible and lowered it over the side, she knew he didn't intend for her to surface again. She immediately activated the life-support systems, while shutting off all nonessential power drains. She was thankful her father had powered down everything when they were brought aboard the *Sea Raker*, leaving her some remaining battery charge.

Once on the seafloor, she realized ninety minutes was a false hope. As the bulk cutter's treads began turning and the big machine lurched forward, she saw the massive pit filled with explosives. Her death would come soon – and violently.

The cutter trudged to the edge of the trench and stopped. Its manipulator arm rotated outward, swinging the *Starfish* from its side. An operator on the surface released the manipulator's grip and the submersible dropped into the trench, landing upright on a carpet of explosives.

A pair of ROVs captured the scene, their lights blinding Summer as they buzzed about the submersible. They gradually pulled away, hovering over the bulk cutter as it crawled into the darkness.

Summer peered out the viewport until the ROVs faded to a small speck of light. Then she went to work.

She had one last gambit: the fact she could still make the submersible buoyant. The ROV may have destroyed the sub's external thrusters on their first encounter, but it hadn't hampered the *Starfish*'s ability to surface.

Summer powered the ballast tank pumps and initiated a purge to empty the flooded tanks. She waited for a reaction, but nothing happened. There was normally a hissing of compressed air, followed by a gurgle of expelled water, but now there was only silence. She checked the power and circuit breakers and tried a second time.

Again nothing. Then she checked the compressed air cylinder that supported the ballast tank. The gauge read zero. The *Sea Raker*'s crew had emptied the cylinder to prevent such an attempt.

Glancing out the viewport at the bed of explosives, she tried not to panic. She took a deep breath – and thought of one more option. The *Starfish* was fitted with twin lead weights that could be jettisoned for lift in an emergency. Her father had released one set of weights when they tried to escape the bulk cutter, but another still remained.

She climbed behind the seat, where under a floor panel she found a secondary release. Grabbing the handle, she twisted it to the drop position.

Nothing happened.

The *Sea Raker*'s crew had done their handiwork there, too, securing the weight so it couldn't be released. Díaz had made sure her last voyage was a one-way trip.

With an angry resignation, Summer slid into the pilot's seat and gazed into the darkness, wondering how much longer she had left to live.

69

A trickle of cold sweat ran down Pitt's back as he watched the *Starfish* being deposited on the pile of explosives. The ROV's underwater cameras tracked the bulk cutter as it left the submersible and crawled to the utility platform, which had been separately lowered to the seafloor. The cutter stopped alongside the platform and used its manipulator to pluck up the end of the coiled detonator tube filled with TNT.

The bulk cutter reversed course and began crawling back toward the explosives trench, unraveling the tube along its side. It eventually pulled the snake-like detonator tube clear of the utility platform, trailing a wire cable. Tagged with small floats, the cable led to the surface, where a console operator a few rows ahead of Pitt could ignite the charge on command.

Pitt glanced around the control room and dismissed any thought of trying to commandeer the bulk cutter. Three men operated its controls from an expanded console near the front of the room. Near it was a side exit door, guarded by a pair of armed soldiers. Farther back was an unoccupied table used for the auxiliary cutter, followed by a half-dozen staggered workstations that controlled the ROVs, the utility platform, and numerous shipboard cameras.

Nearest Pitt was one of the ROV control stations: a large table topped with several monitors and a joystick control system. A slight man in military fatigues and cap hunkered over the controls, engrossed in tracking the movements of the bulk cutter with his ROV's camera.

Pitt watched the camera's view of the detonator tube trailing beside the cutter and had an idea. He'd need some help, but it was all that time allowed.

The key was the ROV and its operator station at the back of the room. Weaponless, Pitt stepped to a nearby bookshelf filled with technical manuals. He selected the thickest one, then crept back to the station. As the operator focused on the controls, he never noticed Pitt step behind him and smash the binder into his temple.

The operator let out a muted grunt as he tumbled from his chair, a communications headset flying off him. Pitt instantly slipped an arm around his throat and squeezed in a tight choke hold. The dazed man gave little resistance as Pitt dragged him out the back door with a few quick steps. The action went undetected. While the front of the control room was brightly illuminated by the video screen, the rear was virtually black.

Outside, the operator regained his bearings and tried to break free. Pitt didn't give him the opportunity, swinging him forward and driving him into a bulkhead. The man didn't throw up an arm in time and connected headfirst with the steel wall. His skull made a loud clang, and Pitt felt him go limp.

'I'm sure Díaz offers workmen's comp,' Pitt muttered. He dragged the man behind a storage locker and removed his cap. Placing it on his own head, he hurried back to the control room and took his place at the ROV controls.

Díaz was yelling and pointing at the big screen, and Pitt immediately saw why. The unmanned ROV had drifted to the bottom and was sitting idle, its main camera pointed at a rock. Pitt kept his face hidden behind the monitors as he groped for the toggle and thruster controls. An experienced hand at operating ROVs, Pitt managed to raise the vehicle and move it forward, quieting Díaz's complaints.

He quickly gained a feel for the ROV, which operated much like a backyard, radio-controlled helicopter. He guided the ROV across the bottom, pursuing the tracks of the bulk cutter until the cutter and its trailing detonator tube came into view.

There were two monitors on his operator's desk, which relayed video feeds from separate cameras on the front and back of the ROV. Only the front view was displayed on the screen at the front of the room. He experimented with the commands and found the drop-down menu for picture quality.

Díaz wanted to see the detonator tube being inserted and he voiced his wishes from his command seat. Pitt began distorting the picture quality. In frustration,

Díaz ordered another ROV to take over and dropped Pitt's ROV from the big screen.

He readjusted the picture and was relieved to see that the bulk cutter was retracing its tracks toward the *Starfish*. Pitt quelled the urge to peek in on Summer and studied the flank of the bulk cutter and its trailing explosives.

The cutter crept slowly past the *Starfish* and proceeded another twenty feet before stopping. Its manipulator reached out to its full lateral extension, swinging the detonator tube from its side.

At Díaz's command, the tube was released. The forward section coiled into the drill hole, disappearing several feet beneath the base of the trench. The remaining section of tube, with its firing line attached, fell at an angle atop the trench filled with ANFO. Once detonated, the TNT in the tube would initiate a concentrated blast at the heart of the thermal vent's fissure – and set off the ANFO in a broad eruption.

Pitt followed the drop with the ROV, turning it to face the trench. He eased the ROV back from the fissure to provide a panoramic view of the trench. Careful to avoid passing the second ROV's camera, he drove the ROV toward the *Starfish*.

As the yellow submersible loomed up, he spotted Summer in the pilot's seat. He feverishly hoped she would help him save her life.

70

The rattling sound on the exterior lock signaled every-one in the *Sargasso Sea*'s lab that the door was about to open. All the occupants scurried to the back of the bay, where they ducked beneath a large desk. Everyone except Dirk and Giordino, who stood at separate angles to the door shielded by a pair of lab benches.

The door flung open and the helmsman Ross was again shoved into the lab at the point of a muzzle. A commando followed him in and looked about. His eyes squinted in puzzlement. It wasn't the concealed crew at the back of the lab that baffled him as much as the attire of Dirk and Giordino.

Each had a shop towel wrapped around his nose and mouth while wearing crude goggles cut from plastic water bottles. Before the commando could respond, Giordino sidearmed a glass beaker in his direction. The gunman ducked as the beaker struck the door above his head, releasing upon him a shower of glass and liquid.

'Ross, get down!' Dirk yelled.

The helmsman dove to the floor as the commando sprayed the room with gunfire. Anticipating the move, Dirk and Giordino dropped beneath the lab benches.

The firing soon stopped as the gunman dropped his weapon and began rubbing his eyes, which were flooding with tears.

At the sound of the shooting, a second commando came rushing through the door. Dirk popped from behind the bench and let his weapon fly. Another sealed glass beaker, it smashed into the doorframe inches above the man. He, too, was instantly overcome, choking and hacking as his eyes swelled.

The pain-inducing liquid was a homemade batch of tear gas concocted from chemicals in the lab. Aided by the ship's biologist Kamala Bhatt, Dirk had mixed iodine with portions of nitric acid and an acetone solvent and heated it in a sealed container with a match. The mixture was a crude facsimile of riot-control tear gas.

They had tested a small sample on a volunteer crewman, whose red, watery eyes an hour later vouched for its efficacy. Giordino had found a pair of empty beakers in a cabinet, which proved the perfect delivery vehicle.

Dirk and Giordino waited briefly for the gas to disperse, then sprang from their cover. The first commando was crawling toward the door while the second staggered after him. Dirk ran over and scooped up the first commando's weapon. Giordino in turn launched himself at the second commando with his elbows flying. He struck the man hard in the side, propelling them both out the doorway.

Dirk sprinted out after them, finding the two

commandos writhing on the deck with Giordino on top. Giordino had already wrestled the AK-47 from his victim as the man clawed at his eyes. Dirk was reaching down to help Giordino to his feet when a burst of gunfire tore into the bulkhead just above their heads.

'Drop your weapons!' Calzado shouted from twenty feet away. Alerted by the gunfire, he had rushed to the scene accompanied by two more commandos. All three stepped closer, each with an assault rifle aimed at Dirk and Giordino. The NUMA men had no choice but to drop their weapons and stand empty-handed.

With considerable effort, the two tear-gassed guards rose to their feet, their eyes red and burning.

'Close and lock the door to the lab,' Calzado ordered.

The guards nodded and did as instructed. After the door was sealed, one of the commandos motioned toward Dirk and Giordino. 'What about them?'

'I have no time for further hindrances,' Calzado said. 'Stand out of the way. I will take care of them right now.'

Raising his rifle, the commando leader took aim at the two captives and tightened his finger on the trigger.

71

Without the normal humming of its heat-producing electronics, the *Starfish* felt like an icebox. Summer sat with her teeth chattering as the bulk cutter made a return appearance, inching past the submersible while dragging the long detonator tube. She tried to watch the cutter insert the end of the tube in the trench, but her view was blocked by one of the ROVs.

The boxy device approached the submersible and hovered outside its viewport. Summer resisted the urge to extend her middle finger at it, instead shielding her eyes from its glaring lights.

Then an odd thing happened. The ROV flashed its lights.

This time, she didn't hesitate, letting loose with her finger while cursing Díaz for his taunting gesture.

Though clearly observing Summer's response, the ROV didn't waver. Instead, it flashed its lights again, in a short-long-short sequence, as if sending a modified SOS signal.

Intrigued, Summer watched the ROV repeat the flashing twice more. She then reached up and toggled a switch, flashing the submersible's forward external lights.

Her mouth dropped when the ROV responded by tilting up and down as if nodding. Somewhere, someone at the other end of the controls was trying to help.

She leaned forward and watched the ROV as it eased closer. It turned slightly to angle its bright lights away from the cockpit and brushed against the submersible's low-mounted manipulator arm. Again, the ROV flashed its lights.

Summer activated the controls, raising the robotic arm from its cradle.

Again the ROV nodded approval. When Summer continued to raise the manipulator, the ROV pivoted side to side, expressing its disapproval.

Through trial and error under the ROV's guidance, Summer extended the manipulator laterally to its full reach and opened its claw grip.

Ahead of the submersible, the bulk cutter had completed its task and was retracing its tracks to the drop point. Those tracks would bring it alongside the *Starfish* in another minute or two.

Summer watched as the ROV seemed to consider the cutter for a moment, then darted to the submersible's side. Summer had to press her face against the viewport to see its next move.

The ROV pivoted and dropped to the seabed. It thrust toward the *Starfish*, shoving a thin layer of sand in front of it like a snowplow. At first baffled, Summer saw the intent. The ROV had begun its push on the opposite side of the detonator tube's firing cable. It was shoving it toward the *Starfish*. Or more specifically, toward the submersible's manipulator arm.

The ROV wanted her to grasp the cable. She waited as the ROV pushed again. When the cable came into reach, she snatched it with the arm's claw grip.

The ROV gave a quick flash of its lights, then rose and hovered over the approaching bulk cutter. As the big mining machine churned close, the ROV dropped along its side and bumped up against a stubby metal appendage that protruded at a forward angle.

It was a spud, or stabilizer leg, that could be lowered for extra leverage when the cutter was battering through hard rock. The ROV moved up and down along the spud's flat metal foot and flashed its lights.

Summer understood. She retracted the manipulator arm clear of the bulk cutter's path and waited.

The churning steel treads shook the seabed as the machine crept across the bottom. The operator held to his previous tracks, driving alongside the *Starfish*. As its forward treads inched past her viewport, Summer raised the manipulator and aimed it toward the bulk cutter.

When the stabilizer assembly drew within reach, she extended the manipulator and draped the firing cable around the spud's foot. The bulk cutter moved so slowly, she had ample time to loop the cable a second time before releasing her grip. As the machine crept forward, the loop drew tight, snagging fast on the metal appendage.

The ROV appeared outside the viewport and nodded its approval. With a final flash, it whirred off to follow the bulk cutter. Summer waited a minute, then flicked on the *Starfish*'s external lights. She saw the detonator tube unraveling from the trench and sliding past her, tailing the cutter. She killed the lights and watched the glow of the assorted mining equipment again recede into the distance.

Summer checked her remaining battery power, then sat back in the cold, dark confines of the submersible, contemplating the mysterious ROV. It had saved her from dying in an explosion, but could it find a way to get her off the bottom?

72

Pitt was contemplating the same question when the rear door of the control room burst open. An armed soldier stepped in, supporting the woozy frame of the ROV operator. The dazed man regained his focus at the sight of Pitt at his workstation.

'That's him!' He pointed a finger at Pitt. 'That's the man who attacked me. Shoot him!'

Pitt jumped to his feet but refrained from further movement when the soldier leveled his assault rifle on him at point-blank range. The two guards at the front of the room sprinted up a second later. Pitt was now surrounded.

'What's going on here?' Díaz stepped over to see what the commotion was about. His jaw dropped when he saw Pitt standing by the ROV console.

'I believe you have a submersible of mine,' Pitt said calmly. 'I'd like it back.'

The ROV operator stepped forward. 'He attacked me and dragged me out of here so he could control the number two ROV.'

Díaz nodded, not taking his eyes off Pitt. 'You may have cheated death once, but you won't a second time. I will personally deliver you to Havana and take a front-row seat at your execution. But before that, you will join me up front . . . to watch your daughter die.'

He turned to the operator. 'Quickly check on the submersible. We're about to raise the equipment.'

Díaz strode to the front of the room, taking a seat in his command chair. The guards were more diligent this time, taking up positions on either side of Pitt.

Pitt looked up at the video screen and watched the feed from the number two ROV as it circled about the *Starfish*. For an instant, Pitt saw Summer peering out of the viewport as if expecting a message from the ROV. But this time, it just looked at her coldly.

Pitt remembered the detonator tube and held his breath that the ROV wouldn't turn the other direction and find it missing. But the ROV operator didn't think to survey the explosives. He hovered the ROV over the submersible a minute or two, then raised it off the bottom and thrust it toward the distant bulk cutter.

Díaz looked on in satisfaction. 'I hope you said good-bye to her, Mr Pitt,' he said, then addressed the entire room. 'All equipment to the surface. Prepare for detonation.'

Four giant winches began turning around the main deck, spooling the cables attached to the bulk cutter, the utility platform, and the two ROVs. Inside the control room, the underwater video feeds turned to snowy images as the equipment was tugged up through the water.

When all four devices were thirty meters off the

bottom, Díaz phoned the bridge. 'Reposition the ship two hundred meters up-current. We are preparing to detonate.'

The *Sea Raker*'s propellers churned the sea as the big ship slowly moved off station. A few minutes later, the captain reported they were holding the new position as ordered. Díaz asked the chief mining engineer for an update on the deployed equipment.

'Both ROVs are aboard and the utility platform has just cleared the water. The bulk cutter is ascending slowly and is presently showing a depth of twenty meters.'

'We're well clear of the shock zone. Let's proceed with the detonation.' Díaz turned to Pitt. 'Would you like the honors?'

Pitt gave him a hard stare. 'No. I think the last act belongs to you.'

Díaz stepped to the utility platform's control panel and placed his finger over the firing cable activator. He smiled at Pitt and pushed the button.

73

Dirk sunk to his knees, waiting for the slugs from Calzado's assault rifle to tear into his chest as he made a desperate grab for his dropped weapon. Instead, an agonizing bolt of pain shot through his head. His ears felt like they were going to explode, while his skull seemed to vibrate with an intensity that rated a ten on the numeric pain scale.

He thought he had been shot in the head, but as he raised his hands to muffle his ears, he felt no blood. Looking up, he saw that Calzado and his commandos, as well as Giordino, had also fallen to their knees and were crushing their hands against their ears.

Compressing his ears did little to alleviate the pain, but it was an instinctive act of survival against the unseen force. Giordino dropped his hands and reached for the gun at his feet, but the painful auditory assault forced him to abandon the act and return his palms to his ears.

As he cringed from the pain, Dirk noticed a trio of figures emerge from the shadows of the aft deck and slowly approach. They were dressed in commando-style fatigues similar to the Cubans, only black. Curiously, they wore motorcycle-type helmets with thick, dark visors. Two carried assault rifles and were following a third man, who led with an octagonal paddle held in front of him that was wired to a bulky backpack.

The intruders were oblivious to the pain. Drawing closer, the two armed men kicked away the Cubans' weapons, pulled out flex cuffs, and bound the commandos as they squirmed on the deck. The third intruder eased alongside Dirk and Giordino, keeping his electronic paddle aimed at the Cubans.

The pain eased from Dirk's ears and he realized the paddle was somehow generating the auditory assault. When all the Cubans were subdued, the man clicked a button on the paddle and lowered it to his side.

Flipping open his visor, Rudi Gunn smiled at his two NUMA friends. 'Sorry for the earache. Your little escape attempt forced us to engage sooner than we planned.'

'Rudi, you're a sight for sore eyes, but that's as far as it goes,' Giordino said, his ears ringing like the bells of Big Ben at high noon. 'What is that torture contraption?'

'It's called an MRAD, or medium range acoustic device. This is a portable version of a system built for the Navy, used to ward off small-boat attacks or Somali-type pirates. It's a high-intensity directional acoustic array capable of emitting sound waves at an extremely high volume, which are in turn relatively focused.'

'A loudspeaker on steroids,' Dirk said, rubbing his ears.

'Pretty much. Jack and I borrowed it from a friend at the Naval Research Laboratory.'

Jack Dahlgren, the burly marine engineer who was old friends with Dirk, approached carrying an assault rifle. 'Glad to see you boys happy and healthy. Rudi, we best move to the bridge. Does anybody know how many commandos are aboard?'

'I counted nine.' Giordino picked up one of the Cuban guns. 'You keep that ear blaster away from me and I'll back you up.'

Gunn passed some small headphones to Dirk and Giordino. 'These will help.'

He reactivated the system and led his armed companions to the forward superstructure. The ship's bulkheads acted as a deterrent to the MRAD system, so Gunn didn't hesitate, scrambling up the companionway and bursting on to the bridge.

The remaining four commandos were on duty and alert to the commotion on deck. Two were standing watch with assault rifles and instantly turned toward Gunn. He dove to the floor, holding the MRAD paddle aloft. Dahlgren and his partner turned the corner and fired. Their aim was true and they took down the two shooters.

The other two Cubans, unarmed, had fallen to the floor during the audio bombardment and now climbed to their feet. They raised their hands as Dirk and Giordino entered with their weapons drawn.

Dirk stepped over and helped Gunn to his feet. 'Rudi, are you okay?'

'I'm good. Is everybody on the ship safe?'

'They won't be for long,' Giordino said. 'Word is, our friends planted explosives on the ship and were about to send her to the bottom.'

He stepped to the smaller of the two Cubans. Grabbing him by the lapel, he raised him off the floor and ground his teeth in the man's face. 'Where are the explosives? *Dónde están los explosivos?*'

The soldier saw the unflinching determination in Giordino's eye. *'La sala de máquinas,'* he grunted.

'The engine room,' Dirk said. 'Let's go.'

He and Giordino sprinted from the top of the ship to the bottom, reaching the engine room two minutes later. They didn't have to search long before finding several crates of explosives positioned beside a seawater induction valve. It would have quickly flooded the ship.

Giordino found a simple digital timer wired to a detonator that was packed into the high explosives. He nervously removed the detonator. 'Two more hours and she'd be on her way to the bottom.'

'Good thing Rudi and Jack arrived when they did.'

They climbed back to the main deck and released the crew from the two labs, but not before Giordino flung the timer and detonator over the side. They helped Dahlgren lock up the surviving Cubans, then rejoined Gunn on the bridge.

He stood over a communications console, shaking

his head. 'The satellite communications system was destroyed in the shoot-out.'

'We've still got marine radios,' Giordino said. 'By the way, how'd you find us?'

'Tracked you with satellite imaging, until we left Bimini on the NUMA research ship *Caroline*. Fortunately, you hadn't moved by the time we crossed the straits.'

'Where's the *Caroline* now?'

'She's holding in friendly waters, about ten miles due north.' He gave Giordino a studious gaze. 'I've been afraid to ask. Where's Pitt and Summer?'

'As of two days ago, a mining ship called the *Sea Raker*,' Giordino said. 'They were abducted aboard the *Starfish* while investigating the sub-sea mining. The *Sea Raker* was operating at the site of the *Alta*'s sinking. We need to find her and fast.'

Gunn nodded as he took the helm and dialed up the ship's engines. He stabbed a finger at a horizontal radar screen that had survived the shoot-out. 'If the *Caroline* doesn't find her first,' he said in a determined voice, 'we will.'

74

Fifty feet beneath the hull of the *Sea Raker*, an electrical charge ignited a lead azide detonator. The small primary detonation instantly ignited the eight hundred pounds of TNT packed into the sleeve that dangled from the bulk cutter.

A shock wave rippled through the water as the explosion created a large gas bubble in the depths. The bubble rose rapidly, expanding in size and power as it ascended through less dense layers of seawater.

On board the *Sea Raker*, the shock wave was felt first, rattling through the ship like a burst of thunder.

'What was that?' Díaz asked as the deck shuddered beneath his feet.

The chief mining engineer shook his head. 'I don't know. There should be no impact to the ship at this range.'

Pitt smiled at the two men and pointed to the video screen. 'Perhaps your explosives got tied up below.'

Díaz looked at the screen. The video feed from the bulk cutter had gone blank.

'What have you done?' he screamed at Pitt. He turned and grabbed an assault rifle from one of the guards.

Pitt didn't have to answer. A second later, the explosives-induced gas bubble struck the underside of the *Sea Raker* like a boot to the belly. The ship's midsection was driven almost out of the sea, its keel fracturing in three places. Hull plates ruptured along the vessel's spine, allowing the sea to flood in from stern to stem. Alarms sounded throughout the ship as power from the main generators was instantly severed.

On the bridge, shipboard diagnostics told the captain his worst fear. Flooding was pervasive and there was no hope of staying afloat. He issued the order to abandon ship, which blared through the vessel's PA system on a recorded message.

In the control room, everyone had been knocked off their feet. The electrical power had vanished, pitching the bay into total darkness. As Díaz climbed to his feet still clutching the rifle, emergency lights slowly flickered on, casting the room in a red glow.

The chief mining engineer stood and grabbed Díaz's arm. 'Come, we must get out of here.'

Díaz shook his head, his face a mask of rage. He knocked the engineer away and swept the room with his weapon. 'Where is he?'

His anger magnified when he realized that Pitt was no longer there.

75

Pitt was already on the run to save his daughter. His only hope, albeit a slim one, was with the auxiliary cutter machine that was aboard the ship. If he could quickly lower and drive the cutter to the *Starfish*, he might be able to latch on to the submersible and raise it to the surface.

It was a big if.

Crawling out of the blackened control room, he found an early state of chaos on deck. There was already a panicked exodus as the crew flocked to the lifeboats. Shouts and curses filled the air as the soldiers, most with no prior seagoing experience, ran about searching for the boats. Whatever loyalty the soldiers owed to Díaz had vanished in a sudden effort to save their own skins.

Pitt realized he was on the opposite deck from the auxiliary cutter and sprinted across an amidships passageway. He stopped momentarily at the rail and radioed Ramsey, requesting he return with the *Gold Digger* to pick up survivors and make an emergency call for a deepwater submersible rescue. He knew the chances of the latter arriving in time were minimal.

As he raced forward across the deck, he saw the *Sea*

Raker had generated a noticeable list but seemed to be settling slowly. She was going to afford Pitt a few minutes afloat.

He fought past a group of men lined up to board a lifeboat, then ran along the explosives barge, still secured to the ship. Just beyond the barge, he found the dark bay where the auxiliary cutter was housed. Only partial power had been restored to the ship, and Pitt feared the machine would be dead. Locating a control station at the edge of the bay, he found that wasn't the case. A row of lights illuminated the control panel, showing the auxiliary cutter still had full power.

Pitt fidgeted with the controls, decoding the machine's drive mechanism and activating its forward lights and camera. A separate overhead hydraulic lift was used to lower the cutter over the side. Searching for its controls, he stopped as several men rushed into the bay.

'There he is,' a voice cried out.

It was Díaz and a guard, both leveling assault rifles.

As he dove to the ground, Pitt punched the winch activation button and slapped the auxiliary cutter's forward control lever. A seam of bullets ripped into the control panel an instant later, showering him with plastic debris. Although the bay was dimly lit, he was still in view of the gunmen and he rolled to the side as more shots followed.

The back of the hangar proved darker, and Pitt

scrambled behind the rear of the cutter. The big machine was surging forward, its steel treads clattering against the wood decking. With its cutter head barely ten feet from the rail, the vehicle was well on its way to marching over the side.

Díaz yelled to one of his men on the right, so Pitt crawled along the cutter's left side. A hail of gunfire sounded through the bay, but it wasn't directed at Pitt. Someone was aiming high, the bullets hitting the ceiling.

The auxiliary cutter ground to a halt as something struck the deck with a thump just in front of Pitt. It was the cutter's overhead power cable, deliberately severed by the gunshots to disable the machine. Sparks flew from the end of the cable, which began spooling loosely about the deck as its supply winch continued to turn.

Pitt heard a noise in front of him. A guard had hopped on to the cutter machine's front frame and was lining up a shot on him.

Pitt lunged forward, grabbing the severed cable lead and jamming it against the steel frame. The gunman screamed as a fatal surge of high-voltage power coursed through the cutter.

Pitt pulled away the cable and stepped to the front of the cutter, intent on grabbing the dead man's weapon. He hesitated at hearing a shuffle on the deck. Díaz was charging around the left side of the cutter, while two others approached from the back.

404

Thinking fast, Pitt snake-whipped the power cable toward the side rail, watching as its sparking tip slipped over the side. Pitt then backed around the right side of the cutter and raised his arms over his head.

The two soldiers converged on him first and held him at gunpoint until Díaz approached.

Díaz saw the dead guard beneath the auxiliary cutter's frame and stared at Pitt with his eyes aglow. 'I'm afraid you won't be going to Havana after all. It ends now.'

He raised his rifle and aimed at Pitt's chest. As he reached for the trigger, a whooshing sound erupted behind him. Then he disappeared in a maelstrom of fire.

When Pitt had thrown the live power cable aside, he hadn't just tossed it over the rail. He had tossed it into the adjacent barge. The unraveling cable snaked around its interior, igniting the scatterings of ANFO that littered the deck. It was only a matter of time before a smoldering pile ignited one of the crates of TNT, detonating the barge's entire contents of explosives.

The barge blew apart in a thunderous blast that sent a thick white cloud heaving into the night sky. It shook the entire length of the *Sea Raker*, shattering her superstructure. The vessel lurched to the side, jettisoning the auxiliary cutter and other loose equipment near the rail, before settling sharply by the bow. The stern rose out of the water a minute later, and the ship glided under the surface on a collision course with the seafloor.

A circle of foam and bubbles rippled the surface in the ship's wake. Then only silence draped the waves for the remaining survivors left floating on a dark sea.

76

The auxiliary cutter saved Pitt's life twice. Standing beside its huge mass, he was shielded from the direct force of the blast while those around him were incinerated. Still, he was knocked off his feet by the concussion, then nearly crushed by one of the steel treads when the cutter began sliding toward the rail.

Choking through the blinding smoke, Pitt heaved himself on to the topsides of the open tread and grabbed an upper brace. He hung on as the cutter slid through the *Sea Raker*'s side rail and toppled over the edge. The cutter tried to carry him to the bottom, but he pushed away and swam to the surface. He stroked away from the *Sea Raker* to avoid its suction, then turned and watched as the last frightened crewmen jumped overboard before the ship slipped under.

He had been treading water only a few minutes when the *Gold Digger* burst on the scene with a throaty roar from its motors. It stopped near one of the *Sea Raker*'s lifeboats as a searchlight on its stern scanned the waters. Desperate to get to Summer, Pitt swam to the yacht and took his place with the *Sea Raker*'s survivors clamoring to get aboard.

Ramsey was on deck leading the rescue. He flashed a

relieved look when Pitt staggered aboard. 'I was worried about you when we saw that second explosion.'

Pitt could only nod. His ears were ringing, his body ached, and he was out of breath. More than that, he knew he had failed Summer, who was trapped on the seafloor beneath them.

'Sorry about the ship,' he finally muttered.

'You . . . you did it?' Ramsey gave Pitt a chagrined look. 'Your friendship is really beginning to cost me.'

Pitt shook off the remark. 'Did you contact the Navy's undersea rescue unit? How soon can they get here?'

Ramsey shook his head. 'I did better than that. I hooked up with a much closer vessel that you might be familiar with.' He pointed off the starboard rail.

For the first time, Pitt noticed the lights of an approaching vessel. Its illuminated profile had a familiar look, and as it drew near, he could make out a hint of its turquoise-colored hull in the darkness. 'The *Sargasso Sea*?'

'Yes. They responded over the radio. It seems they were searching for the *Sea Raker* – looking for you and your daughter.'

'Who's in command?'

'A fellow named Gunn. He seemed surprised when I mentioned your name.'

Ramsey motioned to one of his crewmen, then turned back to Pitt. 'I'll get a Zodiac in the water so you can get to her right away.'

A tired smile crossed Pitt's face. He reached out and shook Ramsey's hand.

'Mark, you're a good man. And if it's any consolation, I'll make you a guarantee.'

'What's that?' Ramsey said.

'I promise you'll never lose to me on the track again.'

77

Pitt gunned the Zodiac's motor, racing to the *Sargasso Sea* as it slowed to a drift near the luxury yacht. Dirk, Gunn and Giordino were all waiting at the rail and helped Pitt aboard.

Giordino eyed Pitt's singed and waterlogged clothes. 'You look like you took a nap in a rock crusher,' he said.

'I needed the sleep.'

'Where's Summer?' Dirk asked. 'The *Gold Digger* said you had a deepwater emergency.'

'She's stuck on the bottom in the *Starfish*,' he said. 'While I'm glad to see the ship, that was the *Sargasso Sea*'s only submersible. We need some outside help – and quick.'

'Actually, we don't.' Gunn extended an arm like a waiter. 'If you'll be kind enough to follow me . . .'

Gunn quickly escorted the group aft with Pitt in a frantic rush to save Summer. At the stern deck, they found Jack Dahlgren inspecting the submersible Gunn had borrowed from the *Caroline*. Named the *Bullet*, it was a hybrid that mated a submersible's cabin to a power-boat's hull. With both conventional and electric motors, the sleek craft was able to skim the surface at high speed.

Pitt was familiar with the vessel, having piloted it in Turkey a few years earlier. 'Where'd this come from?' he asked.

'Jack and I needed something fast and stealthy to get aboard the *Sargasso Sea*. She was operating out of Bimini on the *Caroline*, so we brought the ship in close and piloted her the rest of the way.'

Dahlgren looked up at Pitt and nodded. 'Good to see you, boss. Heard you need a fast ride downstairs.'

'Summer's life depends on it.'

'She's good to go,' Dahlgren said, patting the submersible. 'Hop in and we'll get you over the side.'

Pitt turned to Gunn as he made his way to the *Bullet*'s hatch. 'Ramsey's going to need some help with the survivors.'

Gunn nodded. 'We'll lend a hand, once you're off.'

Giordino joined Pitt in the submersible and they were quickly lowered over the side. Pitt took a bead on Ramsey's yacht and barreled along the surface, descending just as they neared the *Gold Digger*.

The submersible would normally descend by gravity alone, but they lacked the luxury of time. After flooding the ballast tanks, Pitt pushed the nose of the *Bullet* forward and applied full propulsion. The vehicle shot downward. At seven hundred feet, Pitt eased back on the thrusters, and leveled off a minute later as the seafloor loomed beneath them.

The *Bullet* wasn't equipped with sonar, so they had to locate Summer visually. Giordino marked their position as Pitt propelled the submersible in a wide arc.

'There's something on the right.' Giordino pointed out the submersible's large acrylic viewport.

Pitt adjusted course toward a dark object at the fringe of their visibility. It was the auxiliary cutter, which had righted itself during its descent and landed upright on the bottom. Pitt circled around the large cutter head and paused at the gruesome sight. A man was impaled on the blades, his singed uniform indicating he'd been blasted on to them by the barge's explosion.

'Say hello to Juan Díaz,' Pitt said, recognizing the figure. The face was twisted in a final death cry. 'He was responsible for this operation.'

'I see you cut him up with your wit and charm,' Giordino said.

'That and a ton of explosives.'

Giordino marked their position as Pitt accelerated forward. Summer had to be within two or three hundred yards. He traveled that distance, then looped to his left. The bottom became rockier, rising with mounds and hills that showed occasional signs of marine life.

'Water temperature is up a few degrees,' Giordino said. 'We must be in the neighborhood of the thermal vent.'

A few moments later, they came across some tread marks. Pitt followed them to the trench filled with explosives. The yellow *Starfish* was visibly perched on the far side. Pitt zoomed over, bringing the two submersibles nose to nose.

Summer was slumped over in the pilot's seat. As the bright lights shone into the cockpit, she rolled her head back and opened her eyes. She blinked twice, then closed her eyes and leaned back in the seat.

'She looks to be suffering carbon monoxide poisoning,' Giordino said.

'We'll have to find a way to get her up on our own.' Pitt backed the submersible away and slowly circled the *Starfish*.

'Hang on, partner,' Giordino said. 'Take a look at the aft frame.'

Pitt followed Giordino's lead and examined the base of the *Starfish*. Several strands of wire were wrapped around a side frame and extended underneath the submersible. Pitt pivoted around the *Starfish*, observing that the ends of the wires were secured on the opposite side. 'It's the secondary emergency ballast weight. They've wired it up so Summer can't release it.'

'That explains why she's stuck here,' Giordino said. 'They probably spiked the ballast tank, too.'

'You up for some surgery?'

'With no waiting.'

Pitt brought the submersible as close as he could, holding it at an angled hover while Giordino went to work. Using his own small manipulator, Giordino grasped one of the wires, then rotated the mechanical claw. The wire easily snapped under the manipulator's hydraulic power.

Giordino made quick work of the remaining wires. But the *Starfish* failed to ascend.

Pitt brought his submersible in slowly and gave it a firm nudge. Nothing happened.

'She might be stuck in the mud,' Giordino said.

'Then let's pull her out.' He hovered above the *Starfish*, creeping across its top until Giordino could snare a lift ring with the manipulator.

'I got her,' he said, 'though that mechanical arm isn't made for hauling.'

Pitt nodded. He slowly purged his ballast tanks. The *Bullet* rose slightly and stopped as the manipulator reached its full extension.

Pitt kept on the ballast pumps, then tapped his thrusters. The submersible pulled forward, tilting the *Starfish*. Then the yellow submersible broke free of the mud's suction – and started to ascend.

The two submersibles rose together, but the ascent was too slow for Pitt's liking. He powered the thrusters and angled toward the surface. The rise was still agonizing for him. There were no lights on inside the *Starfish*, indicating Summer's battery reserves had expired.

Giordino released the manipulator's grip at fifty feet, and the two vessels broke the surface together. Pitt had Giordino bring them alongside as he opened the hatch and hopped out.

A searchlight from the *Sargasso Sea* illuminated them

as Pitt leaped aboard the *Starfish*. He attacked the main hatch, releasing its safety latch and spinning it open. He quickly slithered into the interior, which had turned icy.

Summer wrapped her arms around her father as he picked her up. She shivered suddenly, breathing hard. 'Dad.'

He carried her to the hatch, where Giordino stood, reaching down with his thick arms.

'Hand her up.' He pulled her out like a rag doll.

Pitt climbed out to see Summer open her eyes and force a smile.

Cradled by the two men atop the submersible, she inhaled deep breaths of night air. 'I don't feel quite as foggy,' she said, 'but I'm getting a headache you wouldn't believe.'

'You nearly slept for good,' Giordino said as the *Sargasso Sea* closed in to pick them up.

'I saw a bright light,' she said in a weak voice. 'I thought it was an angel calling me, then I realized it was something else.'

'What's that?' Pitt asked, leaning close.

'It was you,' she said, reaching up to her father's face and stroking away a tear.

EPILOGUE
Puerto Grande

Challenging the Kelowna

78

General Alberto Gutier walked into the office of the vice president and sized it up for himself. It was a spacious enclave on the top floor of the Cuban Communist Party headquarters, featuring a private bathroom and an impressive city view. Gutier took a quick glance out the window at the José Marti Memorial, which stood illuminated against the night sky. The office would do quite nicely, he thought, once the antiquated décor of its current occupant was removed.

Although Vice President César Alvarez was over eighty and in frail health, his mind was still quick. He remained seated behind a large desk as Gutier was escorted into the room.

'Mr Vice President,' Gutier said, 'you are looking well this evening.'

'Thank you, General,' Alvarez said in a raspy voice. 'Please, take a seat.'

'Why do you wish to see me at this late hour?'

'The news from the Cayman Islands is not good.'

'It is a terrible tragedy.'

'What is the latest information that you have?' Alvarez asked.

'Nothing more than the official reports,' Gutier said.

'There was an explosion on a yacht shortly after the president stepped aboard. No one has seen him since, so it is presumed he perished in the blast.'

'Rescue teams have been unable to identify any remains, so there can be no hope.' The vice president shook his head. 'Who would want to harm the president?'

'Who but the CIA?' Gutier said. 'They tried to kill Fidel and now they have succeeded with Raúl.'

'What are you saying? You can't honestly believe it was the Americans?'

'Most certainly. I had in custody the man responsible. He was an American marine engineer who was found with explosives off our shores. Regrettably, he was killed in transit to Havana in a helicopter crash.'

'That is a serious allegation.'

'Do not worry. We will manage the affairs of state confidently together and stand tall against the cultural intrusion by the Americans. Very soon, we will be stronger than you can imagine.'

'We?'

'When you assume the presidency, Cuba will need a new vice president. I stand ready to serve our nation in this capacity.'

'The president had indicated his desire for a succession that includes Foreign Minister Ruiz. I thought, perhaps, you knew that.'

'Ruiz can hardly be appointed to anything now, given his reckless admiration for America.' Gutier gave the old politician a haughty stare. 'I need not remind you where the Revolutionary Army would stand on the matter.'

Alvarez returned Gutier's look with his own wizened gaze. 'Yes, I see what you mean. That could indeed prove unpopular.' He looked at his watch as if realizing he'd missed an appointment and rose from his chair.

'General, if you'll please excuse me for a moment, I'll be right back.' The aged man shuffled out of the office, closing the door behind him.

Gutier sat back and grinned. The vice presidency would be his. Then it would be only a matter of time before he ascended to the presidency. He would take delight in his first act, demoting Ruiz to serve as a Party representative on a pig farm somewhere in the hinterlands.

His jubilant vision was interrupted by a shuffling sound nearby. A figure emerged from the office's small bathroom.

Dressed in a gray suit and crisp white shirt, Raúl Castro appeared nothing like the ghost he should have been. 'Good evening, General.' Castro settled into Alvarez's chair.

'M-Mr President,' Gutier stammered. 'I thought you were dead.'

'Of course you did. Clever of you to blame the CIA when they are the ones who alerted me to your assassination attempt. I didn't want to believe it, but hearing your aspirations just now confirms the truth.'

'I had nothing to do with that.'

'Of course you did. The official reports from the Cayman Islands all indicate there was a fire aboard the yacht. Nobody said a word about an explosion. Nobody but you.'

Gutier was too stunned to think clearly. 'But I saw a video of you boarding the boat just before it exploded.'

Castro smiled. 'A nice double, wasn't he? Jorge Castenada. A deranged farmer who killed his family several years ago and was serving a life sentence in Boniato Prison. He was recently diagnosed with pancreatic cancer, so he didn't have long to live before you murdered him. Remember the name, though, because now it is yours.'

The door to the office burst open and four security guards charged in, followed by Vice President Alvarez. The guards wrenched Gutier to his feet and cuffed his hands behind his back. As they started to drag him to the door, he cried out to Castro, 'Stop. This is a mistake. You must listen to me.'

'Good-bye, Jorge Castenada,' Castro said.

'What do you mean by calling me that?'

Castro held up his hand to halt the guards. He stepped close and looked Gutier up and down with contempt. 'Yesterday, General Alberto Gutier was killed in the accidental crash of an Army helicopter off the northern coast. Jorge Castenada, meanwhile, is returning to solitary confinement in Boniato Prison, where he will serve out the remainder of his life sentence without parole.'

Castro nodded and the guards dragged the defeated general out of the office. His screams of protest gradually receded down the building's back stairwell.

'I always thought the man was vermin,' Alvarez said quietly.

'He and his brother both, apparently. A healthy lesson, I believe, in where the country shouldn't go.'

'Minister Ruiz believes greater liberty for the people will prevent his type from gaining power.'

'Perhaps he is right.'

'What next, Mr President?'

Castro stared out the open door for several moments. 'I believe my next order of business is to pay a visit to the harbor docks.'

79

The morning sun washed over the *Gold Digger* and the *Sargasso Sea* as they sat moored bow to stern at the Port of Havana's Terminal Sierra Maestra. Shortly after the *Starfish* was recovered, a Cuban Navy corvette had joined the two vessels to assist with the rescue efforts. The corvette then acted as a voluntary escort for the ships' passage to Havana. Military ambulances were waiting on the docks and took the *Sea Raker*'s survivors to an Army hospital under tight security.

Pitt and Gunn stood conversing on the bridge, upwind of Giordino with a freshly lit Ramón Allones he held tightly in his teeth. A crewman entered with a befuddled look. 'Sir, you have a visitor,' he said to Pitt, then stood aside.

Raúl Castro, joined by an aide, walked in without pretense and introduced himself. The startled Americans stepped forward and shook hands, welcoming the Cuban president aboard.

'I'm told you uncovered an unauthorized uranium mining operation in my country and also prevented a great environmental catastrophe,' Castro said.

Pitt nodded. 'I'm glad to hear the mining operation was not of your doing. Unfortunately, several lives were lost, and a rather expensive mining ship was sunk, which may accrue to your government.'

Castro shrugged off the liability. 'My brother and I used to fish the waters off Havana and Matanzas. It would hurt me to see harm done to the sea. The thermal vents there are now safe?'

'Yes, though there are still explosives in place at one site that will have to be removed.'

'What about these mercury releases?' Castro asked.

'That is still a problem,' Gunn said. 'Both here and to the south of Cuba, there are active toxic plumes.'

'We may have a solution,' Pitt said. 'Mark Ramsey believes he can convert one of his underwater mining machines into a type of bulldozer. The machine could fill in a large portion of the currently exposed vents with sediment from the seafloor. This would minimize, if not altogether extinguish, the release of mercury.'

'My government stands ready to assist in any way we can.'

'Thank you, Mr President,' Gunn said.

Castro turned to Pitt. 'My brother once mentioned your name. You helped save Havana from ruin at one time.'

'It was many years ago,' Pitt said.

'You are a true friend of Cuba.' Castro eyed the box of cigars Giordino had brought to the bridge. 'I see you have already partaken in our fine tobacco. Is there anything else I can offer you in appreciation?'

425

'Mr President, there is a Spanish shipwreck off Punta Maisí that we would like to explore. It may be carrying a Meso-American artifact that Juan Díaz was pursuing.'

'I've been told that Díaz kept a warehouse filled with antiquities, which shall now be turned over to our National Museum of Natural History. You have my permission to explore the wreck, but I'd ask that any artifacts you recover be provided to the museum.'

'Of course.'

Castro turned to leave and Pitt escorted him to the bridge wing. The morning light cast the buildings of old Havana in a swath of gold. Castro waved his arm toward the city.

'This is a very special place. I can tell you, the people of Havana and all of Cuba are grateful for the harm you prevented. It is, I suspect, more than you know.'

'The people of Cuba are worthy of good things,' Pitt said. He observed Castro take in the beauty of the old city and a thought occurred to him.

'Mr President, there's nothing more you can do for me, but there is something you could do for Cuba.'

Castro looked at Pitt and nodded. 'For Cuba, anything.'

80

That was the target. *Algonquin*. Haasis wasn't keen on shooting an unarmed merchant ship, but those were his orders. A single torpedo was to be fired to sink her. Pacific Fleet Command wanted it to look like an accident – to the extent that torpedoing a ship could be so disguised. Fat chance, Haasis thought. But at least in the middle of the Pacific, it would take a significant effort on somebody's part to prove the truth.

'Weapons Control, prep torpedo one,' he said.

Haasis remained glued to the periscope as a Mark 48 torpedo was loaded into the number one torpedo tube and the tube flooded. The captain looked at the merchant ship for another minute before calmly calling out, 'Fire number one.'

A faint swoosh sounded from the sub's bow, and Haasis counted the seconds for the torpedo to reach its target. The Liberian-registered ship shuddered and a small plume of black smoke arose amidships. With relief, Haasis saw two lifeboats quickly lowered with a full complement of crew. Its keel shattered by the blast, the heavily loaded ore carrier broke into two pieces, which sank simultaneously ten minutes later.

'Nice shooting, gentlemen,' Haasis said. 'We'll show the video in the mess at dinner tonight.'

He turned to the officer of the deck. 'Parker, alert the *Oregon* to the sinking vessel. They'll be able to pick up the survivors.'

'Yes, sir,' the lieutenant said.

He returned to the captain's side a short time later. 'Message sent and confirmed, sir. The *Oregon* is on her way.'

'Very good.'

'Sir, if I may ask? I recall seeing the *Oregon* when we were in Osaka a few months ago. She's a run-down, dilapidated old freighter. How is it this ship is the only one in the area?'

Haasis shook his head. 'I don't have all the answers, son. I just take my orders and follow them to the best of my ability.'

'Yes, sir.'

Yet the order to sink the ore carrier was one that didn't sit well with Haasis. The captain had been given no explanation, only the required outcome. For the remainder of the *Asheville*'s cruise, the act gnawed at his conscience and kept him turning in his bunk at night. Not until a month later, after the *Asheville* returned to Point Loma Submarine Base, was he told the full nature of the mission. The *Algonquin* was carrying a cargo of high-grade uranium oxide to North Korea, enough to arm dozens of nuclear warheads. After hearing the truth – and accepting a unit commendation on behalf of his boat – the veteran captain never lost a night's sleep again.

81

'It appears someone is guarding the nest,' Gunn said.

He passed a pair of binoculars to Pitt, who stood beside him on the bridge of the *Sargasso Sea*. The NUMA ship was a dozen miles off the eastern tip of Cuba, sailing through a light sea.

Pitt focused the lenses on a modern survey vessel standing at station a half mile ahead. 'We know that Díaz, after stealing Perlmutter's research documents, sent his mining facility manager to locate the *San Antonio*,' Pitt said. 'That must be him.'

'He's the last one to be accounted for,' Gunn said. 'I hear Perlmutter's Cuban burglar didn't fare too well. He was in the country illegally – and being watched by the FBI for industrial spying. They picked him up shortly after Perlmutter's incident, and he will be sent away for a long while.'

Giordino stepped over as the NUMA ship converged on the other vessel. 'Perhaps we should tell those boys thanks for pointing out the wreck site. Saved us a couple of days' searching.'

Gunn smiled. 'I don't suspect they'd consider it too kindly.'

The bridge radio crackled with a gruff, accented

voice. 'Calling the American vessel. You are in protected waters. Leave the vicinity at once or you will be fired upon.'

'I told you they'd be touchy,' Gunn said.

'Reason enough to call in our backup friends,' Pitt said. He switched frequencies and made a call to shore, then dialed back to the survey boat. 'This is the research vessel *Sargasso Sea*. You have twenty minutes to vacate the site and make for Baracoa or we will fire on *you*.'

Pitt's message was met with a flurry of Spanish invectives.

'More than touchy,' Giordino said, 'they're downright grouchy.'

'Then we better dance a bit until the mosquitoes show up.'

Pitt had the NUMA ship turn away and sail slowly toward the Cuban coastline. Twenty minutes later, the ship reversed course, crawling back within a hundred yards of the survey vessel. Blistering threats again emanated from the ship's radio, but Pitt ignored them.

Gunn pointed out the bridge window. 'They're showing their firepower,' he said with a nervous twitch.

A half-dozen men in military garb took up position along the survey ship's rail, pointing assault rifles. One appeared to be wielding a rocket-propelled grenade launcher.

'All crew members off the deck,' Pitt called over the *Sargasso Sea*'s PA system.

The radio blared again. This time, Pitt recognized the voice of Molina.

'This is your last chance. Leave the area at once or we open fire.'

Pitt could see Molina step out of the bridge. A thumping noise sounded as the Cuban leader yelled to his men. The soldiers froze as the ocean in front of them rippled in a fountain of spray. An instant later, a military helicopter burst by, skimming low over the water just feet from the survey ship. The sky darkened briefly as three more helos arrived and circled the ship, firing into the water along her flanks.

They were a squadron of Cuban Mil Mi-24 attack helicopters from a nearby base. Pitt could hear the lead pilot radioing the survey ship and threatening instant destruction if they didn't move.

Molina reluctantly obeyed, getting the ship under way and heading to port with an unwanted airborne escort.

Under Giordino's direction, a side-scan sonar fish was lowered off the stern and the NUMA crew began surveying the seafloor. Within an hour, a small shipwreck appeared on the monitor, not far from the survey ship's stationary position. Molina had indeed been guarding the nest.

The sonar fish was retrieved while the *Starfish*, repaired and refreshed, was prepared for launch. Pitt had his two children meet him at the submersible. 'This is your hunt,' he told them. 'You go down and find it.'

'You don't have to ask twice.' Dirk quickly climbed into the craft. Summer gave her father a quick hug. 'Thanks for indulging us.'

'Just remember to come back up on your own this time.'

A short time later, the submersible reached the seabed at a depth of five hundred feet. Gunn had parked the *Sargasso Sea* right on target. The shipwreck was instantly visible. Dirk guided the submersible over the wreck and inspected its remains.

Perlmutter's research described the *San Antonio* as a steam packet built in Belfast in 1887. The years submerged since her sinking had not been kind. The ship's wood hull and decks had mostly disappeared, leaving little more than a stout keel rising from the sand.

Dirk hovered the *Starfish* over the wreck's midpoint, where the *San Antonio*'s boiler stood upright like a lone sentry in a garden of disintegrating machinery. Off the stern, a bronze propeller glinted under the submersible's floodlights, the only object appearing to have survived the ravages of time unscathed.

'The marine organisms must have left town on a full stomach,' Summer said. 'There's hardly any wood left.'

'Good thing they don't like to eat stone. It might actually help in exposing more of the wreck site.'

Starting at the bow, they began a thorough inspection, poking and prodding the *Starfish*'s manipulator through the scattered debris. Reaching the boiler again,

Summer waved her finger ahead. 'There it is, leaning against the side of the boiler!'

Dirk eased the *Starfish* in for a closer look. A large semicircular stone with a carved surface sat upright among the debris, propped against the side of the boiler. It was identical in size to the stone they'd found at Zimapán.

'It must have been on the main deck and slipped down when the ship disintegrated.' Dirk high-fived his sister. 'Good going, girl.'

Summer gave him a tired grin. 'For all the trouble we've endured in finding it, I sure hope it has something to tell us.'

82

It took several hours before Summer got her answer. The process of securing a sling around the stone and attaching several lift bags required two trips to the surface and considerable finessing with the *Starfish*'s manipulator arm. Assisting the lift bags with a tug on the lines, the submersible helped pull the stone off the bottom and tracked its ascent to the surface.

A crane on the *Sargasso Sea* gently hoisted the stone aboard, then retrieved the submersible. The ship's crew and scientists were crowded around the artifact by the time Dirk and Summer made their way over for a look.

'Looks like a perfect match to the stone in Díaz's office,' Pitt said.

The carvings were less crisp, due to their immersion, but Summer saw much the same patterns and glyphs found on the earlier stone. There was even the completed carving of the bird, which she could see was a heron.

Perhaps more important was the diagram carved at the bottom. It appeared to be a geographic representation of a bay or harbor, with a handful of islands sprinkled about the top. She rubbed her fingertips across the surface, wondering what secret it would reveal.

'Summer, can you kindly stand to the side for a second?' Jack Dahlgren said. 'You're blocking the camera.'

She turned to see Dahlgren standing behind a tripod with a video camera. 'Do you have a satellite link with Dr Madero?'

'He's standing by on the laptop next to the cylinder rack.'

Summer and Dirk stepped to the computer, which showed a live image of Dr Madero in his office in Mexico. His head was bandaged, but he smiled broadly.

'Dirk, Summer, I am just seeing the images. They are wonderful!'

'A long time in coming,' Summer said. 'How are you feeling, Professor?'

'Fine, just fine. I'm still having occasional headaches, but the doctors say those will go away. It's a funny thing, waking up in the hospital after being unconscious for three days. My memory had vacated me, but gradually things have come back.'

'We were shocked to learn Díaz had attacked you in your office.'

'An evil man who got what he deserved. I am glad you both are safe.'

'Safe and anxious to learn what the stone says,' Summer said as Pitt and Giordino joined them for the assessment.

'I've been able to join a still image of the first stone with one your man Dahlgren just sent me of the recovered piece. It finally allows a rough but somewhat complete translation. Of course, Dr Torres could have provided a finer interpretation, God rest his soul.'

'What does it indicate?' Summer asked, unable to contain her excitement.

'I'll summarize as best as I can. It starts with an appearance by Quetzalcoatl, a legendary Toltec ruler, and his army. Motecuhzoma welcomes him but is then killed. There is a rebellion against the intruding forces, where much blood is spilled. Quetzalcoatl is seen to depart during the fighting.

'Afterward, the elders gather gifts and offerings, which are placed in the care of the Eagle and Jaguar Warriors. The offerings are transported in seven vessels across the water to an island marked on the drawing at the base of the stone. There is a representation of Huitzilopochtli, the Aztec ancestral deity. This, along with the image of the heron, suggests they somehow returned to their ancestral home of Aztlán.'

'Any speculation where that island is located?' Dirk asked.

'There is only the image on the bottom – and an indication the voyage may have lasted ten days. Since we don't know where they started from, or which direction they traveled, it is difficult to wager a guess.'

'I just sent an image of the stone to Yaeger,' Dahlgren said as he also joined the group. 'Maybe his computers can find a geographic match.'

'I understand the bit about shipping off some

treasured goodies,' Giordino said, 'but, Professor, who are these Quetzalcoatl, Motecuhzoma, and Huitzilopochtli characters?'

'Huitzilopochtli is the Aztec's ancient founding father, a sort of deified George Washington who led a migration of the Mexica to Tenochtitlan. Quetzalcoatl was a legendary Toltec leader who lived centuries earlier. The Aztecs prophesied he would return someday to regain his throne. He was therefore linked with the arrival of Hernan Cortés and his Spanish conquistadors in 1519. Many historians believe the Aztecs thought Cortés was the second coming of Quetzalcoatl. The stone's inscription would seem to indicate such a belief was true.'

'So if Cortés represented the reincarnation of Quetzalcoatl,' Giordino asked, 'then who was this Motecuhzoma?'

'We know him better as Montezuma,' Pitt said.

Summer looked at her father. 'So that's what you discovered in Díaz's office?'

'It was a guess, but Díaz had a codex page showing a warrior bedecked in jewels and a green feather headdress. I recall seeing photos of a similar headdress attributed to Montezuma.'

'Or Moctezuma, as he's more accurately referred to these days,' Madero said.

'Díaz knew the connection,' Pitt said, 'that's why he nearly killed you for the stone.'

'What value does Moctezuma add to the mix?' Giordino asked.

'A great deal,' Madero said. "You see, the account on the stone correlates with the Spanish record. Cortés and his force of five hundred men landed near Veracruz in 1519. They soon marched to the Aztec capital of Tenochtitlan, a fabulous city built on an island in Lake Texcoco, which is now the heart of Mexico City.

'Moctezuma personally welcomed Cortés and his troops, but the air was thick with mutual distrust. Moctezuma nevertheless brought to Cortés the treasures of the Aztec empire, which included large quantities of gold.

'Moctezuma was shortly thereafter killed, possibly by his own people, and Cortés was unable to maintain the peace. The Spanish were forced to flee for their lives, barely escaping the angry onslaught of the Aztec warriors.'

'So the Spanish didn't get away with the gold?' Giordino said.

'Only a small portion of it. Cortés regrouped and returned a few months later and lay siege to Tenochtitlan, ultimately taking the city in a bloody conquest. But the gold and riches had vanished. The whereabouts of Moctezuma's gold has remained a mystery for centuries.'

'Until now,' Pitt said. 'The codex and stones tell us the story. The Aztecs packed their treasure into large canoes and sailed east into the Caribbean. We found the remains of one of their canoes off Jamaica, so we know they exist – and that they were large and seagoing.'

'A remarkable voyage, to be sure. I'll work up a more thoughtful translation of the stone,' Madero said. 'If I find anything noteworthy, I'll let you know.'

'Thank you, Professor,' Summer replied. 'Perhaps we can meet at the National Museum in Havana and see both stones together.'

'It's a date,' Madero said. He disconnected the video link and faded from the screen.

'So the question is, where did they go?' Summer asked.

A silent pause hung over the group, then Dahlgren turned their attention to the laptop computer. 'I think Hiram may have something for you.'

A live video feed showed Yaeger in his computer center at NUMA headquarters. 'I hear you need some help with your treasure map.'

'I'm afraid the Aztecs didn't leave us any latitude and longitude coordinates,' Pitt said. 'Could you make anything from the diagram on the stones?'

'As a matter of fact, Max gave me an answer in about twelve seconds,' he said, referring to his computer system. 'I conducted a search for a comparable geographic configuration, limiting the scope to the Gulf of Mexico, the Caribbean Sea, and both coasts of Mexico. I found about a dozen near misses and one pretty good match.'

He held up a paper showing the stone diagram on

half the page and a satellite image of a similarly shaped bay on the other. 'Pretty close correlation, if I do say so.'

'It looks dead-on,' Pitt said.

'Are we at all close to it?' Summer asked, elbowing her way to the computer. 'Can we get to the site from here?'

'Oh, you can reach the site all right,' Yaeger said, flashing his teeth in a broad grin. 'It's just leaving there that might pose a problem.'

83

Puerto Grande was the name Christopher Columbus bestowed on the large, crescent-shaped bay he discovered in 1494. It remained under Spanish control for the next four hundred years, serving as an important terminus for the export of cotton and sugar. In June 1898, American Marines stormed ashore and captured the environs in one of the first land battles of the Spanish–American War. By then, the inlet had taken the name of a nearby river and was called Guantánamo Bay.

After the quick defeat of the Spanish, the United States entered into a lease with the newly independent Cuban government for a forty-five-square-mile block of the outer bay for use as a naval refueling station. Occupied today by the Naval Station Guantánamo Bay and its unpopular detention camp, the US pays only a few thousand dollars each year to the Cubans under a perpetual lease – rendered in checks that have long gone uncashed by the Castro government.

Summer stood on the bow of the *Sargasso Sea*, enjoying the sun and breeze as the research ship entered the bay. An Orion P-3 surveillance plane swooped down and landed at a compact airfield to her left, while the ship curled around to the main naval base on her right.

The ship eased into an open dock alongside a Navy frigate.

She joined Pitt, her brother and Giordino in debarking the ship.

Two officers awaited their arrival. To their surprise, standing with them was St Julien Perlmutter, who had flown down from Washington, the first time he'd been in an airplane in ten years.

'Welcome to Gitmo,' the senior of the two officers said in a forced welcome. 'I'm Admiral Stewart, Joint Task Force Commander.'

'Kind of you to welcome us, Admiral,' Pitt said, shaking hands.

'It's not often I receive a call from the Vice President requesting my assistance in a historical goose chase.'

'I can assure you,' Perlmutter said in his best huffy tone, 'there are no geese involved.'

'May I introduce Commander Harold Joyce. Among other duties, he is our de facto base historian. I'm confident Commander Joyce can see to your needs. Now, if you'll excuse me.' Stewart turned and marched off the deck.

'Somebody put some rocks in his porridge?' Dirk asked.

Joyce laughed. 'No, he just doesn't like politicians ordering him around. Especially politicians he once outranked.'

'Vice President Sandecker has been known to stomp on some toes now and then,' Pitt said.

The naval commander, a short man with glasses, gave Summer a friendly smile, then turned to Perlmutter. 'Mr Perlmutter, I am thrilled that you are here visiting Gitmo. I recently read your history of the Roman navy and found it fascinating.'

'You're one of a small minority, but thank you. Did you have any luck with our request?'

'You indicated that you were looking for a cave or repository on one of the islands. There are several islands in the bay, but only two have any real size or elevation – Hospital Cay and Medico Cay. I hiked around both islands, but I'm afraid I didn't find anything resembling a natural cave.'

'Perhaps it's sealed up,' Summer said.

'You may be right.' Joyce said, responding to Summer eagerly. 'There was really only one landmark that may be of interest. It's an old ammunition bunker on Hospital Cay. I didn't think much of it, but when I did some investigating, I found it was built in the earliest days of the base. It remains locked up, but I could find no inventory records that it was ever actually used for munitions storage.'

'Since we're here, could we have a look?' Summer asked.

Perlmutter nodded. 'I think that would be most judicious.'

'Absolutely,' Joyce said. 'I took the liberty of obtaining the old man's approval. The hardest part was finding a key to the lock. I spent four hours rummaging around the base archives. I don't think that place has been swept in a century.'

'Any luck?' Summer asked.

Joyce produced a brass key the size of a hardcover book.

'I've got a launch waiting at the next dock,' he said. 'Let's go have a look.'

The group squeezed into the launch, and Joyce took them across the bay to a small island at its center. Pitt was surprised to see a small freighter traversing the bay, a Cuban flag flying from its staff.

'Per the terms of the lease agreement signed in 1903, the Cubans have full right of passage through the bay even though it cuts right across our base,' Joyce said. 'We used to get refugees floating downstream on rafts, but the Cuban military monitors things pretty tightly now.'

He drove the boat ashore at Hospital Cay, a half-mile-long island with an elevated ridge that ran down its thin length like a spine. The island was arid like the nearby landscape, covered with low shrubs and cacti.

Pitt noticed several deep indentations in the soil near their landing, evidence of an earlier structure. 'This place has some history with the base?'

'It sure does,' Joyce said. 'This was where the original coaling station was built to refuel the Navy's ships. It was the reason they wanted the bay. Several large bunkers were built on the ridge, connected to a gurney that ran out to the docks. It lasted until 1937, when the Navy's coal-burning ships went by the wayside.'

Dirk peered across the now barren island. 'They didn't leave much for posterity.'

'They tore everything down a few years later and the place has sat empty ever since. But one thing they didn't remove was the munitions bunker. It's at the north end of the cay.'

It was a short hike to the other side of the island, but they were all sweating under the warm, humid climate when they reached a small cut in the ridge. Joyce led them to a concrete archway embedded into the side of the hill that was sealed with thick steel doors. He placed the big brass key in the lock and tried to turn it, but he couldn't get the mechanism to budge.

'Let me see that key, young man.' Perlmutter bulled his way to the door. Grabbing the key, he applied some of his four-hundred-pound mass to bear. The lock gave a grinding click and he shoved the door open.

The interior was completely empty. The room stretched twenty feet into the hillside, with walls made of tightly laid stone. There was no treasure or even ammunition present. The group crowded in and looked around in disappointment.

'So much for Montezuma's treasure,' said Summer with disappointment in her voice.

'Obviously, robbers cleaned it out,' Joyce muttered sadly.

'Not the first time thieves have been at work,' Perl-mutter said. 'The pyramids were emptied, too.'

'Probably three thousand years ago,' Pitt said absently as he began walking around the chamber, tapping the stones while studying the tight fit of the seams.

Perlmutter gazed at him, 'Looking for a hidden door?'

Pitt spoke as he rapped the stones with the big brass key. 'Strikes me as odd there's no remnants or indica-tion that anything was ever stored in this chamber. It's as though it was scrubbed clean.'

Giordino aimed his light on the concrete floor. 'Puts my house to shame.'

It took Pitt forty minutes before finding a different dull sound instead of the cling of solid rock.

Giordino went to the launch and returned with a toolbox. With a hammer and chisel, he and Pitt attacked what soon became a loose stone.

Taking turns, Pitt and Giordino carved a hole on one edge of the stone. Jamming the chisel deeper in the hole, Dirk and Al used a large screwdriver to pry the stone from the side. Sweating and on the verge of exhaustion, they slid the stone forward by an inch. Working from the other side, they moved the stone again. Giordino pushed everyone aside and manhan-dled the large stone on to the floor.

For a long moment, they all stood silent and stared at the space beyond. It was as if they were all afraid to peer beyond the wall and find nothing there. Pitt then pushed a flashlight inside and swept its beam across the darkness. Unable to contain her excitement, Summer pushed her face into the opening. 'I see a jaguar,' she said in a hushed voice, 'I think it's standing guard.' She turned and gave her brother and father a knowing grin.

Unable to resist, Dirk moved Summer's head aside. 'And enough gold to fill Fort Knox!' Taking turns, they hacked through enough stones to create an opening large enough to pass through.

Summer was the first to enter, stepping into the chamber. A large yellow and black-spotted feline greeted her, its jaws frozen open. Summer moved her light lower, illuminating a carved figure of a native warrior beneath the jaguar-skin headdress.

She stepped past the carved warrior. A long dark cavern sparkled with an amber reflection under the beam of her flashlight.

Gold.

It was everywhere, in the form of carved figurines, gilded spears and shields, and jewelry draped upon stone plates and bowls. A large wooden canoe was wedged against one of the walls, filled to its gunnels with gold objects, jewel-encrusted masks, and elaborate carved stone disks.

The others followed Summer in and gaped at the artifacts.

Joyce couldn't believe his eyes. 'What is all this?'

Pitt pointed to a large cotton cloak covered in

jewels and bright green feathers. 'The treasure of Montezuma.'

Summer hugged her brother. 'It's a small redemption for Dr Torres.'

Perlmutter gazed at the artifacts with child-like wonder. 'It's all true,' he murmured.

Pitt strode up to the big man. 'St Julien, I believe you may have been holding out on us. You knew it was here all the time, didn't you?'

Perlmutter smiled. 'I wasn't eager to rewrite history, but there is no disputing the facts. As we now know, it seems a Spanish commando force aligned with the archeologist Julio Rodriguez blew up the *Maine* in order to obtain the Aztec stone. The autopsy report on Ellsworth Boyd was the clue. It indicated he died from a gunshot wound, and you very likely found on the wreck itself the Spanish revolver that caused it.'

'It would seem Rodriguez was on his way here in the *San Antonio*,' Pitt said.

'He had performed fieldwork years earlier on a Taíno Indian site in Guantánamo Bay, so he knew the local geography. I believe the diagram on Boyd's stone was sufficient to trigger recognition once he had possession of it and he was beating a path here.'

'But if the *San Antonio* sank with the stone, how did the US know where to find it? And why is the treasure still here?'

'It's apparent that Boyd knew the significance of the stone,' Perlmutter said. 'His partner was an expert in

Meso-American cultures, so they quickly latched on to the link with Moctezuma's treasure. I suspect he was returning to New York with the stone to raise funds for a search. Instead, his ship broke down in Santiago and he was chased to Havana by Rodriguez and ultimately killed for it on the *Maine*.

'But he had already told the Cuban Consul General and the captain of the *Maine* all he knew,' Perlmutter said. 'I discovered several communiqués related to the *Maine*'s sinking that referred to what was called "Boyd's Find." Hence the urgent chase and sinking of the *San Antonio* by the American fleet. Rodriguez lived just long enough after he was pulled from the sea to point the finger at Guantánamo. The military records are quite abundant, after that point, on the strategic necessity of capturing Guantánamo Bay.'

'Are you saying the Spanish–American War was initiated over Moctezuma's treasure?' Pitt said.

Perlmutter nodded. 'It was a key factor any way you slice it. The *Maine* was sunk on account of it, as was our response to invade Cuba.'

'So why was it left here?'

'The powers in Washington didn't want to upset the newly independent Cuban state. On top of that, the US gained an immediate boost as a new world power by its decisive defeat of the Spanish fleet here, and in the Philippines.

'So instead the discovery was covered up. President McKinley figured it would be better to wait a few years

449

before revealing its existence, so he ordered the treasure kept under lock and key until after he left office. Perhaps he didn't count on Theodore Roosevelt succeeding him.'

'Roosevelt became aware of the treasure?'

'Absolutely. But he had a personal motive in squelching the find. As the hero of San Juan Hill, Roosevelt didn't want his own legacy tarnished by a perceived greedy lure for treasure. On top of that, things were deteriorating in Mexico during the last years of his presidency. Insurrection was growing against the Mexican leader Porfirio Díaz, which would eventually lead to the Mexican Revolution. Roosevelt knew that the Mexican public would be outraged at news that the US possessed Moctezuma's treasure, aggravating an already sensitive border situation.'

'So he buried the whole matter.'

'Quite literally. Roosevelt ordered the treasure sealed where it was. Records of its discovery were purged, and those few who knew of its existence were sworn to secrecy . . . not to mention banned from ever setting foot on Guantánamo Bay again. I was clued in when I stumbled upon an Executive Order signed by Roosevelt directing the construction of a secret sealed repository on the base for so-called sensitive items.'

'And after that, time eventually eroded its memory.'

'Precisely.'

Summer stepped up to the two men carrying a carved stone figurine of a heron with jeweled eyes and a gold bill. 'Isn't it beautiful? The craftsmanship is remarkable.'

'There's enough gold here to pay off the national debt,' Dirk said.

'It's quite a collection,' Perlmutter said. 'I just hope World War Three doesn't break out over its disposition.'

'Dirk and I have it all figured out,' Summer said. 'One third will go to the National Museum in Havana, one third will go to the Xalapa Anthropology Museum in Veracruz, and one third will go to the Smithsonian in Washington, with the requirement that the full collection rotate every five years.'

'That sounds like an equitable plan,' Pitt said, 'but what if the Navy wants to keep it all?'

Summer smiled a wicked grin, then reached an arm around Commander Joyce and pulled the diminutive man close. 'In that case, we may have to take a lesson from the Aztecs and cut out a few hearts.'

84

The knock at the door of the hillside home startled its occupants, who seldom received visitors anymore.

'I'll see who it is,' Salvador Fariñas said to his wife, who was in the kitchen filleting a fish for dinner.

Fariñas opened the door and stepped outside to converse with the visitors. After several minutes, he poked his head back through the doorway and called to his wife. 'Maria, you better come see.'

Maria wiped her hands on her apron and strode outside with an impatient gait. She found a delivery truck parked in their drive and two men unloading numerous thin crates.

Fariñas was opening one of the crates with a screwdriver when he noticed his wife. 'Maria, they've come back! They've come back to you!'

She approached with a confused look as he pried off the crate facing. Inside was a painting of an old woman holding a bouquet of flowers. Maria instantly recognized the portrait of her mother, one she had painted forty years earlier. 'My painting of Mama,' she murmured.

She looked to the truck and the other crates being offloaded. 'These are all my paintings?'

'Yes!' Fariñas said. 'They all have been returned.'

Her eyes glistened. 'I don't understand.'

A switch seemed to flick on inside the woman, banishing the tired and defeated heart she had carried for the past several decades. With her husband, she eagerly pried open the crates, looking upon her works as a mother to her children.

When the last crate was unloaded, one of the deliverymen approached. 'This is for you, Señora Fariñas.' He handed her a thick envelope. 'Have a nice day.'

'Thank you,' she replied, opening the envelope. Inside was a note and a thin object wrapped in brown paper. She pulled open the note.

Maria,

    Always remember, the artist who lives within can never die.

Dirk Pitt

She unfurled the brown paper to find a fine Kolinsky sable-hair artist's brush inside.

Tears began cascading down her cheeks. She dabbed them away with her apron until regaining her composure. Then she raised the brush in the air and in a powerful voice said, *'Absolutamente!'*

He just wanted a decent book to read …

Not too much to ask, is it? It was in 1935 when Allen Lane, Managing Director of Bodley Head Publishers, stood on a platform at Exeter railway station looking for something good to read on his journey back to London. His choice was limited to popular magazines and poor-quality paperbacks – the same choice faced every day by the vast majority of readers, few of whom could afford hardbacks. Lane's disappointment and subsequent anger at the range of books generally available led him to found a company – and change the world.

'We believed in the existence in this country of a vast reading public for intelligent books at a low price, and staked everything on it'
Sir Allen Lane, 1902–1970, founder of Penguin Books

The quality paperback had arrived – and not just in bookshops. Lane was adamant that his Penguins should appear in chain stores and tobacconists, and should cost no more than a packet of cigarettes.

Reading habits (and cigarette prices) have changed since 1935, but Penguin still believes in publishing the best books for everybody to enjoy. We still believe that good design costs no more than bad design, and we still believe that quality books published passionately and responsibly make the world a better place.

So wherever you see the little bird – whether it's on a piece of prize-winning literary fiction or a celebrity autobiography, political tour de force or historical masterpiece, a serial-killer thriller, reference book, world classic or a piece of pure escapism – you can bet that it represents the very best that the genre has to offer.

Whatever you like to read – trust Penguin.